THE GREAT STORIES OF RIDER HAGGARD AND ALLAN QUARTERMAIN

British Library Cataloguing-in-Publication Data
A catalogue record for this book is available from
the British Library

Contents

The Real King Solomon's Mines

Over twenty years ago the spirit moved me to attempt a story of African adventure and as a result I wrote the book called *King Solomon's Mines*. Now, one of those old Romans who had such an extraordinary art of summing up gathered wisdom in a single sentence has informed us that books, like men, have their appointed destinies. Certainly, this is so. Thus, for *King Solomon's Mines* I never expected any particular success; it was only a tale of adventure and there seemed to be no reason why I should do so.

Indeed, if I remember right, this pessimistic attitude was shared by sundry publishers, who turned up their experienced noses at what has proved to be a sound investment in the way of fiction, until by chance it fell into the hands of the late Mr W. E. Henley, who recommended it to Messrs Cassell. Even when the manuscript found a publisher, I recollect, so small was my faith that I nearly disposed of the work outright for a small sum of money.

Yet *King Solomon's Mines* has proved curiously successful. Nowadays, it is quite unusual for a novel or romance to live more than twelve months, even when its admirers have announced, as they do several times per season, that it is the book of the year, or perhaps the greatest of its kind that has been published for generations. Well, twenty-two years have gone by, and it still flourishes. Old ladies still buy it under the impression that it is a religious tale – I have seen it included in theological catalogues, even those of German origin – and other people, young and old, because it amuses them.

During my recent journey through America I met scarcely anyone who did not take the opportunity of informing me that he had read *King Solomon's Mines*, but there, of course, it has been pirated by the million, and is, as I gathered from advertisements in the newspapers, frequently given away by grocers as

---

Cassell's Magazine, July 1907.

flavouring to a pound of tea. In countries shackled by the Berne Copyright Convention, where folk must pay fourpence-half-penny (at least) if they wish to make acquaintance with it in its cheapest form, of course its circulation is not so extensive. Still, it is large, and what is more, scarcely varies from year to year. Indeed, I have come to hope that in dim, unborn ages, when much better work, both of my own and other people's, is clean forgotten, I shall still be remembered as a man who in the Victorian era wrote the well-known romance called *King Solomon's Mines*, and some other equally popular tales. All this I say, not because I am in any way puffed up by these facts, but to show how very wise was that old Roman who enunciated the aphorism, *Habent sua fata libelli*. So since this particular *libelli* has reached its majority, and seems set for a long life – for it is during infancy that the mortality among books of fancy is so terrible: if they grow up at all, they are apt to go on living – it may be worthwhile, in connection with the subject of this article, to say how I came to be able to bring about its birth.

When I was a lad and a public servant in Africa I met many men who have long ago passed away, the pioneers of settlement and exploration, or those who had first become acquainted with certain of the great savage races of the interior, or who had helped to shape history when at length these races and the white man found themselves face to face. Being of an inquiring character, I collected from them information which afterwards enabled me to produce such books as *Nada the Lily* or that which I am discussing.

Thus, although I think that Mr Baines, one of the first wanderers in much of the country which is now Rhodesia, died shortly after I reached Natal, and I do not recall ever having spoken to him, I knew his family, and doubtless heard something of that country from them and others, with the result that it must have been ingrained in my mind that it had once been occupied by an ancient people.

How I came to conclude that this people was Phoenician I have now no idea, for I do not believe that anyone suggested this to me. Nor, to the best of my memory, did I ever at any time hear of the great ruin of Zimbabwe, or that the ancients had carried on a vast gold-mining enterprise in the part of Africa where it stands.

Still less did I know that diamonds existed elsewhere than at Kimberley; indeed, that fact has only been discovered within the last year or so. I introduced them only because they were more picturesque and easier to handle than gold.

When I wrote of Solomon's Road I never guessed that the old-world Road of God, as I think that it is called, would be discovered in the Matoppos. When I imagined 'Sheba's Breasts', I was ignorant that so named and shaped they stand – *vide* the latest maps – not far from the Tokwe River, guarding the gate to the Great Zimbabwe, near to which in truth, or so I believe, Solomon, or other ancient kings, had the mines that poured the gold of Ophir into their coffers.

I never knew of the ancient workings, so many of which have been found since, or of that hidden treasury with swinging doors of stone, which now is said to have an actual existence. All of these, so far as this and other books are concerned, were the fruit of imagination, conceived, I suppose, from chance words spoken long ago that lay dormant in the mind; of that imagination which in some occult way so often seems to throw a shadow of the truth.

But of the Matabele, who in the tale are named the Kukuanas, I did know something, even in those days. Indeed, I went very near to knowing too much, for when in 1877 my dear friends Captain Patterson and Mr J. Sergeaunt, were sent by Sir Bartle Frere on an embassy to their king, Lobengula, I begged the Government of the Transvaal, whose servant I was at that time, for leave to accompany them. It was refused, as I could not be spared from my office. So I rode with them a few miles and returned.

Had I gone on, my fate doubtless would have been their fate, for Lobengula murdered them both very cruelly, also my two servants whom I had lent them, and poor young Thomas, the missionary's son. The names of those two servants, Khiva, the Bastard Zulu, and Ventvogel, the Hottentot, I have tried to preserve in the pages of *King Solomon's Mines*. In life they were such men as are there described. But all this is another matter upon which I must not enter here.

So much for legends and romance. Now let us come to facts. If any reader will take the trouble to consult a modern map of central South Africa, he may see a vast block of territory bounded, roughly speaking, by the Zambesi on the north and the Transvaal on the south, by Barotse and Bechuanaland on the west and by Portuguese East Africa on the east, measuring, perhaps, six hundred miles square.

Over all this huge expanse are found spotted ancient ruins, whereof about five hundred are known to exist, while doubtless many more remain to be discovered. These ruins – in spite of the newest theories to the contrary, which are disputed by many experts – it would seem almost certain – or so at least have concluded my late friend, Theodore Bent and other learned persons – were built by people of Semitic race, probably Phoenicians, or to be more accurate, South Arabian Himyarites, a people rendered somewhat obscure by age. At any rate, they worshipped the sun, the moon, the planets, and other forces of Nature which need not be detailed, and took observations of the more distant stars. Also, in the intervals of these pious occupations, they were exceedingly keen business men. Business took them to South Africa, where they were not native, and business kept them there, until at last, while still engaged on business, or so it appears most probable, they were all of them slain.

Their occupation was gold mining, perhaps with a little trading in 'ivory, almug trees, apes, and peacocks' (or ostriches) thrown in. They opened up hundreds of gold reefs, from which it is estimated that they extracted at least seventy-five million pounds' worth of gold, and probably a great deal more.

They built scores of forts to protect their line of communication with the coast. They erected vast stronghold temples, of which the great Zimbabwe, that is situated practically in the centre of the block of territory delimitated above, is the largest discovered. They worshipped the sun and the moon, as I have said. They enslaved the local population by tens of thousands to labour in the mines and other public works; for gold-seeking was evidently their state monopoly.

They came, they dwelt, they vanished. That is all we know about them. What they were like, what were their domestic habits, what land they took ship from, to what land returned, how they spent their leisure, in what dwellings they abode, whither they carried their dead for burial – of all these things and many others we are utterly ignorant.

But Mr Andrew Lang, with that fine touch of his, has put the problem in a little poem that once he wrote at my request for a paper in which I was interested at the time, so much better than I can do, that I will quote a couple of his verses.

Into the darkness whence they came,
    They passed, their country knoweth none;
They and their gods without a name
    Partake the same oblivion.
Their work they did, their work is done;
    Whose gold, it may be, shone like fire,
About the brows of Solomon,
    And in the House of God's Desire.

The pestilence, the desert spear,
    Smote them: they passed, with none to tell
The names of them that labored there:
    Stark walls and crumbling crucible,
Strait gates and graves, and ruined well,
    Abide, dumb monuments of old;
We know but that men fought and fell,
    Like us, like us for love of gold.

The thing is strange, almost terrifying, to think of. We modern folk are very vain of ourselves. We can hardly conceive a state of affairs on this little planet in which we shall not fill a large part; when for practical purposes, excepting some obscure traces of blood, our particular race, the Anglo-Saxon, the Teutonic, the Gallic, whatever it may be, has passed away and been forgotten. Imagine London, Paris, Berlin, Chicago, and those who built them, forgotten! Yet such things may well come about. Indeed, there are forces at work in the world, though few folk give a thought to them, which seem likely to bring them about a great deal sooner than we anticipate.

Well, as we think today, so doubtless these Phoenicians, or Himyarites, or whoever they may have been, thought in their day. Remember, it must have been a great people that without the aid of steam or firearms could have penetrated, not peacefully we may be sure, into the dark heart of Africa, and there have established their dominion over its teeming millions of population.

Probably the struggle was long and fierce – how fierce their fortifications show, for evidently they lived the over-lords, the taskmasters of hostile multitudes – yes, multitudes and multitudes, for there are great districts in Rhodesia where, league after league, even the mountainsides are terraced by the patient, laborious toil of man, that every inch of soil might be made available for the growth of food. Yet these fierce traders broke their spirit and brought them under the yoke; forced them to dig in the dark mines for gold, to pound the quartz with stone hammers, and bake it in crucibles; forced them to quarry the hard granite and iron-stone to the shape and size of the bricks whereto they were accustomed in their land of orgin, and, generation by generation, to build up the mighty immemorial mass of temple-fortresses.

When did they do it? Whatever may be asserted, no one really knows; but from the orientation of the ruins to the winter or the summer solstice, or to northern stars, scholars think that the earliest of them were built somewhere about two thousand years before Christ. And when did they cease from their labours, leaving nothing behind them but these dry-built walls – for although they were proficient in the manufacture of cement they used no mortar – and the hollow pits whence they had dug the gold, and the instruments with which they treated it? That no scholar can tell us, though many scholars have theories on the matter. They vanished. That is all. Probably the subject tribes, having learned their masters' wisdom, rose up and massacred them to the last man, and in those days there was no historian to record it and no novelist to make a story of the thing.

Solemn, awe-inspiring, the great elliptical building of Zimbabwe still stands beneath the moon, which doubtless was worshipped from its courts. In it are the altars and the sacred cone where once the priests made prayer, or perchance offered sacrifice of children to Baal and to Ashtaroth.

On the hill above, amidst the granite boulders, frowns the fortress, and all around stretch the foundation blocks of a dead city. Here the Makalanga, of whom I have written in *Benita* – that is, the People of the Sun, descendants, without doubt, of

the Semitic conquerors and the native races – still make offerings of black oxen to the spirits of their ancestors, or did so till
within a few years gone. The temple, too – or so they hold – is
still haunted by those spirits; none will enter it at night. But of
the beginning of it all these folk know nothing. If questioned,
they say only that the place was built by white men 'when stones
were soft' – that is, countless time ago.

What a place it must have been when the monoliths and the
carven vultures, each upon its soapstone pillar, stood in their
places upon the broad, flat tops of the walls; when the goldsmiths were at work and the merchants trafficked in the courts;
when the processions wound their way through the narrow passages, and the white-robed, tall-capped priests did sacrifice in
the shrines!

Where did they bury their dead, one wonders? Of these as
yet no cemetery has been found. Perhaps they cremated them
and cast their ashes to the winds. Perhaps they embalmed them,
if they were individuals of consequence, and sent them back to
Arabia or to Tyre, as the Chinese do today, while humbler folk
were cast out to the beasts and birds. Or perhaps they still lie in
deep and hidden kloofs among the mountains.

This at least is evident: that during long centuries of
occupation – for all these ruins reveal various periods of building that must have been separated by great stretches of time –
the dead were many.

Indeed, a few have been found – not at the Great Zimbabwe – but at Mundie, at Chum, and at Dhlo-dhlo. These
were interred beneath the granite cement of the floors, perhaps
under the dwelling of the deceased, who was laid on his side with
his head resting upon a stone or wooden pillow of the ancient
Egyptian pattern, earthenware pots standing about him, his
gold ornaments still upon his person, and cakes of gold within
his pouch to pay the expenses of his last long journey. If he were a
high official also, his gold-headed and gold-ferruled rod of
office was laid in the tomb with him.

One of these departed, who dwelt, or at any rate was
buried, at Chum, was a giant. Messrs Hall and Neal say that he
was over seven feet high, his shin-bone being more than two feet
in length. As much as seventy-two ounces of gold have been
found buried with a single ancient, and at Dhlo-dhlo my friend

Major Burnham, DSO, found more than six hundred ounces of that metal, nearly all of it, I think, manufactured. Also he found skeletons, and within them arrow-heads, showing how they met their deaths, some of which arrow-heads I still have, though whether these date from ancient or from mediaeval times I cannot say.

Ages and ages after the ancients had been destroyed or left the country, there was another empire here – that of Mono-motapa – and semi-savage kings, who Mr Wilmot tells us in his book, held their courts in the Zimbabwes. The Portuguese used to fight with these people and to send missionaries to make Christians of those who survived.

Thus from documents preserved in the Vatican it appears that in 1628 one Brother Louis, having defeated the Emperor and his army of a hundred thousand men, went on to the Great Zimbabwe, 'the court of the King, and there,' he says, 'I built a little church and put up a crucifix I had brought with me and a statue of the Blessed Virgin of the Rosary.'

Sixty or seventy years before this also Father Gonsalvo Silvera was murdered by the Emperor of Monomotapa under circumstances which would be well worth relating if I had the space. Two generations later Father Alphonsus, travelling up the Zambesi, into a tributary of which the body was thrown, alleges that he was shown a place where it still lay uncorrupted. He could not visit it, however, as – the report went – it was carefully guarded by tigers which fifty years before had carried the sacred corpse into a wood.

But of these Zimbabwes, ancient and mediaeval, the legends are endless. Now they are the heritage of the Anglo-Saxon race. Major Wilson and his companions who fell fighting against innumerable odds on the banks of the Shangani, lie within the shadow of their walls, which still wrap the secrets of those who built them in time-worn and impenetrable silence.

Hunter Quatermain's Story

Sir Henry Curtis, as everybody acquainted with him knows, is one of the most hospitable men on earth. It was in the course of the enjoyment of his hospitality at his place in Yorkshire the other day that I heard the hunting story which I am now about to transcribe. Many of those who read it will no doubt have heard some of the strange rumours that are flying about to the effect that Sir Henry Curtis and his friend Captain Good, R.N., recently found a vast treasure of diamonds out in the heart of Africa, supposed to have been hidden by the Egyptians, or King Solomon, or some other antique person. I first saw the matter alluded to in a paragraph in one of the society papers the day before I started for Yorkshire to pay my visit to Curtis, and arrived, needless to say, burning with curiosity; for there is something very fascinating to the mind in the idea of hidden treasure. When I reached the Hall, I at once asked Curtis about it, and he did not deny the truth of the story; but on my pressing him to tell it he would not, nor would Captain Good, who was also staying in the house.

'You would not believe me if I did,' Sir Henry said, with one of the hearty laughs which seem to come right out of his great lungs. 'You must wait till Hunter Quatermain comes; he will arrive here from Africa tonight, and I am not going to say a word about the matter, or Good either, until he turns up. Quatermain was with us all through; he has known about the business for years and years, and if it had not been for him we should not have been here today. I am going to meet him presently.'

I could not get a word more out of him, nor could anybody else, though we were all dying of curiosity, especially some of the ladies. I shall never forget how they looked in the drawing-room before dinner when Captain Good produced a great rough diamond, weighing fifty carats or more, and told them that he had many larger than that. If ever I saw curiosity and envy printed on fair faces, I saw them then.

In A Good Cause, 1885.

It was just at this moment that the door was opened, and Mr Allan Quatermain announced, whereupon Good put the diamond into his pocket, and sprang at a little man who limped shyly into the room, convoyed by Sir Henry Curtis himself.

'Here he is, Good, safe and sound,' said Sir Henry, gleefully. 'Ladies and gentlemen, let me introduce you to one of the oldest hunters and the very best shot in Africa, who has killed more elephants and lions than any other man alive.'

Everybody turned and stared politely at the curious-looking little lame man, and though his size was insignificant, he was quite worth staring at. He had short grizzled hair, which stood about an inch above his head like the bristles of a brush, gentle brown eyes that seemed to notice everything, and a withered face, tanned to the colour of mahogany from exposure to the weather. He spoke, too, when he returned Good's enthusiastic greeting, with a curious little accent, which made his speech noticeable.

It so happened that I sat next to Mr Allan Quatermain at dinner, and, of course, did my best to 'draw' him; but he was not to be drawn. He admitted that he had recently been a long journey into the interior of Africa with Sir Henry Curtis and Captain Good, and that they had found treasure; then he politely turned the subject and began to ask me questions about England, where he had never been before – that is, since he came to years of discretion.[1] Of course, I did not find this very interesting, and so cast about for some means to bring the conversation round again.

Now, we were dining in an oak-panelled vestibule, and on the wall opposite to me were fixed two gigantic elephant tusks, and under them a pair of buffalo horns, very rough and knotted, showing that they came off an old bull, and having the tip of one horn split and chipped. I noticed that Hunter Quatermain's eyes kept glancing at these trophies, and took an occasion to ask him if he knew anything about them.

'I ought to,' he answered, with a little laugh; 'the elephant to which those tusks belonged tore one of our party right in two about eighteen months ago, and as for the buffalo horns, they

---

[1] For a full account of the adventures of Mr Quatermain and his companions upon this journey the reader is referred to the book called *King Solomon's Mines* by H. Rider Haggard.

were nearly my death, and were the end of a servant of mine to whom I was much attached. I gave them to Sir Henry when he left Natal some months ago;' and Mr Quatermain sighed and turned to answer a question from the lady whom he had taken down to dinner, and who, needless to say, was also employed in trying to pump him about the diamonds.

Indeed, all around the table there was a simmer of scarcely suppressed excitement, which, when the servants had left the room, could no longer be restrained.

'Now, Mr Quatermain,' said the lady next to him, 'we have been kept in an agony of suspense by Sir Henry and Captain Good, who have persistently refused to tell us a word of this story about the hidden treasure till you came, and we simply can bear it no longer; so, please, begin at once.'

'Yes,' said everybody, 'go on, please.'

Hunter Quatermain glanced round the table apprehensively; he did not seem to appreciate finding himself the object of so much curiosity.

'Ladies and gentlemen,' he said at last, with a shake of his grizzled head, 'I am very sorry to disappoint you, but I cannot do it. It is this way. At the request of Sir Henry and Captain Good I have written down a true and plain account of King Solomon's Mines and how we found them, so you will soon all be able to learn all about that wonderful adventure for yourselves; but until then I will say nothing about it, not from any wish to disappoint your curiosity, or to make myself important, but simply because the whole story partakes so much of the marvellous, that I am afraid to tell it in a piecemeal, hasty fashion, for fear I should be set down as one of those common fellows of whom there are so many in my profession, who are not ashamed to narrate things they have not seen, and even to tell wonderful stories about wild animals they have never killed. And I think that my companions in adventure, Sir Henry Curtis and Captain Good, will bear me out in what I say.'

'Yes, Quatermain, I think you are quite right,' said Sir Henry. 'Precisely the same considerations have forced Good and myself to hold our tongues. We did not wish to be bracketed with – well, with other famous travellers.'

There was a murmur of disappointment at these announcements.

'I believe you are all hoaxing us,' said the young lady next to Mr Quatermain, rather sharply.

'Believe me,' answered the old hunter, with a quaint courtesy and a little bow of his grizzled head; 'though I have lived all my life in the wilderness, and amongst savages, I have neither the heart, nor the want of manners, to wish to deceive one so lovely.'

Whereat the young lady, who was pretty, looked appeased.

'This is very dreadful,' I broke in. 'We ask for bread and you give us a stone, Mr Quatermain. The least that you can do is to tell us the story of the tusks opposite and the buffalo horns underneath. We won't let you off with less.'

'I am but a poor storyteller,' put in the old hunter, 'but if you will forgive my want of skill, I shall be happy to tell you, not the story of the tusks, for it is part of the history of our journey to King Solomon's Mines, but that of the buffalo horns beneath them, which is now ten years old.'

'Bravo, Quatermain!' said Sir Henry. 'We shall all be delighted. Fire away! Fill up your glass first.'

The little man did as he was bid, took a sip of claret, and began:

About ten years ago I was hunting up in the far interior of Africa, at a place called Gatgarra, not a great way from the Chobe River. I had with me four native servants, namely, a driver and voorlooper, or leader who were natives of Matabeleland, a Hottentot called Hans, who had once been the slave of a Transvaal Boer, and a Zulu hunter, who for five years had accompanied me upon my trips, and whose name was Mashune. Now near Gatgarra I found a fine piece of healthy, park-like country, where the grass was very good, considering the time of year; and here I made a little camp or headquarter settlement, from whence I went on expeditions on all sides in search of game, especially elephant. My luck, however, was bad; I got but little ivory. I was therefore very glad when some natives brought me news that a large herd of elephants were feeding in a valley about thirty miles away. At first I thought of trekking down to the valley, waggon and all, but gave up the idea on hearing that it was infested with the deadly 'tsetse' fly, which is certain death to all animals, except men, donkeys, and wild game. So I

reluctantly determined to leave the waggon in the charge of
the Matabele leader and driver, and to start on a trip into the
thorn country, accompanied only by the Hottentot Hans, and
Mashune.

Accordingly on the following morning we started, and on
the evening of the next day reached the spot where the elephants
were reported to be. But here again we were met by ill luck. That
the elephants had been there was evident enough, for their spoor
was plentiful, and so were other traces of their presence in the
shape of mimosa trees torn out of the ground, and placed topsy-
turvy on their flat crowns, in order to enable the great beasts to
feed on their sweet roots; but the elephants themselves were con-
spicuous by their absence. They had elected to move on. This
being so, there was only one thing to do, and that was to move
after them, which we did, and a pretty hunt they led us. For a
fortnight or more we dodged about after those elephants,
coming up with them on two occasions, and a splendid herd they
were – only, however, to lose them again. At length we came up
with them a third time, and I managed to shoot one bull, and
then they started off again, where it was useless to try to follow
them. After this I gave it up in disgust, and we made the best of
our way back to the camp, not in the sweetest of tempers, carrying the tusks of the elephant I had shot.

It was on the afternoon of the fifth day of our tramp that we
reached the little koppie overlooking the spot where the waggon
stood, and I confess that I climbed it with a pleasurable sense of
home-coming, for his waggon is the hunter's home, as much as
his house is that of a civilized person. I reached the top of the
koppie, and looked in the direction where the friendly white tent
of the waggon should be, but there was no waggon, only a black
burnt plain stretching away far as the eye could reach. I rubbed
my eyes, looked again, and made out on the spot of the camp,
not my waggon, but some charred beams of wood. Half wild
with grief and anxiety, followed by Hans and Mashune, I ran at
full speed down the slope of the koppie, and across the space of
plain below to the spring of water, where my camp had been. I
was soon there, only to find that my suspicions were confirmed.

The waggon and all its contents, including my spare guns
and ammunition, had been destroyed by a grass fire.

Now before I started, I had left orders with the driver to

burn off the grass round the camp, in order to guard against accidents of this nature, and here was the reward of my folly: a very proper illustration of the necessity, especially where natives are concerned, of doing a thing one's self if one wants it done at all. Evidently the lazy rascals had not burnt round the waggon; most probably, indeed, they had themselves carelessly fired the tall and resinous tambouki grass near by; the wind had driven the flames on to the waggon tent, and there was quickly an end of the matter. As for the driver and leader, I know not what became of them: probably fearing my anger, they bolted, taking the oxen with them. I have never seen them from that hour to this.

I sat down on the black veldt by the spring, and gazed at the charred axles and disselboom of my waggon, and I can assure you, ladies and gentlemen, I felt inclined to weep. As for Mashune and Hans they cursed away vigorously, one in Zulu and the other in Dutch. Ours was a pretty position. We were nearly three hundred miles away from Bamangwato, the capital of Khama's country, which was the nearest spot where we could get any help, and our ammunition, spare guns, clothing, food, and everything else, were all totally destroyed. I had just what I stood in, which was a flannel shirt, a pair of 'veldt-schoons', or shoes of raw hide, my eight-bore rifle, and a few cartridges. Hans and Mashune had also each a Martini rifle and some cartridges, not many. And it was with this equipment that we had to undertake a journey of three hundred miles through a desolate and almost uninhabited region. I can assure you that I have rarely been in a worse position, and I have been in some queer ones. However, these accidents are natural to a hunter's life, and the only thing to do was to make the best of them.

Accordingly, after passing a comfortless night by the remains of my waggon, we started next morning on our long journey towards civilization. Now if I were to set to work to tell you all the troubles and incidents of that dreadful journey I should keep you listening here till midnight; so I will, with your permission, pass on to the particular adventure of which the pair of buffalo horns opposite are a melancholy memento.

We had been travelling for about a month, living and getting along as best we could, when one evening we camped some forty miles from Bamangwato. By this time we were indeed in a melancholy plight, footsore, half starved, and utterly worn out; and, in addition, I was suffering from a sharp attack of fever, which half blinded me and made me as weak as a babe. Our ammunition, too, was exhausted; I had only one cartridge left for my eight-bore rifle, and Hans and Mashune, who were armed with Martini Henrys, had three between them. It was about an hour from sundown when we halted and lit a fire – for luckily we had still a few matches. It was a charming spot to camp, I remember. Just off the game track we were following was a little hollow, fringed about with flat-crowned mimosa trees, and at the bottom of the hollow, a spring of clear water welled up out of the earth, and formed a pool, round the edges of which grew an abundance of watercresses of an exactly similar kind to those which were handed round the table just now. Now we had no food of any kind left, having that morning devoured the last remains of a little oribe antelope, which I had shot two days previously. Accordingly Hans, who was a better shot than Mashune, took two of the three remaining Martini cartridges, and started out to see if he could not kill a buck for supper. I was too weak to go myself.

Meanwhile Mashune employed himself in dragging together some dead boughs from the mimosa trees to make a sort of 'skerm', or shelter for us to sleep in, about forty yards from the edge of the pool of water. We had been greatly troubled with lions in the course of our long tramp, and only on the previous night had very nearly been attacked by them, which made me nervous, especially in my weak state. Just as we had finished the skerm, or rather something which did duty for one, Mashune and I heard a shot apparently fired about a mile away.

'Hark to it!' sung out Mashune in Zulu, more, I fancy, by way of keeping his spirits up than for any other reason – for he was a sort of black Mark Tapley, and very cheerful under difficulties. 'Hark to the wonderful sound with which the "Maboona" (the Boers) shook our fathers to the ground at the battle of the Blood River. We are hungry now, my father; our stomachs are small and withered up like a dried ox's paunch, but they will soon be full of good meat. Hans is a Hottentot, and an *umfagozan* (that is, a low fellow), but he shoots straight – ah! he certainly shoots straight. Be of a good heart, my father, there will soon be meat upon the fire, and we shall rise up men.'

And so he went on talking nonsense till I told him to stop, because he made my head ache with his empty words.

Shortly after we heard the shot, the sun sank in his red splendour, and there fell upon earth and sky the great hush of the African wilderness. The lions were not up as yet, they would probably wait for the moon, and the birds and beasts were all at rest. I cannot describe the intensity of the quiet of the night: to me in my weak state, and fretting as I was over the non-return of the Hottentot Hans, it seemed almost ominous – as though Nature were brooding over some tragedy which was being enacted in her sight.

It was quiet – quiet as death, and lonely as the grave.

'Mashune,' I said at last, 'where is Hans? my heart is heavy for him.'

'Nay, my father, I know not; mayhap he is weary, and sleeps, or mayhap he has lost his way.'

'Mashune, art thou a boy to talk folly to me?' I answered. 'Tell me, in all the years thou hast hunted by my side, didst thou ever know a Hottentot to lose his path or to sleep upon the way to camp?'

'Nay, Macumazahn,' (that, ladies, is my native name, and means the man who 'gets up by night,' or who 'is always awake') 'I know not where he is.'

But though we talked thus, we neither of us liked to hint at what was in both our minds, namely, that misfortune had overtaken the poor Hottentot.

'Mashune,' I said at last, 'go down to the water and bring me of those green herbs that grow there. I am hungered, and must eat something.'

'Nay, my father; surely the ghosts are there; they come out of the water at the night, and sit upon the banks to dry themselves. An Isanusi[1] told it me.'

Mashune was, I think, one of the bravest men I ever knew in the daytime, but he had a more than civilized dread of the supernatural.

'Must I go myself, thou fool?' I said, sternly.

'Nay, Macumazahn, if thy heart yearns for strange things like a sick woman, I go, even if the ghosts devour me.'

---

1 *Isanusi*, witch-finder.

And accordingly he went, and soon returned with a large bundle of watercresses, of which I ate greedily.

'Art thou not hungry?' I asked the great Zulu presently, as he sat eyeing me eating.

'Never was I hungrier, my father.'

'Then eat,' and I pointed to the watercresses.

'Nay, Macumazahn, I cannot eat those herbs.'

'If thou dost not eat thou wilt starve: eat, Mashune.'

He stared at the watercresses doubtfully for a while, and at last seized a handful and crammed them into his mouth, crying out as he did so, 'Oh, why was I born that I should live to feed on green weeds like an ox? Surely if my mother could have known it she would have killed me when I was born!' and so he went on lamenting between each fistful of watercresses till all were finished, when he declared that he was full indeed of stuff, but it lay very cold on his stomach, 'like snow upon a mountain'. At any other time I should have laughed, for it must be admitted he had a ludicrous way of putting things. Zulus do not like green food.

Just after Mashune had finished his watercress, we heard the loud 'woof! woof!' of a lion, who was evidently promenading much nearer to our little skerm than was pleasant. Indeed, on looking into the darkness and listening intently, I could hear his snoring breath, and catch the light of his great yellow eyes. We shouted loudly, and Mashune threw some sticks on the fire to frighten him, which apparently had the desired effect, for we saw no more of him for a while.

Just after we had had this fright from the lion, the moon rose in her fullest splendour, throwing a robe of silver light over all the earth. I have rarely seen a more beautiful moonrise. I remember that sitting in the skerm I could with ease read faint pencil notes in my pocketbook. As soon as the moon was up game began to trek down to the water just below us. I could, from where I sat, see all sorts of them passing along a little ridge that ran to our right, on their way to the drinking place. Indeed, one buck – a large eland – came within twenty yards of the skerm, and stood at gaze, staring at it suspiciously, his beautiful head and twisted horns standing out clearly against the sky. I had, I recollect, every mind to have a pull at him on the chance of providing ourselves with a good supply of beef; but remembering that we had but two cartridges left, and the extreme uncertainty of a shot by moonlight, I at length decided to refrain. The eland presently moved on to the water, and a minute or two afterwards there arose a great sound of splashing followed by the quick fall of galloping hoofs.

'What's that, Mashune?' I asked.

'That damn lion; buck smell him,' replied the Zulu in English, of which he had a very superficial knowledge.

Scarcely were the words out of his mouth before we heard a sort of whine over the other side of the pool, which was instantly answered by a loud coughing roar close to us.

'By Jove!' I said, 'there are two of them. They have lost the buck; we must look out they don't catch us.' And again we made up the fire, and shouted, with the result that the lions moved off.

'Mashune,' I said, 'do you watch till the moon gets over that tree, when it will be the middle of the night. Then wake me. Watch well, now, or the lions will be picking those worthless bones of yours before you are three hours older. I must rest a little, or I shall die.'

'Koos!' (chief), answered the Zulu. 'Sleep, my father, sleep in peace; my eyes shall be open as the stars; and like the stars shall watch over you.'

Although I was so weak, I could not at once follow his poetical advice. To begin with, my head ached with fever, and I was torn with anxiety as to the fate of the Hottentot Hans; and, indeed, as to our own fate, left with sore feet, empty stomachs, and two cartridges, to find our way to Bamangwato, forty miles off. Then the mere sensation of knowing that there are one or more hungry lions prowling round you somewhere in the dark is disquieting, however well one may be used to it, and, by keeping the attention on the stretch, tends to prevent one from sleeping. In addition to all these troubles, too, I was, I remember, seized with a dreadful longing for a pipe of tobacco, whereas, under the circumstances, I might as well have longed for the moon.

At last, however, I fell into an uneasy sleep as full of bad dreams as a prickly pear is of points, one of which, I recollect, was that I was setting my naked foot upon a cobra which rose upon its tail and hissed my name, 'Macumazahn,' into my ear. Indeed, the cobra hissed with such persistency that at last I roused myself.

'*Macumazahn, nanzia, nanzia!*' (there, there!) whispered Mashune's voice into my drowsy ears. Raising myself, I opened my eyes, and I saw Mashune kneeling by my side and pointing towards the water. Following the line of his outstretched hand, my eyes fell upon a sight that made me jump, old hunter as I was even in those days. About twenty paces from the little skerm was a large ant-heap, and on the summit of the ant-heap, her four feet rather close together, so as to find standing space, stood the massive form of a big lioness. Her head was towards the skerm, and in the bright moonlight I saw her lower it and lick her paws.

Mashune thrust the Martini rifle into my hands, whispering that it was loaded. I lifted it and covered the lioness, but found that even in that light I could not make out the foresight of the Martini. As it would be madness to fire without doing so, for the result would probably be that I should wound the lioness, if, indeed, I did not miss her altogether, I lowered the rifle; and, hastily tearing a fragment of paper from one of the leaves of my pocketbook, which I had been consulting just before I went to sleep, I proceeded to fix it on to the front sight. But all this took a little time, and before the paper was satisfactorily arranged, Mashune again gripped me by the arm, and pointed to a dark heap under the shade of a small mimosa tree which grew not more than ten paces from the skerm.

'Well, what is it?' I whispered; 'I can see nothing.'

'It is another lion,' he answered.

'Nonsense! thy heart is dead with fear, thou seest double;' and I bent forward over the edge of the surrounding fence, and stared at the heap.

Even as I said the words, the dark mass rose and stalked out into the moonlight. It was a magnificent, black-maned lion, one of the largest I had ever seen. When he had gone two or three steps he caught sight of me, halted, and stood there gazing straight towards us; he was so close that I could see the firelight reflected in his wicked, greenish eyes.

'Shoot, shoot!' said Mashune. 'The devil is coming – he is going to spring!'

I raised the rifle, and got the bit of paper on the foresight straight on to a little patch of white hair just where the throat is set into the chest and shoulders. As I did so, the lion glanced back over his shoulders, as, according to my experience, a lion

nearly always does before he springs. Then he dropped his body
a little, and I saw his big paws spread out upon the ground as he
put his weight on them to gather purchase. In haste I pressed the
trigger of the Martini, and not an instant too soon; for, as I did
so, he was in the act of springing. The report of the rifle rang out
sharp and clear on the intense silence of the night, and in
another second the great brute had landed on his head within
four feet of us, and rolling over and over towards us, was sending
the bushes which composed our little fence flying with convulsive strokes of his great paws. We sprang out of the other side
of the skerm, and he rolled on to it and into it and then right
through the fire. Next he raised himself and sat upon his
haunches like a great dog, and began to roar. Heavens! how he
roared! I never heard anything like it before or since. He kept
filling his lungs with air, and then emitting it in the most heart-
shaking volumes of sound. Suddenly, in the middle of one of the
loudest roars, he rolled over on to his side and lay still, and I
knew that he was dead. A lion generally dies upon his side.

With a sigh of relief I looked up towards his mate upon the
ant-heap. She was standing there apparently petrified with
astonishment, looking over her shoulder, and lashing her tail;
but to our intense joy, when the dying beast ceased roaring, she
turned, and, with one enormous bound, vanished into the
night.

Then we advanced cautiously towards the prostrate brute,
Mashune droning an improvised Zulu song as he went, about
how Macumazahn, the hunter of hunters, whose eyes are open
by night as well as by day, put his hand down the lion's stomach
when it came to devour him and pulled out his heart by the
roots, etc., etc., by way of expressing his satisfaction, in his
hyperbolical Zulu way, at the turn events had taken.

There was no need for caution; the lion was as dead as
though he had already been stuffed with straw. The Martini
bullet had entered within an inch of the white spot I had aimed
at, and travelled right through him, passing out at the right
buttock, near the root of the tail. The Martini has wonderful
driving power, though the shock it gives to the system is, comparatively speaking, slight, owing to the smallness of the hole it
makes. But fortunately the lion is an easy beast to kill.

I passed the rest of that night in a profound slumber, my

head reposing upon the deceased lion's flank, a position that had, I thought, a beautiful touch of irony about it, though the smell of his singed hair was disagreeable. When I woke again the faint primrose lights of dawn were flushing in the eastern sky. For a moment I could not understand the chill sense of anxiety that lay like a lump of ice at my heart, till the feel and smell of the skin of the dead lion beneath my head recalled the circumstances in which we were placed. I rose, and eagerly looked round to see if I could discover any signs of Hans, who, if he had escaped accident, would surely return to us at dawn, but there were none. Then hope grew faint, and I felt that it was not well with the poor fellow. Setting Mashune to build up the fire I hastily removed the hide from the flank of the lion, which was indeed a splendid beast, and cutting off some lumps of flesh, we toasted and ate them greedily. Lions' flesh, strange as it may seem, is very good eating, and tastes more like veal than anything else.

By the time that we had finished our much-needed meal the sun was getting up, and after a drink of water and a wash at the pool, we started to try and find Hans leaving the dead lion to the tender mercies of the hyenas. Both Mashune and myself were, by constant practice, pretty good hands at tracking, and we had not much difficulty in following the Hottentot's spoor, faint as it was. We had gone on in this way for half-an-hour or so, and were, perhaps, a mile or more from the site of our camping-place, when we discovered the spoor of a solitary bull buffalo mixed up with the spoor of Hans, and were able from various indications, to make out that he had been tracking the buffalo. At length we reached a little glade in which there grew a stunted old mimosa thorn, with a peculiar and overhanging formation of root, under which a porcupine, or an ant-bear, or some such animal, had hollowed out a wide-lipped hole. About ten or fifteen paces from this thorn-tree there was a thick patch of bush.

'See, Macumazahn! see!' said Mashune, excitedly, as we drew near the thorn; 'the buffalo has charged him. Look, here he stood to fire at him; see how firmly he planted his feet upon the earth; there is the mark of his crooked toe (Hans had one bent toe). Look! here the bull came like a boulder down the hill, his hoofs turning up the earth like a hoe. Hans had hit him: he bled as he came; there are the blood spots. It is all written down there, my father — there upon the earth.'

'Yes,' I said; 'yes; but *where is Hans?*'

Even as I said it Mashune clutched my arm, and pointèd to the stunted thorn just by us. Even now, gentlemen, it makes me feel sick when I think of what I saw.

For fixed in a stout fork of the tree some eight feet from the ground was Hans himself, or rather his dead body, evidently tossed there by the furious buffalo. One leg was twisted round the fork, probably in a dying convulsion. In the side, just beneath the ribs, was a great hole, from which the entrails protruded. But this was not all. The other leg hung down to within five feet of the ground. The skin and most of the flesh were gone from it. For a moment we stood aghast, and gazed at this horrifying sight. Then I understood what had happened. The buffalo, with that devilish cruelty which distinguishes the animal, after his enemy was dead, had stood underneath his body, and licked the flesh off the pendant leg with his file-like tongue. I had heard of such a thing before, but had always treated the stories as hunters' yarns; but I had no doubt about it now. Poor Hans' skeleton foot and ankle were an ample proof.

We stood aghast under the tree, and stared and stared at this awful sight, when suddenly our cogitations were interrupted in a painful manner. The thick bush about fifteen paces off burst asunder with a crashing sound, and uttering a series of ferocious pig-like grunts, the bull buffalo himself came charging out straight at us. Even as he came I saw the blood mark on his side where poor Hans' bullet had struck him, and also, as is often the case with particularly savage buffaloes, that his flanks had recently been terribly torn in an encounter with a lion.

On he came, his head well up (a buffalo does not generally lower his head till he does so to strike); those great black horns — as I look at them before me, gentlemen, I seem to see them come charging at me as I did ten years ago, silhouetted against the green bush behind; — on, on!

With a shout Mashune bolted off sideways towards the bush. I had instinctively lifted my eight-bore, which I had in my hand. It would have been useless to fire at the buffalo's head, for the dense horns must have turned the bullet; but as Mashune bolted, the bull slewed a little, with the momentary idea of following him, and as this gave me a ghost of a chance, I let drive my only cartridge at his shoulder. The bullet struck the shoulder-blade and smashed it up, and then travelled on under the skin into his flank; but it did not stop him, though for a second he staggered.

Throwing myself on to the ground with the energy of despair, I rolled under the shelter of the projecting root of the thorn, crushing myself as far into the mouth of the ant-bear hole as I could. In a single instant the buffalo was after me. Kneeling down on his uninjured knee – for one leg, that of which I had broken the shoulder, was swinging helplessly to and fro – he set to work to try and hook me out of the hole with his crooked horn. At first he struck at me furiously, and it was one of the blows against the base of the tree which splintered the tip of the horn in the way that you see. Then he grew more cunning, and pushing his head as far under the root as possible, made long semi-circular sweeps at me, grunting furiously and blowing saliva and hot steamy breath all over me. I was just out of reach of the horn, though every stroke, by widening the hole and making more room for his head, brought it closer to me, but every now and again I received heavy blows in the ribs from his muzzle. Feeling that I was being knocked silly, I made an effort and seizing his rough tongue, which was hanging from his jaws, I twisted it with all my force. The great brute bellowed with pain and fury, and jerked himself backwards so strongly, that he dragged me some inches further from the mouth of the hole, and again made a sweep at me, catching me this time round the shoulder-joint in the hook of his horn.

I felt that it was all up now, and began to holloa.

'He has got me!' I shouted in mortal terror. '*Gwasa, Mashune, gwasa!*' ('Stab, Mashune, stab!')

One hoist of the great head, and out of the hole I came like a periwinkle out of his shell. But even as I did so, I caught sight of Mashune's stalwart form advancing with his 'bangwan,' or broad stabbing assegai, raised above his head. In another quarter of a second I had fallen from the horn, and heard the blow of the spear, followed by the indescribable sound of steel shearing its way through flesh. I had fallen on my back, and, looking up, I saw that the gallant Mashune had driven the assegai a foot or more into the carcass of the buffalo, and was turning to fly.

Alas! it was too late. Bellowing madly, and spouting blood from mouth and nostrils, the devilish brute was on him, and had thrown him high like a feather, and then gored him twice as he lay. I struggled up with some wild idea of affording help, but before I had gone a step the buffalo gave one long sighing bellow, and rolled over dead by the side of his victim.

Mashune was still living, but a single glance at him told me that his hour had come. The buffalo's horn had driven a great hole in his right lung, and inflicted other injuries.

I knelt down beside him in the uttermost distress, and took his hand.

'Is he dead, Macumazahn?' he whispered. 'My eyes are blind; I cannot see.'

'Yes, he is dead.'

'Did the black devil hurt thee, Macumazahn?'

'No, my poor fellow, I am not much hurt.'

'Ow! I am glad.'

Then came a long silence, broken only by the sound of the air whistling through the hole in his lung as he breathed.

'Macumazah, art thou there? I cannot feel thee.'

'I am here, Mashune.'

'I die, Macumazahn — the world flies round and round. I go — I go out into the dark! Surely, my father, at times in days to come — thou wilt think of Mashune who stood by thy side — when thou killest elephants, as we used — as we used——'

They were his last words, his brave spirit passed with them. I dragged his body to the hole under the tree, and pushed it in, placing his broad assegai by him, according to the custom of his people, that he might not go defenceless on his long journey; and then, ladies — I am not ashamed to confess — I stood alone there before it, and wept like a woman.

Long Odds

The story which is narrated in the following pages came to me from the lips of my old friend Allan Quatermain, or Hunter Quatermain, as we used to call him in South Africa. He told it to me one evening when I was stopping with him at the place he bought in Yorkshire. Shortly after that, the death of his only son so unsettled him that he immediately left England, accompanied by two companions, his old fellow-voyagers, Sir Henry Curtis and Captain Good, and has now utterly vanished into the dark heart of Africa. He is persuaded that a white people, of which he has heard rumours all his life, exists somewhere on the highlands in the vast, still unexplored interior, and his great ambition is to find them before he dies. This is the wild quest upon which he and his companions have departed, and from which I shrewdly suspect they never will return. One letter only have I received from the old gentleman, dated from a mission station high up the Tana, a river on the east coast, about three hundred miles north of Zanzibar. In it he says that they have gone through many hardships and adventures, but are alive and well, and have found traces which go far towards making him hope that the results of their wild quest may be a 'magnificent and unexampled discovery'. I greatly fear, however, that all he has discovered is death; for this letter came a long while ago, and nobody has heard a single word of the party since. They have totally vanished.

It was on the last evening of my stay at his house that he told the ensuing story to me and Captain Good, who was dining with him. He had eaten his dinner and drunk two or three glasses of old port, just to help Good and myself to the end of the second bottle. It was an unusual thing for him to do, for he was a most abstemious man, having conceived, as he used to say, a great horror of drink from observing its effects upon the class of colonists – hunters, transport riders and others – amongst whom he had passed so many years of his life. Consequently the good

Macmillan's Magazine, February 1886.

wine took more effect on him than it would have done on most men, sending a little flush into his wrinkled cheeks, and making him talk more freely than usual.

Dear old man! I can see him now, as he went limping up and down the vestibule, with his grey hair sticking up in scrubbing-brush fashion, his shrivelled yellow face, and his large dark eyes, that were as keen as any hawk's, and yet soft as a buck's. The whole room was hung with trophies of his numerous hunting expeditions, and he had some story about every one of them, if only he could be got to tell it. Generally he would not, for he was not very fond of narrating his own adventures, but tonight the port wine made him more communicative.

'Ah! you brute!' he said, stopping beneath an unusually large skull of a lion, which was fixed just over the mantelpiece, beneath a long row of guns, its jaws distended to their utmost width. 'Ah, you brute! you have given me a lot of trouble for the last dozen years, and will, I suppose, to my dying day.'

'Tell us the yarn, Quatermain,' said Good. 'You have often promised to tell me, and you never have.'

'You had better not ask me to,' he answered, 'for it is a longish one.'

'All right,' I said, 'the evening is young, and there is some more port.'

Thus adjured, he filled his pipe from a jar of coarse-cut Boer tobacco that was always standing on the mantelpiece, and still walking up and down the room, began.

It was, I think, in the March of '69 that I was up in Sikukuni's country. It was just after old Sequati's time, and Sikukuni had got into power – I forget how. Anyway, I was there. I had heard that the Bapedi people had brought down an enormous quantity of ivory from the interior, and so I started with a waggon-load of goods, and came straight away from Middleburg to try and trade some of it. It was a risky thing to go into the country so early, on account of the fever; but I knew that there were one or two others after that lot of ivory, so I determined to have a try for it, and take my chance of fever. I had become so tough from continual knocking about that I did not set it down at much.

Well, I got on all right for a while. It is a wonderfully

beautiful piece of bush veldt, with great ranges of mountains running through it, and round granite koppies starting up here and there, looking out like sentinels over the rolling waste of bush. But it is very hot – hot as a stew-pan – and when I was there that March, which, of course, is autumn in this part of Africa, the whole place reeked of fever. Every morning, as I trekked along down by the Oliphant River, I used to creep from the waggon at dawn and look out. But there was no river to be seen – only a long line of billows of what looked like the finest cotton wool tossed up lightly with a pitchfork. It was the fever mist. Out from among the scrub, too, came little spirals of vapour, as though there were hundreds of tiny fires alight in it – reek rising from thousands of tons of rotting vegetation. It was a beautiful place, but the beauty was the beauty of death; and all those lines and blots of vapour wrote one great word across the surface of the country, and that word was 'fever'.

It was a dreadful year of illness that. I came, I remember, to one little kraal of Knobnoses, and went up to it to see if I could get some *maas*, or curdled butter-milk, and a few mealies. As I drew near I was struck with the silence of the place. No children began to chatter, and no dogs barked. Nor could I see any native sheep or cattle. The place, though it had evidently been inhabited of late, was as still as the bush round it, and some guinea-fowl got up out of the prickly pear bushes right at the kraal gate. I remember that I hesitated a little before going in, there was such an air of desolation about the spot. Nature never looks desolate when man has not yet laid his hand upon her breast; she is only lonely. But when man has been, and has passed away, then she looks desolate.

Well, I passed into the kraal, and went up to the principal hut. In front of the hut was something with an old sheep-skin *kaross* thrown over it. I stooped down and drew off the rug, and then shrank back amazed, for under it was the body of a young woman recently dead. For a moment I thought of turning back, but my curiosity overcame me; so going past the dead woman, I went down on my hands and knees and crept into the hut. It was so dark that I could not see anything, though I could smell a great deal, so I lit a match. It was a 'tandstickor' match, and burnt slowly and dimly, and as the light gradually increased I made out what I took to be a family of people, men, women, and

children, fast asleep. Presently it burnt up brightly, and I saw
that they too, five of them altogether, were quite dead. One was
a baby. I dropped the match in a hurry, and was making my way
from the hut as quick as I could go, when I caught sight of two
bright eyes staring out of a corner. Thinking it was a wild cat, or
some such animal, I redoubled my haste, when suddenly a voice
near the eyes began first to mutter, and then to send up a suc-
cesssion of awful yells.

Hastily I lit another match, and perceived that the eyes
belonged to an old woman, wrapped up in a greasy leather
garment. Taking her by the arm, I dragged her out, for she
could not, or would not, come by herself, and the stench was
overpowering me. Such a sight as she was – a bag of bones,
covered over with black, shrivelled parchment. The only white
thing about her was her wool, and she seemed to be pretty well
dead except for her eyes and her voice. She thought that I was a
devil come to take her, and that is why she yelled so. Well, I got
her down to the waggon, and gave her a 'tot' of Cape smoke, and
then, as soon as it was ready, poured about a pint of beef-tea
down her throat, made from the flesh of a blue vilderbeeste I
had killed the day before, and after that she brightened up wonderfully. She could talk Zulu – indeed, it turned out that she
had run away from Zululand in T'Chaka's time – and she told
me that all the people whom I had seen had died of fever. When
they had died the other inhabitants of the kraal had taken the
cattle and gone away, leaving the poor old woman, who was
helpless from age and infirmity, to perish of starvation or
disease, as the case might be. She had been sitting there for three
days among the bodies when I found her. I took her on to the
next kraal, and gave the headman a blanket to look after her,
promising him another if I found her well when I came back. I
remember that he was much astonished at my parting with two
blankets for the sake of such a worthless old creature. Why did I
not leave her in the bush? he asked. Those people carry the
doctrine of the survival of the fittest to its extreme, you see.

It was the night after I had got rid of the old woman that I
made my first acquaintance with my friend yonder – and he
nodded towards the skull that seemed to be grinning down at us
in the shadow of the wide mantelshelf. I had trekked from dawn
till eleven o'clock – a long trek – but I wanted to get on, and had

turned the oxen out to graze, sending the voorlooper to look after them, my intention being to inspan again about six o'clock, and trek with the moon till ten. Then I got into the waggon and had a good sleep till half-past two or so in the afternoon, when I rose and cooked some meat, and had my dinner, washing it down with a pannikin of black coffee — for it was difficult to get preserved milk in those days. Just as I had finished, and the driver, a man called Tom, was washing up the things, in comes the young scoundrel of a voorlooper driving one ox before him.

'Where are the other oxen?' I asked.

'Koos!' he said, 'Koos! the other oxen have gone away. I turned my back for a minute, and when I looked round again they were all gone except Kaptein, here, who was rubbing his back against a tree.'

'You mean that you have been asleep, and let them stray, you villain. I will rub your back against a stick,' I answered, feeling very angry, for it was not a pleasant prospect to be stuck up in that fever trap for a week or so while we were hunting for the oxen. 'Off you go, and you too, Tom, and mind you don't come back till you have found them. They have trekked back along the Middleburg Road, and are a dozen miles off by now, I'll be bound. Now, no words; go both of you.'

Tom, the driver, swore, and caught the lad a hearty kick, which he richly deserved, and then having tied old Kaptein up to the disselboom with a reim, they took their assegais and sticks, and started. I would have gone too, only I knew that somebody must look after the waggon, and I did not like to leave either of the boys with it at night. I was in a very bad temper, indeed, although I was pretty well used to these sort of occurrences, and soothed myself by taking a rifle and going to kill something. For a couple of hours I poked about without seeing anything that I could get a shot at, but at last, just as I was again within seventy yards of the waggon, I put up an old Impala ram from behind a mimosa thorn. He ran straight for the waggon, and it was not till he was passing within a few feet of it that I could get a decent shot at him. Then I pulled, and caught him half-way down the spine. Over he went, dead as a door-nail, and a pretty shot it was, though I ought not to say it. This little incident put me into rather a better humour, especially as the buck had rolled right against the after-part of the waggon, so I had only to gut him, fix a reim round his legs, and haul him up. By the time I had done this the sun was down, and the full moon was up, and a beautiful moon it was. And then there came that wonderful hush which sometimes falls over the African bush in the early hours of the night. No beast was moving, and no bird called. Not a breath of air stirred the quiet trees, and the shadows did not even quiver, they only grew. It was very oppressive and very lonely, for there was not a sign of the cattle or the boys. I was quite thankful for the society of old Kaptein, who was lying down contentedly against the disselboom, chewing the cud with a good conscience.

Presently, however, Kaptein began to get restless. First he snorted, then he got up and snorted again. I could not make it out, so like a fool I got down off the waggon-box to have a look round, thinking it might be the lost oxen coming.

Next instant I regretted it, for all of a sudden I heard a roar and saw something yellow flash past me and light on poor Kaptein. Then came a bellow of agony from the ox, and a crunch as the lion put his teeth through the poor brute's neck, and I began to understand what had happened. My rifle was in the waggon, and my first thought being to get hold of it, I turned and made a bolt for the box. I got my foot up on the wheel and flung my body forward on to the waggon, and there I stopped as if I were frozen, and no wonder, for as I was about to spring up I heard the lion behind me, and next second I felt the brute, ay, as plainly as I can feel this table. I felt him, I say, sniffing at my left leg that was hanging down.

My word! I did feel queer; I don't think that I ever felt so queer before. I dared not move for the life of me, and the odd thing was that I seemed to lose power over my leg, which developed an insane sort of inclination to kick out of its own mere motion — just as hysterical people want to laugh when they ought to be particularly solemn. Well, the lion sniffed and sniffed, beginning at my ankle and slowly nosing away up to my thigh. I thought that he was going to get hold then, but he did not. He only growled softly, and went back to the ox. Shifting my head a little I got a full view of him. He was about the biggest lion I ever saw, and I have seen a great many, and he had a most tremendous black mane. What his teeth were like you can see — look there, pretty big ones, ain't they? Altogether he was a magnificent animal, and as I lay sprawling on the fore-tongue of the waggon, it occurred to me that he would look uncommonly well in a cage. He stood there by the carcass of poor Kaptein, and deliberately disembowelled him as neatly as a butcher could have done. All this while I dared not move, for he kept lifting his head and keeping an eye on me as he licked his bloody chops. When he had cleaned Kaptein out he opened his mouth and roared, and I am not exaggerating when I say that the sound shook the waggon. Instantly there came back an answering roar.

'Heavens!' I thought, 'there is his mate.'

Hardly was the thought out of my head when I caught sight in the moonlight of the lioness bounding along through the long grass, and after her a couple of cubs about the size of mastiffs. She stopped within a few feet of my head, and stood, waved her tail, and fixed me with her glowing yellow eyes; but just as I thought that it was all over she turned and began to feed on Kaptein, and so did the cubs. There were the four of them within eight feet of me, growling and quarrelling, rending and tearing, and crunching poor Kaptein's bones; and there I lay shaking with terror, and the cold perspiration pouring out of me, feeling like another Daniel come to judgement in a new sense of the phrase. Presently the cubs has eaten their fill, and began to get restless. One went round to the back of the waggon and pulled at the Impala buck that hung there, and the other came round my way and commenced the sniffing game at my leg. Indeed, he did more than that, for, my trouser being hitched up a little, he began to lick the bare skin with his rough tongue. The more he licked the more he liked it, to judge from his increased vigour and the loud purring noise he made. Then I knew that the end had come, for in another second his file-like tongue would have rasped through the skin of my leg – which was luckily pretty tough – and have drawn the blood, and then there would be no chance for me. So I just lay there and thought of my sins, and prayed to the Almighty, and reflected that after all life was a very enjoyable thing.

Then of a sudden I heard a crashing of bushes and the shouting and whistling of men, and there were the two boys coming back with the cattle, which they had found trekking along all together. The lions lifted their heads and listened, then bounded off without a sound – and I fainted.

The lions came back no more that night, and by the next morning my nerves had got pretty straight again; but I was full of wrath when I thought of all that I had gone through at the hands, or rather noses, of those four brutes, and of the fate of my after-ox Kaptein. He was a splendid ox, and I was very fond of him. So wroth was I that like a fool I determined to attack the whole family of them. It was worthy of a greenhorn out on his first hunting trip; but I did it nevertheless. Accordingly after breakfast, having rubbed some oil upon my leg, which was very sore from the cub's tongue, I took the driver, Tom, who did not half like the business, and having armed myself with an ordinary double No. 12 smoothbore, the first breechloader I ever had, I started. I took the smoothbore because it shot a bullet very well; and my experience has been that a round ball from a smoothbore is quite as effective against a lion as an express bullet. The lion is soft, and not a difficult animal to finish if you hit him anywhere in the body. A buck takes far more killing.

Well, I started, and the first thing I set to work to do was to try to discover whereabouts the brutes lay up for the day. About three hundred yards from the waggon was the crest of a rise covered with single mimosa trees, dotted about in a park-like fashion, and beyond this lay a stretch of open plain running down to a dry pan, or water-hole, which covered about an acre of ground, and was densely clothed with reeds, now in the sere and yellow leaf. From the further edge of this pan the ground sloped up again to a great cleft, or nullah, which had been cut out by the action of the water, and was pretty thickly sprinkled with bush, amongst which grew some large trees, I forget of what sort.

It at once struck me that the dry pan would be a likely place to find my friends in, as there is nothing a lion is fonder of than lying up in reeds, through which he can see things without being seen himself. Accordingly thither I went and prospected. Before I had got half-way round the pan I found the remains of a blue vilderbeeste that had evidently been killed within the last three or four days and partially devoured by lions; and from other indications about I was soon assured that if the family were not in the pan that day they spent a good deal of their spare time there. But if there, the question was how to get them out; for it was clearly impossible to think of going in after them unless one was quite determined to commit suicide. Now there was a strong wind blowing from the direction of the waggon, across the reedy pan towards the bush-clad kloof or donga, and this first gave me the idea of firing the reeds, which, as I think I told you, were pretty dry. Accordingly Tom took some matches and began starting little fires to the left, and I did the same to the right. But the reeds were still green at the bottom, and we should never have got them well alight had it not been for the wind, which grew stronger and stronger as the sun climbed higher, and forced the fire into them. At last, after half-an-hour's trouble, the flames got a hold, and began to spread out like a fan, where-upon I went round to the further side of the pan to wait for the lions, standing well out in the open, as we stood at the copse today where you shot the woodcock. It was a rather risky thing to do, but I used to be so sure of my shooting in those days that I did not so much mind the risk. Scarcely had I got round when I heard the reeds parting before the onward rush of some animal. 'Now for it,' said I. On it came. I could see that it was yellow, and prepared for action, when instead of a lion out bounded a beautiful reit bok which had been lying in the shelter of the pan. It must, by the way, have been a reit bok of a peculiarly confid-ing nature to lay itself down with the lion, like the lamb of prophesy, but I suppose the reeds were thick, and that it kept a long way off.

Well, I let the reit bok go, and it went like the wind, and kept my eyes fixed upon the reeds. The fire was burning like a furnace now; the flames crackling and roaring as they bit into the reeds, sending spouts of fire twenty feet and more into the air, and making the hot air dance above in a way that was per-fectly dazzling. But the reeds were still half green, and created an enormous quantity of smoke, which came rolling towards me like a curtain, lying very low on account of the wind. Presently, above the crackling of the fire, I heard a startled roar, then another and another. So the lions were at home.

I was beginning to get excited now, for, as you fellows know, there is nothing in experience to warm up your nerves like a lion at close quarters, unless it is a wounded buffalo; and I became still more so when I made out through the smoke that the lions were all moving about on the extreme edge of the reeds. Occasionally they would pop their heads out like rabbits from a burrow, and then, catching sight of me standing about fifty yards away, draw them back again. I knew that it must be getting pretty warm behind them, and that they could not keep the game up for long; and I was not mistaken, for suddenly all four of them broke cover together, the old black-maned lion leading by a few yards. I never saw a more splendid sight in all my hunting experience than those four lions bounding across the veldt, overshadowed by the dense pall of smoke and backed by the fiery furnace of the burning reeds.

I reckoned that they would pass, on their way to the bushy kloof, within about five and twenty yards of me, so, taking a long breath, I got my gun well on to the lion's shoulder — the black-maned one — so as to allow for an inch or two of motion, and catch him through the heart. I was on, dead on, and my finger was just beginning to tighten on the trigger, when suddenly I went blind — a bit of reed-ash had drifted into my right eye. I danced and rubbed, and succeeded in clearing it more or less just in time to see the tail of the last lion vanishing round the bushes up the kloof.

If ever a man was mad I was that man. It was too bad; and such a shot in the open! However, I was not going to be beaten, so I just turned and marched for the kloof. Tom, the driver, begged and implored me not to go, but though as a general rule I never pretend to be very brave (which I am not), I was determined that I would either kill those lions or they should kill me. So I told Tom that he need not come unless he liked, but I was going; and being a plucky fellow, a Swazi by birth, he shrugged his shoulders, muttered that I was mad or bewitched, and followed doggedly in my tracks.

We soon reached the kloof, which was about three hundred yards in length and but sparsely wooded, and then the real fun began. There might be a lion behind every bush — there certainly were four lions somewhere; the delicate question was, where. I peeped and poked and looked in every possible direction, with my heart in my mouth, and was at last rewarded by catching a glimpse of something yellow moving behind a bush. At the same moment, from another bush opposite me out burst one of the cubs and galloped back towards the burnt pan. I whipped round and let drive a snap shot that tipped him head over heels, breaking his back within two inches of the root of the tail, and there he lay helpless but glaring. Tom afterwards killed him with his assegai. I opened the breech of the gun and hurriedly pulled out the old case, which, to judge from what ensued, must, I suppose, have burst and left a portion of its fabric sticking to the barrel. At any rate, when I tried to get in the new cartridge it would only enter half-way; and — would you believe it? — this was the moment that the lioness, attracted no doubt by the outcry of her cub, chose to put in an appearance. There she stood, twenty paces or so from me, lashing her tail and looking just as wicked as it is possible to conceive. Slowly I stepped backwards, trying to push in the new case, and as I did so she moved on in little runs, dropping down after each run. The danger was imminent, and the case would not go in. At the moment I oddly enough thought of the cartridge maker, whose name I will not mention, and earnestly hoped that if the lion got *me* some condign punishment would overtake *him*. It would not go in, so I tried to pull it out. It would not come out either, and my gun was useless if I could not shut it to use the other barrel. I might as well have had no gun.

Meanwhile I was walking backward, keeping my eye on the lioness, who was creeping forward on her belly without a sound, but lashing her tail and keeping her eye on me; and in it I saw that she was coming in a few seconds more. I dashed my wrist and the palm of my hand against the brass rim of the cartridge till the blood poured from them —

'Look, there are the scars of it to this day!'

Here Quatermain held up his right hand to the light and showed us four or five white cicatrices just where the wrist is set into the hand.

But it was not of the slightest use, he went on: The cartridge would not move. I only hope that no other man will ever be put in such an awful position. The lioness gathered herself together, and I gave myself up for lost, when suddenly Tom shouted out from somewhere in my rear —

'You are walking on to the wounded cub; turn to the right.'

I had the sense, dazed as I was, to take the hint, and slewing round at right-angles, but still keeping my eyes on the lioness, I continued my backward walk.

To my intense relief, with a low growl she straightened herself, turned, and bounded further up the kloof.

'Come on, Macumazahn,' said Tom, 'let's get back to the waggon.'

'All right, Tom,' I answered. 'I will when I have killed those three other lions,' for by this time I was bent on shooting them as I never remember being bent on anything before or since. 'You can go if you like, or you can get up a tree.'

He considered the position a little, and then he very wisely got up a tree. I wish that I had done the same.

Meanwhile I had found my knife, which had an extractor in it, and succeeded after some difficulty in pulling out the cartridge which had so nearly been the cause of my death, and removing the obstruction in the barrel. It was very little thicker than a postage-stamp; certainly not thicker than a piece of writing-paper. This done, I loaded the gun, bound a handkerchief round my wrist and hand to staunch the flowing of the blood, and started on again.

I had noticed that the lioness went into a thick green bush, or rather cluster of bushes, growing near the water, about fifty yards higher up, for there was a little stream running down the kloof, and I walked towards this bush. When I got there, however, I could see nothing, so I took up a big stone and threw it into the bushes. I believe that it hit the other cub, for out it came with a rush, giving me a broadside shot, of which I promptly availed myself, knocking it over dead. Out, too, came the lioness like a flash of light, but quick as she went I managed to put the other bullet into her ribs, so that she rolled right over three times like a shot rabbit. I instantly got two more cartridges into the gun, and as I did so the lioness rose again and came crawling towards me on her fore-paws, roaring and groaning, and with such an expression of diabolical fury on her countenance as I have not often seen. I shot her again through the chest, and she fell over on to her side quite dead.

That was the first and last time that I ever killed a brace of lions right and left, and, what is more, I never heard of anybody else doing it. Naturally I was considerably pleased with myself, and having again loaded up, I went on to look for the black-maned beauty who had killed Kaptein. Slowly, and with the greatest care, I proceeded up the kloof, searching every bush and tuft of grass as I went. It was wonderfully exciting work, for I never was sure from one moment to another but that he would be on me. I took comfort, however, from the reflection that a lion rarely attacks a man – rarely, I say; sometimes he does, as you will see – unless he is cornered or wounded. I must have been nearly an hour hunting after that lion. Once I thought I saw something move in a clump of tambouki grass, but I could not be sure, and when I trod out the grass I could not find him.

At last I worked up to the head of the kloof, which made a *cul-de-sac*. It was formed of a wall of rock about fifty feet high. Down this rock trickled a little waterfall, and in front of it, some seventy feet from its face, rose a great piled-up mass of boulders, in the crevices and on the top of which grew ferns, grasses, and stunted bushes. This mass was about twenty-five feet high. The sides of the kloof here were also very steep. Well, I came to the top of the nullah and looked all round. No signs of the lion. Evidently I had either overlooked him further down or he had escaped right away. It was very vexatious; but still three lions were not a bad bag for one gun before dinner, and I was fain to be content. Accordingly I departed back again, making my way round the isolated pillar of boulders, beginning to feel, as I did so, that I was pretty well done up with excitement and fatigue, and should be more so before I had skinned those three lions. When I had got, as nearly as I could judge, about eighteen yards past the pillar or mass of boulders, I turned to have another look round. I have a pretty sharp eye, but I could see nothing at all.

Then, on a sudden, I saw something sufficiently alarming. On the top of the mass of boulders, opposite to me, standing out clear against the rock beyond, was the huge black-maned lion. He had been crouching there, and now arose as though by magic. There he stood lashing his tail, just like a living repro-duction of the animal on the gateway of Northumberland House that I have seen in a picture. But he did not stand long. Before I could fire – before I could do more than get the gun to my shoulder – he sprang straight up and out from the rock, and driven by the impetus of that one mighty bound came hurtling through the air towards me.

Heavens! how grand he looked, and how awful! High into the air he flew, describing a great arch. Just as he touched the highest point of his spring I fired. I did not dare to wait, for I saw that he would clear the whole space and land right upon me. Without a sight, almost without aim, I fired, as one would fire a snap shot at a snipe. The bullet told, for I distinctly heard its thud above the rushing sound caused by the passage of the lion through the air. Next second I was swept to the ground (luckily I fell into a low, creeper-clad bush, which broke the shock), and the lion was on the top of me, and the next those great white teeth of his had met in my thigh — I heard them grate against the bone. I yelled out in agony, for I did not feel in the least benumbed and happy, like Dr Livingstone — whom, by the way, I knew very well — and gave myself up for dead. But suddenly, at that moment, the lion's grip on my thigh loosened, and he stood over me, swaying to and fro, his huge mouth, from which the blood was gushing, wide open. Then he roared, and the sound shook the rocks.

To and fro he swung, and then the great head dropped on me, knocking all the breath from my body, and he was dead. My bullet had entered in the centre of his chest and passed out on the right side of the spine about half way down the back.

The pain of my wound kept me from fainting, and as soon as I got my breath I managed to drag myself from under him. Thank heavens, his great teeth had not crushed my thigh-bone; but I was losing a great deal of blood, and had it not been for the timely arrival of Tom, with whose aid I loosed the handkerchief from my wrist and tied it round my leg, twisting it tight with a stick, I think that I should have bled to death.

Well, it was a just reward for my folly in trying to tackle a family of lions single-handed. The odds were too long. I have been lame ever since, and shall be to my dying day; in the month of March the wound always troubles me a great deal, and every three years it breaks out raw.

I need scarcely add that I never traded the lot of ivory at Sikukuni's. Another man got it — a German — and made five hundred pounds out of it after paying expenses. I spent the next month on the broad of my back, and was a cripple for six months after that.

'And now I've told you the yarn, so I will have a drop of Hollands and go to bed. Goodnight to you all, goodnight!'

Magepa the Buck

In a preface to the story of the early life of the late Allan Quatermain, known in Africa as Macumazahn, which has recently been published under the name of *Marie*, Mr Curtis, the brother of Sir Henry Curtis, tells of how he found a number of manuscripts that were left by Mr Quatermain in his house in Yorkshire. Of these *Marie* was one, but in addition to it and sundry other completed stories, I, the Editor to whom it was directed that these manuscripts should be handed for publication, have found a quantity of unclassified notes and papers.

One of these notes – it is contained in a book, much soiled and worn, that evidently its owner had carried about with him for years – reminds me of a conversation I had with Mr Quatermain long ago when I was his guest in Yorkshire. The note itself is short; I think that he must have jotted it down within an hour or two of the event to which it refers. It runs thus:

'I wonder whether in the "Land Beyond" any recognition is granted for acts of great courage and unselfish devotion – a kind of spiritual Victoria Cross. If so I think it ought to be accorded to that poor old savage, Magepa, at least it would be if I had any voice in the matter. He has made me feel proud of humanity. And yet he was nothing but a "nigger", as so many call the Kaffirs.'

For a while I, the Editor, wondered to what this entry could allude. Then of a sudden it all came back to me. I saw myself, as a young man, seated in the hall of Quatermain's house one evening after dinner. With me were Sir Henry Curtis and Captain Good. We were smoking, and the conversation had turned upon deeds of heroism. Each of us detailed such acts as he could remember which had made the most impression on him. When we had finished, old Allan said:

With your leave I'll tell you a story of what I think was one of the bravest things I ever saw. It happened at the beginning of the Zulu war, when the troops were marching into Zululand. Now at

Pears' Christmas Annual, 1912.

that time, as you know, I was turning an honest penny transport-riding for the Government, or rather for the military authorities. I hired them three waggons with the necessary voorloopers and drivers, sixteen good salted oxen to each waggon, and myself in charge of the lot. They paid me – well, never mind how much – I am rather ashamed to mention the amount. I asked a good price for my waggons, or rather for the hire of them, of a very well satisfied young gentleman in uniform who had been exactly three weeks in the country, and, to my surprise, got it. But when I went to those in command and warned them what would happen if they persisted in their way of advance, then in their pride they would not listen to the old hunter and transport-rider, but politely bowed me out. If they had, there would have been no Isandhlwana disaster.

He brooded awhile, for, as I knew, this was a sore subject with him, one of which he would rarely talk. Although he escaped himself, Quatermain had lost friends on that fatal field. He went on:

To return to old Magepa. I had known him for many years. The first time we met was in the battle of the Tugela. I was fighting for the king's son, Umbelazi the Handsome, in the ranks of the Amawombe regiment – I mean to write all that story, for it should not be lost.[1] Well, as I have told you before, the Amawombe were wiped out; of the three thousand or so of them I think only about fifty remained alive after they had annihilated the three of Cetywayo's regiments that set upon them. But Magepa was one who survived.

I met him afterwards at old King Panda's kraal and recognised him as having fought by my side. Whilst I was talking with him the Prince Cetywayo came by; to me he was civil enough, for he knew how I chanced to be in the battle, but he glared at Magepa, and said:

'Why, Macumazahn, is not this man one of the dogs with which you tried to bite me by the Tugela not long ago? He must be a cunning dog also, one who can run fast, for how comes it that he lives to snarl when so many will never bark again? *Ow!* if I had my way I would find a strip of hide to fit his neck.'

'Not so,' I answered; 'he has the king's peace and he is a brave man – braver than I am, anyway, Prince, seeing that I ran

---

[1] For this story see the book named *Child of Storm* by H. Rider Haggard.

from the ranks of the Amawombe, while he stood where he was.'

'You mean that your horse ran, Macumazahn. Well, since you like this dog, I will not hurt him.' And with a shrug he went his way.

'Yet soon or late he will hurt me,' said Magepa, when the Prince had gone. 'U'Cetywayo has a memory long as the shadow thrown by a tree at sunset. Moreover, as he knows well, it is true that I ran, Macumazahn, though not till all was finished and I could do no more by standing still. You remember how, after we had eaten up the first of Cetywayo's regiments, the second charged us and we ate that up also. Well, in that fight I got a tap on the head from a kerry. It struck me on my man's ring which I had just put on, for I think I was the youngest soldier in that regiment of veterans. The ring saved me; still, for a while I lost my mind and lay like one dead. When I found it again the fight was over and Cetywayo's people were searching for our wounded that they might kill them. Presently they found me and saw that there was no hurt on me.

' "Here is one who shams dead like a stink-cat," said a big fellow, lifting his spear.

'Then it was that I sprang up and ran, I who was but just married and desired to live. He struck at me, but I jumped over the spear, and the others that they threw missed me. Then they began to hunt me, but, Macumazahn, I, who am named "The Buck" because I am swifter of foot than any man in Zululand, outpaced them all and got away safe.'

'Well done, Magepa,' I said. 'Still, remember the saying of your people, "At last the strong swimmer goes with the stream and the swift runner is run down." '

'I know it, Macumazahn,' he answered, with a nod, 'and perhaps in a day to come I shall know it better.'

I took little heed of his words at the time, but more than thirty years afterwards I remembered them.

Such was my first acquaintance with Magepa. Now, friends, I will tell you how it was renewed at the time of the Zulu war.

As you know, I was attached to the centre column that advanced into Zululand by Rorke's Drift on the Buffalo River. Before war was declared, or at any rate before the advance began, while it might have been and many thought it would be

averted, I was employed transport-riding goods to the little
Rorke's Drift station, that which became so famous afterwards,
and incidentally in collecting what information I could of Cetywayo's intentions. Hearing that there was a kraal a mile or so the
other side of the river, of which the people were said to be very
friendly to the English, I determined to visit it. You may think
this was rash, but I was so well known in Zululand, where for
many years, by special leave of the king, I was allowed to go
whither I would quite unmolested, that I felt no fear for myself
so long as I went alone.

Accordingly one evening I crossed the drift and headed for
a kloof in which I was told the kraal stood. Ten minutes' ride
brought me in sight of it. It was not a large kraal; there may have
been six or eight huts and a cattle enclosure surrounded by the
usual fence. The situation, however, was very pretty, a knoll of
rising ground backed by the wooded slopes of the kloof. As I
approached I saw women and children running to the kraal to
hide, and when I reached the gateway for some time no one
would come out to meet me. At length a small boy appeared who
informed me that the kraal was 'empty as a gourd'.

'Quite so,' I answered; 'still, go and tell the headman that
Macumazahn wishes to speak with him.'

The boy departed, and presently I saw a face that seemed
familiar to me peeping round the gateway. After a careful
inspection its owner emerged.

He was a tall, thin man of indefinite age, perhaps between
sixty and seventy, with a finely-cut face, a little grey beard, kind
eyes and very well shaped hands and feet, the fingers, which
twitched incessantly, being remarkably long.

'Greeting, Macumazahn,' he said. 'I see you do not remember me. Well, think of the battle of the Tugela, and of the last
stand of the Amawombe and of a certain talk at the kraal of our
Father-who-is-dead' (that is, King Panda), 'and of how he who
sits in his place' (he meant Cetywayo) 'told you that if he had his
way he would find a hide rope to fit the neck of a certain one.'

'Ah!' I said, 'I know you now; you are Magepa the Buck. So
the Runner has not yet been run down.'

'No, Macumazahn, not yet; but there is still time. I think
that many swift feet will be at work ere long.'

'How have you prospered?' I asked him.

'Well enough, Macumazahn, in all ways except one. I have three wives, but my children have been few and are dead, except one daughter, who is married and lives with me, for her husband, too, is dead. He was killed by a buffalo, and she has not yet married again. But enter and see.'

So I went in and saw Magepa's wives, old women all of them. Also, at his bidding, his daughter, whose name was Gita, brought me some *maas*, curdled milk, to drink. She was a well-formed woman, very like her father, but sad-faced, perhaps with a prescience of evil to come. Clinging to her finger was a beautiful boy of something under two years of age, who, when he saw Magepa, ran to him and threw his little arms about his legs. The old man lifted the child and kissed him tenderly, saying:

'It is well that this toddler and I should love one another, Macumazahn, seeing that he is the last of my race. All the other children here are those of the people who have come to live in my shadow.'

'Where are their fathers?' I asked, patting the little boy (who, his mother told me, was named Sinala) upon the cheek, an attention that he resented.

'They have been called away on duty,' answered Magepa shortly; and I changed the subject.

Then we began to talk about old times, and I asked him if he had any oxen to sell, saying that this was my reason for visiting his kraal.

'Nay, Macumazahn,' he answered, in a meaning voice. 'This year all the cattle are the king's.'

I nodded and replied that, as it was so, I had better be going; whereon, as I half expected, Magepa announced that he would see me safe to the drift. So I bade farewell to the wives and the widowed daughter, and we started.

As soon as we were clear of the kraal Magepa began to open his heart to me.

'Macumazahn,' he said, looking up at me earnestly, for I was mounted and he walked beside my horse, 'there is to be war. Cetywayo will not consent to the demands of the great White Chief from the Cape' — he meant Sir Bartle Frere. 'He will fight with the English; only he will let them begin the fighting. He will draw them on into Zululand and then overwhelm them with his *impis* and stamp them flat, and eat them up; I, who love the English, am very sorry. Yes, it makes my heart bleed. If it were the Boers now, I should be glad, for we Zulus hate the Boers; but the English we do not hate; even Cetywayo likes them; still he will eat them up if they attack him.'

'Indeed,' I answered; and then, as in duty bound, I proceeded to get what I could out of him, and that was not a little. Of course, however, I did not swallow it all, since I suspected that Magepa was feeding me with news that he had been ordered to disseminate.

Presently we came to the mouth of the kloof in which the kraal stood, and here, for greater convenience of conversation, we halted, for I thought it as well that we should not be seen in close talk on the open plain beyond. The path here, I should add, ran past a clump of green bushes; I remember they bore a white flower that smelt sweet, and were backed by some tall grass, elephant-grass I think it was, among which grew mimosa trees.

'Magepa,' I said, 'if in truth there is to be fighting, why don't you move over the river one night with your people and cattle, and get into Natal?'

'I would if I could, Macumazahn, who have no stomach for this war against the English. But there I should not be safe, since presently the king will come into Natal too, or send thirty thousand assegais as his messengers. Then what will happen to those who have left him?'

'Oh, if you think that,' I answered, 'you had better stay where you are.'

'Also, Macumazahn, the husbands of those women at my kraal have been called up to their regiments, and if their wives fled to the English they would be killed. Again, the king has sent for nearly all our cattle, "to keep it safe". He fears lest we Border Zulus might join our people in Natal, and that is why he is keeping our cattle "safe".'

'Life is more than cattle, Magepa. At least you might come.'

'What! And leave my people to be killed? Macumazahn, you did not use to talk so. Still, hearken Macumazahn, will you do me a service? I will pay you well for it. I would get my daughter Gita and my little grandson Sinala into safety. If I and my wives are wiped out it does not matter, for we are old. But her

I would save, and the boy I would save, so that one may live who will remember my name. Now, if I were to send them across the drift, say at the dawn, not tomorrow, and not the next day, but the day after, would you receive them into your wagon and deliver them safe to some place in Natal? I have money hidden, fifty pieces of gold, and you may take half of these and also half of the cattle if ever I live to get them back out of the keeping of the king.'

'Never mind about the money, and we will speak of the cattle afterward,' I said. 'I understand that you wish to send your daughter and your little grandson out of danger, and I think you wise, very wise. When once the advance begins, if there is an advance, who knows what may happen? War is a rough game, Magepa. It is not the custom of you black people to spare women and children, and there will be Zulus fighting on our side as well as on yours; do you understand?'

'*Ow!* I understand, Macumazahn, I have known the face of war and seen many a little one like my grandson Sinala assegaied upon his mother's back.'

'Very good. But if I do this for you, you must do something for me. Say, Magepa, does Cetywayo *really* mean to fight, and if so, how? Oh yes, I know all you have been telling me, but I want not words, but truth from the heart.'

'You ask secrets,' said the old fellow, peering about him into the gathering gloom. 'Still, "a spear for a spear and a shield for a shield," as our saying runs. I have spoken no lie. The king *does* mean to fight, not because he wants to, but because the regiments swear that they will wash their assegais, they who have never seen blood since that battle of the Tugela in which we two played a part; and if he will not suffer it, well, there are more of his race! Also he means to fight thus,' and he gave me some very useful information; that is, information which would have been useful if those in authority had deigned to pay any attention to it when I passed it on.

Just as he finished speaking I thought that I heard a sound in the dense green bush behind us. It reminded me of the noise a man makes when he tries to stifle a cough, and frightened me. For if we had been overheard by a spy, Magepa was as good as dead, and the sooner I was across the river the better.

'What's that?' I asked.

'A bush buck, Macumazahn. There are lots of them about here.'

Not being satisfied, though it is true that bucks do cough like this, I turned my horse to the bush, seeking an opening. Thereon something crashed away and vanished into the long grass. In those shadows, of course, I could not see what it was, but such light as remained glinted on what might have been the polished tip of the horn of an antelope or – an assegai.

'I told you it was a buck, Macumazahn,' said Magepa. 'Still, if you smell danger, let us come away from the bush, though the orders are that no white man is to be touched as yet.'

Then, while we walked on towards the ford, he set out with great detail, as Kaffirs do, the exact arrangements that he proposed to make for the handing over of his daughter and her child into my care. I remember that I asked him why he would not send her on the following morning, instead of two mornings later. He answered because he expected an outpost of scouts from one of the regiments at his kraal that night, who would probably remain there over the morrow and perhaps longer. While they were in the place it would be difficult for him to send away Gita and her son without exciting suspicion.

Near the drift we parted, and I returned to our provisional camp and wrote a beautiful report of all that I had learned, of which report, I may add, no one took the slightest notice.

I think it was the morning before that whereon I had arranged to meet Gita and the little boy at the drift that just about dawn I went down to the river for a wash. Having taken my dip I climbed on to a flat rock to dress myself, and looked at the billows of beautiful, pearly mist which hid the face of the water, and considered – I almost said listened to – the great silence, for as yet no live thing was stirring.

Ah! if I had known of the hideous sights and sounds that were destined to be heard ere long in this same haunt of perfect peace! Indeed, at that moment there came a kind of hint or premonition of them, since suddenly through the utter quiet broke the blood-curdling wail of a woman. It was followed by other wails and shouts, distant and yet distinct. Then the silence fell again.

Now, thought I to myself, that noise might very well have come from old Magepa's kraal; luckily, however, sounds are deceptive in mist.

Well, the end of it was that I waited there till the sun rose. The first thing on which its bright beams struck was a mighty column of smoke rising to heaven from where Magepa's kraal had stood!

I went back to my waggons very sad, so sad that I could scarcely eat my breakfast. While I walked I wondered hard whether the light had glinted upon the tip of a buck's horn in that patch of green bush with the sweet-smelling white flowers a night or two ago. Or had it perchance fallen upon the point of the assegai of some spy who was watching my movements! In that event yonder column of smoke and the horrible cries which preceded it were easy to explain. For had not Magepa and I talked secrets together, and in Zulu.

On the following morning at the dawn I attended at the drift in the faint hope that Gita and her boy might arrive there as arranged. But nobody came, which was not wonderful, seeing that Gita lay dead, stabbed through and through, as I saw after-wards (she made a good fight for the child), and that her spirit had gone to wherever go the souls of the brave-hearted, be they white or black. Only on the farther bank of the river I saw some Zulu scouts who seemed to know my errand, for they called to me, asking mockingly where was the pretty woman I had come to meet?

After that I tried to put the matter out of my head, which indeed was full enough of other things, since now definite orders had arrived as to the advance, and with these many troops and officers.

It was just then that the Zulus began to fire across the river at such of our people as they saw upon the bank. At these they took aim, and, as a result, hit nobody. A raw Kaffir with a rifle, in my experience, is only dangerous when he aims at nothing, for then the bullet looks after itself, and may catch you. To put a stop to this nuisance a regiment of the friendly natives – there may have been several hundred of them – was directed to cross the river and clear the kloofs and rocks of the Zulu skirmishers who were hidden among them. I watched them go off in fine style.

Towards evening some one told me that our *impi*, as he grandiloquently called it, was returning victorious. Having at the moment nothing else to do, I walked down to the river at a point where the water was deep and the banks were high. Here I climbed to the top of a pile of boulders, whence with my field-glasses I could sweep a great extent of plain which stretched away on the Zululand side till at length it merged into hills and bush.

Presently I saw some of our natives marching homewards in a scattered and disorganised fashion, but evidently very proud of themselves, for they were waving their assegais and singing scraps of war-songs. A few minutes later, a mile or more away, I caught sight of a man running.

Watching him through the glasses I noted three things: first, that he was tall; secondly, that he ran with extraordinary swiftness; and, thirdly, that he had something tied upon his back. It was evident, further, that he had good reason to run, since he was being hunted by a number of our Kaffirs, of whom more and more continually joined in the chase. From every side they poured down upon him, trying to cut him off and kill him, for as they got nearer I could see the assegais which they threw at him flash in the sunlight.

Very soon I understood that the man was running with a definite object and to a definite point; he was trying to reach the river. I thought the sight very pitiful, this one poor creature being hunted to death by so many. Also I wondered why he did not free himself from the bundle on his back, and came to the conclusion that he must be a witch-doctor, and that the bundle contained his precious charms or medicines.

This was while he was yet a long way off, but when he came nearer, within three or four hundred yards, of a sudden I caught the outline of his face against a good background, and knew it for that of Magepa.

'My God!' I said to myself, 'it is old Magepa the Buck, and the bundle in the mat will be his grandson, Sinala!'

Yes, even then I felt certain that he was carrying the child upon his back.

What was I to do? It was impossible for me to cross the river at that place, and long before I could get round by the ford all would be finished. I stood up on my rock and shouted to those brutes of Kaffirs to let the man alone. They were so excited that they did not hear my words; at least, they swore afterwards that they thought I was encouraging them to hunt him down.

But Magepa heard me. At that moment he seemed to be failing, but the sight of me appeared to give him fresh strength. He gathered himself together and leapt forward at a really surprising speed. Now the river was not more than three hundred yards away from him, and for the first two hundred of these he quite outdistanced his pursuers, although they were most of them young men and comparatively fresh. Then once more his strength began to fail.

Watching through the glasses I could see that his mouth was wide open, and that there was red foam upon his lips. The burden on his back was dragging him down. Once he lifted his hands as though to loose it; then with a wild gesture let them fall again.

Two of the pursuers who had outpaced the others crept up to him — lank, lean men of not more than thirty years of age. They had stabbing spears in their hands, such as are used at close quarters, and these of course they did not throw. One of them gained a little on the other.

Now Magepa was not more than fifty yards from the bank, with the first hunter about ten paces behind him and coming up rapidly. Magepa glanced over his shoulder and saw, then put out his last strength. For forty yards he went like an arrow, running straight away from his pursuers, until he was within a few feet of the bank, when he stumbled and fell.

'He's done,' I said, and, upon my word, if I had a rifle in my hand I think I would have stopped one or both of those bloodhounds and taken the consequences.

But, no! Just as the first man lifted his broad spear to stab him through the back on which the bundle lay, Magepa leapt up and wheeled round to take the thrust in his chest. Evidently he did not wish to be speared in the back — for a certain reason. He took it sure enough, for the assegai was wrenched out of the hand of the striker. Still, as he was reeling backwards, it did not go through Magepa, or perhaps it hit a bone. He drew out the spear and threw it at the man, wounding him. Then he staggered on, back and back, to the edge of the little cliff.

It was reached at last. With a cry of 'Help me Macumazahn!'

Magepa turned, and before the other man could spear him, leapt straight into deep water. He rose. Yes, the brave old fellow rose and struck out for the other bank, leaving a little line of red behind him.

I rushed, or rather sprang and rolled down to the edge of the stream, to where a point of shingle ran out into the water. Along this I clambered, and beyond it up to my middle. Now Magepa was being swept past me. I caught his outstretched hand and pulled him ashore.

'The boy!' he gasped; 'the boy! Is he dead?'

I severed the lashings of the mat that had cut right into the old fellow's shoulders. Inside of it was little Sinala, spluttering out water, but very evidently alive and unhurt, for presently he set up a yell.

'No,' I said, 'he lives, and will live.'

'Then all is well, Macumazahn.' (*A pause*) 'It *was* a spy in the bush, not a buck. He overheard our talk. The king's slayers came. Gita held the door of the hut while I took the child, cut a hole through the straw with my assegai, and crept out at the back. She was full of spears before she died, but I got away with the boy. Till your Kaffirs found me I lay hid in the bush, hoping to escape to Natal. Then I ran for the river, and saw you on the further bank. *I* might have got away, but that child is heavy.' (*A pause*) 'Give him food, Macumazahn, he must be hungry.' (*A pause*) 'Farewell. That was a good saying of yours – the swift runner is outrun at last. Ah! yet I did not run in vain.' (*Another pause, the last.*) Then he lifted himself upon one arm and with the other saluted, first the boy Sinala and next me, muttering, 'Remember your promise, Macumazahn.'

'That is how Magepa the Buck died. I never saw any one carrying weight who could run quite so well as he,' and Quatermain turned his head away as though the memory of this incident affected him somewhat.

'What became of the child Sinala?' I asked presently.

'Oh, I sent him to an institution in Natal, and afterwards was able to get some of his property back for him. I believe that he is being trained as an interpreter.'

Black Heart and White Heart

I

A Zulu Idyll

At the date of our introduction to him, Philip Hadden was a transport-rider and a trader in 'the Zulu'. Still on the right side of forty, in appearance he was singularly handsome; tall, dark, upright, with keen eyes, short-pointed beard, curling hair and clear-cut features. His life had been varied, and there were passages in it which he did not narrate even to his most intimate friends. He was of gentle birth, however, and it was said that he had received a public school and university education in England. At any rate he could quote the classics with aptitude on occasion, an accomplishment which, coupled with his refined voice and a bearing not altogether common in the wild places of the world, had earned for him among his rough companions the *soubriquet* of 'The Prince'.

However these things may have been, it is certain that he had emigrated to Natal under a cloud, and equally certain that his relatives at home were content to take no further interest in his fortunes. During the fifteen or sixteen years which he had spent in or about the colony, Hadden followed many trades, and did no good at any of them. A clever man, of agreeable and pre-possessing manner, he always found it easy to form friendships and to secure a fresh start in life. But, by degrees, the friends were seized with a vague distrust of him; and, after a period of more or less application, he himself would close the opening that he had made by a sudden disappearance from the locality, leaving behind him a doubtful reputation and some bad debts.

Before the beginning of this story of the most remarkable episodes in his life, Philip Hadden was engaged for several years in transport-riding – that is, in carrying goods on ox waggons from Durban or Maritzburg to various points in the interior. A difficulty such as had more than once confronted him in the course of his career, led to his temporary abandonment of this

The African Review, January 1896.

means of earning a livelihood. On arriving at the little frontier town of Utrecht in the Transvaal, in charge of two waggon-loads of mixed goods consigned to a storekeeper there, it was discovered that out of six cases of brandy five were missing from his waggon. Hadden explained the matter by throwing the blame upon his Kaffir 'boys', but the storekeeper, a rough-tongued man, openly called him a thief and refused to pay the freight on any of the load. From words the men came to blows, knives were drawn, and before anybody could interfere the storekeeper received a nasty wound in his side. That night, without waiting till the matter could be inquired into by the landdrost or magistrate, Hadden slipped away, and trekked back into Natal as quickly as his oxen would travel. Feeling that even here he was not safe, he left one of his waggons at Newcastle, loaded up the other with Kaffir goods — such as blankets, calico, and hardware — and crossed into Zululand, where in those days no sheriff's officer would be likely to follow him.

Being well acquainted with the language and customs of the natives, he did good trade with them, and soon found himself possessed of some cash and a small herd of cattle, which he received in exchange for his wares. Meanwhile news reached him that the man whom he had injured still vowed vengeance against him, and was in communication with the authorities in Natal. These reasons making his return to civilization undesirable for the moment, and further business being impossible until he could receive a fresh supply of trade stuff, Hadden like a wise man turned his thoughts to pleasure. Sending his cattle and waggon over the border to be left in charge of a native headman with whom he was friendly, he went on foot to Ulundi to obtain permission from the king, Cetywayo, to hunt game in his country. Somewhat to his surprise the Indunas, or headmen, received him courteously — for Hadden's visit took place within a few months of the outbreak of the Zulu war in 1878, when Cetywayo was already showing unfriendliness to the English traders and others, though why the king did so they knew not.

On the occasion of his first and last interview with Cetywayo, Hadden got a hint of the reason. It happened thus. On the second morning after his arrival at the royal kraal, a messenger came to inform him that 'the Elephant whose tread shook the earth' had signified that it was his pleasure to see him.

Accordingly he was led through the thousands of huts and across the Great Place to the little enclosure where Cetywayo, a royal-looking Zulu seated on a stool, and wearing a *kaross* of leopard skins, wäs holding an *indaba*, or conference, surrounded by his counsellors. The Induna who had conducted him to the august presence went down upon his hands and knees, and, uttering the royal salute of *Bayéte*, crawled forward to announce that the white man was waiting.

'Let him wait,' said the king angrily; and, turning, he continued the discussion with his counsellors.

Now, as has been said, Hadden thoroughly understood Zulu; and, when from time to time the king raised his voice, some of the words he spoke reached his ear.

'What!' Cetywayo said, to a wizened and aged man who seemed to be pleading with him earnestly; 'am I a dog that these white hyenas should hunt me thus? Is not the land mine, and was it not my father's before me? Are not the people mine to save or to slay? I tell you that I will stamp out these little white men; my *impis* shall eat them up. I have said!'

Again the withered aged man interposed, evidently in the character of a peacemaker. Hadden could not hear his talk, but he rose and pointed towards the sea, while from his expressive gestures and sorrowful mien, he seemed to be prophesying disaster should a certain course of action be followed.

For a while the king listened to him, then he sprang from his seat, his eyes literally ablaze with rage.

'Hearken,' he cried to the counsellor; 'I have guessed it for long, and now I am sure of it. You are a traitor. You are Sompseu's[1] dog, and the dog of the Natal Government, and I will not keep another man's dog to bite me in my own house. Take him away!'

A slight involuntary murmur rose from the ring of *indunas*, but the old man never flinched, not even when the soldiers, who presently would murder him, came and seized him roughly. For a few seconds, perhaps five, he covered his face with the corner of the *kaross* he wore, then he looked up and spoke to the king in a clear voice.

'O King,' he said, 'I am a very old man; as a youth I served under Chaka the Lion, and I heard his dying prophecy of the

---

[1] Sir Theophilus Shepstone's.

coming of the white man. Then the white men came, and I fought for Dingaan at the battle of the Blood River. They slew Dingaan, and for many years I was the counsellor of Panda, your father. I stood by you, O King, at the battle of the Tugela, when its grey waters were turned to red with the blood of Umbulazi your brother, and of the tens of thousands of his people. Afterwards I became your counsellor, O King, and I was with you when Sompseu set the crown upon your head and you made promises to Sompseu – promises that you have not kept. Now you are weary of me, and it is well; for I am very old, and doubtless my talk is foolish, as it chances to the old. Yet I think that the prophecy of Chaka, your great-uncle, will come true, and that the white men will prevail against you and that through them you shall find your death. I would that I might have stood in one more battle and fought for you, O King, since fight you will, but the end which you choose is for me the best end. Sleep in peace, O King, and farewell. *Bayéte!*'[1]

For a space there was silence, a silence of expectation while men waited to hear the tyrant reverse his judgment. But it did not please him to be merciful, or the needs of policy outweighed his pity.

'Take him away,' he repeated. Then, with a slow smile on his face and one word, 'Good-night,' upon his lips, supported by the arm of a soldier, the old warrior and statesman shuffled forth to the place of death.

Hadden watched and listened in amazement not unmixed with fear. 'If he treats his own servants like this, what will happen to me?' he reflected. 'We English must have fallen out of favour since I left Natal. I wonder whether he means to make war on us or what? If so, this isn't my place.'

Just then the king, who had been gazing moodily at the ground, chanced to look up. 'Bring the stranger here,' he said.

Hadden heard him, and coming forward offered Cetywayo his hand in as cool and nonchalant a manner as he could command.

Somewhat to his surprise it was accepted. 'At least, White Man,' said the king, glancing at his visitor's tall spare form and cleanly cut face, 'you are no *umfagozan* (low fellow); you are of the blood of chiefs.'

---

[1] The royal salute of the Zulus.

'Yes, King,' answered Hadden, with a little sigh, 'I am of the blood of chiefs.'

'What do you want in my country, White Man?'

'Very little, King. I have been trading here, as I daresay you have heard, and have sold all my goods. Now I ask your leave to hunt buffalo, and other big game, for a while before I return to Natal.'

'I cannot grant it,' answered Cetywayo, 'you are a spy sent by Sompseu, or by the Queen's Induna in Natal. Get you gone.'

'Indeed,' said Hadden, with a shrug of his shoulders; 'then I hope that Sompseu, or the Queen's Induna, or both of them, will pay me when I return to my own country. Meanwhile I will obey you because I must, but I should first like to make you a present.'

'What present?' asked the king. 'I want no presents. We are rich here, White Man.'

'So be it, King. It was nothing worthy of your taking, only a rifle.'

'A rifle, White Man? Where is it?'

'Without. I would have brought it, but your servants told me that it is death to come armed before the "Elephant who shakes the Earth".'

Cetywayo frowned, for the note of sarcasm did not escape his quick ear.

'Let this white man's offering be brought; I will consider the thing.'

Instantly the Induna who had accompanied Hadden darted to the gateway, running with his body bent so low that it seemed as though at every step he must fall upon his face. Presently he returned with the weapon in his hand and presented it to the king, holding it so that the muzzle was pointed straight at the royal breast.

'I crave leave to say, O Elephant,' remarked Hadden in a drawling voice, 'that it might be well to command your servant to lift the mouth of that gun from your heart.'

'Why?' asked the king.

'Only because it is loaded, and at full cock, O Elephant, who probably desires to continue to shake the Earth.'

At these words the 'Elephant' uttered a sharp exclamation, and rolled from his stool in a most unkingly manner, whilst the

terrified Induna, springing backwards, contrived to touch the
trigger of the rifle and discharge a bullet through the exact spot
that a second before had been occupied by his monarch's head.

'Let him be taken away,' shouted the incensed king from
the ground, but long before the words had passed his lips the
Induna, with a cry that the gun was bewitched, had cast it down
and fled at full speed through the gate.

'He has already taken himself away,' suggested Hadden,
while the audience tittered. 'No, King, do not touch it rashly; it
is a repeating rifle. Look – ' and lifting the Winchester, he fired
the four remaining shots in quick succession into the air, striking
the top of a tree at which he aimed with every one of them.

'*Wow*, it is wonderful!' said the company in astonishment.

'Has the thing finished?' asked the king.

'For the present it has,' answered Hadden. 'Look at it.'

Cetywayo took the repeater in his hand, and examined it
with caution, swinging the muzzle horizontally in an exact line
with the stomachs of some of his most eminent Indunas, who
shrank to this side and that as the barrel was brought to bear
upon them.

'See what cowards they are, White Man,' said the king with
indignation; 'they fear lest there should be another bullet in this
gun.'

'Yes,' answered Hadden, 'they are cowards indeed. I
believe that if they were seated on stools they would tumble off
them as it chanced to your Majesty to do just now.'

'Do you understand the making of guns, White Man?'
asked the king hastily, while the Indunas one and all turned
their heads, and contemplated the fence behind them.

'No, King, I cannot make guns, but I can mend them.'

'If I paid you well, White Man, would you stop here at my
kraal, and mend guns for me?' asked Cetywayo anxiously.

'It might depend on the pay,' answered Hadden; 'but for a
while I am tired of work, and wish to rest. If the king gives me the
permission to hunt for which I asked, and men to go with me,
then when I return perhaps we can bargain on the matter. If
not, I will bid the king farewell, and journey to Natal.'

'In order to make report of what he has seen and learned
here,' muttered Cetywayo.

At this moment the talk was interrupted, for the soldiers

who had led away the old Induna returned at speed, and pro-strated themselves before the king.

'Is he dead?' he asked.

'He has travelled the king's bridge,' they answered grimly; 'he died singing a song of praise of the king.'

'Good,' said Cetywayo, 'that stone shall hurt my feet no more. Go, tell the tale of its casting away to Sompseu and to the Queen's Induna in Natal,' he added with bitter emphasis.

'*Baba!* Hear our Father speak. Listen to the rumbling of the Elephant,' said the Indunas taking the point, while one bolder than the rest added: 'Soon we will tell them another tale, the white Talking Ones, a red tale, a tale of spears, and the regiments shall sing it in their ears.'

At the words an enthusiasm caught hold of the listeners, as the sudden flame catches hold of dry grass. They sprang up, for the most of them were seated on their haunches, and stamping their feet upon the ground in unison, repeated:

> *Indaba ibomwu — indaba ye mikonto*
> *Lizo dunyiswa nge impi ndhlebeni yaho.*
> (A red tale! A red tale! A tale of spears,
> And the *impis* shall sing it in their ears.)

One of them, indeed, a great fierce-faced yellow, drew near to Hadden and shaking his fist before his eyes — fortunately being in the royal presence he had no assegai — shouted the sentences at him.

The king saw that the fire he had lit was burning too fiercely.

'Silence,' he thundered in the deep voice for which he was remarkable, and instantly each man became as if he were turned to stone, only the echoes still answered back: 'And the *impis* shall sing it in their ears — in their ears.'

'I am growing certain that this is no place for me,' thought Hadden; 'if that scoundrel had been armed he might have temporarily forgotten himself. Hullo! who's this?'

Just then there appeared through the gate of the fence a splendid specimen of the Zulu race. The man, who was about thirty-five years of age, was arrayed in a full war dress of a captain of the Umcityu regiment. From the circlet of otter skin on his brow rose his crest of plumes, round his middle, arms and

knees hung the long fringes of black oxtails, and in one hand he
bore a little dancing shield, also black in colour. The other was
empty, since he might not appear before the king bearing arms.
In countenance the man was handsome, and though just now
they betrayed some anxiety, his eyes were genial and honest, and
his mouth sensitive. In height he must have measured six foot
two inches, yet he did not strike the observer as being tall,
perhaps because of his width of chest and the solidity of his
limbs, that were in curious contrast to the delicate and almost
womanish hands and feet which so often mark the Zulu of noble
blood. In short the man was what he seemed to be, a savage
gentleman of birth, dignity and courage.

In company with him was another man plainly dressed in a
moocha and a blanket, whose grizzled hair showed him to be
over fifty years of age. His face also was pleasant and even
refined, but the eyes were timorous, and the mouth lacked
character.

'Who are these?' asked the king.

The two men fell on their knees before him, and bowed till
their foreheads touched the ground – the while giving him his
sibonga or titles of praise.

'Speak,' he said impatiently.

'O King,' said the young warrior, seating himself Zulu
fashion, 'I am Nahoon, the son of Zomba, a captain of the
Umcityu, and this is my uncle, Umgona, the brother of one of
my mothers, my father's youngest wife.'

Cetywayo frowned. 'What do you here away from your
regiment, Nahoon?'

'May it please the king, I have leave of absence from the
head captains, and I come to ask a boon of the king's bounty.'

'Be swift, then, Nahoon.'

'It is this, O King,' said the captain with some embarrass-
ment: 'A while ago the king was pleased to make a *keshla* of me
because of certain service that I did out yonder . . .' and he
touched the black ring which he wore in the hair of his head.
'Being now a ringed man and a captain, I crave the right of a
man at the hands of the king – the right to marry.'

'Right? Speak more humbly, son of Zomba; my soldiers and
my cattle have no rights.'

Nahoon bit his lip, for he had made a serious mistake.

'Pardon, O King. The matter stands thus: My uncle Umgona here has a fair daughter named Nanea, whom I desire to wife, and who desires me to husband. Awaiting the king's leave I am betrothed to her and in earnest of it I have paid to Umgona a *lobola* of fifteen head of cattle, cows and calves together. But Umgona has a powerful neighbour, an old chief named Maputa, the warden of the Crocodile Drift, who doubtless is known to the king, and this chief also seeks Nanea in marriage and harries Umgona, threatening him with many evils if he will not give the girl to him. But Umgona's heart is white towards me, and towards Maputa it is black, therefore together we come to crave this boon of the king.'

'It is so; he speaks the truth,' said Umgona.

'Cease,' answered Cetywayo angrily. 'Is this a time that my soldiers should seek wives in marriage, wives to turn their hearts to water? Know that but yesterday for this crime I commanded that twenty girls who had dared without my leave to marry men of the Undi regiment, should be strangled and their bodies laid upon the crossroads and with them the bodies of their fathers, that all might know their sin and be warned thereby. Ay, Umgona, it is well for you and for your daughter that you sought my word before she was given in marriage to this man. Now this is my award: I refuse your prayer, Nahoon, and since you, Umgona, are troubled with one whom you would not take as son-in-law, the old chief Maputa, I will free you from his importunity. The girl, says Nahoon, is fair – good, I myself will be gracious to her, and she shall be numbered among the wives of the royal house. Within thirty days from now, in the week of the next new moon, let her be delivered into the *Sigodhla*, the royal house of the women, and with her those cattle, the cows and the calves together, that Nahoon has given you, of which I fine him because he has dared to think of marriage without the leave of the king.'

II

The Bee Prophesies

' "A Daniel come to judgment" indeed,' reflected Hadden, who had been watching this savage comedy with interest; 'our love-sick friend has got more than he bargained for. Well, that comes of appealing to Caesar,' and he turned to look at the two suppliants.

The old man, Umgona, merely started, then began to pour out sentences of conventional thanks and praise to the king for his goodness and condescension. Cetywayo listened to his talk in silence, and when he had done answered by reminding him tersely that if Nanea did not appear at the date named, both she and he, her father, would in due course certainly decorate a crossroad in their own immediate neighbourhood.

The captain, Nahoon, afforded a more curious study. As the fatal words crossed the king's lips, his face took on an expression of absolute astonishment, which was presently replaced by one of fury — the just fury of a man who suddenly has suffered an unutterable wrong. His whole frame quivered, the veins stood out in knots on his neck and forehead, and his fingers closed convulsively as though they were grasping the handle of a spear. Presently the rage passed away — for as well might a man be wroth with fate as with a Zulu despot — to be succeeded by a look of the most hopeless misery. The proud dark eyes grew dull, the copper-coloured face sank in and turned ashen, the mouth drooped, and down one corner of it there trickled a little line of blood springing from the lip bitten through in the effort to keep silence. Lifting his hand in salute to the king, the great man rose and staggered rather than walked towards the gate.

As he reached it, the voice of Cetywayo commanded him to stop. 'Stay,' he said, 'I have a service for you, Nahoon, that shall drive out of your head these thoughts of wives and marriage. You see this white man here; he is my guest, and would hunt buffalo and big game in the bush country. I put him in your charge; take men with you, and see that he comes to no hurt. See also that you bring him before me within a month, or your life shall answer for it. Let him be here at my royal kraal in the first week of the new moon — when Nanea comes — and then I will tell you whether or no I agree with you that she is fair. Go now, my child, and you, White Man, go also; those who are to accompany you shall be with you at the dawn. Farewell, but remember we meet again at the new moon, when we will settle what pay you shall receive as keeper of my guns. Do not fail me, White Man, or I shall send after you, and my messengers are sometimes rough.'

'This means that I am a prisoner,' thought Hadden, 'but it will go hard if I cannot manage to give them the slip somehow. I don't intend to stay in this country if war is declared, to be pounded into *mouti* (medicine), or have my eyes put out, or any little joke of that sort.'

*   *   *

Ten days had passed, and one evening Hadden and his escort were encamped in a wild stretch of mountainous country lying between the Blood and Unvunyana Rivers, not more than eight miles from that 'Place of the Little Hand' which within a few weeks was to become famous throughout the world by its native name of Isandhlwana. For three days they had been tracking the spoor of a small herd of buffalo that still inhabited the district, but as yet they had not come up with them. The Zulu hunters had suggested that they should follow the Unvunyana down towards the sea where game was more plentiful, but this neither Hadden, nor the captain, Nahoon, had been anxious to do, for reasons which each of them kept secret to himself. Hadden's object was to work gradually down to the Buffalo River across which he hoped to effect a retreat into Natal. That of Nahoon was to linger in the neighbourhood of the kraal of Umgona, which was situated not very far from their present camping place, in the vague hope that he might find an opportunity of speaking with or at least of seeing Nanea, the girl to whom he was affianced, who within a few weeks must be taken from him, and given over to the king.

A more eerie-looking spot than that where they were encamped Hadden had never seen. Behind them lay a tract of land — half-swamp and half-bush — in which the buffalo were supposed to be hiding. Beyond, in lonely grandeur, rose the mountain of Isandhlwana, while in front was an amphitheatre of the most gloomy forest, ringed round in the distance by sheer-sided hills. Into this forest there ran a river which drained the swamp, placidly enough upon the level. But it was not always level, for within three hundred yards of them it dashed suddenly over a precipice, of no great height but very steep, falling into a boiling rock-bound pool that the light of the sun never seemed to reach.

'What is the name of that forest, Nahoon?' asked Hadden.

'It is named *Emagudu*, The Home of the Dead,' the Zulu replied absently, for he was looking towards the kraal of Nanea, which was situated an hour's walk away over the ridge to the right.

'The Home of the Dead! Why?'

'Because the dead live there, those whom we name the *Esemkofu*, the Speechless Ones, and with them other Spirits, the *Amahlosi*, from whom the breath of life has passed away, and who yet live on.'

'Indeed,' said Hadden, 'and have you ever seen these ghosts?'

'Am I mad that I should go to look for them, White Man? Only the dead enter that forest, and it is on the borders of it that our people make offerings to the dead.'

Followed by Nahoon, Hadden walked to the edge of the cliff and looked over it. To the left lay the deep and dreadful-looking pool, while close to the bank of it, placed upon a narrow strip of turf between the cliff and the commencement of the forest, was a hut.

'Who lives there?' asked Hadden.

'The great *Isanusi* — she who is named *Inyanga* or Doctoress; she who is named *Inyosi* (the Bee), because she gathers wisdom from the dead who grow in the forest.'

'Do you think that she could gather enough wisdom to tell me whether I am going to kill any buffalo, Nahoon?'

'Mayhap, White Man, but,' he added with a little smile, 'those who visit the Bee's hive may hear nothing, or they may hear more than they wish for. The words of that Bee have a sting.'

'Good; I will see if she can sting me.'

'So be it,' said Nahoon; and turning, he led the way along the cliff till he reached a native path which zig-zagged down its face.

By this path they climbed till they came to the sward at the foot of the descent, and walked up it to the hut which was surrounded by a low fence of reeds, enclosing a small courtyard paved with ant-heap earth beaten hard and polished. In this courtyard sat the Bee, her stool being placed almost at the mouth of the round opening that served as a doorway to the hut. At first all that Hadden could see of her, crouched as she was in the shadow, was a huddled shape wrapped round with a greasy and tattered catskin *kaross*, above the edge of which appeared two eyes, fierce and quick as those of a leopard. At her feet smouldered a little fire, and ranged around it in a semi-circle were a number of human skulls, placed in pairs as though they were talking together, whilst other bones, to all appearance also human, were festooned about the hut and the fence of the courtyard.

'I see that the old lady is set up with the usual properties,' thought Hadden, but he said nothing.

Nor did the witch-doctoress say anything; she only fixed her beady eyes upon his face. Hadden returned the compliment, staring at her with all his might, till suddenly he became aware that he was vanquished in this curious duel. His brain grew confused, and to his fancy it seemed that the woman before him had shifted shape into the likeness of a colossal and horrid spider sitting at the mouth of her trap, and that these bones were the relics of her victims.

'Why do you not speak, White Man?' she said at last in a slow clear voice. 'Well, there is no need, since I can read your thoughts. You are thinking that I who am called the Bee should be better named the Spider. Have no fear; I did not kill these men. What would it profit me when the dead are so many? I suck the souls of men, not their bodies, White Man. It is their living hearts I love to look on, for therein I read much and thereby I grow wise. Now what would you of the Bee, White Man, the Bee that labours in this Garden of Death, and – what brings *you* here, son of Zomba? Why are you not with the Umcityu now that they doctor themselves for the great war – the last war – the war of the white and the black – or if you have no stomach for fighting, why are you not at the side of Nanea the tall, Nanea the fair?'

Nahoon made no answer, but Hadden said:

'A small thing, mother. I would know if I shall prosper in my hunting.'

'In your hunting, White Man; what hunting? The hunting of game, of money, or of women? Well, one of them, for a-hunting you must ever be; that is your nature, to hunt and be hunted. Tell me now, how goes the wound of that trader who tasted of your steel yonder in the town of the Maboon (Boers)? No need to answer, White Man, but what fee, Chief, for the poor witch-doctoress whose skill you seek,' she added in a whining voice. 'Surely you would not that an old woman should work without a fee?'

'I have none to offer you, mother, so I will be going,' said Hadden, who began to feel himself satisfied with this display of the Bee's powers of observation and thought-reading.

'Nay,' she answered with an unpleasant laugh, 'would you ask a question, and not wait for the answer? I will take no fee from you at present, White Man; you shall pay me later on when we meet again,' and once more she laughed. 'Let me look in your face, let me look in your face,' she continued, rising and standing before him.

Then of a sudden Hadden felt something cold at the back of his neck, and the next instant the Bee had sprung from him, holding between her thumb and finger a curl of dark hair which she had cut from his head. The action was so instantaneous that he had neither time to avoid nor to resent it, but stood still staring at her stupidly.

'That is all I need,' she cried, 'for like my heart my magic is white. Stay — son of Zomba, give me also of your hair, for those who visit the Bee must listen to her humming.'

Nahoon obeyed, cutting a little lock from his head with the sharp edge of his assegai, though it was very evident that he did this not because he wished to do so, but because he feared to refuse.

Then the Bee slipped back her *kaross*, and stood bending over the fire before them, into which she threw herbs taken from a pouch that was bound about her middle. She was still a finely-shaped woman, and she wore none of the abominations which Hadden had been accustomed to see upon the persons of witch-doctoresses. About her neck, however, was a curious ornament, a small live snake, red and grey in hue, which her visitors recognised as one of the most deadly to be found in that part of the country. It is not unusual for Bantu witch-doctors thus to decorate themselves with snakes, though whether or not their fangs have first been extracted no one seems to know.

Presently the herbs began to smoulder, and the smoke of them rose up in a thin straight stream, that, striking upon the face of the Bee, clung about her head enveloping it as though with a strange blue veil. Then of a sudden she stretched out her hands, and let fall the two locks of hair upon the burning herbs, where they writhed themselves to ashes like things alive. Next she opened her mouth, and began to draw the fumes of the hair and herbs into her lungs in great gulps; while the snake, feeling the influence of the medicine, hissed and, uncoiling itself from about her neck, crept upwards and took refuge among the black *saccaboola* feathers of her head-dress.

Soon the vapours began to do their work; she swayed to and fro muttering, then sank back against the hut, upon the straw of which her head rested. Now the Bee's face was turned upwards towards the light, and it was ghastly to behold, for it had become blue in colour, and the open eyes were sunken like the eyes of one dead, whilst above her forehead the red snake wavered and hissed, reminding Hadden of the Uraeus crest on the brow of statues of Egyptian kings. For ten seconds or more she remained thus, then she spoke in a hollow and unnatural voice:

'O Black Heart and body that is white and beautiful, I look into your heart, and it is black as blood, and it shall be black with blood. Beautiful white body with a black heart, you shall find your game and hunt it, and it shall lead you into the House of the Homeless, into the Home of the Dead, and it shall be shaped as a bull, it shall be shaped as a tiger, it shall be shaped as a woman whom kings and waters cannot harm. Beautiful white body and black heart, you shall be paid your wages, money for money, and blow for blow. Think of my word when the spotted cat purrs above your breast; think of it when the battle roars about you; think of it when you grasp your great reward, and for the last time stand face to face with the ghost of the dead in the Home of the Dead.

'O White Heart and black body, I look into your heart and it is white as milk, and the milk of innocence shall save it. Fool, why do you strike that blow? Let him be who is loved of the tiger, and whose love is as the love of a tiger, Ah! what face is that in the battle? Follow it, follow it, O swift of foot; but follow warily, for the tongue that has lied will never plead for mercy, and the hand that can betray is strong in war. White Heart, what is death? In death life lives, and among the dead you shall find the life you lost, for there awaits you she whom kings and waters cannot harm.'

As the Bee spoke, by degrees her voice sank lower and lower till it was almost inaudible. Then it ceased altogether, and she seemed to pass from trance to sleep. Hadden, who had been listening to her with an amused and cynical smile, now laughed aloud.

'Why do you laugh, White Man?' asked Nahoon angrily.

'I laugh at my own folly in wasting time listening to the nonsense of that lying fraud.'

'It is no nonsense, White Man.'

'Indeed? Then will you tell me what it means?'

'I cannot tell you what it means yet, but her words have to do with a woman and a leopard, and with your fate and my fate.'

Hadden shrugged his shoulders, not thinking the matter worth further argument, and at that moment the Bee woke up shivering, drew the red snake from her head-dress and coiling it about her throat wrapped herself again in the greasy *kaross*.

'Are you satisfied with my wisdom, *Inkoos?*' she asked of Hadden.

'I am satisfied that you are one of the cleverest cheats in Zululand, mother,' he answered coolly. 'Now, what is there to pay?'

The Bee took no offence at this rude speech, though for a second or two the look in her eyes grew strangely like that which they had seen in those of the snake when the fumes of the fire made it angry.

'If the white lord says I am a cheat, it must be so,' she answered, 'for he of all men should be able to discern a cheat. I have said that I ask no fee – yet, give me a little tobacco from your pouch.'

Hadden opened the bag of antelope hide and drawing some tobacco from it, gave it to her. In taking it she clasped his hand and examined the gold ring that was upon the third finger, a ring fashioned like a snake with two little rubies set in the head to represent the eyes.

'I wear a snake about my neck, and you wear one upon your hand, *Inkoos*. I should like to have this ring to wear upon my hand, so that the snake about my neck may be less lonely there.'

'Then I am afraid you will have to wait till I am dead,' said Hadden.

'Yes, yes,' she answered in a pleased voice, 'it is a good word. I will wait till you are dead and then I will take the ring, and none can say that I have stolen it, for Nahoon there will bear me witness that you gave me permission to do so.'

For the first time Hadden started, since there was something about the Bee's tone that jarred upon him. Had she addressed him in her professional manner, he would have thought nothing of it; but in her cupidity she had become natural, and it was evident that she spoke from conviction, believing her own words.

She saw him start, and instantly changed her note.

'Let the white lord forgive the jest of a poor old witch-doctoress,' she said in a whining voice. 'I have so much to do with Death that his name leaps to my lips,' and she glanced first at the circle of skulls about her, then towards the waterfall that fed the gloomy pool upon whose banks her hut was placed.

'Look,' she said simply.

Following the line of her outstretched hand Hadden's eyes fell upon two withered mimosa trees which grew over the fall almost at right angles to its rocky edge. These trees were joined together by a rude platform made of logs of wood lashed down with *riems* of hide. Upon this platform stood three figures: not-withstanding the distance and the spray of the fall, he could see that they were those of two men and a girl, for their shapes stood out distinctly against the fiery red of the sunset sky. One instant there were three, the next there were two — for the girl had gone, and something dark rushing down the face of the fall, struck the surface of the pool with a heavy thud, while a faint and piteous cry broke upon his ear.

'What is the meaning of that?' he asked, horrified and amazed.

'Nothing,' answered the Bee with a laugh. 'Do you not know, then, that this is the place where faithless women, or girls who have loved without the leave of the king, are brought to meet their death, and with them their accomplices. Oh! they die here thus each day, and I watch them die and keep the count of the number of them,' and drawing a tally-stick from the thatch of the hut, she took a knife and added a notch to the many that appeared upon it, looking at Nahoon the while with a half-questioning, half-warning gaze.

'Yes, yes, it is a place of death,' she muttered. 'Up yonder the quick die day by day and down there' – and she pointed along the course of the river beyond the pool to where the forest began some two hundred yards from her hut – 'the ghosts of them have their home. Listen!'

As she spoke, a sound reached their ears that seemed to swell from the dim skirts of the forests, a peculiar and unholy sound which it is impossible to define more accurately than by saying that it seemed beastlike, and almost inarticulate.

'Listen,' repeated the Bee, 'they are merry yonder.'

'Who?' asked Hadden; 'the baboons?'

'No, *Inkoos*, the *Amatongo* – the ghosts that welcome her who has just become of their number.'

'Ghosts,' said Hadden roughly, for he was angry at his own tremors, 'I should like to see those ghosts. Do you think that I have never heard a troop of monkeys in the bush before, mother? Come, Nahoon, let us be going while there is light to climb the cliff. Farewell.'

'Farewell *Inkoos*, and doubt not that your wish will be fulfilled. Go in peace *Inkoos* – to sleep in peace.'

III
The End of the Hunt

The prayer of the Bee notwithstanding, Philip Hadden slept ill that night. He felt in the best of health, and his conscience was not troubling him more than usual, but rest he could not. Whenever he closed his eyes, his mind conjured up a picture of the grim witch-doctoress, so strangely named the Bee and the sound of her evil-omened words as he had heard them that afternoon. He was neither a superstitious nor a timid man, and any supernatural beliefs that might linger in his mind were, to say the least of it, dormant. But do what he might, he could not shake off a certain eerie sensation of fear, lest there should be some grains of truth in the prophesyings of this hag. What if it were a fact that he was near his death, and that the heart which beat so strongly in his breast must soon be still for ever – no, he would not think of it. This gloomy place, and the dreadful sight which he saw that day, had upset his nerves. The domestic customs of these Zulus were not pleasant, and for his part he was determined to be clear of them so soon as he was able to escape the country.

In fact, if he could in any way manage it, it was his intention to make a dash for the border on the following night. To do this with a good prospect of success, however, it was necessary that he should kill a buffalo, or some other head of game. Then, as he knew well, the hunters with him would feast upon meat until they could scarcely stir, and that would be his opportunity. Nahoon, however, might not succumb to this temptation; therefore he must trust to luck to be rid of him. If it came to the worst, he could put a bullet through him, which he considered he would be justified in doing, seeing that in reality the man was his jailor. Should this necessity arise, he felt indeed that he could face it without undue compunction, for in truth he disliked Nahoon; at times he even hated him. Their natures were antagonistic, and he knew that the great Zulu distrusted and looked down upon him, and to be looked down upon by a savage 'nigger' was more than his pride could stomach.

At the first break of dawn Hadden rose and roused his escort, who were still stretched in sleep around the dying fire, each man wrapped in his kaross or blanket. Nahoon stood up and shook himself, looking gigantic in the shadows of the morning.

'What is your will, *Umlungu* (white man), that you are up before the sun?'

'My will, *Muntumpofu* (yellow man), is to hunt buffalo,' answered Hadden coolly. It irritated him that this savage should give him no title of any sort.

'Your pardon,' said the Zulu reading his thoughts, 'but I cannot call you *Inkoos* because you are not my chief, or any man's; still if the title 'white man' offends you, we will give you a name.'

'As you wish,' answered Hadden briefly.

Accordingly they gave him a name, *Inhlizin-mgama*, by which he was known among them thereafter, but Hadden was not best pleased when he found that the meaning of those soft-sounding syllables was 'Black Heart'. That was how the *inyanga* had addressed him – only she used different words.

An hour later, and they were in the swampy bush country that lay behind the encampment searching for their game. Within a very little while Nahoon held up his hand, then pointed to the ground. Hadden looked; there, pressed deep in the marshy soil, and to all appearance not ten minutes old, was the spoor of a small herd of buffalo.

'I knew that we should find game today,' whispered Nahoon, 'because the Bee said so.'

'Curse the Bee,' answered Hadden below his breath. 'Come on.'

For a quarter of an hour or more they followed the spoor through thick reeds, till sudenly Nahoon whistled very softly and touched Hadden's arm. He looked up, and there, about two hundred yards away, feeding on some higher ground among a patch of mimosa trees, were the buffaloes – six of them – an old bull with a splendid head, three cows, a heifer and a calf about four months old. Neither the wind nor the nature of the veldt were favourable for them to stalk the game from their present position, so they made a detour of half a mile and very carefully crept towards them up the wind, slipping from trunk to trunk of the mimosas and when these failed them, crawling on their stomachs under cover of the tall *tambuti* grass. At last they were within forty yards, and a further advance seemed impracticable; for although he could not smell them, it was evident from his movements that the old bull heard some unusual sound and was growing suspicious. Nearest to Hadden, who alone of the party had a rifle, stood the heifer broadside on – a beautiful shot. Remembering that she would make the best beef, he lifted his Martini, and aiming at her immediately behind the shoulder, gently squeezed the trigger. The rifle exploded, and the heifer fell dead, shot through the heart. Strangely enough the other buffaloes did not at once run away. On the contrary, they seemed puzzled to account for the sudden noise; and, not being able to wind anything, lifted their heads and stared round them.

The pause gave Hadden space to get in a fresh cartridge and to aim again, this time at the old bull. The bullet struck him somewhere in the neck or shoulder, for he came to his knees, but in another second was up and having caught sight of the cloud of smoke he charged straight at it. Because of this smoke, or for some other reason, Hadden did not see him coming, and in consequence would most certainly have been trampled or gored, had not Nahoon sprung forward, at the imminent risk of his own life, and dragged him down behind an ant-heap. A moment more and the great beast had thundered by, taking no further notice of them.

'Forward,' said Hadden, and leaving most of the men to cut up the heifer and carry the best of her meat to camp, they started on the blood spoor.

For some hours they followed the bull, till at last they lost the trail on a patch of stony ground thickly covered with bush, and exhausted by the heat, sat down to rest and to eat some *biltong* or sun-dried flesh which they had with them. They finished their meal, and were preparing to return to the camp, when one of the four Zulus who were with them went to drink at a little stream that ran at a distance of not more than ten paces away. Half a minute later they heard a hideous grunting noise and a splashing of water, and saw the Zulu fly into the air. All the while that they were eating, the wounded buffalo had been lying in wait for them under a thick bush on the banks of the streamlet, knowing – cunning brute that he was – that sooner or later his turn would come. With a shout of consternation they rushed forward to see the bull vanish over the rise before Hadden could get a chance of firing at him, and to find their companion dying, for the great horn had pierced his lung.

'It is not a buffalo, it is a devil,' the poor fellow gasped, and expired.

'Devil or not, I mean to kill it,' exclaimed Hadden. So leaving the others to carry the body of their comrade to camp, he started on accompanied by Nahoon only. Now the ground was more open and the chase easier, for they sighted their quarry frequently, though they could not come near enough to fire. Presently they travelled down a steep cliff.

'Do you know where we are?' asked Nahoon, pointing to a belt of forest opposite. 'That is *Emagudu*, the Home of the Dead – and look, the bull heads thither.'

Hadden glanced round him. It was true; yonder to the left were the Fall, the Pool of Doom, and the hut of the Bee.

'Very well,' he answered; 'then we must head for it too.'

Nahoon halted. 'Surely you would not enter there,' he exclaimed.

'Surely I will,' replied Hadden, 'but there is no need for you to do so if you are afraid.'

'I am afraid – of ghosts,' said the Zulu, 'but I will come.'

So they crossed the strip of turf, and entered the haunted wood. It was a gloomy place indeed; great wide-topped trees grew thick there shutting out the sight of the sky; moreover, the air in it which no breeze stirred, was heavy with the exhalations of rotting foliage. There seemed to be no life here and no sound – only now and again a loathsome spotted snake would uncoil itself and glide away, and now and again a heavy rotten bough fell with a crash.

Hadden was too intent upon the buffalo, however, to be much impressed by his surroundings. He only remarked that the light would be bad for shooting, and went on.

They must have penetrated a mile or more into the forest when the sudden increase of blood upon the spoor told them that the bull's wound was proving fatal to him.

'Run now,' said Hadden cheerfully.

'Nay, *hamba gachle* – go softly – ' answered Nahoon, 'the devil is dying, but he will try to play us anoher trick before he dies.' And he went on peering ahead of him cautiously.

'It is all right here, anyway,' said Hadden, pointing to the spoor that ran straight forward printed deep in the marshy ground.

Nahoon did not answer, but stared steadily at the trunks of two trees a few paces in front of them and to their right. 'Look,' he whispered.

Hadden did so, and at length made out the outline of something brown that was crouched behind the trees.

'He is dead,' he exclaimed.

'No,' answered Nahoon, 'he has come back on his own path and is waiting for us. He knows that we are following his spoor. Now if you stand here, I think that you can shoot him through the back between the tree trunks.'

Hadden knelt down, and aiming very carefully at a point just below the bull's spine, he fired. There was an awful bellow, and the next instant the brute was up and at them. Nahoon flung his broad spear, which sank deep into its chest, then they fled this way and that. The buffalo stood still for a moment, its fore legs straddled wide and its head down, looking first after the one and then the other, till of a sudden it uttered a low moaning sound and rolled over dead, smashing Nahoon's assegai to fragments as it fell.

'There! he's finished,' said Hadden, 'and I believe it was your assegai that killed him. Hullo! what's that noise?'

Nahoon listened. In several quarters of the forest, but from how far away it was impossible to tell, there rose a curious sound, as of people calling to each other in fear but in no articulate language. Nahoon shivered.

'It is the *Esemkofu*,' he said, 'the ghosts who have no tongue, and who can only wail like infants. Let us be going; this place is bad for mortals.'

'And worse for buffaloes,' said Hadden, giving the dead bull a kick, 'but I suppose that we must leave him here for your friends, the *Esemkofu*, as we have got meat enough, and can't carry his head.'

So they started back towards the open country. As they threaded their way slowly through the tree trunks, a new idea came into Hadden's mind. Once out of this forest, he was within an hour's run of the Zulu border, and once over the Zulu border, he would feel a happier man than he did at that moment. As has been said, he had intended to attempt to escape in the darkness, but the plan was risky. All the Zulus might not over-eat themselves and go to sleep, especially after the death of their comrade; Nahoon, who watched him day and night, certainly would not. This was his opportunity – there remained the question of Nahoon.

Well, if it came to the worst, Nahoon must die: it would be easy – he had a loaded rifle, and now that his assegai was gone, Nahoon had only a kerry. He did not wish to kill the man, though it was clear to him, seeing that his own safety was at stake, that he would be amply justified in so doing. Why should he not put it to him – and then be guided by circumstances?

Nahoon was walking across a little open space about ten paces ahead of him where Hadden could see him very well, whilst he himself was under the shadow of a large tree with low horizontal branches running out from the trunk.

'Nahoon,' he said.

The Zulu turned round, and took a step towards him.

'No, do not move, I pray. Stand where you are, or I shall be obliged to shoot you. Listen now: do not be afraid for I shall not fire without warning. I am your prisoner, and you are charged to take me back to the king to be his servant. But I believe that a war is going to break out between your people and mine; and this being so, you will understand that I do not wish to go to Cetywayo's kraal, because I should either come to a violent death there, or my own brothers will believe that I am a traitor and treat me accordingly. The Zulu border is not much more than an hour's journey away – let us say an hour and a half's: I mean to be across it before the moon is up. Now, Nahoon, will you lose me in the forest and give me this hour and a half's start – or will you stop here with that ghost people of whom you talk? Do you understand? No, please do not move.'

'I understand you,' answered the Zulu, in a perfectly composed voice, 'and I think that was a good name which we gave you this morning, though, Black Heart, there is some justice in your words and more wisdom. Your opportunity is good, and one which a man named as you are should not let fall.'

'I am glad to find that you take this view of the matter, Nahoon. And now will you be so kind as to lose me, and to promise not to look for me till the moon is up?'

'What do you mean, Black Heart?'

'What I say. Come, I have no time to spare.'

'You are a strange man,' said the Zulu reflectively. 'You heard the king's order to me: would you have me disobey the order of the king?'

'Certainly, I would. You have no reason to love Cetywayo, and it does not matter to you whether or not I return to his kraal to mend guns there. If you think that he will be angry because I am missing, you had better cross the border also; we can go together.'

'And leave my father and all my brethen to his vengeance? Black Heart, you do not understand. How can you, being so named? I am a soldier, and the king's word is the king's word. I hoped to have died fighting, but I am the bird in your noose. Come, shoot, or you will not reach the border before moonrise,' and he opened his arms and smiled.

'If it must be, so let it be. Farewell, Nahoon, at least you are a brave man, but every one of us must cherish his own life,' answered Hadden calmly.

Then with much deliberation he raised his rifle and covered the Zulu's breast.

Already — whilst his victim stood there still smiling, although a twitching of his lips betrayed the natural terrors that no bravery can banish — already his finger was contracting on the trigger, when of a sudden, as instantly indeed as though he had been struck by lightning, Hadden went down backwards, and behold! there stood upon him a great spotted beast that waved its long tail to and fro and glared down into his eyes.

It was a leopard — a tiger as they call it in Africa — which, crouched upon a bough of the tree above, had been unable to resist the temptation of satisfying its savage appetite on the man below. For a second or two there was silence, broken only by the purring, or rather the snoring sound made by the leopard. In those seconds, strangely enough, there sprang up before Hadden's mental vision a picture of the *inyanga* called *Inyosi* or the Bee, her death-like head resting against the thatch of the hut, and her death-like lips muttering 'think of my word when the great cat purrs above your face'.

Then the brute put out its strength. The claws of one paw it drove deep into the muscles of his left thigh, while with another it scratched at his breast, tearing the clothes from it and furrowing the flesh beneath. The sight of the white skin seemed to madden it, and in its fierce desire for blood it drooped its square muzzle and buried its fangs in its victim's shoulder. Next moment there was a sound of rushing feet and of a club falling heavily. Up reared the leopard with an angry snarl, up till it stood as high as the attacking Zulu. At him it came, striking out savagely and tearing the black man as it had torn the white. Again the kerry fell full on its jaws, and down it went backwards. Before it could rise again, or rather as it was in the act of rising, the heavy knob-stick struck it once more, and with fearful force, this time as it chanced, full on the nape of the neck, and paralysing the brute. It writhed and bit and twisted, throwing up the earth and leaves, while blow after blow was rained upon it, till at length with a convulsive struggle and a stifled roar it lay still — the brains oozing from its shattered skull.

Hadden sat up, the blood running from his wounds.

'You have saved my life, Nahoon,' he said faintly, 'and I thank you.'

'Do not thank me, Black Heart,' answered the Zulu, 'it was the king's word that I should keep you safely. Still this tiger has been hardly dealt with, for certainly *he* has saved *my* life,' and lifting the Martini he unloaded the rifle.

At this juncture Hadden swooned away.

*　*　*

Twenty-four hours had gone by when, after what seemed to him to be but a little time of troubled and dreamful sleep, through which he could hear voices without understanding what they said, and feel himself borne he knew not whither, Hadden awoke to find himself lying upon a *kaross* in a large and beautifully clean Kaffir hut with a bundle of furs for a pillow. There was a bowl of milk at his side and tortured as he was by thirst, he tried to stretch out his arm to lift it to his lips, only to find to his astonishment that his hand fell back to his side like that of a dead man. Looking round the hut impatiently, he found that there was nobody in it to assist him, so he did the only thing which remained for him to do – he lay still. He did not fall asleep, but his eyes closed, and a kind of gentle torpor crept over him, half obscuring his recovered senses. Presently he heard a soft voice speaking; it seemed far away, but he could clearly distinguish the words.

'Black Heart still sleeps,' the voice said, 'but there is colour in his face; I think that he will wake soon, and find his thoughts again.'

'Have no fear, Nanea, he will surely wake, his hurts are not dangerous,' answered another voice, that of Nahoon. 'He fell heavily with the weight of the tiger on top of him, and that is why his senses have been shaken for so long. He went near to death, but certainly he will not die.'

'It would have been a pity if he had died,' answered the soft voice, 'he is so beautiful; never have I seen a white man who was so beautiful.'

'I did not think him beautiful when he stood with his rifle pointed at my heart,' answered Nahoon sulkily.

'Well, there is this to be said,' she replied, 'he wished to

76

escape from Cetywayo, and that is not to be wondered at,' and
she sighed. 'Moreover he asked you to come with him, and it
might have been well if you had done so, that is, if you would
have taken me with you!'

'How could I have done it, girl?' he asked angrily. 'Would
you have me set at nothing the order of the king?'

'The king!' she replied raising her voice. 'What do you owe
to the king? You have served him faithfully, and your reward
is that within a few days he will take me from you – me, who
should have been your wife, and I must – I must . . .' And she
began to weep softly, adding between her sobs, 'If you loved me
truly, you would think more of me and of yourself, and less of the
Black One and his orders. Oh! let us fly, Nahoon, let us fly to
Natal before this spear pierces me.'

'Weep not, Nanea,' he said; 'why do you tear my heart in
two between my duty and my love? You know that I am a soldier,
and that I must walk the path whereon the king has set my feet.
Soon I think I shall be dead, for I seek death, and then it will
matter nothing.'

'Nothing to you, Nahoon, who are at peace, but to me? Yet,
you are right, and I know it, therefore forgive me, who am no
warrior, but a woman who must also obey the will of the king.'
And she cast her arms about his neck, sobbing her fill upon his
breast.

IV
Nanea

Presently, muttering something that the listener could not
catch, Nahoon left Nanea, and crept out of the hut by its bee-
hole entrance. Then Hadden opened his eyes and looked around
him. The sun was sinking and a ray of its red light streaming
through the little opening filled the place with a soft and
crimson glow. In the centre of the hut – supporting it – stood a
thorn-wood roof-tree coloured black by the smoke of the fire;
and against this, the rich light falling full upon her, leaned the
girl Nanea – a very picture of gentle despair.

As is occasionally the case among Zulu women, she was

beautiful – so beautiful that the sight of her went straight to the white man's heart, for a moment causing the breath to catch in his throat. Her dress was very simple. On her shoulders, hanging open in front, lay a mantle of soft white stuff edged with blue beads, about her middle was a buck-skin moocha, also embroidered with blue beads, while round her forehead and left knee were strips of grey fur, and on her right wrist a shining bangle of copper. Her naked bronzed-hued figure was tall and perfect in its proportions; while her face had little in common with that of the ordinary native girl, showing as it did strong traces of the ancestral Arabian or Semitic blood. It was oval in shape, with delicate aquiline features, arched eyebrows, a full mouth, that drooped a little at the corners, tiny ears, behind which the wavy coal-black hair hung down to the shoulders, and the very loveliest pair of dark and liquid eyes that it is possible to imagine.

For a minute or more Nanea stood thus, her sweet face bathed in the sunbeam, while Hadden feasted his eyes upon its beauty. Then sighing heavily, she turned, and seeing that he was awake, started, drew her mantle over her breast and came, or rather glided, towards him.

'The chief is awake,' she said in her soft Zulu accents. 'Does he need aught?'

'Yes, Lady,' he answered; 'I need to drink, but alas! I am too weak.'

She knelt down beside him, and supporting him with her left arm, with her right held the gourd to his lips.

How it came about Hadden never knew, but before that draught was finished a change passed over him. Whether it was the savage girl's touch, or her strange and fawn-like loveliness, or the tender pity in her eyes, matters not – the issue was the same. She struck some cord in his turbulent uncurbed nature, and of a sudden it was filled full with passion for her – a passion which if, not elevated, at least was real. He did not for a moment mistake the significance of the flood of feeling that surged through his veins. Hadden never shirked facts.

'By Heaven!' he said to himself, 'I have fallen in love with a black beauty at first sight – more in love than I have ever been before. It's awkward, but there will be compensations. So much the worse for Nahoon, or for Cetywayo, or for both of them.

After all, I can always get rid of her if she becomes a nuisance.'

Then, in a fit of renewed weakness, brought about by the turmoil of his blood, he lay back upon the pillow of furs, watching Nanea's face while with a native salve of pounded leaves she busied herself dressing the wounds that the leopard had made.

It almost seemed as though something of what was passing in his mind communicated itself to that of the girl. At least, her hand shook a little at her task, and getting done with it as quickly as she could, she rose from her knees with a courteous 'It is finished, *Inkoos*,' and once more took up her position by the roof-tree.

'I thank you, Lady,' he said; 'your hand is kind.'

'You must not call me lady, *Inkoos*,' she answered, 'I am no chieftainess, but only the daughter of a headman, Umgona.'

'And named Nanea,' he said. 'Nay, do not be surprised, I have heard of you. Well, Nanea, perhaps you will soon become a chieftainess – up at the king's kraal yonder.'

'Alas! and alas!' she said, covering her face with her hands.

'Do not grieve, Nanea, a hedge is never so tall and thick but that it can be climbed or crept through.'

She let fall her hands and looked at him eagerly, but he did not pursue the subject.

'Tell me, how did I come here, Nanea?'

'Nahoon and his companions carried you, *Inkoos*.'

'Indeed, I begin to be thankful to the leopard that struck me down. Well, Nahoon is a brave man, and he has done me a great service. I trust that I may be able to repay it – to you, Nanea.'

*　*　*

This was the first meeting of Nanea and Hadden; but, although she did not seek them, the necessities of his sickness and of the situation brought about many another. Never for a moment did the white man waver in his determination to get into his keeping the native girl who had captivated him, and to attain his end he brought to bear all his powers and charm to detach her from Nahoon, and win her affections for himself. He was no rough wooer, however, but proceeded warily, weaving her about with a web of flattery and attention that must, he thought, produce the desired effect upon her mind. Without a doubt, indeed, it would have done so – for she was but a woman, and an untutored one – had it not been for a simple fact which dominated her whole nature. She loved Nahoon, and there was no room in her heart for any other man, white or black. To Hadden she was courteous and kindly but no more, nor did she appear to notice any of the subtle advances by which he attempted to win a foot-hold in her heart. For a while this puzzled him, but he remembered that the Zulu women do not usually permit themselves to show feeling towards an undeclared suitor. Therefore it became necessary that he should speak out.

His mind once made up, he had not to wait long for an opportunity. He was now quite recovered from his hurts, and accustomed to walk in the neighbourhood of the kraal. About two hundred yards from Umgona's huts rose a spring, and thither it was Nanea's habit to resort in the evening to bring back drinking-water for the use of her father's household. The path between this spring and the kraal ran through a patch of bush, where on a certain afternoon towards sundown Hadden took his seat under a tree, having first seen Nanea go down to the little stream as was her custom. A quarter of an hour later she reappeared carrying a large gourd upon her head. She wore no garment now except her moocha, for she had but one mantle and was afraid lest the water should splash it. He watched her advancing along the path, her hands resting on her hips, her splendid naked figure outlined against the westering sun, and wondered what excuse he could make to talk with her. As it chanced fortune favoured him, for when she was near him a snake glided across the path in front of the girl's feet, causing her to spring backwards in alarm and overset the gourd of water. He came forward, and picked it up.

'Wait here,' he said laughing; 'I will bring it to you full.'

'Nay, *Inkoos*,' she remonstrated, 'that is a woman's work.' .

'Among my people,' he said, 'the men love to work for the women,' and he started for the spring, leaving her wondering.

Before he reached her again, he regretted his gallantry, for it was necessary to carry the handleless gourd upon his shoulder, and the contents of it spilling over the edge soaked him. Of this, however, he said nothing to Nanea.

'There is your water, Nanea, shall I carry it for you to the kraal?'

'Nay, *Inkoos*, I thank you, but give it to me, you are weary with its weight.'

'Stay awhile, and I will accompany you. Ah! Nanea, I am still weak, and had it not been for you I think that I should be dead.'

'It was Nahoon who saved you – not I, *Inkoos*.'

'Nahoon saved my body, but you, Nanea, you alone can save my heart.'

'You talk darkly, *Inkoos*.'

'Then I must make my meaning clear, Nanea. I love you.' She opened her brown eyes wide.

'You, a white lord, love me, a Zulu girl? How can that be?'

'I do not know, Nanea, but it is so, and were you not blind you would have seen it. I love you, and I wish to take you to wife.'

'Nay, *Inkoos*, it is impossible. I am already betrothed.'

'Ay,' he answered, 'betrothed to the king.'

'No, betrothed to Nahoon.'

'But it is the king who will take you within a week; is it not so? And would you not rather that I should take you than the king?'

'It seems to be so, *Inkoos*, and I would rather go with you than with the king, but most of all I desire to marry Nahoon. It may be that I shall not be able to marry him, but if that is so, at least I will never become one of the king's women.'

'How will you prevent it, Nanea?'

'There are waters in which a maid may drown, and trees upon which she can hang,' she answered with a quick setting of the mouth.

'That were a pity, Nanea, you are too fair to die.'

'Fair or foul, yet I die, *Inkoos*.'

'No, no, come with me – I will find a way – and be my wife,' and he put his arm about her waist, and strove to draw her to him.

Without any violence of movement, and with the most perfect dignity, the girl disengaged herself from his embrace.

'You have honoured me, and I thank you, *Inkoos*,' she said quietly, 'but you do not understand. I am the wife of Nahoon – I belong to Nahoon; therefore, I cannot look on any other man while Nahoon lives. It is not our custom, *Inkoos*, for we are not as the white women, but ignorant and simple, and when we vow ourselves to a man, we abide by that vow till death.'

'Indeed,' said Hadden; 'and so now you go to tell Nahoon that I have offered to make you my wife.'

'No, *Inkoos*, why should I tell Nahoon your secrets? I have said "nay" to you, not "yea", therefore he has no right to know,' and she stooped to lift the gourd of water.

Hadden considered the situation rapidly, for his repulse only made him the more determined to succeed. Of a sudden under the emergency he conceived a scheme, or rather its rough outline. It was not a nice scheme, and some men might have shrunk from it, but as he had no intention of suffering himself to be defeated by a Zulu girl, he decided – with regret, it is true – that having failed to attain his ends by means which he considered fair, he must resort to others of more doubtful character.

'Nanea,' he said, 'you are a good and honest woman, and I respect you. As I have told you, I love you also, but if you refuse to listen to me there is nothing more to be said, and after all, perhaps it would be better that you should marry one of your own people. But, Nanea, you will never marry him, for the king will take you; and, if he does not give you to some other man, either you will become one of his "sisters", or to be free of him, as you say, you will die. Now hear me, for it is because I love you and wish your welfare that I speak thus. Why do you not escape into Natal, taking Nahoon with you, for there as you know you may live in peace out of reach of the arm of Cetywayo?'

'That is my desire, *Inkoos*, but Nahoon will not consent. He says that there is to be war between us and you white men, and he will not break the command of the king and desert from his army.'

'Then he cannot love you much, Nanea, and at least you have to think of yourself. Whisper into the ear of your father and fly together, for be sure that Nahoon will soon follow you. Ay! and I myself will fly with you, for I too believe that there must be war, and then a white man in this country will be as a lamb among the eagles.'

'If Nahoon will come, I will go, *Inkoos*, but I cannot fly without Nahoon; it is better I should stay here and kill myself.'

'Surely then being so fair and loving him so well, you can teach him to forget his folly and to escape with you. In four days' time we must start for the king's kraal, and if you win over Nahoon, it will be easy for us to turn our faces southwards and cross the river that lies between the land of the Amazulu and Natal. For the sake of all of us, but most of all for your own sake, try to do this, Nanea, whom I have loved and whom I now would save. See him and plead with him as you know how, but as yet do not tell him that I dream of flight, for then I should be watched.'

'In truth, I will, *Inkoos*,' she answered earnestly, 'and oh! I thank you for your goodness. Fear not that I will betray you — first would I die. Farewell.'

'Farewell, Nanea,' and taking her hand he raised it to his lips.

*   *   *

Late that night, just as Hadden was beginning to prepare himself for sleep, he heard a gentle tapping at the board which closed the entrance to his hut.

'Enter,' he said, unfastening the door, and presently by the light of the little lantern that he had with him, he saw Nanea creep into the hut, followed by the great form of Nahoon.

'*Inkoos*,' she said in a whisper when the door was closed again, 'I have pleaded with Nahoon, and he has consented to fly; moreover, my father will come also.'

'Is it so, Nahoon?' asked Hadden.

'It is so,' answered the Zulu, looking down shamefacedly; 'to save this girl from the king, and because the love of her eats out my heart, I have bartered away my honour. But I tell you, Nanea, and you, White Man, as I told Umgona just now, that I think no good will come of this flight, and if we are caught or betrayed, we shall be killed every one of us.'

'Caught we can scarcely be,' broke in Nanea anxiously, 'for who could betray us, except the *Inkoos* here——'

'Which he is not likely to do,' said Hadden quietly, 'seeing that he desires to escape with you, and that his life is also at stake.'

'That is so, Black Heart,' said Nahoon, 'otherwise I tell you that I should not have trusted you.'

Hadden took no notice of this outspoken saying, but until very late that night they sat there together making their plans.

*   *   *

On the following morning Hadden was awakened by sounds of violent altercation. Going out of his hut he found that the disputants were Umgona and a fat and evil-looking Kaffir chief who had arrived at the kraal on a pony. This chief, he soon discovered, was named Maputa, being none other than the man who had sought Nanea in marriage and brought about Nahoon's and Umgona's unfortunate appeal to the king. At present he was engaged in abusing Umgona furiously, charging him with having stolen certain of his oxen and bewitched his cows so that they would not give milk. The alleged theft it was comparatively easy to disprove, but the wizardry remained a matter of argument.

'You are a dog, and a son of a dog,' shouted Maputa, shaking his fat fist in the face of the trembling but indignant Umgona. 'You promised me your daughter in marriage, then having vowed her to that *umfagozan* — that low lout of a soldier, Nahoon, the son of Zomba — you went, the two of you, and poisoned the king's ear against me, bringing me into trouble with the king, and now you have bewitched my cattle. Well, wait, I will be even with you, Wizard; wait till you wake up in the cold morning to find your fence red with fire, and the slayers standing outside your gates to eat up you and yours with spears——'

At this juncture Nahoon, who till now had been listening in silence, intervened with effect.

'Good,' he said, 'we will wait, but not in your company Chief Maputa. *Hamba!* (go)' and seizing the fat old ruffian by the scruff of his neck, he flung him backwards with such violence that he rolled over and over down the little slope.

Hadden laughed, and passed on towards the stream where he proposed to bathe. Just as he reached it, he caught sight of Maputa riding along the footpath, his head-ring covered with mud, his lips purple and his black face livid with rage.

'There goes an angry man,' he said to himself. 'Now, how would it be . . .' and he looked upwards like one seeking an inspiration. It seemed to come; perhaps the devil finding it open whispered in his ear, at any rate — in a few seconds his plan was formed, and he was walking through the bush to meet Maputa.

'Go in peace, Chief,' he said; 'they seem to have treated you roughly up yonder. Having no power to interfere, I came away

for I could not bear the sight. It is indeed shameful that an old
and venerable man of rank should be struck into the dirt, and
beaten by a soldier drunk with beer.'

'Shameful, White Man!' gasped Maputa; 'your words are
true indeed. But wait a while. I, Maputa, will roll that stone
over, I will throw that bull upon its back. When next the harvest
ripens, this I promise, that neither Nahoon nor Umgona, nor
any of his kraal shall be left to gather it.'

'And how will you manage that, Maputa?'

'I do not know, but I will find a way. Oh! I tell you, a way
shall be found.'

Hadden patted the pony's neck meditatively, then leaning
forward, he looked the chief in the eyes and said:

'What will you give me, Maputa, if I show you that way,
a sure and certain one, whereby you may be avenged to the
death upon Nahoon, whose violence I also have seen, and upon
Umgona, whose witchcraft brought sore sickness upon me?'

'What reward do you seek, White Man?' asked Maputa
eagerly.

'A little thing, Chief, a thing of no account, only the girl
Nanea, to whom as it chances I have taken a fancy.'

'I wanted her for myself, White Man, but he who sits at
Ulundi has laid his hand upon her.'

'That is nothing, Chief; I can arrange with him who "sits at
Ulundi". It is with you who are great here that I wish to come to
terms. Listen: if you grant my desire, not only will I fulfil yours
upon your foes, but when the girl is delivered into my hands I
will give you this rifle and a hundred rounds of cartridges.'

Maputa looked at the sporting Martini, and his eyes
glistened.

'It is good,' he said; 'it is very good. Often have I wished for
such a gun that will enable me to shoot game, and to talk with
my enemies from far away. Promise it to me, White Man, and
you shall take the girl if I can give her to you.'

'You swear it, Maputa?'

'I swear it by the head of Chaka, and the spirits of my
fathers.'

'Good. At dawn on the fourth day from now it is the purpose of Umgona, his daughter Nanea, and Nahoon, to cross the
river into Natal by the drift that is called Crocodile Drift, taking

their cattle with them and flying from the king. I also shall be of their company, for they know that I have learned their secret, and would murder me if I tried to leave them. Now you who are chief of the border and guardian of that drift, must hide at night with some men among the rocks in the shallows of the drift and await our coming. First Nanea will cross driving the cows and calves, for so it is arranged, and I shall help her; then will follow Umgona and Nahoon with the oxen and heifers. On these two you must fall, killing them and capturing the cattle, and afterwards I will give you the rifle.'

'What if the king ask for the girl, White Man?'

'Then you shall answer that in the uncertain light you did not recognise her and so she slipped away from you; moreover, that at first you feared to seize the girl lest her cries should alarm the men and they should escape you.'

'Good, but how can I be sure that you will give me the gun once you are across the river?'

'Thus: before I enter the ford I will lay the rifle and cartridges upon a stone by the bank, telling Nanea that I shall return to fetch them when I have driven over the cattle.'

'It is well, White Man; I will not fail you.'

So the plot was made, and after some further conversation upon points of detail, the two conspirators shook hands and parted.

'That ought to come off all right,' reflected Hadden to himself as he plunged and floated in the waters of the stream, 'but somehow I don't quite trust our friend Maputa. It would have been better if I could have relied upon myself to get rid of Nahoon and his respected uncle – a couple of shots would do it in the water. But then that would be murder and murder is unpleasant; whereas the other thing is only the delivery to justice of two base deserters, a laudable action in a military country. Also personal interference upon my part might turn the girl against me; while after Umgona and Nahoon have been wiped out by Maputa, she *must* accept my escort. Of course there is a risk, but in every walk of life the most cautious have to take risks at times.'

As it chanced, Philip Hadden was correct in his suspicions of his coadjutor, Maputa. Even before that worthy chief reached his own kraal, he had come to the conclusion that the white man's plan, though attractive in some ways, was too dangerous, since it was certain that if the girl Nanea escaped, the king would be indignant. Moreover, the men he took with him to do the killing in the drift would suspect something and talk. On the other hand he would earn much credit with his majesty by revealing the plot, saying that he had learned it from the lips of the white hunter, whom Umgona and Nahoon had forced to participate in it, and of whose coveted rifle he must trust to chance to possess himself.

An hour later two discreet messengers were bounding across the plains, bearing words from the Chief Maputa, the Warden of the Border, to the 'great Black Elephant' at Ulundi.

V

The Doom Pool

Fortune showed itself strangely favourable to the plans of Nahoon and Nanea. One of the Zulu captain's perplexities was as to how he should lull the suspicions and evade the vigilance of his own companions, who together with himself had been detailed by the king to assist Hadden in his hunting and to guard against his escape. As it chanced, however, on the day after the incident of the visit of Maputa, a messenger arrived from no less a person than the great military Induna, Tvingwayo ka Marolo, who afterwards commanded the Zulu army at Isandhlwana; ordering these men to return to their regiment, the Umcityu Corps, which was to be placed upon full war footing. Accordingly Nahoon sent them, saying that he himself would follow with Black Heart in the course of a few days, as at present the white man was not sufficiently recovered from his hurts to allow of his travelling fast and far. So the soldiers went, doubting nothing.

Then Umgona gave it out that in obedience to the command of the king he was about to start for Ulundi, taking with him his daughter Nanea to be delivered over into the *Sigodhla*, and also those fifteen head of cattle that had been *lobola'd* by Nahoon in consideration of his forthcoming marriage, whereof he had been fined by Cetywayo. Under pretence that they required a change of veldt, the rest of his cattle he sent away in charge of a Basuto herd who knew nothing of their plans, telling him to keep them by the Crocodile Drift, as there the grass was good and sweet.

All preparations being completed, on the third day the party started, heading straight for Ulundi. After they had travelled some miles, however, they left the road and turning sharp to the right, passed unobserved of any through a great stretch of uninhabited bush. Their path now lay not far from the Pool of Doom, which, indeed, was close to Umgona's kraal, and the forest that was called Home of the Dead, but out of sight of these. It was their plan to travel by night, reaching the broken country near the Crocodile Drift on the following morning. Here they proposed to lie hid that day and through the night; then, having first collected the cattle which had preceded them, to cross the river at the break of dawn and escape into Natal. At least this was the plan of his companions; but, as we know, Hadden had another programme, wherein after one last appearance two of the party would play no part.

During that long afternoon's journey Umgona, who knew every inch of the country, walked ahead driving the fifteen cattle and carrying in his hand a long travelling stick of black and white *umzimbeet* wood, for in truth the old man was in a hurry to reach his journey's end. Next came Nahoon, armed with a broad assegai, but naked except for his moocha and necklet of baboon's teeth, and with him Nanea in her white bead-bordered mantle. Hadden, who brought up the rear, noticed that the girl seemed to be under the spell of an imminent apprehension, for from time to time she clasped her lover's arm, and looking up into his face, addressed him with vehemence, almost with passion.

Curiously enough, the sight touched Hadden, and once or twice he was shaken by so sharp a pang of remorse at the thought of his share in this tragedy, that he cast about in his mind seeking a means to unravel the web of death which he himself had woven. But ever that evil voice was whispering at his ear. It reminded him that he, the white *Inkoos*, had been refused by this dusky beauty, and that if he found a way to save him, within some few hours she would be the wife of the savage gentleman at her side, the man who had named him Black Heart and who despised him, the man whom he had meant to murder and who immediately repaid his treachery by rescuing him from the jaws of the leopard at the risk of his own life. Moreover, it was a law of Hadden's existence never to deny himself anything that he desired if it lay within his power to take it — a law which had led him always deeper into sin. In other respects, indeed, it had not carried him far, for in the past he had desired much, and he had won little; but this particular flower was to his hand, and he would pluck it. If Nahoon stood between him and the flower, so much the worse for Nahoon, and if it should wither in his grasp, so much the worse for the flower; it could always be thrown away. Thus it came about that, not for the first time in his life, Philip Hadden discarded the somewhat spasmodic prickings of conscience and listened to that evil whispering at his ear.

About half-past five o'clock in the afternoon the four refugees passed the stream that a mile or so down fell over the little precipice into the Doom Pool; and, entering a patch of thorn trees on the further side, walked straight into the midst of two-and-twenty soldiers, who were beguiling the tedium of expectancy by the taking of snuff and the smoking of *dakka* or native hemp. With these soldiers, seated on his pony, for he was too fat to walk, waited the Chief Maputa.

Observing that their expected guests had arrived, the men knocked out the *dakka* pipe, replaced the snuff boxes in the slits made in the lobes of their ears, and secured the four of them.

'What is the meaning of this, O King's soldiers?' asked Umgona in a quavering voice. 'We journey to the kraal of U'Cetywayo; why do you molest us?'

'Indeed. Wherefore then are your faces set towards the south? Does the Black One live in the south? Well, you will journey to another kraal presently,' answered the jovial-looking captain of the party with a callous laugh.

'I do not understand,' stammered Umgona.

'Then I will explain while you rest,' said the captain. 'The Chief Maputa yonder sent word to the Black One at Ulundi that he had learned of your intended flight to Natal from the lips of this white man, who had warned him of it. The Black One was angry, and despatched us to catch you and make an end of you. That is all. Come on now, quietly, and let us finish the matter.

As the Doom Pool is near, your deaths will be easy.'

Nahoon heard the words, and sprang straight at the throat of Hadden; but he did not reach it, for the soldiers pulled him down. Nanea heard them also, and turning, looked the traitor in the eyes; she said nothing, she only looked, but he could never forget that look. The white man for his part was filled with a fiery indignation against Maputa.

'You wicked villain,' he gasped, whereat the chief smiled in a sickly fashion, and turned away.

Then they were marched along the banks of the stream till they reached the waterfall that fell into the Pool of Doom.'

Hadden was a brave man after his fashion, but his heart quailed as he gazed into that abyss.

'Are you going to throw me in there?' he asked of the Zulu captain in a thick voice.

'You, White Man?' replied the soldier unconcernedly. 'No, our orders are to take you to the king, but what he will do with you I do not know. There is to be war between your people and ours, so perhaps he means to pound you into medicine for the use of the witch-doctors, or to peg you over an ant-heap as a warning to other white men.'

Hadden received this information in silence, but its effect upon his brain was bracing, for instantly he began to search out some means of escape.

By now the party had halted near the two thorn trees that hung over the waters of the pool.

'Who dives first?' asked the captain of the Chief Maputa.

'The old wizard,' he replied, nodding at Umgona; 'then his daughter after him, and last of all this fellow,' and he struck Nahoon in the face with his open hand.

'Come on, Wizard,' said the captain, grasping Umgona by the arm, 'and let us see how you can swim.'

At the words of doom Umgona seemed to recover his self-command, after the fashion of his race.

'No need to lead me, soldier,' he said, shaking himself loose, 'who am old and ready to die.' Then he kissed his daughter at his side, wrung Nahoon by the hand, and turning from Hadden with a gesture of contempt walked out upon the platform that joined the two thorn trunks. Here he stood for a moment looking at the setting sun, then suddenly, and without a sound, he hurled himself into the abyss below and vanished.

'That was a brave one,' said the captain with admiration. 'Can you spring too, girl, or must we throw you?'

'I can walk my father's path,' Nanea answered faintly, 'but first I crave leave to say one word. It is true that we were escaping from the king, and therefore by the law we must die; but it was Black Heart here who made the plot, and he who has betrayed us. Would you know why he has betrayed us? Because he sought my favour, and I refused him, and this is the vengeance that he takes – a white man's vengeance.'

'*Wow!*' broke in the Chief Maputa, 'this pretty one speaks truth, for the white man would have made a bargain with me under which Umgona, the wizard, and Nahoon, the soldier, were to be killed at the Crocodile Drift, and he himself suffered to escape with the girl. I spoke him softly and said "yes", and then like a loyal man I reported to the king.'

'You hear,' sighed Nanea. 'Nahoon, fare you well, though presently perhaps we shall be together again. It was I who tempted you from your duty. For my sake you forgot your honour, and I am repaid. Farewell, my husband, it is better to die with you than to enter the house of the king's women,' and Nanea stepped on to the platform.

Here, holding to a bough of one of the thorn trees, she turned and addressed Hadden saying:

'Black Heart, you seem to have won the day, but me at least you lose and – the sun is not yet set. After sunset comes the night, Black Heart, and in that night I pray that you may wander eternally, and be given to drink of my blood and the blood of Umgona my father, and the blood of Nahoon my husband, who saved your life, and whom you have murdered. Perchance, Black Heart, we may yet meet yonder – in the House of the Dead.'

Then uttering a low cry Nanea clasped her hands and sprang upwards and outwards from the platform. The watchers bent their heads forward to look. They saw her rush headlong down the face of the fall to strike the water fifty feet below. A few seconds, and for the last time, they caught sight of her white garment glimmering on the surface of the gloomy pool. Then the shadows and mist-wreaths hid it, and she was gone.

'Now, husband,' cried the cheerful voice of the captain,

'yonder is your marriage bed, so be swift to follow a bride who is so ready to lead the way. *Wow!* but you are good people to kill; never have I had to do with any who gave less trouble. You——' and he stopped, for mental agony had done its work, and suddenly Nahoon went mad before his eyes.

With a roar like that of a lion the great man cast off those who held him and seizing one of them round the waist and thigh, he put out all his terrible strength. Lifting him as though he had been an infant, he hurled him over the edge of the cliff to find his death on the rocks of the Pool of Doom. Then crying:

'Black Heart! your turn, Black Heart the traitor!' he rushed at Hadden, his eyes rolling and foam flying from his lips, as he passed striking the Chief Maputa from his horse with a backward blow of his hand. Ill would it have gone with the white man if Nahoon had caught him. But he could not come at him, for the soldiers sprang upon him and notwithstanding his fearful struggles they pulled him to the ground, as at certain festivals the Zulu regiments with their naked hands pull down a bull in the presence of the king.

'Cast him over before he can work more mischief,' said a voice. But the captain cried out, 'Nay, nay, he is sacred; the fire from Heaven has fallen on his brain, and we may not harm him, else evil would overtake us all. Bind him hand and foot, and bear him hence tenderly to where he can be cared for. Surely I thought that these evil-doers were giving us too little trouble, and thus it has proved.'

So they set themselves to make fast Nahoon's hands and wrists, using as much gentleness as they might, for among the Zulus a lunatic is accounted holy. It was no easy task, and it took time.

Hadden glanced around him, and saw his opportunity. On the ground close beside him lay his rifle, where one of the soldiers had placed it, and about a dozen yards away Maputa's pony was grazing. With a swift movement, he seized the Martini and five seconds later he was on the back of the pony, heading for the Crocodile Drift at a gallop. So quickly indeed did he execute this masterly retreat, that occupied as they all were in binding Nahoon, for half a minute or more none of the soldiers noticed what had happened. Then Maputa chanced to see, and waddled after him to the top of the rise, screaming:

'The white thief, he has stolen my horse, and the gun too, the gun that he promised to give me.'

Hadden, who by this time was a hundred yards away, heard him clearly, and a rage filled his heart. This man had made an open murderer of him; more, he had been the means of robbing him of the girl for whose sake he had dipped his hands in these iniquities. He glanced over his shoulder; Maputa was still running, and alone. Yes, there was time; at any rate he would risk it.

Pulling up the pony with a jerk, he leapt from its back, slipping his arms through the rein with an almost simultaneous movement. As it chanced, and as he had hoped would be the case, the animal was a trained shooting horse, and stood still. Hadden planted his feet firmly on the ground and drawing a deep breath, he cocked the rifle and covered the advancing chief. Now Maputa saw his purpose and with a yell of terror turned to fly. Hadden waited a second to get the sight fair on to his broad back, then just as the soldiers appeared above the rise he pressed the trigger. He was a noted shot, and in this instance his skill did not fail him; for, before he heard the bullet tell, Maputa flung his arms wide and plunged to the ground dead.

Three seconds more, and with a savage curse, Hadden had remounted the pony and was riding for his life towards the river, which a while later he crossed in safety.

VI

The Ghost of the Dead

When Nanea leapt from the dizzy platform that overhung the Pool of Doom, a strange fortune befell her. Close in to the precipice were many jagged rocks, and on these the waters of the fall fell and thundered, bounding from them in spouts of spray into the troubled depths of the foss beyond. It was on these stones that the life was dashed out of the bodies of the wretched victims who were hurled from above. But Nanea, it will be remembered, had not waited to be treated thus, and as it chanced the strong spring with which she had leapt to death carried her clear of the rocks. By a very little she missed the edge of them and striking the deep water head first like some practised diver, she sank down and down till she thought that she would never rise again. Yet she did rise, at the end of the pool in the mouth of the rapid, along which she sped swiftly, carried down by the rush of the water. Fortunately there were no rocks here; and, since she was a skilful swimmer, she escaped the danger of being thrown against the banks.

For a long distance she was borne thus till at length she saw that she was in a forest, for trees cut off the light from the water, and their drooping branches swept its surface. One of these Nanea caught with her hand, and by the help of it she dragged herself from the River of Death whence none had escaped before. Now she stood upon the bank gasping but quite unharmed; there was not a scratch on her body; even her white garment was still fast about her neck.

But though she had suffered no hurt in her terrible voyage, so exhausted was Nanea that she could scarcely stand. Here the gloom was that of night, and shivering with cold she looked around helplessly to find some refuge. Close to the water's edge grew an enormous yellow-wood tree, and to this she staggered — thinking to climb it, and seek shelter in its boughs where, as she hoped, she would be safe from wild beasts. Again fortune befriended her, for at a distance of a few feet from the ground there was a great hole in the tree which, she discovered, was hollow. Into this hole she crept, taking her chance of its being the home of snakes or other evil creatures, to find that the interior was wide and warm. It was dry also, for at the bottom of the cavity lay a foot or more of rotten tinder and moss brought there by rats or birds. Upon this tinder she lay down, and covering herself with the moss and leaves soon sank into sleep or stupor.

How long Nanea slept she did not know, but at length she was awakened by a sound as of guttural human voices talking in a language that she could not understand. Rising to her knees she peered out of the hole in the tree. It was night, but the stars shone brilliantly, and their light fell upon an open circle of ground close by the edge of the river. In this circle there burned a great fire, and at a little distance from the fire were gathered eight or ten horrible-looking beings, who appeared to be rejoicing over something that lay upon the ground. They were small in stature, men and women together, but no children, and all of them were nearly naked. Their hair was long and thin, growing down almost to the eyes, their jaws and teeth protruded and the girth of their black bodies was out of all proportion to their height. In their hands they held sticks with sharp stones lashed on to them, or rude hatchet-like knives of the same material.

Now Nanea's heart shrank within her, and she nearly fainted with fear, for she knew that she was in the haunted forest, and without a doubt these were the *Esemkofu*, the evil ghosts that dwelt therein. Yes, that was what they were, and yet she could not take her eyes off them — the sight of them held her with a horrible fascination. But if they were ghosts, why did they sing and dance like men? Why did they wave those sharp stones aloft, and quarrel and strike each other? And why did they make a fire as men do when they wish to cook food? More, what was it that they rejoiced over, that long dark thing which lay so quiet upon the ground? It did not look like a head of game, and it could scarcely be a crocodile, yet clearly it was food of some sort, for they were sharpening the stone knives in order to cut it up.

While she wondered thus, one of the dreadful-looking little creatures advanced to the fire, and taking from it a burning bough, held it over the thing that lay upon the ground, to give light to a companion who was about to do something to it with the stone knife. Next instant Nanea drew back her head from the hole, a stifled shriek upon her lips. She saw what it was now — it was the body of a man. Yes, and these were not ghosts; they were cannibals of whom when she was little, her mother had told her tales to keep her from wandering away from home.

But who was the man they were about to eat? It could not be one of themselves, for his stature was much greater. Oh! now she knew; it must be Nahoon, who had been killed up yonder, and whose dead body the waters had brought down to the haunted forest as they had brought her alive. Yes, it must be Nahoon, and she would be forced to see her husband devoured before her eyes. The thought of it overwhelmed her. That he should die by order of the king was natural, but that he should be buried thus! Yet what could she do to prevent it? Well, if it cost her her life, it should be prevented. At the worst they could only kill and eat her also, and now that Nahoon and her father were gone, being untroubled by any religious or spiritual hopes and fears, she was not greatly concerned to keep her own breath in her.

Slipping through the hole in the tree, Nanea walked quietly towards the cannibals — not knowing in the least what she should do when she reached them. As she arrived in line with the fire this lack of programme came home to her mind forcibly, and she paused to reflect. Just then one of the cannibals looked up to see a tall and stately figure wrapped in a white garment which, as the flame-light flickered on it, seemed now to advance from the dense background of shadow, and now to recede into it. The poor savage wretch was holding a stone knife in his teeth when he beheld her, but it did not remain there long, for opening his great jaws he uttered the most terrified and piercing yell that Nanea had ever heard. Then the others saw her also, and presently the forest was ringing with shrieks of fear. For a few seconds the outcasts stood and gazed, then they were gone this way and that, bursting their path through the undergrowth like startled jackals. The *Esemkofu* of Zulu tradition had been routed in their own haunted home by what they took to be a spirit.

Poor *Esemkofu!* they were but miserable and starving bushmen who, driven into that place of ill omen many years ago, had adopted this means, the only one open to them, to keep the life in their wretched bodies. Here at least they were unmolested, and as there was little other food to be found amid that wilderness of trees, they took what the river brought them. When executions were few in the Pool of Doom, times were hard for them indeed — for then they were driven to eat each other. That is why there were no children.

As their inarticulate outcry died away in the distance, Nanea ran forward to look at the body that lay on the ground, and staggered back with a sigh of relief. It was not Nahoon, but she recognised the face for that of one of the party of executioners. How did he come here? Had Nahoon killed him? Had Nahoon escaped? She could not tell, and at the best it was improbable, but still the sight of this dead soldier lit her heart with a faint ray of hope, for how did he come to be dead if Nahoon had no hand in his death? She could not bear to leave him lying so near her hiding-place, however; therefore, with no small toil, she rolled the corpse back into the water, which carried it swiftly away. Then she returned to the tree, having first replenished the fire, and awaited the light.

At last it came — so much of it as ever penetrated this

darksome den – and Nanea, becoming aware that she was hungry, descended from the tree to search for food. All day long she searched, finding nothing, till towards sunset she remembered that on the outskirts of the forest there was a flat rock where it was the custom of those who had been in any way afflicted, or who considered themselves or their belongings to be bewitched, to place propitiatory offerings of food wherewith the *Esemkofu* and *Amalhosi* were supposed to satisfy their spiritual cravings. Urged by the pinch of starvation, to this spot Nanea journeyed rapidly, and found to her joy that some neighbouring kraal had evidently been in recent trouble, for the Rock of Offering was laden with cobs of corn, gourds of milk, porridge and even meat. Helping herself to as much as she could carry, she returned to her lair, where she drank of the milk and cooked meat and mealies at the fire. Then she crept back into the tree, and slept.

For nearly two months Nanea lived thus in the forest, since she could not venture out of it – fearing lest she should be seized, and for a second time taste of the judgement of the king. In the forest at least she was safe, for none dared enter there, nor did the *Esemkofu* give her further trouble. Once or twice she saw them, but on each occasion they fled shrieking from her presence – seeking some distant retreat, where they hid themselves or perished. Nor did food fail her, for finding that it was taken, the pious givers brought it in plenty to the Rock of Offering.

But, oh! the life was dreadful, and the gloom and loneliness coupled with her sorrows at times drove her almost to insanity. Still she lived on, though often she desired to die, for if her father was dead, the corpse she had found was not the corpse of Nahoon, and in her heart there still shone that spark of hope. Yet what she hoped for she could not tell.

*　*　*

When Philip Hadden reached civilised regions, he found that war was about to be declared between the Queen and Cetywayo, King of the Amazulu; also that in the prevailing excitement his little adventure with the Utrecht store-keeper had been overlooked or forgotten. He was the owner of two good buck-waggons with spans of salted oxen, and at that time vehicles were much in request to carry military stores for the columns which were to advance into Zululand; indeed the transport authorities were

97

glad to pay £90 a month for the hire of each waggon and to guarantee the owners against all loss of cattle. Although he was not desirous of returning to Zululand, this bait proved too much for Hadden, who accordingly leased out his waggons to the Commissariat, together with his own services as conductor and interpreter.

He was attached to No. 3 column of the invading force, which it may be remembered was under the immediate command of Lord Chelmsford, and on the 20 January, 1879, he marched with it by the road that runs from Rorke's Drift to the Indeni forest, and encamped that night beneath the shadow of the steep and desolate mountain known as Isandhlwana.

That day also a great army of King Cetywayo's, numbering twenty thousand men and more, moved down from the Upindo Hill and camped upon the stony plain that lies a mile and a half to the east of Isandhlwana. No fires were lit, and it lay there in utter silence, for the warriors were 'sleeping on their spears'.

With that *impi* was the Umcityu regiment, three thousand five hundred strong. At the first break of dawn the Induna in command of the Umcityu looked up from beneath the shelter of the black shield with which he had covered his body, and through the thick mist he saw a great man standing before him, clothed only in a moocha, a gaunt wild-eyed man who held a rough club in his hand. When he was spoken to, the man made no answer; he only leaned upon his club looking from left to right along the dense array of innumerable shields.

'Who is this *Silwana* (wild creature)?' asked the Induna of his captains wondering.

The captains stared at the wanderer, and one of them replied, 'This is Nahoon-ka-Zomba, it is the son of Zomba who not long ago held rank in this regiment of the Umcityu. His betrothed, Nanea, daughter of Umgona, was killed together with her father by order of the Black One, and Nahoon went mad with grief at the sight of it, for the fire of Heaven entered his brain, and mad he has wandered ever since.'

'What would you here, Nahoon-ka-Zomba?' asked the Induna.

Then Nahoon spoke slowly. 'My regiment goes down to war against the white men; give me a shield and a spear, O Captain of the king, that I may fight with my regiment, for I seek a face in the battle.'

So they gave him a shield and a spear, for they dared not turn away one whose brain was alight with the fire of Heaven.

When the sun was high that day, bullets began to fall among the ranks of the Umcityu. Then the black-shielded, black-plumed Umcityu arose, company by company, and after them arose the whole vast Zulu army, breast and horns together, and swept down in silence upon the doomed British camp, a moving sheen of spears. The bullets pattered on the shields, the shells tore long lines through their array, but they never halted nor wavered. Forward on either side shot out the horns of armed men, clasping the camp in an embrace of steel. Then as these began to close, out burst the war cry of the Zulus, and with the roar of a torrent and the rush of a storm, with a sound like the humming of a billion bees, wave after wave the deep breast of the *impi* rolled down upon the white men. With it went the black-shielded Umcityu and with them went Nahoon, the son of Zomba. A bullet struck him in the side, glancing from his ribs, he did not heed; a white man fell from his horse before him, he did not stab, for he sought but one face in the battle.

He sought – and at last he found. There, among the waggons where the spears were busiest, there standing by his horse and firing rapidly was Black Heart, he who had given Nanea his betrothed to death. Three soldiers stood between them, one of them Nahoon stabbed, and two he brushed aside; then he rushed straight at Hadden.

But the white man saw him come, and even through the mask of his madness he knew Nahoon again, and terror took hold of him. Throwing away the empty rifle, for his ammunition was spent, he leaped upon his horse and drove his spurs into its flanks. Away it went among the carnage, springing over the dead and bursting through the lines of shields, and after it came Nahoon, running long and low with head stretched forward and trailing spear, running as a hound runs when the buck is at view.

Hadden's first plan was to head for Rorke's Drift, but a glance to the left showed him that the masses of the Undi barred that way, so he fled straight on, leaving his path to fortune. In five minutes he was over a ridge, and there was nothing of the battle to be seen, in ten all sounds of it had died away, for few

- - -

guns were fired in the dread race to Fugitive's Drift, and the assegai makes no noise. In some strange fashion, even at this moment, the contrast between the dreadful scene of blood and turmoil that he had left, and the peaceful face of Nature over which he was passing, came home to his brain vividly. Here birds sang and cattle grazed; here the sun shone undimmed by the smoke of cannon, only high up in the blue and silent air long streams of vultures could be seen winging their way to the Plain of Isandhlwana.

The ground was very rough, and Hadden's horse began to tire. He looked over his shoulder — there some two hundred yards behind came the Zulu, grim as Death, unswerving as Fate. He examined the pistol in his belt; there was but one undis-charged cartridge left, all the rest had been fired and the pouch was empty. Well, one bullet should be enough for one savage: the question was should he stop and use it now? No, he might miss or fail to kill the man; he was on horseback and his foe on foot, surely he could tire him out.

A while passed, and they dashed through a little stream. It seemed familiar to Hadden. Yes, that was the pool where he used to bathe when he was the guest of Umgona, the father of Nanea; and there on the knoll to his right were the huts, or rather the remains of them, for they had been burnt with fire. What chance had brought him to this place, he wondered; then again he looked behind him at Nahoon, who seemed to read his thoughts, for he shook his spear and pointed to the ruined kraal.

On he went at speed for here the land was level, and to his joy he lost sight of his pursuer. But presently there came a mile of rocky ground, and when it was past, glancing back he saw that Nahoon was once more in his old place. His horse's strength was almost spent, but Hadden spurred it forward blindly, whither he knew not. Now he was travelling along a strip of turf and ahead of him he heard the music of a river, while to his left rose a high bank. Presently the turf belt bent inwards and there, not twenty yards away from him, was a Kaffir hut standing on the brink of a river. He looked at it, yes, it was the hut of that accursed *inyanga*, the Bee, and standing by the fence of it was none other than the Bee herself. At the sight of her the exhausted horse swerved violently, stumbled and came to the ground, where it lay panting. Hadden was thrown from the saddle but sprang to his feet unhurt.

'Ah! Black Heart, is it you? What news of the battle, Black Heart?' cried the Bee in a mocking voice.

'Help me, mother, I am pursued,' he gasped.

'What of it, Black Heart, it is but by one tired man. Stand then and face him, for now Black Heart and White Heart are together again. You will not? Then away to the forest and seek shelter among the dead who await you there. Tell me, tell me, was it the face of Nanea that I saw beneath the waters a while ago? Good! bear my greetings to her when you two meet in the House of the Dead.'

Hadden looked at the stream; it was in flood. He could not swim it, so followed by the evil laugh of the prophetess, he sped towards the forest. After him came Nahoon, his tongue hanging from his jaws like the tongue of a wolf.

Now he was in the shadow of the forest, but still he sped on following the course of the river, till at length his breath failed, and he halted on the further side of a little glade, beyond which a great tree grew. Nahoon was more than a spear's throw behind him: therefore he had time to draw his pistol and make ready.

'Halt, Nahoon,' he cried, as once before he had cried; 'I would speak with you.'

The Zulu heard his voice, and obeyed.

'Listen,' said Hadden. 'We have run a long race and fought a long fight, you and I, and we are still alive both of us. Very soon, if you come on, one of us must be dead, and it will be you, Nahoon, for I am armed and as you know I can shoot straight. What do you say?'

Nahoon made no answer, but stood still at the edge of the glade, his wild and glowering eyes fixed on the white man's face and his breath coming in short gasps.

'Will you let me go, if *I* let *you* go?' Hadden asked once more. 'I know why you hate me, but the past cannot be undone, nor can the dead be brought to earth again.'

Still Nahoon made no answer, and his silence seemed more fateful and more crushing than any speech; no spoken accusation would have been so terrible in Hadden's ear. He made no answer, but lifting his assegai he stalked grimly toward his foe.

When he was within five paces Hadden covered him and fired. Nahoon sprang aside, but the bullet struck him somewhere, for his right arm dropped, and the stabbing spear that he held was jerked from it harmlessly over the white man's head. But still making no sound, the Zulu came on and gripped him by the throat with his left hand. For a space they struggled terribly, swaying to and fro, but Hadden was unhurt and fought with the fury of despair, while Nahoon had been twice wounded, and there remained to him but one sound arm wherewith to strike. Presently forced to earth by the white man's iron strength, the soldier was down, nor could he rise again.

'Now we will make an end,' muttered Hadden savagely, and he turned to seek the assegai, then staggered slowly back with starting eyes and reeling gait. For there before him, still clad in her white robe, a spear in her hand, stood the spirit of Nanea!

'Think of it,' he said to himself, dimly remembering the words of the *inyanga*, 'when you stand face to face with the ghost of the dead in the Home of the Dead.'

There was a cry and a flash of steel; the broad spear leapt towards him to bury itself in his breast. He swayed, he fell, and presently Black Heart clasped that great reward which the word of the Bee had promised Him.

'Nahoon! Nahoon!' murmured a soft voice, 'awake, it is no ghost, but I – Nanea – I, your living wife, to whom my *Ehlose*[1] has given it me to save you.'

Nahoon heard and opened his eyes to look and his madness left him.

'Welcome, wife,' he said faintly, 'now I will live since Death has brought you back to me in the House of the Dead.'

*　*　*

Today Nahoon is one of the Indunas of the English Government in Zululand, and there are children about his kraal. It was from the lips of none other than Nanea his wife that the teller of this tale heard its substance.

The Bee also lives and practises as much magic as she dares under the white man's rule. On her black hand shines a golden ring shaped like a snake with ruby eyes, and of this trinket the Bee is very proud.

---

[1] Guardian Spirit.

The Kiss of Fate

There came a man to Philae. Watching from a pylon top whither I had gone to pray alone, I saw him land upon the island and from far off noted that he was a godlike man, clad in armour such as the Grecians used, over which was thrown a common cloak, hooded as though to disguise him; one who had the air of a warrior. At a distance from the temple gate he halted and looked upward as though something drew his glance to me standing high above him upon the pylon top. I could not see his face because of the shadow thrown by the great walls behind which the sun was sinking, but doubtless he could see me well enough, whose shape was outlined against the veil of golden light that must have touched me with its glory, though, as that light was behind me, my face also would be hidden from him. At least he stood a little while as though amazed, staring upward steadily, then bowed his head and passed into the temple, followed by men bearing burdens.

Some pilgrim to the shrine, I thought to myself, then turned my mind to other matters, remembering that with men I had no more to do. Thus for the first time here in the body, all unknowing, I looked upon Kallikrates and he looked on me, but often I have thought that there was a veiled lesson or a parable in the fashion of this meeting.

For did I not stand far above him, clothed in the glory of heaven's gold, and did he not stand far beneath in the gloom of the shadows that lay upon the lowly earth, so that between us there was space unclimbable? And has it not been ever thus throughout the centuries, for am I not still upon the pylon top clad in the splendour of the spirit, and is he not still far beneath me wrapped with the shadows of the flesh? And since as yet the secret of the pylon stair is hidden from him, must I not descend to earth if we would meet, leaving the light and my pride of place that I may walk humbly with him in the shadow? And is it not often so between those that love, that one is set far above the

---

other, though still this rope of love draws them together, uplifting the one, or dragging down the other?

The man passed into the temple and that night I heard he was a Grecian captain of high blood, one who though young had seen much service in the wars and done great deeds, Kallikrates by name, who had come to seek the counsel of the goddess, bringing precious gifts of gold and Eastern silks, the spoils of battle in which he had fought.

I asked why such a one sought the wisdom of Isis, and was told that it was because his heart was troubled. It seemed that he had been dwelling at Pharaoh's court as a captain of the Grecian guard, and that there he had quarrelled with and slain one who was as a brother to him, if indeed he were not his very brother. This ill deed, it was said, preyed upon his soul and drove him into the arms of Mother Isis, seeking for pardon and that comfort which he could not find at the hand of any of the gods of the Greeks.

Again I asked idly enough why this Kallikrates had killed his familiar friend or his brother, whichever it might be. The answer was — because of some highly-placed maiden whom both of them loved, so that they fought from jealousy, after the fashion of men. For this reason the life of Kallikrates was held to be forfeit according to the stern military law of the Grecian soldiers, and he must fly. Also the deed had tarnished that great lady's name; also his heart was broken with remorse and hither he came to pray Isis to mend it of her mercy, he who had forsaken the world.

The tale moved a little, but again I cast it from my mind, for are not such common among men? Always the story is the same; two men and a woman, or two women and a man, and bloodshed and remorse and memories which will not die and the cry for pardon that is so hard to find.

Yes, I cast it from my mind, saying lightly — oh! those evil-omened words — that doubtless his own blood in a day to come would pay for that which he had spilt.

For a while, some months indeed, this Grecian Kallikrates vanished from my sight and even from my thoughts, save when, from time to time, I heard of him as studying the Mysteries among the priests, having, it was said, determined to renounce the world and be sworn to the service of the goddess. Noot, the high priest, told me that he was very earnest in this design and made great progress in the faith, which pleased the priests who desired above everything to convert those that served Grecian gods with whom the deities of Egypt, and most of all Isis, were at war. Therefore they hastened his preparation, so that as soon as might be he should be bound to the heavenly Queen by bonds that could not be loosed.

At length his fasts and instruction were finished; his trials had been passed and the hour came when he must make his last confession to the goddess and swear the awful oaths to her very self.

Now as Isis did not descend to earth to stand face to face with every neophyte, it was needful in this great ceremony that one filled with her spirit should take her place and, as may be guessed, that one was I, Ayesha the Arab. To speak truth, in all Egypt because of my beauty, my learning and the grace that was given to me, there was none so fitting to wear her mantle as myself. Indeed afterward this was acknowledged when, with a single voice, the Colleges of her servants throughout the land, men and women together promoted me to be her high-priestess, and gave me, who at first among them was known by the title of Wisdom's Daughter, the new name of *Isis come to earth*, or in shorter words, *The Isis*. For my own name of Ayesha I kept hid lest it should be discovered that I was that chieftainess, the child of Yarab, who had defeated the army of Nectanebes.

Therefore at a certain hour of the night, draped in the holy robes, wearing on my brow the vulture cap and the bent symbol of the moon, holding in my hands the *sistrum* and the cross of Life, I was conducted to the pillared sanctuary and seated alone upon a throne of blackest marble, with the round symbol of the world for my footstool.

Thus, having learned my part and the ancient hallowed words that I must say, I sat awhile, wondering in my heart whether Isis herself could be more glorious or more fair. So indeed did the priests and priestesses who saw me thus arrayed and bent the knee to me as though I were the very goddess, which in truth some of the humbler among them half believed.

Thus I sat in the moonlight that flowed from the unroofed hall beyond, while the carven gods watched me with their quiet eyes.

At length I heard the sound of footsteps whereon there came a priestess and flung over me the white veil of innocence sewn with golden stars that, until the appointed moment, must hide Isis from her worshipper. The priestess withdrew and, wrapped in the dark, hooded robe that signified the stained flesh about to be cast away, which hid all of him so that his face could not be seen, appeared that tall neophyte led by two priests who held his right hand and his left. I noted those hands because they were so white against the blackness of the robe, and even by the moonlight saw that they were beautiful, long, thin and shapely, though one, the right, was somewhat broadened as though by the long handling of the tools of war.

The priests led him to the entrance to the shrine and in hushed whispers bade him kneel upon a footstool and make his sacrifice and confession to the goddess as he had been taught to do. Then they departed leaving us alone.

There followed silence which at length I broke, whispering:

'Who is this that comes to visit the Mother in her earthly shrine and what is his prayer to the Queen of Heaven and Earth?'

Though I spoke so gently and so low, perhaps because of their quiet sweetness, my words seemed to frighten him; or perhaps he believed that he stood in the very presence of the goddess; at least he answered in a trembling voice:

'O holy Queen adored, in the world I was named Kalli-krates the comely. But the priests, O Queen, have given me a new name, and it is, *Lover of Isis.*'

'What have you to say to Isis, O Lover of Isis?'

'O Queen eternal, I come to tell my sins and ask her pardon for them, I who have passed the Trials and am accepted by her servants. If it is granted, then to her I must make the oath, binding myself eternally to love and serve her, her and no other in heaven or on earth.'

'Set out those sins, O Lover of Isis, that my Majesty may judge of them, whether they can be forgiven or are beyond for-giveness,' I answered in the words of the appointed ritual.

Then he began and told a tale that made me redden behind my veil, for all of it had to do with women, and never before had I learned what wantons those Greeks could be. Also he told me of men whom he had slain in war, one of them in the battle against my tribe, in which strangely enough it seemed he had fought as a lad, for this man was a great warrior. Of these killings, however, I took no account, because they had been of those who were the enemies of himself or of his cause.

In stern silence I listened, noting that save for these matters of light love and fightings, the man seemed innocent enough, for in his story there was naught of baseness or of betrayal. Moreover it seemed that he was one in whom the spirit had striven against the flesh, and who, however much his feet were tangled in the bitter snares of earth, from time to time had set his eyes on Heaven.

At length he paused and I asked of him:

'Is the black count finished? Tell now the truth and dare to hold nothing back from the goddess who notes all.'

'Nay, O Queen,' he answered, 'the worst is yet to speak. I came to Egypt as a captain of the Grecian guard that watches the House of Pharaoh of Sais. With me came another captain, my half-brother, for our father was the same, with whom I was brought up and loved as never I loved any other man, and who loved me. He was a glorious warrior, though some held that I was more handsome in my person. Tisisthenes by name, that in my Grecian tongue in which I speak, means the Avenger. Thus was he called because my father, whose firstborn he was, desired that he might grow up to work vengeance upon the Persians who slew his father named like myself, Kallikrates, the most beauteous Spartan that was ever born. Foully they slew him before the battle of Plataea, whilst he was aiding the great Pausanius to make sacrifice to the gods. This Tisisthenes my brother I killed with my own hand.'

'For what cause did you kill him?'

'There was a royal maiden at that Court, one fairer than any woman has been, is or will be — ask not her name, O Mother, though doubtless it is known to you already. This lady both of us saw at the same time and by the decree of Aphrodite, both of us loved. As it chanced it was I who won her favour, not my brother. We were spied upon; the tale was told; trouble fell upon that royal maiden who, when she should be old enough, was sworn in marriage to a distant king. To save her name she made denial, as she must do. She swore there was naught between her and me, and to prove it turned her face from me and towards my brother. I came upon them together in a garden. She had plucked a flower which she gave to him and he kissed the hand that held the flower. She saw me and fled away. I, maddened with jealousy, smote my beloved brother in the face and forced him to fight with me. We fought. He guarded himself but ill, as though he cared nothing of the end of that fray. I cut him down. He lay before me dying, but before he died he spoke:

' "This is a very evil business," he said. "Know, Kallikrates, my most beloved brother, that what you saw in the garden between that royal maid and myself was but a plot to save you both, since thereby I proposed to take on to my own head the weight of your transgression against the law of this land, because she prayed it and it was my wish. This I have done and for this reason I suffered you to slay me, though during that fight twice I could have pierced you, because you were blind with rage and forgot your swordsmanship. Now it will be said that you found me pursuing this royal maiden and rightly slew me according to your duty and that it was I who loved her and not you, as has been commonly reported. Yet in truth I love her well and am glad to die because it was to you that her heart turned and not to me; also because thereby I save both her and you. Yet, Kallikrates, my brother, in this the hour of my death, the gods give me wisdom and foresight and I say that you will do well to have done with this lady and all women, and to seek rest in the bosom of the gods, since if you do not, great trouble will come upon you, and through this same curse of jealousy, such a death as mine shall be yours also. Now let us who are the victims of Fate, kiss each other on the brow as we used to do when we were children playing together in the happy fields of Greece, from whom death was yet a long way off, forgiving each other all and hoping that we may meet once more in the region of the Shades."

'So we embraced and my brother Tisisthenes gave up his spirit in my arms and looking on him I wished that I were dead in his place. Then as I turned to go the soldiers of our company found me and seeing that I had slain my brother, would have brought me to trial, not because we had fought together, but because he was my superior in rank and therefore I who, being under his command, drew sword on him, by the law of the Greeks must die. Yet before I could be put upon my trial, some of those who loved me and guessed the truth of the business, thrust me out of our camp disguised, with all the treasure that I had won in war, bidding me hide myself awhile till the matter was forgotten. O Queen, I did not desire to go; nay, I desired to stay and to pay the price of my sin. But they would not have it so. I think indeed that there were others behind, great ones of Egypt, moving in this matter; at least I was thrust forth all being made easy for me, and all eyes growing blind.'

Again he paused and I, Ayesha, clothed as the goddess, asked:

'And what did you then, you who could slay your brother for the sake of a woman?'

'Then, divine One, I fled up Nile where, because of the trouble that was in the land, Pharaoh's arm could not reach me, nor the arm of the commander of the Greeks. Tarrying not and without speech with that high maiden who was the cause of my sin, I fled up Nile.'

'Why did you fly up Nile and not back to your own people, O most sinful man?'

'Because my heart was broken, Queen, and I desired to seek the mercy of Isis whose law I had learned already and to become her priest. I knew that those who bow themselves to her may look no more on woman, but henceforth must live virgin to the death, and it was my own will to look no more on woman, since woman had stained my hands with a brother's blood, and therefore I hated her.'

Now I, Ayesha, asked:

'What gods did you worship before your heart was turned to Isis, Queen of Heaven?'

'I worshipped the gods of Greece and first among them Aphrodite, Lady of Love.'

'Who has paid you well for your service, making of you a murderer of one of your own blood who, before she blinded your eyes, was more to you than any on the earth. Do you then renounce this wanton Aphrodite?'

'Aye, Queen, I renounce her for ever. Never more will I offer at her altars or look on woman in the way of love. If I may have pardon for my sins, here and now I vow myself to Isis as her faithful priest and servant. Here and now I blot out the name of Aphrodite; yea, I reject her gifts and tread down all her memories beneath my aspiring feet that at last shall bear my heart to peace.'

Thus the man spoke in a quivering and earnest voice, and was silent. Yes, deep silence reigned in that holy place, whilst I, Ayesha, although it is true that as a woman I misdoubted me of such rash oaths, as the minister of the goddess, prepared myself to grant pardon to this seeker in the hallowed, immemorial words, and to open to his troubled soul the doors of purity and eternal rest.

Then suddenly in that silence clearly I heard the sound of silvern laughter; soft, sweet laughter that seemed to come from the skies above and though it was so low to fill the shrine and all the hall beyond. I looked about me but could see nothing. It would seem that the Greek heard also, for he turned his head and glanced behind him, then once more let it fall upon his hands.

Whence came that sound? Could it be that the queen of love. . .? Nay, it was impossible, and not thus would I be turned from my office, I who was clothed with the robe and for that hour wielded the might of Isis.

'Hearken, O man, in the world named Kallikrates,' I said. 'On behalf of Isis, the All-Mother, Goddess of virtue and of wisdom, speaking with her voice, hearing with her ears, and filled with her soul, I wash you clean of all your sins and accept you as her priest, promising to you light burdens on the earth and beyond the earth great rewards for ever. First swear the oath that may not be broken, and then draw near that I may kiss you on the brow, accepting you as the slave and lover of Isis, from this day until the moon, her heavenly throne, shall crumble into nothingness.'

Having spoken thus, letting the words fall one by one, slowly as the tears of that penitent fell upon the ground, I uttered the oath, the form of which even now I will not write.

It was a dreadful oath covering all things, and binding him who took it to Isis alone, an oath that if it were forgot, wrought upon the traitor the age-long doom of death in this world and woe in the worlds to come, till by slow steps, with pierced heart and bleeding feet, the holy height from which he had fallen should be climbed again.

At length it was finished and he said faintly:

'I swear! With fear and trembling still I swear!'

Then I beckoned to him with the *sistrum* of which the little shaken bells made a faint compelling music that already he had learned to follow, and he came and kneeled before me. There I laid the Cross of Life upon his head and gave him blessing, laid it upon his lips and gave him wisdom, laid it upon his heart and gave him breath for thousands upon thousands of years. All these things I did in the name and with the strength of Isis the Mother.

Came the last rite, the greeting of the Mother to her child new born in spirit, the rite of the Kiss of Welcome. At that moment supreme a light fell on me from above: perchance it came from Heaven, perchance it was but an art of the watching priests; I do not know. At least it fell upon me illumining my glittering robes and jewelled head-dress with a soft splendour in the darkness of that shrine. At that moment, too, at a touch my veil fell down, so that the moonlight struck full upon my face making it mystical and lovely in the frame of my flowing hair.

The priest new-ordained lifted his bent head that I might consecrate his brow with the kiss of welcome, and his hood fell back. The moonlight shone on his face also, his beautiful face like that of a sculptured Grecian god; shapely, fine-featured, large-eyed and crowned with little golden curls — for as yet he was unshorn; yes, a face more beautiful than that which I had seen on any man, set above a warrior's tall and sinewy form.

By Isis! I knew this face; it was that which had haunted me from my childhood, that which often I had seen in a dream of halls beyond the earth, that of a man who in this dream had been sworn to me to complete my womanhood. Oh! I could not doubt, it was the same, the very same, and looking on it, the curse of Aphrodite fell upon me and for the first time I knew the madness of our mortal flesh. Yea, my being was rent and shattered like a cedar beneath the lightning stroke; I was smitten through and through. I, the priestess of Isis, proud and pure, was as lost as any village maid within her lover's arms.

The man, too! He saw me and his aspect changed; the holy fervour went out of his eyes and into them entered something more human, something more fateful. It was as though he too remembered — I know not what.

By a mighty effort of the will, aware that the eyes of the

goddess and perhaps of her priests also were upon me, I conquered myself and with beating heart and heaving breast bent down to touch his brow with the Kiss of Ceremony. Yet, I know not how – I know not if the fault were his or mine or perchance that of both of us – I touched his *lips* and not his brow, just touched them and no more.

It was nothing, or at any rate but a little thing, in one instant come and gone, and yet to me it was all. For in that touch I broke my holy vows, and he, new-sworn to the worship of the goddess, broke his, yes, in the very act of sacrifice. What drove us to it? I do not know, but once again I thought I heard that low, triumphant laughter and it came into my mind that we were the sport of an indomitable power greater than ourselves and all the oaths that mortals swear to gods or men.

I waved my sceptre. The new-made priest rose, bowed and withdrew, I wondering of whom he was the priest – of Isis or of Aphrodite. The singing of a distant choir broke out upon the silence, the heirophants came and led him away to be of their company till his death: the ceremony was ended. My attendants, arrayed as the goddesses Hathor and Nut, conducted me from the shrine. I was unrobed of my sacred panoplies and once more from a goddess became a woman. Then as a woman I sought my couch and wept and wept.

For in my heart, had I not at the first temptation broken the law and betrayed the trust of her who, as then I believed, is and was and shall be; her whose veil no mortal man had lifted, the Mother of the sun and all its stars?

The Tale of Philo

This tale is a sequel to that called The Kiss of Fate. *Egypt has been invaded; Noot, the high priest of Isis, and the new priest Kallikrates have sailed away down the Nile. Ayesha, high priestess of Isis, guided by the sea captain Philo, is endeavouring to find them.*

Once more it was the night of full moon. As we had done for many days, we were sailing before that steady wind along the coast of Libya, having this upon our right hand, and upon our left at a distance a line of rocky reef upon which breakers fell continually.

It was a very splendid moon that turned the sea to silver and lit up the palm-grown shore almost as brightly as does the sun. I sat upon the deck near to my cabin and by me stood Philo watching that shore.

'For what do you seek, Philo? Are you in fear of sunken rocks?'

'Nay, child of Isis, yet it is true that I seek a certain rock of which, by my reckoning, we should now be in sight. Ah!'

Then suddenly he ran foward and shouted an order. Men leaped and sprang to the ropes while the rowers began to get out the sweeps. As they did this the *Hapi* came round so that her bow pointed to the shore and the great sail sank to the deck. Then the long oars drove us shorewards.

Philo returned.

'Look, lady,' he said. 'Now that the moon has risen higher you can see well,' and he pointed to a headland in front of us.

Following his outstreched hand with my eyes I perceived a great rock many cubits in height and, carven on the crest of it, a head far larger than that of the huge Sphinx of Egypt. Or perchance it was not carved; perchance Nature had fashioned it thus. At least there it stood and will stand, a terrible and hideous thing, having the likeness of an Ethiopian's head gazing eternally across the sea.

'What is it?' I asked.

'Lady, it is the guardian of the gate of the land whither we go. Legend tells that it is shaped to the likeness of the first king of that land who lived thousands upon thousands of years before the pyramids were built; also that his bones lie in it, or at least, that it is haunted by his spirit. For this reason none dare to touch and much less to climb yonder monstrous rock.'

Then he left me to see to the matters of the ship, because, as he said in going, the entrance to the place was narrow and dangerous. But I sat on alone upon the deck watching this strange new sight.

Within an hour, rowing carefully, we entered the mouth of a river, having the rock shaped like a negro's head upon our right. Then it was that I saw something which put me in mind of Philo's tale about an ancient king. For there, unless I dreamed, upon the very point of the skull of the effigy, of a sudden I perceived a tall form clad in armour which shone silvery bright in the moon's rays. It leaned upon a great spear and when we were opposite to it, it straightened itself and bent forward as though to stare at our ship beneath. Next, thrice it lifted the spear in salutation; thrice it bowed, as I thought in obeisance to me, and having done so, threw its arms wide and was gone.

Afterwards I asked Philo if he also had seen this shape.

'Nay,' he answered in a doubtful voice as though the matter were one of which he did not wish to talk, adding:

'It is not the custom of mariners to study that head in moonlight, because the story goes that if they do and chance to see some such ghost as that you tell of, it casts a spear towards them, who then are doomed to die within the year. Yet at you, child of Isis, he cast no spear, only bowed and gave the salute of kings, or so you tell me. Therefore doubtless neither you nor any of us, your companions, are marked for death.'

I smiled and said that I whose soul was in touch with heaven, feared not the wraith of any ancient king, nor did we speak more of this matter. Yet in the after ages it came into my mind that there was truth in the story and that this long-dead chieftain appeared thus to give greeting to her who was destined to rule his land through many generations; also that perchance

he was not dead at all, but, having drunk of a certain cup of life
of which I was to learn, lived eternally there upon the rock.

I laid me down and slept and when I woke in the bright
morning, it was to find that we had passed from that river into a
canal dug by man, which, though deep, was too narrow for the
sweeps to work. Therefore the *Hapi* must be pushed along with
poles and towed by ropes dragged at by the mariners from a path
that ran upon the bank.

For three days we travelled thus making but slow progress,
since the toil of dragging so large a ship was great, and at night
we tied up to the bank, as boats do upon the Nile. All this while
we saw no habitation though of ruins there were many. Indeed,
that country was very desolate and full of great swamps that were
tenanted by wild beasts, the haunt of owls and bitterns, where
lions roared and serpents crept, great serpents such as I had
never seen.

At length at noon on the fourth day we came to a lake where
the canal ended, which lake once had been a harbour, for we
saw stone quays to which were tied some boats that seemed to be
little used. Here Philo said that we must disembark and travel on
by land. So we left the *Hapi*, sadly enough for my part, because
those were happy, quiet days that I had spent on board of her,
veritable oases in the storm-swept desert of my life.

Scarcely had we set foot upon the land when appeared, I
knew not whence, a company of men, handsome, hook-nosed,
sombre men, such as I had seen among the crew upon the *Hapi*.
These men, though so fierce of countenance, were not barbarians for they wore linen garments that gave to them the aspects
of priests. Moreover, their leaders could speak Arabic in its most
ancient form which, having studied it as it chanced, I knew.
With this army, who bore bows and spears, came a multitude of
folk of a baser sort that carried litters, or burdens, also a guard of
great fellows who, Philo told me, were my escort. Now my
patience failed so that I turned to Philo saying angrily,

'Hitherto, friend, I have trusted myself to you, because it
seemed decreed that I should do so. Tell me, I pray you, for what
reason I journey over countless leagues of sea into a land untrod,
and whither I go in the fellowship of these barbarians? Because
you brought me a certain writing in an acceptable hour, I gave
myself into your keeping, nor did I so much as ask light from the

goddess or seek to solve the mystery of its spells. Yet, now, as the Prophetess of Isis, I demand the truth of you, her humbler servant.'

'Lady divine,' answered Philo, bowing himself before me, 'what I have withheld is by command, the command of a very great one, of none less than Noot, the aged and holy. You go to an old land that is yet new, to find Noot, your master and mine.'

'In the flesh or in the spirit?' I asked.

'In the flesh, prophetess, if he lives, as these men say, and see, I accompany you, I whom you have found faithful in the past. If I fail you, let my life pay forfeit, and for the rest, ask it of the holy Noot.'

'It is enough,' I said. 'Lead on.'

We entered the litters; we laded the bearers with the treasures of Isis and with my own peculiar wealth, and having placed the ship *Hapi* under guard, marched into the unknown, like to some great caravan of merchants. For days we marched, following a broad road that was broken down in places, over plains and through vast swamps, at night sleeping in caves, or covered by tents which we had brought with us.

This was a strange journey which I made surrounded by that host of hook-nosed, silent, ghost-like men, who, as I noted, loved the night better than they did the day. Almost I might have thought that they had been sent from Hades to conduct us to those gates from which for mortals there is no return. My fellowship of the priests and priestesses grew afraid and clustered round me at night, praying to be led back to familiar lands and faces.

I answered them that what I dared, they must dare also, and that the goddess was as near to us here as she had been in Egypt, nor could death be closer to us than it was in Egypt. Yea, I bade them have faith, since without faith we could not be at peace one hour, who, lacking it, must be overwhelmed with terrors, even within the walls of citadels.

They listened, bowing their heads and saying that whatever else they might doubt, they trusted themselves to me.

So we went on, passing through a country where more of these half-savage men, that I learned were called *Amahagger*, surrounded by their cattle, dwelt in villages or by colonies in caves. At last there arose before us a mighty mountain whose towering cliffs had the appearance of a wall so vast that the eye could not compass it. By a gorge we penetrated that mountain and found within it an enormous, fertile plain, and on the plain a city larger than Memphis or than Thebes, but a city half in ruins.

Passing over a great bridge spanning a wide moat, once filled with water, that now here and there was dry, we entered the walls of that city and by a street broader than any I had ever seen, bordered by many noble, broken houses, though some of these seemed still to be inhabited, came to a glorious temple like to those of Egypt, only greater, and with taller columns. Across its grass-grown courts that were set one within another, we were carried to an inner sanctuary. Here we descended from the litters and were led to sculptured chambers that seemed to have been made ready to receive us, where we cleansed ourselves of the dust of travel, and ate. Then came Philo who conducted me to a little lamp-lit hall, for now the night had fallen, where was a chair of state such as high-priests used, in which at his bidding I sat myself.

I think that being weary with travel, I must have slept in that chair, since I dreamed or seemed to dream, that I received worship such as is given to a queen, or even to a goddess. Heralds hailed me, sweet voices sang to me, spirits appeared in troops to talk to me, the spirits of those who thousands of years before had departed from the earth. They told me strange stories of the past and of the future; tales of a fallen people, of a worship and a glory that had gone by and been swallowed in the gulfs of time. Then gathering in a multitude they seemed to hail me, crying,

'Welcome, appointed queen! Build thou up that which has fallen. Discover thou that which is lost. Thine is the strength, thine the opportunity, yet beware of the temptations, beware of the flesh, lest the flesh should overcome the spirit and by its fall add ruin unto ruin, the ruin of the soul to the ruin of the body.'

I awoke from my vision and saw Philo standing before me.

'Hearken, Philo,' I said. 'I can bear no more of these mysteries. The time has come when you must speak, or face my wrath. Why have I been brought to this strange and distant land where it seems that I must dwell in a place of ruins?'

'Because the holy Noot so commanded, O child of wisdom,'

he answered. 'Was it not set down in the writing I gave you at the Isle of Reeds upon the Nile?'

'Where then is the holy Noot?' I asked. 'I see him not. Is he dead?'

'I do not think that he is dead, lady. Yet to the world he is dead. He has become a hermit, one who dwells in a cave in a perilous place not very far from this city. Tomorrow I will bring you to him, if that be your will. Thus only can you see him who now for years has never left that cave, or so I think, unless it be to fetch the food which is prepared for him.'

'A strange tale, Philo, though that Noot should become a hermit does not amaze me, for such was ever his desire. Now tell me how he came here, and you with him?'

'Lady, you will remember that in the bygone years when Nectanebes, he who was Pharaoh, fled up Nile, the holy Noot embarked upon my ship, the *Hapi*, to sail to the northern cities, that there he might treat with the Persians for the ransom of those temples of Egypt that remained unravished.'

'I remember, Philo. What chanced to you upon that journey?'

'This, lady: that we were very nearly slain, every one of us, for whom the Persians had set a trap, thinking to snare Noot and his company, and torture him till he revealed where the treasures of the temples of Isis were buried. Nevertheless, because I am a good sailor and because that warrior priest, Kallikrates, was brave, we escaped into the canal which is called the *Road of Rameses*, and so at last out to sea, for to return up Nile was impossible. Then Noot commanded that I should sail on southerly upon a course he seemed to know well enough; or perhaps the goddess taught it to him; I cannot say. At least I obeyed, so that in the end we reached that harbour which is guarded by a rock carved to the likeness of an Ethiopian's head, and thence travelled to this place, still guided by the wisdom of Noot who knew the road.'

'And Kallikrates? What chanced to Kallikrates – who, it seems, was with you?' I asked in an indifferent voice, though my heart burned to hear his answer.

'Lady, so far as it is known to me, this is the story of Kallikrates and the Princess Amenartas.'

'*The Princess Amenartas!* By all the gods, what is your meaning, Philo? She went up Nile with Nectanebes her father, he who was Pharaoh.'

'Nay, lady, she went *down* Nile with Kallikrates, or perhaps with Noot, or perhaps with herself alone. I do not know with whom she hid, since I never saw her, nor learned that she was aboard my ship until we were two days' journey out to sea, with the coasts of Egypt far behind us.'

'Is it so?' I asked coldly, though I was filled with bitter anger. 'And what did the holy Noot when he found that this woman was aboard his vessel?'

'Nothing, lady, except look on her somewhat doubtfully and lead her to the cabin — that which was yours.'

'And the priest, Kallikrates? Did he strive to be rid of her?'

'Nay, lady, indeed that would have been impossible, unless he had cast her overboard. He, too, did nothing except talk with her — that is, so far as I saw.'

'Then, Philo, where is she now, and where is Kallikrates? I do not see him in this place?'

'Lady, I cannot tell you, but I think it probable that they are dead and in the fellowship of Osiris. When we had been some weeks at sea we were driven by storm to an island off the coast under the lee of which we took shelter, a very fertile and beautiful island, peopled by kindly folk. After we had sailed again from that island it was discovered that the priest Kallikrates and the royal Princess Amenartas were missing from the ship, nor because of the strong wind that blew us forward, was it possible for us to return to seek for them. I enquired of the matter and the sailors told me that they had been fishing together and that a shark which took their bait, pulled them both into the sea; in which case doubtless they were drowned.'

'And did you believe that story, Philo?'

'Nay, lady. I understood at once that it was one which the sailors had been bribed to tell. Myself I think that they went to the island in one of the boats of the people who dwell there; perhaps because they could no longer bear the cold eyes of Noot fixed upon them, or perhaps to gather fruit, for which those who have been long upon the sea often conceive a great desire. But,' he added simply, 'I do not know why they should have done this, seeing that the island-dwellers brought us aplenty of fruits in their boats.'

'Doubtless they preferred to pluck them fresh with their own hands, Philo.'

'Perhaps, lady; or perhaps they wished to stay awhile upon that island. At least I noted that the Princess took her garments and her jewels with her, which she could scarcely have done if the shark had dragged her into the sea.'

'Are you so sure, Philo, that she did not leave some of those jewels behind – in *your* keeping, Philo? It is very strange to me that the Princess Amenartas could have come aboard your ship and have left your ship and you know nothing.'

Now Philo looked up innocently and said,

'Surely it is lawful for a captain to receive faring money from his passengers, and that I admit I did. But I do not understand why the child of wisdom is so wroth because a Greek and a great lady were by chance left together upon an island where, for aught I know, one or other of them may have had friends.'

'Am I not the guardian of the honour of the goddess?' I answered. 'And do you not know that under our law Kallikrates was sworn to her alone?'

'If so, prophetess, doubtless that captain, or that priest, remembers his oaths and deals with this princess as though she were his sister or his mother. At the least, the goddess can guard her own honour, so why should you fret your soul concerning it, prophetess? Lastly, it is probable that by now both of them are dead and have made all things clear to Isis in the heavenly halls.'

Thus he prattled on, adding lie to lie as only a Greek can do. I listened until I could bear no more. Then I said but one word. It was 'Begone!'.

He went humbly, yet, as I thought, smiling.

Oh! now I understood. Noot had made a plot to remove Kallikrates far from me, so that I might never look upon him again. Philo knew of this plot, and through him Amenartas knew it also. Unknown to Noot, she bribed Philo to hide her upon his ship till they were far from land, though whether the plan was known to Kallikrates I could not say, nor did it greatly matter. Then the rest followed. Amenartas appeared upon the ship and cast her net about Kallikrates who had sworn to have done with her, and the end can be guessed. Noot was wroth with them, so wroth that when the chance came, they fled away, purposing to stay upon that island until they could find a ship to take them back to Egypt, or elsewhere. Thus I was sure, ran the story, and, as it proved afterwards, I was right.

Well, they were gone and as I hoped, dead, since only death could cover up such a sin, and for my part I was glad that I had done with Kallikrates and his light-of-love. And yet there, seated on the couch of state, I wept — because of the outrage done to Isis whom I served. Or was it for myself that I wept? I cannot say, I only know that my tears were bitter. Also I was very lonely in this strange and desolate place. Why had I been brought here, I wondered. Because Noot had commanded it, sending for me from afar, and what he commanded, that I must obey. Where, then, was Noot, who Philo swore, still lived? Why had he not appeared to greet me? I covered my eyes with my hands and threw out my soul to Noot, saying,

'Come to me, Noot. Come to me, my beloved master.'

Lo! a voice, a well-remembered voice answered.

'Daughter, I am here.'

I let fall my hands. I gazed with my tear-stained eyes, and behold! before me, white-robed, gold-filleted, snowy-bearded; grown very ancient and ethereal, stood the prophet and high-priest, my master. For a moment I thought that it was his spirit which I saw. Then he moved and I heard his white robes rustle, and knew that there stood Noot himself whom I had travelled far to find.

I rose; I ran to him; I seized his thin hand and kissed it, while he, murmuring, 'My daughter, at last, at last!' leaned forward and with his lips touched me on the brow.

'Far away your summons reached me in an hour of peril,' I said. 'Behold! I obeyed, I came. In faith I came, asking no questions, and I am here in safety, for I think the goddess herself was with me on that journey. Tell me all, O Noot. What is this place? How were you brought to it and why have you called me to you?'

'Hearken, daughter,' he said, seating himself beside me on the throne-like couch. 'This city is named Kôr. Once she was queen of the world, as after her Babylon, Tyre, Thebes, and Athens are, or have been queens. From Kôr thousands of years ago in the black, lost ages Egypt was peopled, as were other lands. In those dim days, by another title, her citizens worshipped Isis, queen of heaven, only they named her *Truth* whom in Egypt you know as Maat. Then apostasy arose and many of this great people, abandoning the pure and gentle worship of Isis wrapped in the veil of truth, set up another god under the name of Rezu, a fierce sun-demon, to whom they made human sacrifices, as the Sidonians did to Moloch. Yea, they sacrificed men, women, and children by thousands, and even learned to eat their flesh, first as a sacred rite, and afterwards to satisfy their appetites. Heaven saw and grew wrath. Heaven smote the people with a mighty pestilence, so that they perished and perished till few were left. Thus Kôr fell by the sword of God as, for like cause, fell Sidon.'

'Of all this afterwards,' I answered impatiently. 'Tell me first, how came you here? Long years ago you sailed down Nile to treat with the Persians for the ransom of the temples of Isis, a mission in which it seems you failed, my father.'

'Aye, Ayesha, I failed. It was but a trap, since those false-hearted fire-worshippers thought to take me captive and hold my life in gage against all the treasures of Isis. By the cunning and seamanship of Philo and the courage of a priest named Kallikrates, whom you may still remember after all these years . . .' here he glanced at me sharply, 'I escaped when a gang of them disguised as envoys, strove to snare me. But the road up Nile being barred, we were forced to fly south, down Pharaoh's great ditch, till at length, after many wanderings and adventures, we came to this land, as it was fated that I should do. You will remember daughter that I told you I believed that we were parting for a long while, although I believed also that we should meet again in the flesh.'

'I remember well,' I answered, 'also that I swore to come to you at the appointed hour.'

'I came to this land,' went on Noot, 'but Kallikrates, the Greek captain who was a priest of Isis, never reached it. He was lost on the way.'

'With another, my father. I have heard that story from Philo.'

'With another who caused him to break his vows. Be sure, daughter, that I knew nothing of her plot or that she was hidden aboard the ship, though perchance Philo knew. The goddess hid it from me, doubtless for her own purposes.'

'Are this pair dead, or do they still live, my father?'

'I cannot say; that also is hidden from me. Better for them

if they are dead, since soon or late for such sacrilege vengeance will fall upon the head of one, if not of both of them. Peace be to them. May they be forgiven! At least, as I think they loved each other much and, since love is very strong, all should have pity on them who have ever loved where they ought not,' and again his questioning eyes played upon my face.

The Trade in the Dead

What appearance, the traveller in Egypt wonders, did 'Thebes of the Hundred Gates' present to the tourist of, say, 500 years BC, and similarly its Necropolis on the Western Hills and also the valley of Dead Kings?

Thanks to the labours of the learned, it is now possible to any who have imagination to reconstruct them after a sort. The limestone cliffs would be the same, and all the place as unutterably solemn as it is now.

But then that solemnity was ordered. Everywhere appeared the portals of some of the million tombs of great men — for that number or more this place is estimated to contain — while among them, bringing offerings, passed the relatives of the dead on their way to greet the Shades which they knew full surely awaited them beyond the grave.

How different now is that holy place! Of those million tombs, scarce any remain unviolated, and we Christians hunt over what the Persians, the Romans, the Mahommedans, and the desecrating thieves of all ages have left to us.

See the spot today! Everywhere groups of blue-robed fellaheen, many of them children, are at work upon the mouths or in the shafts of ancient sepulchres. Standing in a cloud of choking dust, the men loosen the rubble with their picks, while the children carry it away in baskets. Look! Something appears — the head of an ox that once was an offering, a piece of painted wood that once was a coffin, a hand or a foot that once belonged to a man or a woman.

Long, long ago this grave was rifled: still there may be things to find in it — shattered vases with inscriptions, ornaments overlooked, or even papyri cast aside as worthless. Step to where these black objects lie in the burning sunshine on yonder white bank of débris. They are three bodies recently disinterred, and not yet reburied decently away. Their mummy wrappings are still about them, but their coffins, if any were left to them, are

---

Daily Mail, 4 June, 1904.

gone. So are their heads. One of these, scarcely more than a skull, lies at its owner's side – or it may have belonged to someone else. Melancholy relics of mortality, who lived and died long before Christ was born, arisen from the sepulchre that they thought so inviolable and holy to affront the sunlight with the horror of their shrouded bones!

A splendid tomb has but just been found and Mr Howard Carter, the Director of Antiquities here, and the Italian gentleman who discovered it take us down the grave unvisited by men for perhaps two thousand years. It is the burying-place of one who was great enough in her day, Nefretari, the first and most beloved wife of Rameses II, who died some three thousand five hundred years ago. See, there are her titles painted on the walls – 'Royal Wife, Royal Mother, Great Queen' – and close to them she sits playing at chess, the pawns and principal pieces upon the board before her. Everywhere she stands and sits, alone or with her mighty husband, making offerings to the gods, receiving offerings as woman or as goddess, passing down the dreadful ways of death, triumphing over her mortality, and received at last as pure and just and perfect into the holy and eternal habitations of the Under-World.

It is a wonderful thing to crawl across the rubbish with which some of these chambers are still filled and look upon those paintings as fresh today as when the artist left them a hundred generations since. But this tomb, like most, has been opened. The sarcophagus of granite has been broken into fragments, the body of Nefretari, 'Royal Wife, Royal Mother, Great Queen', · has been taken away; probably, since it has not been found in any other royal sepulchre, to be broken up by thieves and when its ornaments of gold and heart scarab had been torn from it, cast out to melt into dust amid the limestone sands. Look, there lie the fragments of the mummy cases, and there amid the débris the Ushabti figures of her Majesty, wood all of them and painted in black and gold, there, too, the bones of some funeral offering which at first we thought were hers – these and no more.

Let us pass on from the sepulchre of Nefretari, so brilliant with its paintings, so heavy with its silence, to another tomb also new-found, though plundered in old days. It is that of the Prince Amon-Repeshfu. He lived in a later generation, for he was the son of the third Rameses. Here he, too, stands upon the painted walls, a boy holding the ostrich feather, the emblem of a prince. It was the conventional way of representing one of his rank, but in fact he died young. We know it, for yonder in his plundered sarcophagus lie his bones, and the finely formed skull is that of a lad of perhaps fourteen years of age. One wonders if the child was always sickly and if this sepulchre was made ready for a death that was seen to be inevitable, or whether the splendid graves of princes were commenced as soon as they appeared upon earth.

At length the tomb of Queen Hatshepu has been opened. She in her day was perhaps as great a woman as Queen Elizabeth, and the builder of the lovely temple of Deir-el-Bahari, the wife and guardian of her half-brother Thotmes II and the aunt or the sister of Thotmes III. For a year and a half gangs of men have been excavating in this tomb, one of the earliest in the Valley of Kings, for its length is over 200 yards, and it was filled with débris. And now, after all these weary months of toil and of expenditure, which has been borne by a private person, save for the sarcophagi of Hatshepu and her father, the First Thotmes, and some tablets of the Book of Hours which I saw, it has been proved to be empty.

Where, then, is the body of Hatshepu? In the recently-discovered tomb of Amenophis II were found a number of royal mummies, moved thither, doubtless by the priests in troublous times, which are now in the Cairo Museum. Also there were found three naked bodies – those of a woman of mature age, a child wearing the single lock of royalty, and a young man – which can still be seen in a side chamber. I suggest that the shrivelled thing with the long hair is none other than the mortal shape of the famed Hatshepu.

The guidebooks tell us the body of Amenophis II is to be seen 'wrapped in its shroud, and still adorned with garlands.' In fact, what is to be seen is his royal though somewhat ghastly countenance staring upwards, but no longer through the darkness, since above it now glows an electric lamp. I asked Mr Carter how the discrepancy was to be explained. It seems that shortly after the mummy was discovered some of the Luxor thieves broke into the tomb at night and stripped the royal body in search of its ornaments.

Whether they found any or no I cannot say, nor are they

likely to tell the truth as to that matter, but they destroyed the sacred boat in the antechamber and the mummy that lay thereon. M. Legrain at Karnak has had a similar experience. Two of the statues of his recent wonderful find there were stolen by thieves, who broke through the wall of his house. I am glad to report that they have been recovered.

There are, fortunately, still many relics of some 5,000 years of the ancient history of Egypt to be found in the new Museum of Antiquities at Cairo. Here within its lofty walls are the mementoes of the rule of no fewer than 297 kings and Caesars; say, from Mena, who flourished about 4400 BC to the Roman Decius who reigned about 250 AD. To study all these would occupy volumes. So I confine myself to the royal mummies, not from a wish to be gruesome, but because I desire to make some suggestions concerning them.

There they lie, very many of them, some stripped, others still in their ancient wrappings; Rameses and Seti, the generations of the family of Thotmes and the rest; kings, queens, princes and little children, once famous in the land, every one of them.

There, stripped of their royal ornaments and state, they repose in their glass cases for the visitor to stare at. There, for instance, is Menephtah, whose 'heart was hardened' so that he withstood Moses; that Pharaoh, it is believed, who saw the first-born die and heard the march of the departing Israelites. But he did not perish in the Red Sea, when of 'all the host of Pharaoh . . . there remained not so much as one of them'.

No, for we may still look upon his body, with his name scribbled on its yellow wrappings, as I did the other day. It has never been unrolled, and one wonders whether within it is hidden any key to those great events recorded in the book of Exodus, as to which Egyptian history is so strangely silent.

Among these mummies Seti is beautiful to look on, 'black but comely', with his smile and placid brow of pride, and there is much majesty in the withered countenance of that mighty monarch, the aged Rameses, his son. But what of the rest?

To be frank, all are repulsive, and some are horrible to see.

Is it right, then, that kings and queens, and high priests and priestesses, prophets and prophetesses of God as they understood

Him, should be thus dragged from the sepulchres they fashioned with so much thought and care, and for so high a purpose; stripped, too, even of their shrouds and made a show of in the very land they ruled? Should not we English shudder if some seer told us that within a given number of years, say 3,000 (which to the dead, for whom time does not exist, whatever we believe, can be but as a moment's sleep), those who rest in Westminster Abbey were destined to be treated in just this fashion, to satisfy the curiosity of men unborn? I think so. Yet where these Egyptian departed are concerned we hear no voice of public protest.

Why were they thus preserved? Because above all people that ever lived, the old Egyptians believed in the Resurrection of the Body, and conceived, foolishy enough perhaps, that on this account the body itself must be held back from corruption in order that, at the time appointed, it might once more receive the spirit. Therefore, they built themselves 'everlasting houses', and lavished their wealth upon their burials, and believed that no crime was more heinous than to disturb the dead. Yet we who are Christians and share the cardinal doctrines of their faith treat them thus.

Everywhere in Egypt it is the same. At Luxor the other day I saw the naked body of a little child lying in a wooden box outside a shop, to be purchased for a few piastres. Within was the corpse of a priestess in her painted coffin; for a penny the Arab would lift the lid and show her with a ghoulish laugh. At Beni-Hassan the deep tombs are being violated by the score, and those who have slept within them for 4,000 years or so dragged forth. We saw them lying in some of the larger sepulchres, adults and children together; saw also many long deal boxes being nailed up. To guess their contents was not difficult. And so forth. Within another score of years scarcely a grave in Egypt that can be discovered will be left unrifled.

I suggest, therefore, that these excesses should be modified, and more particularly that the royal bodies should be restored to their sepulchres. What are the arguments against such a course?

That robbers would get at them and break them up? This can be prevented by proper iron gates. Also, when it is known that no object of value remains, human flesh and bone have no great worth in the eyes of thieves.

That the museum would lose an attraction and the curiosity of visitors be baulked? Though these distorted, withered corpses are not, in fact, agreeable — much the contrary, indeed — this objection, such as it is, could to a great extent be overcome by modelling each body of importance carefully in wax and exhibiting the reproduction, which it would be difficult to distinguish from the original.

That science would suffer? Why? The mummies can first be unrolled, photographed, measured, weighed, Röntgen-rayed, etc. After that what more has science to learn from them? That there are various difficulties in the way of restoring these princes to their tombs? I do not agree, but if so, then place them all in the central chamber of the Great Pyramid, which is a cavity of no great interest, and pump it full of cement, so that it may remain inviolate for ever!

I venture to hope that this plea for the dead will not be dismissed as mere 'sentiment'. At least, it is a sentiment that is shared by many people, and among them, as I am aware, by some who are in the best position to know about the matter in all its bearings.

Lastly, if something is not done, the question will settle itself ultimately in another fashion. I quote from the new guide to the Cairo Museum. It says (p. 412, speaking of the royal mummies found at Deir-el-Bahari, which were unwrapped in 1886): 'Every precaution was taken to ensure their preservation. But notwithstanding all this, they have been seriously damaged since they were found, and in spite of all the care that has been taken to surround them with substances likely to preserve them, most of them have been attacked by insects: some day they will disappear altogether.' I may add that after a period of seventeen years it seems to me that those mummies which I saw first but just unrolled are much deteriorated.

I quote one more pregnant passage from the same page of the guide. It describes the removal of the mummies, and seems to me to furnish an additional reason for the adoption of the course I have proposed: 'The museum barge arrived . . . and . . . was laden with its cargo of kings! It was remarkable that between Luxor and Kaft on both sides of the Nile the fellaheen women followed the boat, uttering loud cries, and with their hair all dishevelled, while the men fired guns as they do at funerals.'

Fallen as they may be, these poor folk could still mourn over the desecration of the relics of their ancestors' ancient kings. Is it not possible for the representatives of a great Christian Power to so arrange that this desecration shall forthwith cease? Perhaps, if the English Press sees fit to urge the matter.

Smith and the Pharaohs

I

Scientists, or some scientists — for occasionally one learned person differs from other learned persons — tell us they know all that is worth knowing about man, which statement, of course, includes woman. They trace him from his remotest origin; they show us how his bones changed and his shape modified, also how, under the influence of his needs and passions, his intelligence developed from something very humble. They demonstrate conclusively that there is nothing in man which the dissecting-table will not explain; that his aspirations towards another life have their root in the fear of death, or, say others of them, in that of earthquake or thunder; that his affinities with the past are merely inherited from remote ancestors who lived in that past, perhaps a million years ago; and that everything noble about him is but the fruit of expediency or of a veneer of civilisation, while everything base must be attributed to the instincts of his dominant and primeval nature. Man, in short, is an animal who, like every other animal, is finally subdued by his environment and takes his colour from his surroundings, as cattle do from the red soil of Devon. Such are the facts, they (or some of them) declare; all the rest is rubbish.

At times we are inclined to agree with these sages, especially after it has been our privilege to attend a course of lectures by one of them. Then perhaps something comes within the range of our experience which gives us pause and causes doubts, the old divine doubts, to arise again deep in our hearts, and with them a yet diviner hope.

Perchance when all is said, so we think to ourselves, man *is* something more than an animal. Perchance he has known the past, the far past, and will know the future, the far, far future. Perchance the dream is true, and he does indeed possess what for convenience is called an immortal soul, that may manifest

Strand Magazine, February 1913.

itself in one shape or another; that may sleep for ages, but, waking or sleeping, still remains itself, indestructible as the matter of the Universe.

An incident in the career of Mr James Ebenezer Smith might well occasion such reflections, were any acquainted with its details, which until this, its setting forth, was not the case. Mr Smith is a person who knows when to be silent. Still, undoubtedly it gave cause for thought to one individual – namely, to him to whom it happened. Indeed, James Ebenezer Smith is still thinking over it, thinking very hard indeed.

J.E. Smith was well born and well educated. When he was a good-looking and able young man at college, but before he had taken his degree, trouble came to him, the particulars of which do not matter, and he was thrown penniless, also friendless, upon the rocky bosom of the world. No, not quite friendless, for he had a godfather, a gentleman connected with business whose Christian name was Ebenezer. To him, as a last resource, Smith went, feeling that Ebenezer owed him something in return for the awful appellation wherewith he had been endowed in baptism.

To a certain extent Ebenezer recognised the obligation. He did nothing heroic, but he found his godson a clerkship in a bank of which he was one of the directors – a modest clerkship, no more. Also, when he died a year later, he left him a hundred pounds to be spent upon some souvenir.

Smith, being of a practical turn of mind, instead of adorning himself with memorial jewellery for which he had no use, invested the hundred pounds in an exceedingly promising speculation. As it happened, he was not misinformed, and his talent returned to him multiplied by ten. He repeated the experiment, and, being in a position to know what he was doing, with considerable success. By the time that he was thirty he found himself possessed of a fortune of something over twenty-five thousand pounds. Then (and this shows the wise and practical nature of the man) he stopped speculating and put out his money in such a fashion that it brought him a safe and clear four per cent.

By this time Smith, being an excellent man of business, was well up in the service of his bank – as yet only a clerk, it is true, but one who drew his four hundred pounds a year, with prospects. In short, he was in a position to marry had he wished to do so. As it happened, he did not wish – perhaps because, being very friendless, no lady who attracted him crossed his path; perhaps for other reasons.

Shy and reserved in temperament, he confided only in himself. None, not even his superiors at the bank or the Board of Management, knew how well off he had become. No one visited him at the flat which he was understood to occupy somewhere in the neighbourhood of Putney; he belonged to no club, and possessed not a single intimate. The blow which the world had dealt him in his early days, the harsh repulses and the rough treatment he had then experienced, sank so deep into his sensitive soul that never again did he seek close converse with his kind. In fact, while still young, he fell into a condition of old-bachelorhood of a refined type.

Soon, however, Smith discovered – it was after he had given up speculating – that a man must have something to occupy his mind. He tried philanthropy, but found himself too sensitive for a business which so often resolves itself into rude inquiry as to the affairs of other people. After a struggle, therefore, he compromised with his conscience by setting aside a liberal portion of his income for anonymous distribution among deserving persons and objects.

While still in this vacant frame of mind Smith chanced one day, when the bank was closed, to drift into the British Museum, more to escape the vile weather that prevailed without than for any other reason. Wandering hither and thither at hazard, he found himself in the great gallery devoted to Egyptian stone objects and sculpture. The place bewildered him somewhat, for he knew nothing of Egyptology; indeed, there remained upon his mind only a sense of wonderment not unmixed with awe. It must have been a great people, he thought to himself, that executed these works, and with the thought came a desire to know more about them. Yet he was going away when suddenly his eye fell on the sculptured head of a woman which hung upon the wall.

Smith looked at it once, twice, thrice, and at the third look he fell in love. Needless to say, he was not aware that such was his condition. He knew only that a change had come over him, and never, never could he forget the face which that carven mask portrayed. Perhaps it was not really beautiful save for its wondrous and mystic smile; perhaps the lips were too thick and the nostrils too broad. Yet to him that face was Beauty itself, beauty which drew him as with a cart-rope, and awoke within him all kinds of wonderful imaginings, some of them so strange and tender that almost they partook of the nature of memories. He stared at the image, and the image smiled back sweetly at him, as doubtless it, or rather its original − for this was but a plaster cast − had smiled at nothingness in some tomb or hiding-hole for over thirty centuries, and as the woman whose likeness it was had once smiled upon the world.

A short, stout gentleman bustled up and, in tones of authority, addressed some workmen who were arranging a base for a neighbouring statue. It occurred to Smith that he must be someone who knew about these objects. Overcoming his natural diffidence with an effort, he raised his hat and asked the gentleman if he could tell him who was the orginal of the mask.

The official − who, in fact, was a very great man in the Museum − glanced at Smith shrewdly, and, seeing that his interest was genuine, answered:

'I don't know. Nobody knows. She has been given several names, but none of them have authority. Perhaps one day the rest of the statue may be found, and then we shall learn − that is, if it is inscribed. Most likely, however, it has been burnt for lime long ago.'

'Then you can't tell me anything about her?' said Smith.

'Well, only a little. To begin with, that's a cast. The original is in the Cairo Museum. Mariette found it, I believe at Karnak, and gave it a name after his fashion. Probably she was a queen − of the eighteenth dynasty, by the work. But you can see her rank for yourself from the broken *uroeus*.' (Smith did not stop him to explain that he had not the faintest idea what a *uroeus* might be, seeing that he was utterly unfamiliar with the snake-headed crest of Egyptian royalty.) 'You should go to Egypt and study the head for yourself. It is one of the most beautiful things that ever was found. Well, I must be off. Good day.'

And he bustled down the long gallery.

Smith found his way upstairs and looked at mummies and other things. Somehow it hurt him to reflect that the owner of yonder sweet, alluring face must have become a mummy long, long before the Christian era. Mummies did not strike him as attractive.

He returned to the statuary and stared at his plaster cast till one of the workmen remarked to his fellow that if he were the gent he'd go and look at 'a live'un' for a change.

Then Smith retired abashed.

On his way home he called at his bookseller's and ordered 'all the best works on Egyptology'. When, a day or two later, they arrived in a packing-case, together with a bill for thirty-eight pounds, he was somewhat dismayed. Still, he tackled those books like a man, and, being clever and industrious, within three months had a fair working knowledge of the subject, and had even picked up a smattering of hieroglyphics.

In January — that was, at the end of those three months — Smith astonished his Board of Directors by applying for ten weeks' leave, he who had hitherto been content with a fortnight in the year. When questioned he explained that he had been suffering from bronchitis, and was advised to take a change in Egypt.

'A very good idea,' said the manager; 'but I'm afraid you'll find it expensive. They fleece one in Egypt.'

'I know,' answered Smith; 'but I've saved a little and have only myself to spend it upon.'

So Smith went to Egypt and saw the original of the beauteous head and a thousand other fascinating things. Indeed, he did more. Attaching himself to some excavators who were glad of his intelligent assistance, he actually dug for a month in the neighbourhood of ancient Thebes, but without finding anything in particular.

It was not till two years later that he made his great discovery, that which is known as Smith's Tomb. Here it may be explained that the state of his health had become such as to necessitate an annual visit to Egypt, or so his superiors understood.

However, as he asked for no summer holiday, and was always ready to do another man's work or to stop overtime, he found it easy to arrange for these winter excursions.

On this, his third visit to Egypt, Smith obtained from the Director-General of Antiquities at Cairo a licence to dig upon his own account. Being already well known in the country as a skilled Egyptologist, this was granted upon the usual terms — namely, that the Department of Antiquities should have a right to take any of the objects which might be found, or all of them, if it so desired.

Such preliminary matters having been arranged by correspondence, Smith, after a few days spent in the Museum at Cairo, took the night train to Luxor, where he found his headman, an ex-dragoman named Mahomet, waiting for him and his fellaheen labourers already hired. There were but forty of them, for his was a comparatively small venture. Three hundred pounds was the amount that he had made up his mind to expend, and such a sum does not go far in excavations.

During his visit of the previous year Smith had marked the place where he meant to dig. It was in the cemetery of old Thebes, at the wild spot not far from the temple of Medinet Habu, that is known as the Valley of the Queens. Here, separated from the resting-places of their royal lords by the bold mass of the intervening hill, some of the greatest ladies of Egypt have been laid to rest, and it was their tombs that Smith desired to investigate. As he knew well, some of these must yet remain to be discovered. Who could say? Fortune favours the bold. It might be that he would find the holy grave of that beauteous, unknown Royalty whose face had haunted him for three long years!

For a whole month he dug without the slightest success. The spot that he selected had proved, indeed, to be the mouth of a tomb. After twenty-five days of laborious exploration it was at length cleared out, and he stood in a rude unfinished cave. The queen for whom it had been designed must have died quite young and been buried elsewhere, or she had chosen herself another sepulchre, or mayhap the rock had proved unsuitable for sculpture.

Smith shrugged his shoulders and moved on, sinking trial pits and trenches here and there, but still finding nothing. Two-thirds of his time and money had been spent when at last the luck turned. One day, towards evening, with some half-dozen of his best men he was returning after a fruitless morning of labour, when something seemed to attract him towards a little *wadi*, or bay, in the hillside that was filled with tumbled rocks and sand. There were scores of such places, and this one looked no more promising than any of the others had proved to be. Yet it attracted him. Thoroughly dispirited, he walked past it twenty paces or more, then turned.

'Where go you, sah?' asked his head-man, Mahomet.

He pointed to the recess in the cliff.

'No good, sah,' said Mahomet. 'No tomb there. Bed-rock too near top. Too much water run in there; dead queen like keep dry!'

But Smith went on, and the others followed obediently.

He walked down the little slope of sand and boulders and examined the cliff. It was virgin rock; never a tool mark was to be seen. Already the men were going, when the same strange instinct which had drawn him to the spot caused him to take a spade from one of them and begin to shovel away the sand from the face of the cliff – for here, for some unexplained reason, were no boulders or débris. Seeing their master, to whom they were attached, at work, they began to work too, and for twenty minutes or more dug on cheerfully enough, just to humour him, since all were sure that here there was no tomb. At length Smith ordered them to desist, for, although now they were six feet down, the rock remained of the same virgin character.

With an exclamation of disgust he threw out a last shovelful of sand. The edge of his spade struck on something that projected. He cleared away a little more sand, and there appeared a rounded ledge which seemed to be a cornice. Calling back the men, he pointed to it, and without a word all of them began to dig again. Five minutes more of work made it clear that it was a cornice, and half an hour later there appeared the top of the doorway of a tomb.

'Old people wall him up,' said Mahomet, pointing to the flat stones set in mud for mortar with which the doorway had been closed, and to the undecipherable impress upon the mud of the scarab seals of the officials whose duty it had been to close the last resting-place of the royal dead for ever.

'Perhaps queen all right inside,' he went on, receiving no answer to his remark.

'Perhaps,' replied Smith, briefly. 'Dig, man, dig! Don't waste time in talking.'

So they dug on furiously till at length Smith saw something

which caused him to groan aloud. There was a hole in the masonry — the tomb had been broken into. Mahomet saw it too, and examined the top of the aperture with his skilled eye.

'Very old thief,' he said. 'Look, he try build up wall again, but run away before he have time finish.' And he pointed to certain flat stones which had been roughly and hurriedly replaced.

'Dig . . . dig!' said Smith.

Ten minutes more and the aperture was cleared. It was only just big enough to admit the body of a man.

By now the sun was setting. Swiftly, swiftly it seemed to tumble down the sky. One minute it was above the rough crests of the western hills behind them; the next, a great ball of glowing fire, it rested on their topmost ridge. Then it was gone. For an instant a kind of green spark shone where it had been. This too went out, and the sudden Egyptian night was upon them.

The fellaheen muttered among themselves, and one or two of them wandered off on some pretext. The rest threw down their tools and looked at Smith. 'Men say they no like stop here. They afraid of ghost! Too many *afreet* live in these tomb. That what they say. Come back finish tomorrow morning when it light. Very foolish people, these common fellaheen,' remarked Mahomet, in a superior tone.

'Quite so,' replied Smith, who knew well that nothing that he could offer would tempt his men to go on with the opening of a tomb after sunset. 'Let them go away. You and I will stop and watch the place till morning.'

'Sorry, sah,' said Mahomet, 'but I not feel quite well inside; I think I got fever. I go to camp and lie down and pray under plenty blanket.'

'All right, go,' said Smith; 'but if there is anyone who is not a coward, let him bring me my big coat, something to eat and drink, and the lantern that hangs in my tent. I will meet him there in the valley.'

Mahomet, though rather doubtfully, promised that this should be done, and, after begging Smith to accompany them, lest the spirit of whoever slept in the tomb should work him a mischief during the night, they departed quickly enough.

Smith lit his pipe, sat down on the sand, and waited. Half

an hour later he heard a sound of singing, and through the darkness, which was dense, saw lights coming up the valley.

'My brave men,' he thought to himself, and scrambled up the slope to meet them.

He was right. These were his men, no less than twenty of them, for with a fewer number they did not dare to face the ghosts which they believed haunted the valley after nightfall. Presently the light from the lantern which one of them carried (not Mahomet, whose sickness had increased too suddenly to enable him to come) fell upon the tall form of Smith, who, dressed in his white working clothes, was leaning against a rock. Down went the lantern, and with a howl of terror the brave company turned and fled.

'Sons of cowards!' roared Smith after them, in his most vigorous Arabic. 'It is I, your master, not an *afreet*.'

They heard, and by degrees crept back again. Then he perceived that in order to account for their number each of them carried some article. Thus one had the bread, another the lantern, another a tin of sardines, another the sardine-opener, another a box of matches, another a bottle of beer, and so on. As even thus there were not enough things to go round, two of them bore his big coat between them, the first holding it by the sleeves and the second by the tail as though it were a stretcher.

'Put them down,' said Smith, and they obeyed. 'Now', he added, 'run for your lives; I thought I heard two *afreets* talking up there just now of what they would do to any followers of the Prophet who mocked their gods, if perchance they should meet them in their holy place at night.'

This kindly counsel was accepted with much eagerness. In another minute Smith was alone with the stars and the dying desert wind.

Collecting his goods, or as many of them as he wanted, he thrust them into the pockets of the greatcoat and returned to the mouth of the tomb. Here he made his simple meal by the light of the lantern, and afterwards tried to go to sleep. But sleep he could not. Something always woke him. First it was a jackal howling amongst the rocks; next a sand-fly bit him on the ankle so sharply that he thought he must have been stung by a scorpion. Then, notwithstanding his warm coat, the cold got hold of him, for the clothes beneath were wet through with perspiration, and it occurred to him that unless he did something he would probably contract an internal chill or perhaps fever. He rose and walked about.

By now the moon was up, revealing all the sad, wild scene in its every detail. The mystery of Egypt entered his soul and oppressed him. How much dead majesty lay in the hill upon which he stood? Were they all really dead, he wondered, or were those fellaheen right? Did their spirits still come forth at night and wander through the land where once they ruled? Of course that was the Egyptian faith according to which the *Ka*, or Double, eternally haunted the place where its earthly counterpart had been laid to rest. When one came to think of it, beneath a mass of unintelligible symbolism there was much in the Egyptian faith which it was hard for a Christian to disbelieve. Salvation through a Redeemer, for instance, and the resurrection of the body. Had he, Smith, not already written a treatise upon these points of similarity which he proposed to publish one day, not under his own name? Well, he would not think of them now; the occasion seemed scarcely fitting – they came home too pointedly to one who was engaged in violating a tomb.

His mind, or rather his imagination – of which he had plenty – went off at a tangent. What sights had this place seen thousands of years ago! Once, thousands of years ago, a procession had wound up along the roadway which was doubtless buried beneath the sand whereon he stood towards the dark door of this sepulchre. He could see it as it passed in and out between the rocks. The priests, shaven-headed and robed in leopards' skins, or some of them in pure white, bearing the mystic symbols of their office. The funeral sledge drawn by oxen, and on it the great rectangular case that contained the outer and the inner coffins, and within them the mummy of some departed Majesty; in the Egyptian formula, 'the hawk that had spread its wings and flown into the bosom of Osiris', God of Death. Behind, the mourners, rending the air with their lamentations. Then those who bore the funeral furniture and offerings. Then the high officers of State and the first priests of Amen and of the other gods. Then the sister queens, leading by the hand a wondering child or two. Then the sons of Pharaoh, young men carrying the emblems of their rank.

Lastly, walking alone, Pharaoh himself in his ceremonial

robes, his apron, his double crown of linen surmounted by the golden snake, his inlaid bracelets and his heavy, tinkling earrings. Pharaoh, his head bowed, his feet travelling wearily, and in his heart — what thoughts? Sorrow, perhaps, for her who had departed. Yet he had other queens and fair women without count. Doubtless she was sweet and beautiful, but sweetness and beauty were not given to her alone. Moreover, was she not wont to cross his will and to question his divinity? No, surely it is not only of her that he thinks, her for whom he had prepared this splendid tomb with all things needful to unite her with the gods. Surely he thinks also of himself and that other tomb on the farther side of the hill whereat the artists labour day by day — yes, and have laboured these many years; that tomb to which before so very long he too must travel in just this fashion, to seek his place beyond the doors of Death, who lays his equal hand on king and queen and slave.

The vision passed. It was so real that Smith thought he must have been dreaming. Well, he was awake now, and colder than ever. Moreover, the jackals had multiplied. There were a whole pack of them, and not far away. Look! One crossed in the ring of the lamplight, a slinking, yellow beast that smelt the remains of dinner. Or perhaps it smelt him. Moreover, there were bad characters who haunted these mountains, and he was alone and quite unarmed. Perhaps he ought to put out the light which advertised his whereabouts. It would be wise and yet in this particular he rejected wisdom. After all, the light was some company.

Since sleep seemed to be out of the question, he fell back upon poor humanity's other anodyne, work, which has the incidental advantage of generating warmth. Seizing a shovel, he began to dig at the doorway of the tomb, whilst the jackals howled louder than ever in astonishment. They were not used to such a sight. For thousands of years, as the old moon above could have told, no man, or at least no solitary man, had dared to rob tombs at such an unnatural hour.

When Smith had been digging for about twenty minutes something tinkled on his shovel with a noise which sounded loud in that silence.

'A stone which may come in handy for the jackals,' he thought to himself, shaking the sand slowly off the spade until it appeared. There it was, and not large enough to be of much service. Still, he picked it up, and rubbed it in his hands to clear off the encrusting dirt. When he opened them he saw that it was no stone, but a bronze.

'Osiris,' reflected Smith, 'buried in front of the tomb to hallow the ground. No, an Isis. No, the head of a statuette, and a jolly good one, too – at any rate, in moonlight. Seems to have been gilded.' And, reaching out for the lamp, he held it over the object.

Another minute, and he found himself sitting at the bottom of the hole, lamp in one hand and statuette, or rather head, in the other.

'The Queen of the Mask!' he gasped. 'The same – the same! By heavens, the very same!'

Oh, he could not be mistaken. There were the identical lips, a little thick and pouted; the identical nostrils, curved and quivering, but a little wide; the identical arched eyebrows and dreamy eyes set somewhat far apart. Above all, there was the identical alluring and mysterious smile. Only on this master-piece of ancient art was set a whole crown of *uræi* surrounding the entire head. Beneath the crown and pressed back behind the ears was a full-bottomed wig or royal head-dress, of which the ends descended to the breasts. The statuette, that, having been gilt, remained quite perfect and uncorroded, was broken just above the middle, apparently by a single violent blow, for the fracture was very clean.

At once it occurred to Smith that it had been stolen from the tomb by a thief who thought it to be gold; that outside of the tomb doubt had overtaken him and caused him to break it upon a stone or otherwise. The rest was clear. Finding that it was but gold-washed bronze he had thrown away the fragments, rather than be at the pains of carrying them. This was his theory, probably not a correct one, as the sequel seems to show.

Smith's first idea was to recover the other portion. He searched quite a long while, but without success. Neither then nor afterwards could it be found. He reflected that perhaps this lower half had remained in the thief's hand, who, in his vexa-tion, had thrown it far away, leaving the head to lie where it fell. Again Smith examined this head, and more closely. Now he saw that just beneath the breasts was a delicately cut cartouche.

Being by this time a master of hieroglyphics, he read it without trouble. It ran: 'Ma-Mee, Great Royal Lady. Beloved of . . .' Here the cartouche was broken away.

'Ma-Mé, or it might be Ma-Mi,' he reflected. 'I never heard of a queen called Ma-Mé, or Ma-Mi, or Ma-Mu. She must be quite new to history. I wonder of whom she was beloved? Amen, or Horus, or Isis, probably. Of some god, I have no doubt, at least I hope so!'

He stared at the beautiful portrait in his hand, as once he had stared at the cast on the Museum wall, and the beautiful portrait, emerging from the dust of ages, smiled back at him there in the solemn moonlight as once the cast had smiled from the Museum wall.

Only that had been but a cast, whereas this was real. This had slept with the dead from whose features it had been fashioned, the dead who lay, or who had lain, within.

A sudden resolution took hold of Smith. He would explore that tomb, at once and alone. No one should accompany him on this his first visit; it would be a sacrilege that anyone save himself should set foot there until he had looked on what it might contain.

Why should he not enter? His lamp, of what is called the 'hurricane' brand, was very good and bright, and would burn for many hours. Moreover, there had been time for the foul air to escape through the hole that they had cleared. Lastly, something seemed to call on him to come and see. He placed the bronze head in his breast-pocket over his heart, and, thrusting the lamp through the hole, looked down. Here there was no difficulty, since sand had drifted in to the level of the bottom of the aperture. Through it he struggled, to find himself upon a bed of sand that only just left him room to push himself along between it and the roof. A little farther on the passage was almost filled with mud.

Mahomet had been right when, from his knowledge of the bed-rock, he said that any tomb made in this place must be flooded. It *had* been flooded by some ancient rain-storm, and Smith began to fear that he would find it quite filled with soil caked as hard as iron. So, indeed, it was to a certain depth, a result that apparently had been anticipated by those who hollowed it, for this entrance shaft was left quite undecorated.

Indeed, as Smith found afterwards, a hole had been dug beneath the doorway to allow the mud to enter after the burial was completed. Only a miscalculation had been made. The natural level of the mud did not quite reach the roof of the tomb, and therefore still left it open.

After crawling for forty feet or so over this caked mud, Smith suddenly found himself on a rising stair. Then he understood the plan; the tomb itself was on a higher level.

Here began the paintings. Here the Queen Ma-Mee, wearing her crowns and dressed in diaphanous garments, was presented to god after god. Between her figure and those of the divinities the wall was covered with hieroglyphs as fresh today as on that when the artist had limned them. A glance told him that they were extracts from the Book of the Dead. When the thief of bygone ages had broken into the tomb, probably not very long after the interment, the mud over which Smith had just crawled was still wet. This he could tell, since the clay from the rascal's feet remained upon the stairs, and that upon his fingers had stained the paintings on the wall against which he had supported himself; indeed, in one place was an exact impression of his hand, showing its shape and even the lines of the skin.

At the top of the flight of steps ran another passage at a higher level, which the water had never reached, and to right and left were the beginnings of unfinished chambers. It was clear to him that this queen had died young. Her tomb, as she or the king had designed it, was never finished. A few more paces, and the passage enlarged itself into a hall about thirty feet square. The ceiling was decorated with vultures, their wings outspread, the looped Cross of Life hanging from their talons. On one wall her Majesty Ma-Mee stood expectant while Anubis weighed her heart against the feather of truth, and Thoth, the Recorder, wrote down the verdict upon his tablets. All her titles were given to her here, such as 'Great Royal Heiress, Royal Sister, Royal Wife, Royal Mother, Lady of the Two Lands, Palm-branch of Love, Beautiful exceedingly.'

Smith read them hurriedly and noted that nowhere could he see the name of the king who had been her husband. It would almost seem as though this had been purposely omitted. On the other walls Ma-Mee, accompanied by her *Ka*, or Double, made offerings to the various gods, or uttered propitiatory speeches to the hideous demons of the underworld, declaring their names to them and forcing them to say: 'Pass on. Thou art pure!'

Lastly, on the end wall, triumphant, all her trials done, she, the justified Osiris, or Spirit, was received by the god Osiris, Saviour of Spirits.

All these things Smith noted hurriedly as he swung the lamp to and fro in that hallowed place. Then he saw something else which filled him with dismay. On the floor of the chamber where the coffins had been — for this was the burial chamber — lay a heap of black fragments charred with fire. Instantly he understood. After the thief had done his work he had burned the mummy-cases, and with them the body of the queen. There could be no doubt that this was so, for look! among the ashes lay some calcined human bones, while the roof above was blackened with the smoke and cracked by the heat of the conflagration. There was nothing left for him to find!

Oppressed with the closeness of the atmosphere, he sat down upon a little bench or table cut in the rock that evidently had been meant to receive offerings to the dead. Indeed, on it still lay the scorched remains of some votive flowers. Here, his lamp between his feet, he rested a while, staring at those calcined bones. See, yonder was the lower jaw, and in it some teeth, small, white, regular, and but little worn. Yes, she had died young. Then he turned to go, for disappointment and the holiness of the place overcame him; he could endure no more of it that night.

Leaving the burial hall, he walked along the painted passage, the lamp swinging and his eyes fixed upon the floor. He was disheartened, and the paintings could wait till the morrow. He descended the steps and came to the foot of the mud slope. Here suddenly he perceived, projecting from some sand that had drifted down over the mud, what seemed to be the corner of a reed box or basket. To clear away the sand was easy, and — yes, it was a basket, a foot or so in length, such a basket as the old Egyptians used to contain the funeral figures which are called *ushaptis*, or other objects connected with the dead. It looked as though it had been dropped, for it lay upon its side. Smith opened it — not very hopefully, for surely nothing of value would have been abandoned thus.

The first thing that met his eyes was a mummied hand, broken off at the wrist, a woman's little hand, most delicately shaped. It was withered and paper-white, but the contours still remained; the long fingers were perfect, and the almond-shaped nails had been stained with henna, as was the embalmers' fashion. On the hand were two gold rings, and for those rings it had been stolen. Smith looked at it for a long while, and his heart swelled within him, for here was the hand of that royal lady of his dreams.

Indeed, he did more than look; he kissed it, and as his lips touched the holy relic it seemed to him as though a wind, cold but scented, blew upon his brow. Then, growing fearful of the thoughts that arose within him, he hurried his mind back to the world, or rather to the examination of the basket.

Here he found other objects roughly wrapped in fragments of mummy-cloth that had been torn from the body of the queen. These it is needless to describe, for are they not to be seen in the gold room of the Museum, labelled 'Bijouterie de la Reine Ma-Mé, XVIIIème Dynastie. Thebes (Smith's Tomb)'? It may be mentioned, however, that the set was incomplete. For instance, there was but one of the great gold ceremonial ear-rings fashioned like a group of pomegranate blooms, and the most beautiful of the necklaces had been torn in two – half of it was missing.

It was clear to Smith that only a portion of the precious objects which were buried with the mummy had been placed in this basket. Why had these been left where he found them? A little reflection made that clear also. Something had prompted the thief to destroy the desecrated body and its coffin with fire, probably in the hope of hiding his evil handiwork. Then he fled with his spoil. But he had forgotten how fiercely mummies and their trappings can burn. Or perhaps the thing was an accident. He must have had a lamp, and if its flame chanced to touch this bituminous tinder!

At any rate, the smoke overtook the man in that narrow place as he began to climb the slippery slope of clay. In his haste he dropped the basket, and dared not return to search for it. It could wait till the morrow, when the fire would be out and the air pure. Only for this desecrator of the royal dead that morrow never came, as was discovered afterwards.

When at length Smith struggled into the open air the stars were paling before the dawn. An hour later, after the sky was well up, Mahomet (recovered from his sickness) and his myrmidons arrived.

'I have been busy while you slept,' said Smith, showing them the mummied hand (but not the rings which he had removed from the shrunk fingers), and the broken bronze, but not the priceless jewellery which was hidden in his pockets.

For the next ten days they dug till the tomb and its approach were quite clear. In the sand, at the head of a flight of steps which led down to the doorway, they found the skeleton of a man, who evidently had been buried there in a hurried fashion. His skull was shattered by the blow of an axe, and the shaven scalp that still clung to it suggested that he might have been a priest.

Mahomet thought, and Smith agreed with him, that this was the person who had violated the tomb. As he was escaping from it the guards of the holy place surprised him after he had covered up the hole by which he had entered and purposed to return. There they executed him without trail and divided up the plunder, thinking that no more was to be found. Or perhaps his confederates killed him.

Such at least were the theories advanced by Mahomet. Whether they were right or wrong none will ever know. For instance, the skeleton may not have been that of the thief, though probability appears to point the other way.

Nothing more was found in the tomb, not even a scarab or a mummy-bead. Smith spent the remainder of his time in photographing the pictures and copying the inscriptions, which for various reasons proved to be of extraordinary interest. Then, having reverently buried the charred bones of the queen in a secret place of the sepulchre, he handed it over to the care of the local Guardian of Antiquities, paid off Mahomet and the fellaheen, and departed for Cairo. With him went the wonderful jewels of which he had breathed no word, and another relic to him yet more precious – the hand of her Majesty Ma-Mee, Palm-branch of Love.

And now follows the strange sequel of this story of Smith and the queen Ma-Mee.

II

Smith was seated in the sanctum of the distinguished Director-General of Antiquities at the new Cairo Museum. It was a very interesting room. Books piled upon the floor; objects from tombs awaiting examination, lying here and there; a hoard of Ptolemaic silver coins, just dug up at Alexandria, standing on the table in the pot that had hidden them for two thousand years; in the corner the mummy of a royal child, aged six or seven, not long ago discovered, with some inscription scrawled upon the wrappings (brought here to be deciphered by the Master), and the withered lotus-bloom, love's last offering, thrust beneath one of the pink retaining bands.

'A touching object,' thought Smith to himself. 'Really, they might have left the dear little girl in peace.'

Smith had a tender heart, but even as he reflected he became aware that some of the jewellery hidden in an inner pocket of his waistcoat (designed for bank notes) was fretting his skin. He had a tender conscience also.

Just then the Director, a French savant, bustled in, alert, vigorous, full of interest.

'Ah, my dear Mr Smith!' he said, in his excellent English. 'I am indeed glad to see you back again, especially as I understand that you are come rejoicing and bringing your sheaves with you. They tell me you have been extraordinarily successful. What do you say is the name of this queen whose tomb you have found — Ma-Mee? A very unusual name. How do you get the extra vowel? Is it for euphony, eh? Did I not know how good a scholar you are, I should be tempted to believe that you had misread it. Me-Mee, Ma-Mee! That would be pretty in French, would it not? *Ma mie* — my darling! Well, I dare say she was somebody's *mie* in her time. But tell me the story.'

Smith told him shortly and clearly; also he produced his photographs and copies of inscriptions.

'This is interesting — interesting truly,' said the Director, when he had glanced through them. 'You must leave them with me to study. Also you will publish them, is it not so? Perhaps one of the Societies would help you with the cost, for it should be done in facsimile. Look at this vignette! Most unusual. Oh, what a pity that scoundrelly priest got off with the jewellery and burnt her Majesty's body!'

148

'He didn't get off with all of it.'

'What, Mr Smith? Our inspector reported to me that you found nothing.'

'I dare say, sir; but your inspector did not know what I found.'

'Ah, you are a discreet man! Well, let us see.'

Slowly Smith unbuttoned his waistcoat. From its inner pocket and elsewhere about his person he extracted the jewels wrapped in mummy-cloth as he had found them. First he produced a sceptre-head of gold, in the shape of a pomegranate fruit and engraved with the throne name and titles of Ma-Mee.

'What a beautiful object!' said the Director. 'Look! the handle was of ivory, and that *sacré* thief of a priest smashed it out at the socket. It was fresh ivory then; the robbery must have taken place not long after the burial. See, this magnifying-glass shows it. Is that all?'

Smith handed him the surviving half of the marvellous necklace that had been torn in two.

'I have re-threaded it,' he muttered, 'but every bead is in its place.'

'Oh, heavens! How lovely! Note the cutting of those cornelian heads of Hathor and the gold lotus-blooms between — yes, and the enamelled flies beneath. We have nothing like it in the Museum.'

So it went on.

'Is that all?' gasped the Director at last, when every object from the basket glittered before them on the table.

'Yes,' said Smith. 'That is — no. I found a broken statuette hidden in the sand outside the tomb. It is of the queen, but I thought perhaps you would allow me to keep this.'

'But certainly, Mr Smith; it is yours indeed. We are not niggards here. Still, if I might see it . . .'

From yet another pocket Smith produced the head. The Director gazed at it, then he spoke with feeling.

'I said just now that you were discreet, Mr Smith, and I have been reflecting that you are honest. But now I must add that you are very clever. If you had not made me promise that this bronze should be yours before you showed it to me — well, it would never have gone into that pocket again. And, in the public interest, won't you release me from the promise?'

'*No*,' said Smith.

'You are perhaps not aware,' went on the Director, with a groan, 'that this is a portrait of Mariette's unknown queen whom we are thus able to identify. It seems a pity that the two should be separated; a replica we could let you have.'

'I am quite aware,' said Smith, 'and I will be sure to send *you* a replica, with photographs. Also I promise to leave the original to some museum by will.'

The Director clasped the image tenderly, and, holding it to the light, read the broken cartouche beneath the breasts.

' "Ma-Mé, Great Royal Lady. Beloved of . . ." Beloved of whom? Well, of Smith, for one. Take it, monsieur, and hide it away at once, lest soon there should be another mummy in this collection, a modern mummy called Smith; and, in the name of Justice, let the museum which inherits it be not the British, but that of Cairo, for this queen belongs to Egypt. By the way, I have been told that you are delicate in the lungs. How is your health now? Our cold winds are very trying. Quite good? Ah, that is excellent! I suppose that you have no more articles that you can show me?'

'I have nothing more except a mummied hand, which I found in the basket with the jewels. The two rings off it lie there. Doubtless it was removed to get at that bracelet. I suppose you will not mind my keeping the hand?'

'Of the beloved of Smith,' interrupted the Director drolly. 'No, I suppose not, though for my part I should prefer one that was not quite so old. Still, perhaps *you* will not mind my seeing it. That pocket of yours still looks a little bulky; I thought that it contained books!'

Smith produced a cigar-box; in it was the hand wrapped in cotton wool.

'Ah,' said the Director, 'a pretty, well-bred hand. No doubt this Ma-Mee was the real heiress to the throne, as she describes herself. The Pharaoh was somebody of inferior birth, half-brother – she is called 'Royal Sister', you remember – son of one of the Pharaoh's slave-women, perhaps. Odd that she never mentioned him in the tomb. It looks as though they didn't get on in life, and that she was determined to have done with him in death. Those were the rings upon that hand, were they not?'

He replaced them on the fingers, then took off one, a royal signet in a cartouche, and read the inscription on the other: ' "Bes Ank, Ank Bes." Bes the Living, the living Bes.'

'Your Ma-Mee had some human vanity about her,' he added. 'Bes, among other things, as you know, was the god of beauty and of the adornments of women. She wore that ring that she might remain beautiful, and that her dresses might always fit, and her rouge never cake when she was dancing before the gods. Also it fixes her period pretty closely, but then so do other things. It seems a pity to rob Ma-Mee of her pet ring, does it not? The royal signet will be enough for us.'

With a little bow he gave the hand back to Smith, leaving the Bes ring on the finger that had worn it for more than three thousand years. At least, Smith was so sure it was the Bes ring that at the time he did not look at it again.

Then they parted, Smith promising to return upon the morrow, which, owing to events to be described, he did not do.

'Ah!' said the Master to himself, as the door closed behind his visitor. 'He's in a hurry to be gone. He has fear lest I should change my mind about that ring. Also there is the bronze. Monsieur Smith was *rusé* there. It is worth a thousand pounds, that bronze. Yet I do not believe he was thinking of the money. I believe he is in love with that Ma-Mee and wants to keep her picture. *Mon Dieu!* A well-established affection. At least he is what the English call an odd fish, one whom I could never make out, and of whom no one seems to know anything. Still, honest, I am sure — quite honest. Why, he might have kept every one of those jewels and no one have been the wiser. And what things! What a find! *Ciel!* what a find! There has been nothing like it for years. Benedictions on the head of Odd-fish Smith!'

Then he collected the precious objects, thrust them into an inner compartment of his safe, which he locked and double-locked, and, as it was nearly five o'clock, departed from the Museum to his private residence in the grounds, there to study Smith's copies and photographs, and to tell some friends of the great things that had happened.

When Smith found himself outside the sacred door, and had presented its venerable guardian with a baksheesh of five piastres, he walked a few paces to the right and paused a while to watch some native labourers who were dragging a huge sarcophagus upon an improvised tramway. As they dragged they sang an echoing rhythmic song, whereof each line ended with an invocation to Allah.

Just so, reflected Smith, had their forefathers sung when, millenniums ago, they dragged that very sarcophagus from the quarries to the Nile, and from the Nile to the tomb whence it reappeared today, or when they slid the casing blocks of the pyramids up the great causeway and smooth slope of sand, and laid them in their dizzy resting-places. Only then each line of the immemorial chant of toil ended with an invocation to Amen, now transformed to Allah.

The East may change its masters and its gods, but its customs never change, and if today Allah wore the feathers of Amen one wonders whether the worshippers would find the difference so very great.

Thus thought Smith as he hurried away from the sarcophagus and those blue-robed, dark-skinned fellaheen, down the long gallery that is filled with a thousand sculptures. For a moment he paused before the wonderful white statue of Queen Amenartas, then, remembering that his time was short, hastened on to a certain room, one of those which opened out of the gallery.

In a corner of this room, upon the wall, amongst many other beautiful objects, stood that head which Mariette had found, whereof in past years the cast had fascinated him in London. Now he knew whose head it was; to him it had been given to find the tomb of her who had sat for that statue. Her very hand was in his pocket — yes, the hand that had touched yonder marble, pointing out its defects to the sculptor, or perhaps swearing that he flattered her. Smith wondered who that sculptor was; surely he must have been a happy man. Also he wondered whether the statuette was also this master's work. He thought so, but he wished to make sure.

Near to the end of the room he stopped and looked about him like a thief. He was alone in the place; not a single student or tourist could be seen, and its guardian was somewhere else. He drew out the box that contained the hand. From the hand he slipped the ring which the Director-General had left there as a gift to himself. He would much have preferred the other with the signet, but how could he say so, especially after the episode of the statuette.

Replacing the hand in his pocket without looking at the ring — for his eyes were watching to see whether he was observed

– he set it upon his little finger, which it exactly fitted. (Ma-Mee had worn both of them upon the third finger of her left hand, the Bes ring as a guard to the signet.) He had the fancy to approach the effigy of Ma-Mee wearing a ring which she had worn and that came straight from her finger to his own.

Smith found the head in its accustomed place. Weeks had gone by since he looked upon it, and now, to his eyes, it had grown more beautiful than ever, and its smile was more mystical and loving. He drew out the statuette and began to compare them point by point. Oh, no doubt was possible! Both were like-nesses of the same woman, though the statuette might have been executed two or three years later than the statue. To him the face of it looked a little older and more spiritual. Perhaps illness, or some premonition of her end had then thrown its shadow on the queen. He compared and compared. He made some rough measurements and sketches in his pocket-book, and set himself to work out a canon of proportions.

So hard and earnestly did he work, so lost was his mind that he never heard the accustomed warning sound which announces that the Museum is about to close. Hidden behind an altar as he was, in his distant, shadowed corner, the guardian of the room never saw him as he cast a last perfunctory glance about the place before departing till the Saturday morning; for the morrow was Friday, the Mohammedan Sabbath, on which the Museum remains shut, and he would not be called upon to attend. So he went. Everybody went. The great doors clanged, were locked and bolted, and, save for a watchman outside, no one was left in all that vast place except Smith in his corner, engaged in sketching and in measurements.

The difficulty of seeing, owing to the increase of shadow, first called his attention to the fact that time was slipping away. He glanced at his watch and saw that it was ten minutes to the hour.

'Soon be time to go,' he thought to himself, and resumed his work.

How strangely silent the place seemed! Not a footstep to be heard or the sound of a human voice. He looked at his watch again, and saw that it was six o'clock, not five, or so the thing said. But that was impossible, for the Museum shut at five; evidently the desert sand had got into the works. The room in

which he stood was that known as Room I, and he had noticed
that its Arab custodian often frequented Room K or the gallery
outside. He would find him and ask what was the real time.

Passing round the effigy of the wonderful Hathor cow,
perhaps the finest example of an ancient sculpture of a beast in
the whole world, Smith came to the doorway and looked up and
down the gallery. Not a soul to be seen. He ran to Room K, to
Room H, and others. Still not a soul to be seen. Then he made
his way as fast as he could go to the great entrance. The doors
were locked and bolted.

'Watch must be right after all. I'm shut in,' he said to himself. 'However, there's sure to be someone about somewhere.
Probably the *salle des ventes* is still open. Shops don't shut till
they are obliged.'

Thither he went, to find its door as firmly closed as a door
can be. He knocked on it, but a sepulchral echo was the only
answer.

'I know,' he reflected. 'The Director must still be in his
room. It will take him a long while to examine all that jewellery
and put it away.'

So for the room he headed, and, after losing his path twice,
found it by help of the sarcophagus that the Arabs had been
dragging, which now stood as deserted as it had done in the
tomb, a lonesome and impressive object in the gathering
shadows. The Director's door was shut, and again his knockings
produced nothing but an echo. He started on a tour round the
Museum, and, having searched the ground floors, ascended to
the upper galleries by the great stairway.

Presently he found himself in that devoted to the royal
mummies, and, being tired, rested there a while. Opposite to
him, in a glass case in the middle of the gallery, reposed Rameses
II. Near to, on shelves in a side case, were Rameses's son,
Meneptah, and above, his son, Seti II, while in other cases were
the mortal remains of many more of the royalties of Egypt. He
looked at the proud face of Rameses and at the little fringe of
white locks turned yellow by the embalmer's spices, also at the
raised left arm. He remembered how the Director had told him
that when they were unrolling this mighty monarch they went
away to lunch, and that presently the man who had been left in
charge of the body rushed into the room with his hair on end,

and said that the dead king had lifted his arm and pointed at him.

Back they went, and there, true enough, was the arm lifted; nor were they ever able to get it quite into its place again. The explanation given was that the warmth of the sun had contracted the withered muscles, a very natural and correct explanation.

Still, Smith wished that he had not recollected the story just at this moment, especially as the arm seemed to move while he contemplated it — a very little, but still to move.

He turned round and gazed at Meneptah, whose hollow eyes stared at him from between the wrappings carelessly thrown across the parchment-like and ashen face. There, probably, lay the countenance that had frowned on Moses. There was the heart which God had hardened. Well, it was hard enough now, for the doctors said he died of ossification of the arteries, and that the vessels of the heart were full of lime!

Smith stood upon a chair and peeped at Seti II above. His weaker countenance was very peaceful, but it seemed to wear an air of reproach. In getting down Smith managed to upset the heavy chair. The noise it made was terrific. He would not have thought it possible that the fall of such an article could produce so much sound. Satisfied with his inspection of these particular kings, who somehow looked quite different now from what they had ever done before — more real and imminent, so to speak — he renewed his search for a living man.

On he went, mummies to his right, mummies to his left, of every style and period, till be began to feel as though he never wished to see another dried remnant of mortality. He peeped into the room where lay the relics of Iouiya and Touiyou, the father and mother of the great Queen Taia. Cloths had been drawn over these, and really they looked worse and more suggestive thus draped than in their frigid and unadorned blackness. He came to the coffins of the priest-kings of the twentieth dynasty, formidable painted coffins with human faces. There seemed to be a vast number of these priest-kings, but perhaps they were better than the gold masks of the great Ptolemaic ladies which glinted at him through the gathering gloom.

Really, he had seen enough of the upper floors. The statues

downstairs were better than all these dead, although it was true that, according to the Egyptian faith, every one of those statues was haunted eternally by the *Ka* or Double, of the person whom it represented. He descended the great stairway. Was it fancy, or did something run across the bottom step in front of him – an animal of some kind, followed by a swift-moving and indefinite shadow? If so, it must have been the Museum cat hunting a Museum mouse. Only then what on earth was that very peculiar and unpleasant shadow?

He called, 'Puss! puss! puss!' for he would have been quite glad of its company; but there came no friendly 'miau' in response. Perhaps it was only the *Ka* of a cat and the shadow was – oh! never mind what. The Egyptians worshipped cats, and there were plenty of their mummies about on the shelves. But the shadow!

Once he shouted in the hope of attracting attention, for there were no windows to which he could climb. He did not repeat the experiment, for it seemed as though a thousand voices were answering him from every corner and roof of the gigantic edifice.

Well, he must face the thing out. He was shut in a museum, and the question was in what part of it he should camp for the night. Moreover, as it was growing rapidly dark, the problem must be solved at once. He thought with affection of the lavatory, where, before going to see the Director, only that afternoon he had washed his hands with the assistance of a kindly Arab who watched the door and gracefully accepted a piastre. But there was no Arab there now, and the door, like every other in this confounded place, was locked. He marched on to the entrance.

Here, opposite to each other, stood the red sarcophagi of the great Queen Hatshepu and her brother and husband, Thotmes III. He looked at them. Why should not one of these afford him a night's lodging? They were deep and quiet, and would fit the human frame very nicely. For a while Smith wondered which of these monarchs would be the more likely to take offence at such a use of a private sarcophagus, and, acting on general principles, concluded that he would rather throw himself on the mercy of the lady.

Already one of his legs was over the edge of that solemn

coffer, and he was squeezing his body beneath the massive lid that was propped above it on blocks of wood, when he remembered a little, naked, withered thing with long hair that he had seen in a side chamber of the tomb of Amenhotep II in the Valley of Kings at Thebes. This caricature of humanity many thought, and he agreed with them, to be the actual body of the mighty Hatshepu as it appeared after the robbers had done with it.

Supposing now, that when he was lying at the bottom of that sarcophagus, sleeping the sleep of the just, this little personage should peep over its edge and ask him what he was doing there! Of course the idea was absurd; he was tired, and his nerves were a little shaken. Still, the fact remained that for centuries the hallowed dust of Queen Hatshepu had slept where he, a modern man, was proposing to sleep.

He scrambled down from the sarcophagus and looked round him in despair. Opposite to the main entrance was the huge central hall of the Museum. Now the cement roof of this hall had, he knew, gone wrong, with the result that very extensive repairs had become necessary. So extensive were they, indeed, that the Director-General had informed him that they would take several years to complete. Therefore this hall was boarded up, only a little doorway being left by which the workmen could enter. Certain statues, of Seti II and others, too large to be moved, were also roughly boarded over, as were some great funeral boats on either side of the entrance. The rest of the place, which might be two hundred feet long with a proportionate breadth, was empty save for the colossi of Amenhotep III and his queen Taia that stood beneath the gallery at its farther end.

It was an appalling place in which to sleep, but better, reflected Smith, than a sarcophagus or those mummy chambers. If, for instance, he could creep behind the deal boards that enclosed one of the funeral boats he would be quite comfortable there. Lifting the curtain, he slipped into the hall, where the gloom of evening had already settled. Only the skylights and the outline of the towering colossi at the far end remained visible. Close to him were the two funeral boats which he had noted when he looked into the hall earlier on that day, standing at the head of a flight of steps which led to the sunk floor of the centre. He groped his way to that on the right. As he expected, the projecting planks were not quite joined at the bow. He crept in between them and the boat and laid himself down.

Presumably, being altogether tired out, Smith did ultimately fall asleep, for how long he never knew. At any rate, it is certain that, if so, he woke up again. He could not tell the time, because his watch was not a repeater, and the place was as black as the pit. He had some matches in his pocket, and might have struck one and even have lit his pipe. To his credit be it said, however, he remembered that he was the sole tenant of one of the most valuable museums in the world, and his responsibilities with reference to fire. So he refrained from striking that match under the keel of a boat which had become very dry in the course of five thousand years.

Smith found himself very wide awake indeed. Never in all his life did he remember being more so, not even in the hour of its great catastrophe, or when his godfather, Ebenezer, after much hesitation, had promised him a clerkship in the bank of which he was a director. His nerves seemed strung tight as harp-strings, and his every sense was painfully acute. Thus he could even smell the odour of mummies that floated down from the upper galleries and the earthly scent of the boat which had been buried for thousands of years in sand at the foot of the pyramid of one of the fifth dynasty kings.

Moreover, he could hear all sorts of strange sounds, faint and far-away sounds which at first he thought must emanate from Cairo without. Soon, however, he grew sure that their origin was more local. Doubtless the cement work and the cases in the galleries were cracking audibly, as is the unpleasant habit of such things at night.

Yet why should these common manifestations be so universal and affect him so strangely? Really, it seemed as though people were stirring all about him. More, he could have sworn that the great funeral boat beneath which he lay had become repeopled with the crew that once it bore.

He heard them at their business above him. There were trampings and a sound as though something heavy were being laid on the deck, such, for instance, as must have been made

when the mummy of Pharaoh was set there for its last journey to
the western bank of the Nile. Yes, and now he could have sworn
again that the priestly crew were getting out the oars.

Smith began to meditate flight from the neighbourhood of
that place when something occurred which determined him to
stop where he was.

The huge hall was growing light, but not, as at first he
hoped, with the rays of dawn. This light was pale and ghostly,
though very penetrating. Also it had a blue tinge, unlike any
other he had ever seen. At first it arose in a kind of fan or foun-
tain at the far end of the hall, illumining the steps there and the
two noble colossi which sat above.

But what was this that stood at the head of the steps,
radiating glory? By heavens! it was Osiris himself or the image of
Osiris, god of the Dead, the Egyptian saviour of the world!

There he stood, in his mummy-cloths, wearing the feath-
ered crown, and holding in his hands, which projected from an
opening in the wrappings, the crook and the scourge of power.
Was he alive, or was he dead? Smith could not tell, since he never
moved, only stood there, splendid and fearful, his calm, benig-
nant face staring into nothingness.

Smith became aware that the darkness between him and
the vision of this god was peopled; that a great congregation was
gathering, or had gathered there. The blue light began to grow;
long tongues of it shot forward, which joined themselves
together, illumining all that huge hall.

Now, too, he saw the congregation. Before him, rank upon
rank of them, stood the kings and queens of Egypt. As though at
a given signal, they bowed themselves to the Osiris, and ere the
tinkling of their ornaments had died away, lo! Osiris was gone.
But in his place stood another, Isis, the Mother of Mystery, her
deep eyes looking forth from beneath the jewelled vulture-cap.
Again the congregation bowed, and, lo! she was gone. But in her
place stood yet another, a radiant, lovely being, who held in her
hand the Sign of Life, and wore upon her head the symbol of the
shining disc – Hathor, Goddess of Love. A third time the congregation bowed, and she, too, was gone; nor did any other
appear in her place.

The Pharaohs and their queens began to move about and
speak to each other; their voices came to his ears in one low,
sweet murmur.

In his amazement Smith had forgotten fear. From his hiding-place he watched them intently. Some of them he knew by their faces. There, for instance, was the long-necked Khu-en-aten, talking somewhat angrily to the imperial Rameses II. Smith could understand what he said, for this power seemed to have been given to him. He was complaining in a high, weak voice that on this, the one night of the year when they might meet, the gods, or the magic images of the gods who were put up for them to worship, should not include *his* god, symbolized by the 'Aten', or the sun's disc.

'I have heard of your Majesty's god,' replied Rameses; 'the priests used to tell me of him, also that he did not last long after your Majesty flew to heaven. The Fathers of Amen gave you a bad name; they called you 'the heretic' and hammered out your cartouches. They were quite rare in my time. Oh, do not let your Majesty be angry! So many of us have been heretics. My grandson, Seti, there,' — and he pointed to a mild, thoughtful-faced man — 'for example. I am told that he really worshipped the god of those Hebrew slaves whom I used to press to build my cities. Look at that lady with him. Beautiful, isn't she? Observe her large, violet eyes! Well, she was the one who did the mischief, a Hebrew herself. At least, they tell me so.'

'I will talk with him,' answered Khu-en-aten. 'It is more than possible that we may agree on certain points. Meanwhile, let me explain to your Majesty——'

'Oh, I pray you, not now. There is my wife.'

'Your wife?' said Khu-en-aten, drawing himself up. 'Which wife? I am told that your Majesty had many and left a large family; indeed, I see some hundreds of them here tonight. Now, I — but let me introduce Nefertiti to your Majesty. I may explain that she was my *only* wife.'

'So I have understood. Your Majesty was rather an invalid, were you not? Of course, in those circumstances, one prefers the nurse whom one can trust. Oh, pray, no offence! Nefertari, my love — oh, I beg pardon! — Astnefert — Nefertari has gone to speak to some of her children — let me introduce you to your predecessor, the Queen Nefertiti, wife of Amenhotep IV — I mean Khu-en-aten (he changed his name, you know, because half of it was that of the father of the gods). She is interested in the question of plural marriage. Goodbye! I wish to have a word with my grandfather, Rameses I. He was fond of me as a little boy.'

At this moment Smith's interest in that queer conversation died away, for of a sudden he beheld none other than the queen of his dreams, Ma-Mee. Oh! there she stood, without a doubt, only ten times more beautiful than he had ever pictured her. She was tall and somewhat fair-complexioned, with slumbrous, dark eyes, and on her face gleamed the mystic smile he loved. She wore a robe of simple white and a purple-broidered apron, a crown of golden *uræi* with turquoise eyes was set upon her dark hair as in her statue, and on her breast and arms were the very necklace and bracelets that he had taken from her tomb. She appeared to be somewhat moody, or rather thoughtful, for she leaned by herself against a balustrade, watching the throng without much interest.

Presently a Pharaoh, a black-browed, vigorous man with thick lips, drew near.

'I greet your Majesty,' he said.

She started, and answered:

'Oh, it is you! I make my obeisance to your Majesty,' and she curtsied to him, humbly enough, but with a suggestion of mockery in her movements.

'Well, you do not seem to have been very anxious to find me, Ma-Mee, which, considering that we meet so seldom——'

'I saw that your Majesty was engaged with my sister queens,' she interrupted, in a rich, low voice, 'and with some other ladies in the gallery there, whose faces I seem to remember, but who I think were *not* queens. Unless, indeed, you married them after I was drawn away.'

'One must talk to one's relations,' replied the Pharaoh.

'Quite so. But, you see, I have no relations – at least, none whom I know well. My parents, you will remember, died when I was young, leaving me Egypt's heiress, and they are still vexed at the marriage which I made on the advice of my counsellors. But, is it not annoying? I have lost one of my rings, that which had the god Bes on it. Some dweller on the earth must be wearing it today, and that is why I cannot get it back from him.'

'Him! Why 'him'? Hush; the business is about to begin.'

'What business, my lord?'

'Oh, the question of the violation of our tombs, I believe.'

'Indeed! That is a large subject, and not a very profitable one, I should say. Tell me, who is that?' And she pointed to a lady who had stepped forward, a very splendid person, magnificently arrayed.

'Cleopatra the Greek,' he answered, 'the last of Egypt's Sovereigns, one of the Ptolemys. You can always know her by that Roman who walks about after her.'

'Which?' asked Ma-Mee. 'I see several — also other men. She was the wretch who rolled Egypt in the dirt and betrayed her. Oh, if it were not for the law of peace by which we abide when we meet thus!'

'You mean that she would be torn to shreds, Ma-Mee, and her very soul scattered like the limbs of Osiris? Well, if it were not for that law of peace, so perhaps would many of us, for never have I heard a single king among these hundreds speak altogether well of those who went before or followed after him.'

'Especially of those who went before if they happen to have hammered out their cartouches and usurped their monuments,' said the queen, dryly, and looking him in the eyes.

At this home-thrust the Pharaoh seemed to wince. Making no answer, he pointed to the royal woman who had mounted the steps at the end of the hall.

Queen Cleopatra lifted her hand and stood thus for a while. Very splendid she was, and Smith, on his hands and knees behind the boarding of the boat, thanked his stars that alone among modern men it had been his lot to look upon her rich and living loveliness. There she shone, she who had changed the fortunes of the world, she who, whatever she did amiss, at least had known how to die.

Silence fell upon that glittering galaxy of kings and queens and upon all the hundreds of their offspring, their women, and their great officers who crowded the double tier of galleries around the hall.

'Royalties of Egypt,' she began, in a sweet, clear voice which penetrated to the farthest recesses of the place, 'I, Cleopatra, the sixth of that name and the last monarch who ruled over the Upper and the Lower Lands before Egypt became a home of slaves, have a word to say to your Majesties, who, in your mortal days, all of you more worthily filled the throne on which once I sat. I do not speak of Egypt and its fate, or of our sins — whereof mine were not the least — that brought her to the dust. Those sins I and others expiate elsewhere, and of them, from age to age, we hear enough. But on this one night of the year, that of the feast of him whom we call Osiris, but whom other nations have known and know by different names, it is given to us once more to be mortal for an hour, and, though we be but shadows, to renew the loves and hates of our long-perished flesh. Here for an hour we strut in our forgotten pomp; the crowns that were ours still adorn our brows, and once more we seem to listen to our people's praise. Our hopes are the hopes of mortal life, our foes are the foes we feared, our gods grow real again, and our lovers whisper in our ears. Moreover, this joy is given to us – to see each other as we are, to know as the gods know, and therefore to forgive, even where we despise and hate. Now I have done, and I, the youngest of the rulers of ancient Egypt, call upon him who was the first of her kings to take my place.'

She bowed, and the audience bowed back to her. Then she descended the steps and was lost in the throng. Where she had been appeared an old man, simply-clad, long-bearded, wise-faced, and wearing on his grey hair no crown save a plain band of gold, from the centre of which rose the snake-headed *urœus* crest.

'Your Majesties who came after me,' said the old man, 'I am Menes, the first of the accepted Pharaohs of Egypt, although many of those who went before me were more truly kings than I. Yet as the first who joined the Upper and the Lower Lands, and took the royal style and titles, and ruled as well as I could rule, it is given to me to talk with you for a while this night whereon our spirits are permitted to gather from the uttermost parts of the uttermost worlds and see each other face to face. First, in dark-ness and in secret, let us speak of the mystery of the gods and of its meanings. Next, in darkness and in secret, let us speak of the mystery of our lives, of whence they come, of where they tarry by the road, and whither they go at last. And afterwards, let us speak of other matters face to face in light and openness, as we were wont to do when we were men. Then hence to Thebes, there to celebrate our yearly festival. Is such your will?'

'Such is our will,' they answered.

It seemed to Smith that dense darkness fell upon the place, and with it a silence that was awful. For a time that he could not reckon, that might have been years or might have been moments, he sat there in the utter darkness and the utter silence.

At length the light came again, first as a blue spark, then in upward pouring rays, and lastly pervading all. There stood Menes on the steps, and there in front of him was gathered the same royal throng.

'The mysteries are finished,' said the old king. 'Now, if any have aught to say, let it be said openly.'

A young man dressed in the robes and ornaments of an early dynasty came forward and stood upon the steps between the Pharaoh Menes and all those who had reigned after him. His face seemed familiar to Smith, as was the side lock that hung down behind his right ear in token of his youth. Where had he seen him? Ah, he remembered. Only a few hours ago lying in one of the cases of the Museum, together with the bones of the Pharaoh Unas.

'Your Majesties,' he began, 'I am the King Metesuphis. The matter that I wish to lay before you is that of the violation of our sepulchres by those men who live upon the earth. The mortal bodies of many who are gathered here tonight lie in this place to be stared at and mocked by the curious. I myself am one of them, jawless, broken, hideous to behold. Yonder, day by day, must my *Ka* sit watching my desecrated flesh, torn from the pyramid that, with cost and labour, I raised up to be an eternal house wherein I might hide till the hour of resurrection. Others of us lie in far lands. Thus, as he can tell you, my predecessor, Man-kau-ra, he who built the third of the great pyramids, the Pyramid of Her, sleeps, or rather wakes in a dark city, called London, across the seas, a place of murk where no sun shines. Others have been burnt with fire, others are scattered in small dust. The ornaments that were ours are stole away and sold to the greedy; our sacred writings and our symbols are their jest. Soon there will not be one holy grave in Egypt that remains undefiled.'

'That is so,' said a voice from the company. 'But four months gone the deep, deep pit was opened that I had dug in the shadow of the Pyramid of Cephren, who begat me in the world. There in my chamber I slept alone, two handfuls of white bones, since when I died they did not preserve the body with wrappings and with spices. Now I see those bones of mine, beside which my

Double has watched for these five thousand years, hid in the blackness of a great ship and tossing on a sea that is strewn with ice.'

'It is so.' echoed a hundred other voices.

Then,' went on the young king, turning to Menes, 'I ask of your Majesty whether there is no means whereby we may be avenged on those who do us this foul wrong.'

'Let him who has wisdom speak,' said the old Pharaoh.

A man of middle age, short in stature and of a thoughtful brow, who held in his hand a wand and wore the feathers and insignia of the heir to the throne of Egypt and of a high priest of Amen, moved to the steps. Smith knew him at once from his statues. He was Khaemuas, son of Rameses the Great, the mightiest magician that ever was in Egypt, who of his own will withdrew himself from earth before the time came that he should sit upon the throne.

'I have wisdom, your Majesties, and I will answer,' he said. 'The time draws on when, in the land of Death which is Life, the land that we call Amenti, it will be given to us to lay our wrongs as to this matter before Those who judge, knowing that they will be avenged. On this night of the year also, when we resume the shapes we were, we have certain powers of vengeance, or rather of executing justice. But our time is short, and there is much to say and do before the sun-god Ra arises and we depart each to his place. Therefore it seems best that we should leave these wicked ones in their wickedness till we meet them face to face beyond the world.'

Smith, who had been following the words of Khaemuas with the closest attention and considerable anxiety, breathed again, thanking Heaven that the engagements of these departed monarchs were so numerous and pressing. Still, as a matter of precaution, he drew the cigar-box which contained Ma-Mee's hand from his pocket, and pushed it as far away from him as he could. It was a most unlucky act. Perhaps the cigar-box grated on the floor, or perhaps the fact of his touching the relic put him into psychic communication with all these spirits. At any rate, he became aware that the eyes of that dreadful magician were fixed upon him, and that a bone had a better chance of escaping the search of a Röntgen ray than he of hiding himself from their baleful glare.

'As it happens, however,' went on Khaemuas, in a cold voice, 'I now percieve that there is hidden in this place, and spying on us, one of the worst of these vile thieves. I say to your Majesties that I see him crouched beneath your funeral barge, and that he has with him at this moment the hand of one of your Majesties, stolen by him from her tomb at Thebes.'

Now every queen in the company became visibly agitated (Smith, who was watching Ma-Mee, saw her hold up her hands and look at them), while all the Pharaohs pointed with their fingers and exclaimed together, in a voice that rolled round the hall like thunder:

'Let him be brought forth to judgment!'

Khaemuas raised his wand and, holding it towards the boat where Smith was hidden, said:

'Draw near, Vile One, bringing with thee that thou hast stolen.'

Smith tried hard to remain where he was. He sat himself down and set his heels against the floor. As the reader knows, he was always shy and retiring by disposition, and never had these weaknesses oppressed him more than they did just then. When a child his favourite nightmare had been that the foreman of a jury was in the act of proclaiming him guilty of some dreadful but unstated crime. Now he understood what that nightmare foreshadowed. He was about to be convicted in a court of which all the kings and queens of Egypt were the jury, Menes was Chief Justice, and the magician Khaemuas played the *rôle* of Attorney-General.

In vain did he sit down and hold fast. Some power took possession of him which forced him first to stretch out his arm and pick up the cigar-box containing the hand of Ma-Mee, and next drew him from the friendly shelter of the deal boards that were about the boat.

Now he was on his feet and walking down the flight of steps opposite to those on which Menes stood far away. Now he was among all that throng of ghosts, which parted to let him pass, looking at him as he went with cold and wondering eyes. They were very majestic ghosts; the ages that had gone by since they laid down their sceptres had taken nothing from their royal dignity. Moreover, save one, none of them seemed to have any pity for his plight. She was a little princess who stood by her mother, that same little princess whose mummy he had seen and pitied in the Director's room with a lotus flower thrust beneath her bandages. As he passed Smith heard her say:

'This Vile One is frightened. Be brave, Vile One!'

Smith understood, and pride come to his aid. He, a gentleman of the modern world, would not show the white feather before a crowd of ancient Egyptian ghosts. Turning to the child, he smiled at her, them drew himself to his full height and walked on quietly. Here it may be stated that Smith was a tall man, still comparatively young, and very good-looking, straight and spare in frame, with dark, pleasant eyes and a little black beard.

'At least he is a well-favoured thief,' said one of the queens to another.

'Yes,' answered she who had been addressed. 'I wonder that a man with such a noble air should find pleasure in disturbing graves and stealing the offerings of the dead,' words that gave Smith much cause for thought. He had never considered the matter in this light.

Now he came to the place where Ma-Mee stood, the black-browed Pharaoh who had been her husband at her side. On his left hand which held the cigar-box was the gold Bes ring, and that box he felt constrained to carry pressed against him just over his heart.

As he went by he turned his head, and his eyes met those of Ma-Mee. She started violently. Then she saw the ring upon his hand and again started still more violently.

'What ails your Majesty?' asked the Pharaoh.

'Oh, naught,' she answered. 'Yet does this earth-dweller remind you of anyone?'

'Yes, he does,' answered the Pharaoh. 'He reminds me very much of that accursed sculptor about whom we had words.'

'Do you mean a certain Horu, the Court artist; he who worked the image that was buried with me, and whom you sent to carve your statues in the deserts of Kush, until he died of fevers — or was it poison?'

'Aye; Horu and no other, may Set take and keep him!' growled the Pharaoh.

Then Smith passed on and heard no more. Now he stood before the venerable Menes. Some instinct caused him to bow to this Pharaoh, who bowed back to him. Then he turned and bowed to the royal company, and they also bowed back to him, coldly, but very gravely and courteously.

'Dweller on the world where once we had our place, and therefore brother of us, the dead,' began Menes, 'this divine priest and magician' – and he pointed to Khaemuas – 'declares that you are one of those who foully violate our sepulchres and desecrate our ashes. He declares, moreover, that at this very moment you have with you a portion of the mortal flesh of a certain Majesty whose spirit is present here. Say, now, are these things true?'

To his astonishment Smith found that he had not the slightest difficulty in answering in the same sweet tongue.

'O King, they are true, and not true. Hear me, rulers of Egypt. It is true that I have searched in your graves, because my heart has been drawn towards you, and I would learn all that I could concerning you, for it comes to me *now* that once I was one of you – no king, indeed, yet perchance of the blood of kings. Also – for I would hide nothing even if I could – I searched for one tomb above all others.'

'Why, O man?' asked the Judge.

'Because a face drew me, a lovely face that was cut in stone.'

Now all that great audience turned their eyes towards him and listened as though his words moved them.

'Did you find that holy tomb?' asked Menes. 'If so, what did you find therein?'

'Aye, Pharaoh, and in it I found these,' and he took from the box the withered hand, from his pocket the broken bronze, and from his finger the ring.

'Also I found other things which I delivered to the keeper of this place, articles of jewellery that I seem to see tonight upon one who is present here among you.'

'Is the face of this figure the face you sought?' asked the Judge.

'It is the lovely face,' he answered.

Menes took the effigy in his hand and read the cartouche that was engraved beneath its breast.

'If there be here among us,' he said, presently, 'one who long after my day ruled as queen in Egypt, one who was named Ma-Mé, let her draw near.'

Now from where she stood glided Ma-Mee and took her

place opposite to Smith.

'Say, O Queen,' asked Menes, 'do you know aught of this matter?'

'I know that hand; it was my own hand,' she answered. 'I know that ring; it was my ring. I know that image in bronze; it was my image. Look on me and judge for yourselves whether this be so. A certain sculptor fashioned it, the son of a king's son, who was named Horu, the first of sculptors and the head artist of my Court. There, clad in strange garments, he stands before you. Horu, or the Double of Horu, he who cut the image when I ruled in Egypt, is he who found the image and the man who stands before you; or, mayhap, his Double cast in the same mould.'

The pharaoh Menes turned to the magician Khaemuas and said:

'Are these things so, O Seer?'

'They are so,' answered Khaemuas. 'This dweller on the earth is he who, long ago, was the sculptor Horu. But what shall that avail? He, once more a living man, is a violator of the hallowed dead. I say, therefore, that judgment should be executed on his flesh, so that when the light comes here tomorrow he himself will again be gathered to the dead.'

Menes bent his head upon his breast and pondered. Smith said nothing. To him the whole play was so curious that he had no wish to interfere with its development. If these ghosts wished to make him of their number, let them do so. He had no ties on earth, and now when he knew full surely that there was a life beyond this of earth he was quite prepared to explore its mysteries. So he folded his arms upon his breast and awaited the sentence.

But Ma-Mee did not wait. She raised her hand so swiftly that the bracelets jingled on her wrists, and spoke out with boldness.

'Royal Khaemuas, prince and magician,' she said, 'hearken to one who, like you, was Egypt's heir centuries before you were born, one also who ruled over the Two Lands, and not so ill — which, Prince, never was your lot. Answer me! Is all wisdom centred in your breast? Answer me! Do you alone know the mysteries of Life and Death? Answer me! Did your god Amen teach you that vengeance went before mercy? Answer me! Did he teach you that men should be judged unheard? That they should be hurried by violence to Osiris ere their time, and thereby separated from the dead ones whom they loved and forced to return to live again upon this evil Earth?

'Listen: when the last moon was near her full my spirit sat in my tomb in the burying-place of queens. My spirit saw this man enter into my tomb, and what he did there. With bowed head he looked upon my bones that a thief of the priesthood of Amen had robbed and burnt within twenty years of their burial, in which he himself had taken part. And what did this man with those bones, he who was once Horu? I tell you that he hid them away there in the tomb where he thought they could not be found again. Who, then, was the thief and the violator? He who robbed and burnt my bones, or he who buried them with reverence? Again, he found the jewels that the priest of your brotherhood had dropped in his flight, when the smoke of the burning flesh and spices overpowered him, and with them the hand which that wicked one had broken off from the body of my Majesty. What did this man then? He took the jewels. Would you have had him leave them to be stolen by some peasant? And the hand? I tell you that he kissed that poor dead hand which once had been part of the body of my Majesty, and that now he treasures it as a holy relic. My spirit saw him do these things and made report thereof to me. I ask you, therefore, Prince, I ask you all, Royalties of Egypt — whether for such deeds this man should die?'

Now Khaemuas, the advocate of vengeance, shrugged his shoulders and smiled meaningly, but the congregation of kings and queens thundered an answer, and it was:

'No!'

Ma-Mee looked to Menes to give judgment. Before he could speak the dark-browed Pharaoh who had named her wife strode forward and addressed them.

'Her Majesty, Heiress of Egypt, Royal Wife, Lady of the Two Lands, has spoken,' he cried. 'Now let me speak who was the husband of her Majesty. Whether this man was once Horu the sculptor I know not. If so he was also an evil-doer who, by my decree, died in banishment in the land of Kush. Whatever be the truth as to that matter, he admits that he violated the tomb of her Majesty and stole what the old thieves had left. Her Majesty says also — and he does not deny it — that he dared to kiss her hand, and for a man to kiss the hand of a wedded Queen of Egypt the punishment is death. I claim that this man should die to the World before his time, that in a day to come again he may live and suffer in the World. Judge, O Menes.'

Menes lifted his head and spoke, saying:

'Repeat to me the law, O Pharaoh, under which a living man must die for the kissing of a dead hand. In my day and in that of those who went before me there was no such law in Egypt. If a living man, who was not her husband, or of her kin, kissed the living hand of a wedded Queen of Egypt, save in ceremony, then perchance he might be called upon to die. Perchance for such a reason a certain Horu once was called upon to die. But in the grave there is no marriage, and therefore even if he had found her alive within the tomb and kissed her hand, or even her lips, why should he die for the crime of love?

'Hear me, all; this is my judgment in the matter. Let the soul of that priest who first violated the tomb of the royal Ma-Mee be hunted down and given to the jaws of the Destroyer, that he may know the last depths of Death, if so the gods declare. But let this man go from among us unharmed, since what he did he did in reverent ignorance and because Hathor, Goddess of Love, guided him from of old. Love rules this world wherein we meet tonight, with all the worlds whence we have gathered or whither we still must go. Who can defy its power? Who can refuse its rites? Now hence to Thebes!'

There was a rushing sound as of a thousand wings, and all were gone.

No, not all, since Smith yet stood before the draped colossi and the empty steps, and beside him, glorious, unearthly, gleamed the vision of Ma-Mee.

'I, too, must away,' she whispered; 'yet ere I go a word with you who once were a sculptor in Egypt. You loved me then, and that love cost you your life, you who once dared to kiss this hand of mine that again you kissed in yonder tomb. For I was Pharaoh's wife in name only; understand me well, in name only; since that title of Royal Mother, which they gave me is but a graven lie. Horu, I never was a wife, and when you died, swiftly I followed you to the grave. Oh, you forget, but I remember! I remember many things. You think that the priestly thief broke this figure of me which you found in the sand outside my tomb. Not so. *I* broke it, because, daring greatly, you had written thereon, "Beloved " not "of *Horus* the God " as you should have done, but of "*Horu* the Man". So when I came to be buried, Pharaoh, knowing all, took the image from my wrappings and hurled it away. I remember, too, the casting of that image, and how you threw a gold chain I had given you into the crucible with the bronze, saying that gold alone was fit to fashion me. And this signet that I bear – it was you who cut it. Take it, take it, Horu, and in its place give me back that which is on your hand, the Bes ring that I also wore. Take it and wear it ever till you die again, and let it go to the grave with you as once it went to the grave with me.

'Now hearken. When Ra the great sun arises again and you awake you will think that you have dreamed a dream. You will think that in this dream you saw and spoke with a lady of Egypt who died more than three thousand years ago, but whose beauty, carved in stone and bronze, has charmed your heart today. So let it be, yet know, O man, who once was named Horu, that such dreams are oft-times a shadow of the truth. Know that this Glory which shines before you is mine indeed in the land that is both far and near, the land wherein I dwell eternally, and that what is mine has been, is, and shall be yours for ever. Gods may change their kingdoms and their names; men may live and die, and live again once more to die; empires may fall and those who ruled them be turned to forgotten dust. Yet true love endures immortal as the souls in which it was conceived, and from it for you and me, the night of woe and separation done, at the daybreak which draws on, there shall be born the splendour and the peace of union. Till that hour foredoomed seek me no more, though I be ever near you, as I have ever been. Till that most blessed hour, Horu, farewell.'

She bent towards him; her sweet lips touched his brow; the perfume from her breath and hair beat upon him; the light of her wondrous eyes searched out his very soul, reading the answer that was written there.

He stretched out his arms to clasp her, and lo! she was gone.

It was a very cold and a very stiff Smith who awoke on the following morning, to find himself exactly where he had lain down –

namely, on a cement floor beneath the keel of a funeral boat in the central hall of the Cairo Museum. He crept from his shelter shivering, and looked at this hall, to find it quite as empty as it had been on the previous evening. Not a sign or a token was there of Pharaoh Menes and all those kings and queens of whom he had dreamed so vividly.

Reflecting on the strange fantasies that weariness and excited nerves can summon to the mind in sleep, Smith made his way to the great doors and waited in the shadow, praying earnestly that, although it was the Mohammedan Sabbath, someone might visit the Museum to see that all was well.

As a matter of fact, someone did, and before he had been there a minute – a watchman going about his business. He unlocked the place carelessly, looking over his shoulder at a kite fighting with two nesting crows. In an instant Smith, who was not minded to stop and answer questions, had slipped past him and was gliding down the portico, from monument to monument, like a snake between boulders, still keeping in the shadow as he headed for the gates.

The attendant caught sight of him and uttered a yell of fear; then, since it is not good to look upon an *afreet*, appearing from whence no mortal man could be, he turned his head away. When he looked again Smith was through those gates and had mingled with the crowd in the street beyond.

The sunshine was very pleasant to one who was conscious of having contracted a chill of the worst Egyptian order from long contact with a damp stone floor. Smith walked on through it towards his hotel – it was Shepheard's, and more than a mile away – making up a story as he went to tell the hall-porter of how he had gone to dine at Mena House by the Pyramids, missed the last tram, and stopped the night there.

Whilst he was thus engaged his left hand struck somewhat sharply against the corner of the cigar-box in his pocket, that which contained the relic of the queen Ma-Mee. The pain caused him to glance at his fingers to see if they were injured, and to perceive on one of them the ring he wore. Surely, surely it was not the same that the Director-General had given him! *That* ring was engraved with the image of the god Bes. On *this* was cut the cartouche of her Majesty Ma-Mee! And he had dreamed – oh, he had dreamed . . .

To this day Smith is wondering whether, in the hurry of the moment, he made a mistake as to which of those rings the Director-General had given him as part of his share of the spoil of the royal tomb he discovered in the Valley of Queens. Afterwards Smith wrote to ask, but the Director-General could only remember that he gave him one of the two rings, and assured him that that inscribed '*Bes Ank, Ank Bes*,' was with Ma-Mee's other jewels in the Gold Room of the Museum.

Also Smith is wondering whether any other bronze figure of an old Egyptian royalty shows so high a percentage of gold as, on analysis, the broken image of Ma-Mee was proved to do. For had she not seemed to tell him a tale of the melting of a golden chain when that effigy was cast?

Was it all only a dream, or was it – something more – by day and by night he asks of Nothingness?

But, be she near or far, no answer comes from the Queen Ma-Mee, whose proud titles were 'Her Majesty the Good God, the justified Dweller in Osiris; Daughter of Amen, Royal Heiress, Royal Sister, Royal Wife, Royal Mother; Lady of the Two Lands; Wearer of the Double Crown; of the White Crown, of the Red Crown; Sweet Flower of Love, Beautiful Eternally.'

So, like the rest of us, Smith must wait to learn the truth concerning many things, and more particularly as to which of those two circles of ancient gold the Director-General gave him yonder at Cairo.

It seems but a little matter, yet it is more than all the worlds to him!

To the astonishment of his colleagues in antiquarian research, Smith has never returned to Egypt. He explains to them that his health is quite restored, and that he no longer needs this annual change to a more temperate clime.

Now, *which* of the two royal rings did the Director-General return to Smith on the mummied hand of her late Majesty Ma-Mee?

A Ghostly Connection

The Times, 21 July, 1904.

The following story is so strange and its sequel so extraordinary that I have hesitated to write it down although I know its circumstances to be well worthy of record. I have considered telling it anonymously, yet after much thought I have made up my mind to publish it over my own name, although I am aware that by doing so I may expose myself to ridicule and disbelief.

On the night of Saturday, 9 July, I went to bed about 12.30, and suffered from what I took to be a nightmare. I was awakened by my wife's voice calling me from her own bed upon the other side of the room. As I awoke, the nightmare itself, which had been long and vivid, faded from my brain. All I could remember of it was a sense of awful oppression and of desperate and terrified struggling for life such as the act of drowning would probably involve. But between the time that I heard my wife's voice and the time that my consciousness answered to it, or so it seemed to me, I had another dream.

I dreamed that a black retriever dog, a most amiable and intelligent beast named Bob, which was the property of my eldest daughter, was lying on its side among brushwood, or rough growth of some sort, by water. My own personality in some mysterious way seemed to me to be arising from the body of the dog, which I knew quite surely to be Bob and no other, so much so that my head was against its head, which was lifted up at an unnatural angle.

In my vision the dog was trying to speak to me in words; and, failing, transmitted to my mind in an undefined fashion the knowledge that it was dying. Then everything vanished, and I woke to hear my wife asking me why on earth I was making those horrible and weird noises. I replied that I had had a nightmare about a fearful struggle, and that I had dreamed that old Bob was in a dreadful way, and was trying to talk to me and to tell me about it. Finally, seeing that it was still quite dark, I asked what the time was. She said she did not known, and shortly afterwards I went to sleep again and was disturbed no more.

On the Sunday morning, my wife told the tale of my nightmare at breakfast, and I repeated my story in a few words.

Thinking that the whole thing was nothing more than a disagreeable dream, I made no inquiries about the dog and never learned even that it was missing until that Sunday night, when my little girl, who was in the habit of feeding it, told me so. At breakfast-time, I may add, nobody knew that it was gone, as it had been seen late on the previous evening. Then I remembered my dream, and the following day inquiries were set on foot.

To be brief, on the morning of Thursday, the 14th, my servant, Charles Bedingfield, and I discovered the body of the dog floating in the Waveney against a weir about a mile and a quarter away.

On Friday, the 15th, I was going into Bungay when at the level crossing on the Bungay road I was hailed by two plate-layers, who are named respectively George Arterton and Harry Alger. These men informed me that the dog had been killed by a train, and took me on a trolly down to a certain open-work bridge which crosses the water between Ditchingham and Bungay, where they showed me evidence of its death. This is the sum of their evidence:

It appears that about 7 o'clock upon the Monday morning, very shortly after the first train had passed, in the course of his duties Harry Alger was on the bridge, where he found a dog's collar torn off and broken by the engine (since produced and positively identified as that worn by Bob), coagulated blood, and bits of flesh, of which remnants he cleaned the rails. On search also I personally found portions of black hair from the coat of a dog.

On the Monday afternoon and subsequently his mate saw the body of the dog floating in the water beneath the bridge, whence it drifted down to the weir, it having risen with the natural expansion of gases, such as, in this hot weather, might be expected to occur within about forty hours of death. It would seem that the animal must have been killed by an excursion train that left Ditchingham at 10.25 on Saturday night, returning empty from Harleston a little after 11 o'clock. This was the last train which ran that night. No trains run on Sunday, and it is practically certain that it cannot have been killed on the

Monday morning, for then the blood would have been still fluid. Further, if it was living, the dog would almost certainly have come home during Sunday, and its body would not have risen so quickly from the bottom of the river, or presented the appearance it did on Thursday morning.

From traces left upon the piers of the bridge it appears that the animal was knocked or carried along some yards by the train and fell into the brink of the water where reeds grow. Here, if it were still living – and, although the veterinary thinks that death was practically instantaneous, its life may perhaps have lingered for a few minutes – it must have suffocated and sunk, undergoing, I imagine, much the same sensations as I did in my dream, and in very similar surroundings to those that I saw therein – namely, amongst a scrubby growth at the edge of water.

Both in a judicial and a private capacity I have been accustomed all my life to the investigation of evidence, and, if we may put aside our familiar friend 'the long arm of coincidence', which in this case would surely be strained to dislocation, I confess that what is available upon this matter forced me to the following conclusions.

The dog Bob, between whom and myself there existed a mutual attachment, either at the moment of his death, if his existence can conceivably have been prolonged till after one in the morning, or, as seems more probable, about three hours after that event, *did* succeed in calling my attention to its actual or recent plight by placing whatever portion of my being is capable of receiving such impulses when enchained by sleep, into its own terrible position. That subsequently, as that chain of sleep was being broken by the voice of my wife calling me back to a normal condition of our human existence, with some last despairing effort, while that indefinable part of me was being withdrawn from it (it will be remembered that in the dream I seemed to rise from the dog) it spoke to me, first trying to make use of my own tongue, and, failing therein, by some subtle means of communication whereof I have no knowledge, telling me that it was dying, for I saw no blood or wounds which would suggest this to my mind.

I recognise, further, that, if its dissolution took place at the moment when I dreamt, this communication must have been a form of telepathy which is now generally acknowledged to occur between human beings from time to time and under special circumstances, but which I have never heard of occurring between a human being and one of the lower animals. If, on the other hand, that dissolution happened, as I believe, over three hours previously – what am I to say? Then it would seem it must have been some non-bodily but surviving part of the life or the spirit of the dog which, so soon as my deep sleep gave it an opportunity, reproduced those things in my mind, as they had already occurred, I presume, to advise me of the manner of its end or to bid me farewell.

On the remarkable issues opened up by this occurrence I cannot venture to speak further than to say that, although it is dangerous to generalise from a particular instance however striking and well supported by evidence which is so rarely obtainable in such obscure cases, it does seem to suggest that there is a more intimate ghostly connection between all members of the animal world, including man, than has hitherto been believed, at any rate by Western peoples. That they may be, in short, all of them different manifestations of some central, informing life, though inhabiting the universe in such various forms.

The Mahatma and the Hare

I

The Mahatma

Everyone has seen a hare, either crouched or running in the fields, or hanging dead in a poulterer's shop, or lastly pathetic, even dreadful-looking and in this form almost indistinguishable from a skinned cat, on the domestic table. But not many people have met a Mahatma, at least to their knowledge. Not many people know even who or what a Mahatma is. The majority of those who chance to have heard the title are apt to confuse it with another, that of Mad Hatter.

This is even done of malice prepense (especially, for obvious reasons, if a hare is in any way concerned) in scorn, not in ignorance, by persons who are well acquainted with the real meaning of the word and even with its Sanscrit origin. The truth is that an incredulous Western world puts no faith in Mahatmas. To it a Mahatma is a kind of spiritual Mrs Harris, giving an address in Tibet at which no letters are delivered. Either, it says, there is no such person, or he is a fraudulent scamp with no greater occult powers — well, than a hare.

I confess that this view of Mahatmas is one that does not surprise me in the least. I never met, and I scarcely expect to meet, an individual entitled to set 'Mahatma' after his name. Certainly *I* have no right to do so, who only took that title on the spur of the moment when the Hare asked me how I was called, and now make use of it as a *nom-de-plume*. It is true there is Jorsen, by whose order, for it amounts to that, I publish this history. For aught I know Jorsen may be a Mahatma, but he does not in the least look the part.

Imagine a bluff person with a strong, hard face, piercing grey eyes, and very prominent, bushy eyebrows, of about fifty or

---

Longman's Magazine, October 1911

sixty years of age. Add a Scotch accent and a meerschaum pipe, which he smokes even when he is wearing a frock coat and a tall hat, and you have Jorsen. I believe that he lives somewhere in the country, is well off, and practises gardening. If so he has never asked me to his place, and I only meet him when he comes to Town, as I understand, to visit flower-shows.

Then I always meet him because he orders me to do so, not by letter or by word of mouth but in quite a different way. Suddenly I receive an impression in my mind that I am to go to a certain place at a certain hour, and that there I shall find Jorsen. I do go, sometimes to an hotel, sometimes to a lodging, sometimes to a railway station or to the corner of a particular street, and there I do find Jorsen smoking his big meerschaum pipe. We shake hands and he explains why he has sent for me, after which we talk of various things. Never mind what they are, for that would be telling Jorsen's secrets as well as my own, which I must not do.

It may be asked how I came to know Jorsen. Well, in a strange way. Nearly thirty years ago a dreadful thing happened to me. I was married and, although still young, a person of some mark in literature. Indeed even now one or two of the books which I wrote are read and remembered, although it is supposed that their author has long left the world.

The thing which happened was that my wife and our daughter were coming over from the Channel Islands, where they had been on a visit (she was a Jersey woman), and, and — well, the ship was lost, that's all. The shock broke my heart, in such a way that it has never been mended again, but unfortunately did not kill me.

Afterwards I took to drink and sank, as drunkards do. Then the river began to draw me. I had a lodging in a poor street at Chelsea, and I could hear the river calling me at night, and — I wished to die as the others had died. At last I yielded, for the drink had rotted out all my moral sense. About one o'clock of a wild, winter morning I went to a bridge I knew where in those days policemen rarely came, and listened to that call of the water.

'Come!' it seemed to say. 'This world is the real hell, ending in an eternal naught. The dreams of a life beyond and of reunion there are but a demon's mocking breathed into the mortal heart, lest by its universal suicide mankind should rob him of his torture-pit. There is no truth in all your father taught you' (he was a clergyman and rather eminent in his profession), 'there is no hope for man, there is nothing he can win except the deep happiness of sleep. Come and sleep.'

Such were the arguments of that Voice of the river, the old, familiar arguments of desolation and despair. I leant over the parapet; in another moment I should have been gone, when I became aware that someone was standing near to me. I did not see the person because it was too dark. I did not hear him because of the raving of the wind. But I knew that he was there. So I waited until the moon shone out for a while between the edges of two ragged clouds, the shapes of which I can see to this hour. It showed me Jorsen, looking just as he does today, for he never seems to change – Jorsen, on whom, to my knowledge, I had not set eyes before.

'Even a year ago,' he said, in his strong, rough voice, 'you would not have allowed your mind to be convinced by such arguments as those which you have just heard in the Voice of the river. That is one of the worst sides of drink; it decays the reason as it does the body. You must have noticed it yourself.'

I replied that I had, for I was surprised into acquiescence. Then I grew defiant and asked him what he knew of the arguments which were or were not influencing me. To my surprise – no, that is not the word – to my bewilderment, he repeated them to me one by one just as they had arisen a few minutes before in my heart. Moreover, he told me what I had been about to do, and why I was about to do it.

'You know me and my story,' I muttered at last.

'No,' he answered, 'at least not more than I know that of many men with whom I chance to be in touch. That is, I have not met you for nearly eleven hundred years. A thousand and eighty-six, to be correct. I was a blind priest then and you were the captain of Irene's guard.'

At this news I burst out laughing and the laugh did me good.

'I did not know I was so old,' I said.

'Do you call that old?' answered Jorsen. 'Why, the first time that we had anything to do with each other, so far as I can learn, that is, was over eight thousand years ago, in Egypt before the beginning of recorded history.'

'I thought that I was mad, but you are madder,' I said.

'Doubtless. Well, I am so mad that I managed to be here in time to save you from suicide, as once in the past you saved me, for thus things come round. But your rooms are near, are they not? Let us go there and talk. This place is cold and the river is always calling.'

That was how I came to know Jorsen, whom I believe to be one of the greatest men alive. On this particular night that I have described he told me many things, and since then he has taught me much, me and a few others. But whether he is what is called a Mahatma I am sure I do not know. He has never claimed such a rank in my hearing, or indeed to be anything more than a man who has succeeded in winning a knowledge of his own powers out of the depths of the dark that lies behind us. Of course I mean out of his past in other incarnations long before he was Jorsen. Moreover, by degrees, as I grew fit to bear the light, he showed me something of my own, and of how the two were intertwined.

But all these things are secrets of which I have perhaps no right to speak at present. It is enough to say that Jorsen changed the current of my life on that night when he saved me from death.

For instance, from that day onwards to the present time I have never touched the drink which so nearly ruined me. Also the darkness has rolled away, and with it every doubt and fear; I know the truth, and for that truth I live. Considered from certain aspects such knowledge, I admit, is not altogether desirable. Thus it has deprived me of my interest in earthly things. Ambition has left me altogether; for years I have had no wish to succeed in the profession which I adopted in my youth, or in any other. Indeed I doubt whether the elements of worldly success still remain in me; whether they are not entirely burnt away by that fire of wisdom in which I have bathed. How can we strive to win a crown we have no longer any desire to wear? Now I desire other crowns and at times I wear them, if only for a little while. My spirit grows and grows. It is dragging at its strings.

What am I to look at? A small, white-haired man with a thin and rather plaintive face in which are set two large, dark eyes that continually seem to soften and develop. That is my picture. And what am I in the world? I will tell you. On certain days of the week I employ myself in editing a trade journal that has to do with haberdashery. On another day I act as auctioneer to a firm which imports and sells cheap Italian statuary; modern, very modern copies of the antique, florid marble vases, and so forth. Some of you who read may have passed such marts in different parts of the city, or even have dropped in and purchased a bust or a tazza for a surprisingly small sum. Perhaps I knocked it down to you, only too pleased to find a *bona fide* bidder amongst my company.

As for the rest of my time – well, I employ it in doing what good I can among the poor and those who need comfort or who are bereaved, especially among those who are bereaved, for to such I am sometimes able to bring the breath of hope that blows from another shore.

Occasionally also I amuse myself in my own fashion. Thus sure knowledge has come to me about certain epochs in the past in which I lived in other shapes, and I study those epochs, hoping that one day I may find time to write of them and of the parts I played in them. Some of these parts are really extremely interesting, especially as I am of course able to contrast them with our modern modes of thought and action.

They do not all come back to me with equal clearness, the earlier lives being, as one might expect, the more difficult to recover and the comparatively recent ones the easiest. Also they seem to range over a vast stretch of time, back indeed to the days of primeval, prehistoric man. In short, I think the subconscious in some ways resembles the conscious and natural memory; that which is very far off to it grows dim and blurred, that which is comparatively close remains clear and sharp, although of course this rule is not invariable. Moreover there is foresight as well as memory. At least from time to time I seem to come in touch with future events and states of society in which I shall have my share.

I believe some thinkers hold a theory that such conditions as those of past, present, and future do not in fact exist; that everything already is, standing like a completed column between earth and heaven; that the sum is added up, the equation worked out. At times I am tempted to believe in the truth of this proposition. But if it be true, of course it remains difficult to obtain a clear view of other parts of the column than that in which we happen to find ourselves objectively conscious at any given period, and needless to say impossible to see it from base to capital.

However this may be, no individual entity pervades all the column. There are great sections of it with which that entity has nothing to do, although it always seems to appear again above. I suppose that those sections which are empty of an individual and his atmosphere represent the intervals between his lives which he spends in sleep, or in states of existence with which this world is not concerned, but of such gulfs of oblivion and states of being I know nothing.

To take a single instance of what I do know: once this spirit of mine, that now by the workings of destiny for a little while occupies the body of a fourth-rate auctioneer, and of the editor of a trade journal, dwelt in that of a Pharaoh of Egypt — never mind which Pharaoh. Yes, although you may laugh and think me mad to say it, for me the legions fought and thundered; to me the peoples bowed and the secret sanctuaries were opened that I and I alone might commune with the gods; I who in the flesh and after it myself was worshipped as a god.

Well, of this forgotten Royalty of whom little is known save what a few inscriptions have to tell, there remains a portrait statue in the British Museum. Sometimes I go to look at that statue and try to recall exactly under what circumstances I caused it to be shaped, puzzling out the story bit by bit.

Not long ago I stood thus absorbed and did not notice that the hour of the closing of the great gallery had come. Still I stood and gazed and dreamt till the policeman on duty, seeing and suspecting me, came up and roughly ordered me to be gone.

The man's tone angered me. I laid my hand on the foot of the statue, for it had just come back to me that it was a 'Ka' image, a sacred thing, any Egyptologist will know what I mean, which for ages had sat in a chamber of my tomb. Then the Ka that clings to it eternally awoke at my touch and knew me, or so I suppose. At least I felt myself change. A new strength came into me; my shape, battered in this world's storms, put on something of its ancient dignity; my eyes grew royal. I looked at that man as Pharaoh may have looked at one who had done him insult. He saw the change and trembled — yes, trembled. I believe he thought I was some imperial ghost that the shadows of evening had caused him to mistake for man; at any rate he gasped out:

'I beg your pardon, I was only obeying orders. I hope your Majesty won't hurt me. Now I think of it I have been told that things come out of these old statues in the night.'

Then turning he ran, literally ran, where to I am sure I do not know, probably to seek the fellowship of some other policeman. In due course I followed, and, lifting the bar at the end of the hall, departed without further question asked. Afterwards I was very glad to think that I had done the man no injury. At the moment I knew that I could hurt him if I would, and what is more I had the desire to do so. It came to me, I suppose, with that breath of the past when I was so great and absolute. Perhaps I, or that part of me then incarnate, was a tyrant in those days, and this is why now I must be so humble. Fate is turning my pride to its hammer and beating it out of me.

For thus in the long history of the soul it serves all our vices.

II

The Great White Road

Now, as I have hinted, under the teaching of Jorsen, who saved me from degradation and self-murder, yes, and helped me with money until once again I could earn a livelihood, I have acquired certain knowledge and wisdom of a sort that are not common. That is, Jorsen taught me the elements of these things; he set my feet upon the path which thenceforward, having the sight, I have been able to follow for myself. How I followed it does not matter, nor could I teach others if I would.

I am no member of any mystic brotherhood, and, as I have explained, no Mahatma, although I have called myself thus for present purposes because the name is a convenient cloak. I repeat that I am ignorant if there are such people as Mahatmas, though if so I think Jorsen must be one of them. Still he never told me this. What he has told me is that every individual spirit must work out its own destiny quite independently of others. Indeed, being rather fond of fine phrases, he has sometimes spoken to me of, or rather, insisted upon what he calls 'the lonesome splendour of the human soul,' which it is our business to perfect through various lives till it reaches a glory and a might that I can scarcely appreciate and am certainly unable to describe.

To tell the truth, the thought of this 'lonesome splendour' to which it seems some of us may attain, alarms me. I have had enough of being lonesome, and I do not ask for any particular splendour. My only ambitions are to find those whom I have lost, and in whatever life I live to be of use to others. However, as I gather that the exalted condition to which Jorsen alludes is thousands of ages off for any of us, and may after all mean something quite different to what it seems to mean, the thought of it does not trouble me over much. Meanwhile what I seek is the vision of those I love.

Now I have this power. Occasionally when I am in deep sleep some part of me seems to leave my body and to be transported quite outside the world. It travels, as though I were already dead, to the Gates that all who live must pass, and there takes its stand, on the Great White Road, watching those who have been called speed by continually. Those upon the earth know nothing of that Road. Blinded by their pomps and vanities, they cannot see, they will not see it always growing towards the feet of every one of them. But I see and know. Of course you who read will say that this is but a dream of mine, and it may be. Still, if so, it is a very wonderful dream, and except for the change of the passing people, or rather of those who have been people, always very much the same.

There, straight as the way of the Spirit and broad as the breast of Death, is the Great White Road running I know not whence, up to those Gates that gleam like moonlight and are higher than the Alps. There beyond the Gates the radiant Presences move mysteriously. Thence at the appointed time the Voice cries and they are opened with a sound like to that of deepest thunder, or sometimes are burned away, while from the Glory that lies beyond flow the sweet-faced welcomers to greet those for whom they wait, bearing the cups from which they give to drink. I do not know what is in the cups, whether it be a draught of Lethe or some baptismal water of new birth, or both; but always the thirsting, world-worn soul appears to change, and then as it were to be lost in the Presence that gave the cup. At least they are lost to my sight. I see them no more.

Why do I watch those Gates, in truth or in dream, before my time? Oh! you can guess. That perchance I may behold those for whom my heart burns with a quenchless, eating fire. And once I beheld – not the mother but the child, my child, changed indeed, mysterious, wonderful, gleaming like a star, with eyes so deep that in their depths my humanity seemed to swoon.

She came forward; she knew me; she smiled and laid her finger on her lips. She shook her hair about her and in it vanished as in a cloud. Yet as she vanished a voice spoke in my heart, her voice, and the words it said were:

'Wait, our Beloved! Wait!'

Mark well. 'Our Beloved', not 'My Beloved'. So there are others by whom I am beloved, or at least one other, and I know well who that one must be.

After this dream, perhaps I had better call it a dream, I was ill for a long while, for the joy and the glory of it overpowered me and brought me near to the death I had always sought. But I recovered, for my hour is not yet. Moreover, for a long while as we reckon time, some years indeed, I obeyed the injunction and sought the Great White Road no more. At length the longing grew too strong for me and I returned thither, but never again did the vision come. Its word was spoken, its mission was fulfilled. Yet from time to time I, a mortal, seem to stand upon the borders of that immortal Road and watch the newly dead who travel it towards the glorious Gates.

Once or twice there have been among them people whom I had known. As these pass me I appear to have the power of looking into their hearts, and there I read strange things. Sometimes they are beautiful things and sometimes ugly things. Thus I have learned that those I thought bad were really good in the main, for who can claim to be quite good? And on the other hand that those I believed to be as honest as the day – well, had their faults.

To take an example which I quote because it is so absurd. The rooms I live in were owned by a prim old woman who for more than twenty years was my landlady. She and I were great friends, indeed she tended me like a mother, and when I was so ill nursed me as perhaps few mothers would have done. Yet while I was watching on the Road suddenly she came by, and with horror I saw that during all those years she had been robbing me, taking, I am sorry to say, many things, in money, trinkets, and food. Often I had discussed with her where these articles could possibly have gone, till finally suspicion settled upon the man who cleaned the windows. Yes, and worst of all, he was prosecuted, and I gave evidence against him, or rather strengthened her evidence, on faith of which the magistrate sent him to prison for a month.

'Oh! Mrs Smithers,' I said to her, 'how *could* you do it, Mrs Smithers?'

She stopped and looked about her terrified, so that my heart smote me and I added in haste, 'Don't be frightened, Mrs Smithers; I forgive you.'

'I can't see you, sir,' she exclaimed, or so I dreamed, 'but there! I always knew you would.'

'Yes, Mrs Smithers,' I replied; 'but how about the window-cleaner who went to jail and lost his situation?'

Then she passed on or was drawn away without making any answer.

Now comes the odd part of the story. When I woke up on the following morning in my rooms, it was to be informed by the frightened maid-of-all-work that Mrs Smithers had been found dead in her bed. Moreover, a few days later I learned from a lawyer that she had made a will leaving me everything she possessed, including the lease of her house and nearly £1000, for she had been a saving old person during all her long life.

Well, I sought out that window-cleaner and compensated him handsomely, saying that I had found I was mistaken in the evidence I gave against him. The rest of the property I kept, and I hope that it was not wrong of me to do so. It will be remembered that some of it was already my own, temporarily diverted into another channel, and for the rest I have so many to help. To be frank I do not spend much upon myself.

III

The Hare

Now I have done with myself, or rather with my own insignificant present history, and come to that of the Hare. It impressed me a good deal at the time, which is not long ago, so much indeed that I communicated the facts to Jorsen. He ordered me to publish them, and what Jorsen orders must be done. I don't know why this should be, but it is so. He has authority of a sort that I am unable to define.

One night after the usual aspirations and concentration of mind, which by the way are not always successful, I passed into what occultists call spirit, and others a state of dream. At any rate I found myself upon the borders of the Great White Road, as near to the mighty Gates as I am ever allowed to come. How far that may be away I cannot tell. Perhaps it is but a few yards and perhaps it is the width of this great world, for in that place which my spirit visits time and distance do not exist. There all things are new and strange, not to be reckoned by our measures. There the sight is not our sight nor the hearing our hearing. I repeat that all things are different, but that difference I cannot describe, and if I could it would prove past comprehension.

There I sat by the borders of the Great White Road, my eyes fixed upon the Gates above which the towers mount for miles on miles, outlined against an encircling gloom with the radiance of the world beyond the worlds. Four-square they stand, those towers, and fourfold are the roads that run to them, and fourfold the gates that open to the denizens of other earths. But of these I have no knowledge beyond the fact that it is so in my visions.

I sat upon the borders of the Road, my eyes fixed in hope upon the Gates, though well I knew that the hope would never be fulfilled, and watched the dead go by.

They were many that night. Some plague was working in the East and unchaining thousands. The folk that it loosed were strange to me who in this particular life have seldom left England, and I studied them with curiosity; high-featured, dark-hued people with a patient air. The knowledge which I have told me that one and all they were very ancient souls who often and often had walked this Road before, and therefore, although as yet they did not know it, were well accustomed to the journey. No, I am wrong, for here and there an individual did know. Indeed one deep-eyed, wistful little woman, who carried a baby in her arms, stopped for a moment and spoke to me.

'The others cannot see you as I do,' she said. 'Priest of the Queen of queens, I know you well; hand in hand we climbed by the seven stairways to the altars of the moon.'

'Who is the Queen of queens?' I asked.

'Have you forgotten her of the hundred names whose veils we lifted one by one; her whose breast was beauty and whose eyes were truth? In a day to come you will remember. Farewell till we walk this Road no more.'

'Stay — when did we meet?'

'When our souls were young,' she answered, and faded from my ken like a shadow from the sea.

After the Easterns came many others from all parts of the earth. Then suddenly appeared a company of about six hundred folk of every age and English in their looks. They were not so calm as are the majority of those who make this journey. When I read the papers a few days later I understood why. A great passenger ship had sunk suddenly in mid ocean and they were all cut off, unprepared.

When, followed by a few stragglers, these had passed and gathered themselves in the red shadow beneath the gateway towers waiting for the summons, an unusual thing occurred. For a few moments the Road was left quite empty. After that last great stroke Death seemed to be resting on his laurels. When thus unpeopled it looked a very vast place like to a huge arched causeway, bordered on either side by blackness, but itself gleaming with a curious phosphorescence such as once or twice I have seen in the waters of a summer sea at night.

Presently in the very centre of this illuminated desolation, whilst it was as yet far away, something caught my eye, something so strange to the place, so utterly unfamiliar that I watched it earnestly, wondering what it might be. Nearer and nearer it came, with curious, uncertain hops; yes, a little brown object that hopped.

'Well,' I said to myself, 'if I were not where I am I should say that yonder thing was a hare. Only what would a hare be doing on the Great White Road? How could a hare tread the pathway of eternal souls? I must be mistaken.'

So I reflected whilst still the thing hopped on, until I became certain that either I suffered from delusions, or that it was a hare; indeed a particularly fine hare, much such a one as a friend of my old landlady, Mrs Smithers, had once sent her as a Christmas present from Norfolk, which hare I ate.

A few more hops brought it opposite to my post of observation. Here it halted as though it seemed to see me. At any rate it sat up in the alert fashion that hares have, its forepaws hanging absurdly in front of it, with one ear, on which there was a grey blotch, cocked and one dragging, and sniffed with its funny little nostrils. Then it began to talk to me. I do not mean that it really talked, but the thoughts which were in its mind were flashed on to my mind so that I understood perfectly, yes, and could answer them in the same fashion. It said, or thought, thus:

'You are real. You are a man who yet lives beneath the sun, though how you came here I do not know. I hate men, all hares do, for men are cruel to them. Still it is a comfort in this strange place to see something one has seen before and to be able to talk even to a man, which I could never do until the change came, the dreadful change – I mean because of the way of it,' and it seemed to shiver. 'May I ask you some questions?'

'Certainly,' I said or rather thought back.

'You are sure that they won't make you angry so that you hurt me?'

'I can't hurt you, even if I wished to do so. You are not a hare any longer, if you ever were one, but only the shadow of a hare.'

'Ah! I thought as much, and that's a good thing anyhow. Tell me, Man, have you ever been torn to pieces by dogs?'

'Good gracious! no.'

'Or coursed, or hunted, or caught in a trap, or shot all over your back, or twisted up in nets and choked in snares? Or have you swum out to sea to die more easily, or seen your mate and mother and father killed?'

'No, no. Please stop, Hare; your questions are very unpleasant.'

'Not half so unpleasant as the things are themselves, I can assure you, Man. I will tell you my story if you like; then you can judge for yourself. But first, if you will, do you tell me why I am here. Have you seen more hares about this place?'

'Never, nor any other animals. No, I am wrong, once I saw a dog.'

The Hare looked about it anxiously.

'A dog. How horrible! What was it doing? Hunting? If there are no hares here what could it be hunting? A rabbit, or a pheasant with a broken wing, or perhaps a fox? I should not mind so much if it were a fox. I hate foxes; they catch young hares when they are asleep and eat them.'

'None of these things. I was told that it belonged to a little girl who died. That broke its heart, so that it died also when they shut her up in a box. Therefore it was allowed to accompany her here because it had loved so much. Indeed I saw them together, both very happy, and together they went through those gates.'

'If dogs love little girls why don't they love hares, at least as anything likes to be loved, for the dog didn't want to eat the little girl, did it? I see you can't answer me. Now would you like me to tell you my story? Something inside of me is saying that I am to do so if you will listen; also that there is plenty of time, for I am not wanted at present, and when I am I can run to those gates much quicker than you could.'

'I should like it very much, Hare. Once a prophet heard an ass speak in order to warn him. But since then, except very, very rarely in dreams, no creature has talked to a man, so far as I know. Perhaps you wish to warn me about something, or others through me, as the ass warned Balaam.'

'Who is Balaam? I never heard of Balaam. He wasn't the man who fetches dead pheasants in the donkey-cart, was he? If so, I've seen him make the ass talk — with a thick stick. No? Well, never mind, I daresay I should not understand about him if you told me. Now for my story.'

Then the Hare sat itself down, planting its forepaws firmly in front of it, as these animals do when they are on the watch, looked up at me and began to pour the contents of its mind into mine.

I was born, it said, or rather told me by thought transference, in a field of growing corn near to a big wood. At least I suppose I was born there, though the first thing I remember is playing about in the wheat with two other little ones of my own size, a brother and a sister that were born with me. It was at night, for a great, round, shining thing which I now know was the moon, hung in the sky above us. We gambolled together and were very happy, till presently my mother came — I remember how big she looked — and cuffed me with her paw because I had led the others away from the place where she had told us to stop, and given her a great hunt to find us. That is the first thing I remember about my mother. Afterwards she seemed sorry because she had hurt me, and nursed us all three, letting me have the most milk. My mother always loved me the best of us, because I was such a fine leveret, with a pretty grey patch on my left ear. Just as I had finished drinking another hare came who was my father. He was very large, with a glossy coat and big shining eyes that always seemed to see everything, even when it was behind him.

He was frightened about something, and hustled my mother and us little ones out of the wheat-field into the big wood by which it is bordered. As we left the field I saw two tall creatures that afterwards I came to know were men. They were placing wire-netting round the field — you see I understand now what all these things were, although of course I did not at the time. The two ends of the wire-netting had nearly come together. There was only a little gap left through which we could run. Another young hare, or it may have been a rabbit, had got entangled in it, and one of the men was beating it to death with a stick. I remember that the sound of its screams made me feel cold down the back, for I had never heard anything like that before, and this was the first that I had seen of pain and death.

The other man saw us slipping through and ran at us with his stick. My mother went first and escaped him. Then came my sister, then I, then my brother. My father was last of all. The man hit with his stick and it came down thud along side of me, just touching my fur. He hit again and broke the foreleg of my brother. Still we all managed to get through into the wood, except my father who was behind.

'There's the old buck!' cried one of the men (I understand what he said now, though at the time it meant nothing to me). 'Knock him on the head!'

So leaving us alone they ran at him. But my father was much too quick for them. He rushed back into the corn and afterwards joined us in the wood, for he had seen wire before and knew how to escape it. Still he was terribly frightened and made us keep in the wood till the following evening, not even allowing my mother to go to her form in the rough pasture on its other side and lie up there.

Also we were in trouble because my brother's forepaw was broken. It gave him a great deal of pain, so that he could not rest or sleep. After a while, however, it mended up in a fashion, but he was never able to run as fast as we could, nor did he grow so big. In the end the mother fox killed him, as I shall tell.

My mother asked my father what the men with the sticks were doing – for, you know, many animals can talk to each other in their own way, even if they are of different kinds. He told her that they were protecting the wheat to prevent us from eating it, to which she answered angrily that hares must live somehow, especially when they had young ones to nurse. My father replied that men did not seem to think so, and perhaps they had young ones also. I see now that my father was a philosophic hare.

'But are you tired of my story?'

'Not at all,' I answered; 'go on, please. It is very interesting to hear things described from the animal's point of view, especially when that animal has grown wise and learned to understand.'

'Ah,' answered the Hare. 'I see what you mean. And it is odd, but I do understand. All has become clear to me. I don't know what happened when I died, but there came a change, and I knew that I who was but a beast always have been and still am a necessary part of everything as much as you are, though more helpless and humble. Yes, I am as ancient and as far-reaching as yourself, but how I began and how I shall end is dark to me. Well, I will go on with my story.'

It must have been a moon or so later, after my mother had given up nursing me, that I went to lie out by myself. There was a big house on the hillside overlooking the sea, and near to it were gardens surrounded by a wall. Also outside of this wall was another patch of garden where cabbages grew. I found a way to those cabbages and kept it secret, for I was greedy and wanted them all for myself. I used to creep in at night and eat them, also some flowers with spiky leaves that grew round them which had a very fine flavour. Then after the dawn came I went to a form which I had made under a furze bush on the slope that ran down to the sea, and slept there.

One day I was awakened by something white, hard, and round which rolled gently and stopped still quite close to me. It was not alive, although it had a queer smell, and I wondered why it moved at all. Presently I heard voices and there appeared a little man, and with him somebody who was not a man because it was differently dressed and spoke in a higher voice. I saw that they had sticks in their hands and thought of running away, then that it would be safer to lie quite close. They came up to me and the little man said:

'There's the ball; pick it up, Ella, the lie is too bad.'

She, for now I know it was what is called a girl, stooped to obey and saw my back.

'Tom,' she said in a whisper, 'here's a young hare on its form.'

'Get out of the light,' he answered, 'and I'll kill it,' and he lifted the stick he held, which had a twisted iron end.

'No,' she said, 'catch it alive; I want a hare to be a friend to my rabbit, which has lost all its little ones.'

'Lost them? Eaten them, you mean, because you would always go and stare at it,' said Tom. 'Where's the leveret? Oh! I see. Now, look out!'

A moment later and I was in darkness. Tom had thrown himself upon the top of me and was grabbing at me with his hands. I nearly got away, but as my head poked up under his arm the girl caught hold of it.

'Oh! it's scratching,' she cried, as indeed I was with all my might. 'Hold it, Tom, hold it!'

'Hold it yourself,' said Tom, 'my face is full of furze prickles.' So she held and presently he helped her, till in the end I was tied up in a pocket-handkerchief and carried I knew not whither. Indeed I was almost mad with fear.

When I came to myself I found that I was within a kind of wire run which smelt foully, as though hundreds of things had lived in it for years. There was a hutch at the end of the run in which sat an enormous she-rabbit, quite as big as my mother, a fierce-looking brute with long yellow teeth. I was afraid of that rabbit and got as far from it as I could. Presently it hopped out and looked at me.

'What are you doing here?' it asked. 'Can't you talk? Well, it doesn't matter. If I get hungry I'll eat you. Do you hear that? I'll eat you, as I did all the others,' and it showed its big yellow teeth and hopped back into the hutch.

After that Tom and the girl came and gave us plenty of food which the big rabbit ate, for I could touch nothing. For two days they came, and then I think they forgot all about us. I grew very hungry, and at night filled myself with some of the remaining food, such as stale cabbage leaves. By next morning all was gone, and the big rabbit grew hungry also. All that day it hopped about sniffing at me and showing its yellow teeth.

'I shall eat you tonight,' it said.

I ran round and round the pen in terror, till at last I found a place where rats had been working under the wire, almost big enough for me to squeeze through, but not quite.

The sun went down and the big she-rabbit came out.

'Now I am going to eat you,' it said, 'as I ate all the others. I am hungry, very hungry,' and it prodded me about with its nose and rolled me over.

At last with a little squeal it drove its big yellow teeth into me behind. Oh! how they hurt! I was near the rat-hole. I rushed at it, scrabbling and wriggling. The big rabbit pounced on me with its forefeet, trying to hold me, but too late, for I was through, leaving some of my fur behind me. I ran, how I ran! without stopping, till at length I found my mother in the rough pasture by the wood and told her everything.

'Ah!' she said, 'that's what comes of greediness and of trying to be too clever. Now, perhaps, you will learn to stop at home.'

So I did for a long while.

The summer went by without anything particular happening, except that my brother with the lame foot was eaten by the mother fox. That great red beast was always prowling about, and at night surprised us in a field near the wood where we were feeding on some beautiful turnips. The rest of us got away, but my brother, being lame, was not quick enough. The fox caught him, and I heard her sharp white teeth crunch into his bones. The sound made me quite sick, and my mother was very sad afterwards. She complained to my father of the cruelty of foxes, but he, who, as I have said, was a philosopher, answered her almost in her own words.

'Foxes must live, and this one has young to feed, and therefore is always hungry. There are three of them in a hole at the top of the wood,' he remarked. 'Also our son was lame and would certainly have been caught when the hunting begins.'

'What's the hunting?' I asked.

'Never mind,' said my father sharply.

'No doubt you'll find out in time, that is if you live through the shooting.'

'What's the shooting?' I began, but my father cuffed me over the head and I was silent.

I may tell you that my mother soon got over the loss of my brother, for just about that time she had four new little ones, after which neither she nor my father seemed to think any more about us. My sister and I hated those little ones. We two alone remembered my brother, and sometimes wondered whether he were quite gone or would one day come back. The fox, I am glad to say, got caught in a trap. At least I am not glad now – I was glad because, you see, I was so much afraid of her.

IV

The Shooting

I was quite close by one morning when the fox, who was smelling about after me, I suppose because it had liked my brother so much, got caught in the big trap which was covered over artfully with earth and baited with some stuff which stank horribly. I remember it looked very like my own hind-legs. The fox, not being able to find me, went to this filth and tried to eat it.

Then suddenly there was a dreadful fuss. The fox yelped and flew into the air. I saw that a great black thing was fast on its forepaw. How that fox did jump and roll! It was quite wonderful to see her. She looked like a great yellow ball, except for a lot of white marks about the head, which were her teeth. But the trap would not come away, because it was tied to a root with a chain.

At last the fox grew tired and, lying down, began to think, licking its paw as it thought and making a kind of moaning noise. Next it commenced gnawing at the root after trying the chain and finding that its teeth would not go into it. While it was doing this I heard the sound of a man somewhere in the wood. So did the fox, and oh! it looked so frightened. It lay down panting, its tongue hanging out and its ears pressed back against its head, and whisked its big tail from side to side. Then it began to gnaw again, but this time at its own leg. It wanted to bite it off and so get away. I thought this very brave of the fox, and though I hated it because it had eaten my brother and tried to eat me, I felt quite sorry.

It was about half through its leg when the man came. I remember that he had a cat with a little red collar on its neck, and an owl in his hand, both of them dead, for he was Giles, the head-keeper, going round his traps. He was a tall man with sandy whiskers and a rough voice, and he carried a single-barrelled gun under his arm.

You see, now that I am dead I know the use of these things, just as I understand all that was said, though of course at the time it had no meaning for me. Still I find that I have forgotten nothing, not one word from the beginning of my life to the end.

The keeper, who was on his way to the place where he nailed the creatures he did not like by dozens upon poles, looked down and saw the fox. 'Oh! my beauty,' he said, 'so I have got you at last. Don't you think yourself clever trying to bite off that leg. You'd have done it too, only I came along just in time. Well, good night, old girl, you won't have no more of my pheasants.'

Then he lifted the gun. There was a most dreadful noise and the fox rolled over and lay still.

'There you are, all neat and tidy, my dear,' said the keeper. 'Now I must just tuck you away in the hollow tree before old Grampus sneaks round and sees you, for if he should it will be almost as much as my place is worth.'

Next he set his foot on the trap and, opening it, took hold of the fox by the forelegs to carry it off. The cat and the owl he stuffed away into a great pocket in his coat.

'Jemima! don't you wholly stink,' he said, then gave a most awful yell.

The fox wasn't quite dead after all, it was only shamming dead. At any rate it got Giles's hand in its mouth and made its teeth meet through the flesh.

Now the keeper began to jump about just as the fox had done when it set its paw in the trap, shouting and saying all sorts of things that somehow I don't think I ought to repeat here. Round and round he went with the fox hanging to his hand, like hares do when they dance together, for he couldn't get it off anyhow. At last he tumbled down into a pool of mud and water, and when he got up again all wet through I saw that the fox was really dead. But it had died biting, and now I know that this pleased it very much.

It was just then that the man whom the keeper had called Grampus came up. He was a big, fat man with a very red face, who made a kind of blowing noise when he walked fast. I know now that he was the lord of all the other men about that place, that he lived in the house which looked over the sea, and that the boy and girl who put me in with the yellow-toothed rabbit were his children. He was what the farmers called 'a first-rate all-round sportsman,' which means, my friend . . .

'But what is your name?'

'Oh! Mahatma,' I answered at hazard.

Which means, my friend Mahatma, that he spent most of the year in killing the lower animals such as me. Yes, he spent quite eight months out of the twelve in killing us one way and another, for when there was no more killing to be done in his own country, he would travel to others and kill there. He would even kill pigeons from a trap, or young rooks just out of their nests, or rats in a stack, or sparrows among ivy, rather than not kill anything. I've heard Giles say so to the under-keeper and call him 'a regular slaughterer' and 'a true-blood Englishman'.

Yet, my friend Mahatma, I say in the light of the truth which has come to me, that according to his knowledge Grampus was a good man. Thus, what little time he had to spare from sport he passed in helping his brother men by sending them to prison. Although of course he never worked or earned anything, he was very rich, because money flowed to him from other people who had been very rich, but who at last were forced to travel this Road and could not bring it with them. If they could have brought it, I am sure that Grampus would never have got any. However, he did get it, and he aided a great many people with that part of it which he found he could not spend upon himself. He was a very good man, only he liked killing us lower creatures, whom he bred up with his money to be killed.

'Go on with your story, Hare,' I said; 'when I see this Red-faced Man I will judge of him for myself. Probably you are prejudiced about him.'

'I daresay I am,' answered the Hare, rubbing its nose; 'but please observe that I am not speaking unkindly of Grampus, although before I have done you may think that I might have reason to do so. However, you will be able to form your own opinion when he comes here, which I am sure he does not mean to do for many, many years. The world is much too comfortable for him. He does not wish to leave it.'

'Still he may be obliged to do so, Hare.'

'Oh! no, people like that áre never obliged to do anything they do not like. It is only poor things such as you and I, Mahatma, which must suffer. I can see that you have had a great deal to bear, and so have I, for we were born to suffering as the Red-faced Man was born to happiness.'

'Go on with your story, Hare,' I repeated. 'You are becoming metaphysical and therefore dull. The time is short and I want to hear what happened.'

'Quite so, Mahatma.' Well, Grampus came up breathing very heavily and looking very red in the face. He held his hat in one hand and a large crooked stick in the other, and even the top of his head, on which no hair grew, was red, for he had been running.

'What the deuce is the matter?' he puffed. 'Oh! it is you, Giles, is it? What are you doing, sir, looking like that, all covered with blood and mud? Has a poacher shot you, or what?'

'No, Squire,' answered Giles humbly, touching his hat. 'I have shot a poacher, that's all, and it has given me what for,' and he lifted the body of the fox from the water.

'A fox,' said Grampus, 'a fox! Do you mean to say, Giles, that you have dared to shoot a fox, and a vixen with a litter too? How often have I told you that, although I keep harriers and not foxhounds, you are never to touch a fox. You will get me into trouble with all my neighbours. I give you a month's notice. You will leave on this day month.'

'Very well, Squire,' said Giles, 'I'll leave, and I hope you'll find some one to serve you better. Meanwhile I didn't shoot the dratted fox. At least I only shot her after she'd gone and got herself into a trap which I had set for that there Rectory dog what you told me to make off with on the quiet, so that the young lady might never know what become of it and cry and make a fuss as she did about the last. Then seeing that she was finshed, with her leg half chewed off, I shot her, or rather I didn't shoot her as well as I should, for the beggar gave a twist as I fired, and now she's bit me right through the hand. I only hopes you won't

have to pay my widow for it, Squire, under the Act, as foxes'
bites is uncommon poisonous, especially when they've been
a-eating of rotten rabbit.'

'Dear me!' said the Red-faced Man softening, 'dear me, the
beast does seem to have bitten you very badly. You must go and
be cauterised with a red-hot iron. It is painful but the best thing
to do. Meanwhile, suck it, Giles, suck it! I daresay that will draw
out the poison, and if it doesn't, thank my stars! I am insured.
Look here, a minute or two can make no difference, for if you
are poisoned, you are poisoned. Where can we put this brute? I
wouldn't have it seen for ten pounds.'

'There's an old pollard, Squire, about five yards away down
near the fence, which is hollow and handy,' said Giles.

'Quite so,' he answered, 'I know it well. You bring the —
dog, Giles. Remember, it was a dog, not a fox.'

Then they went to the pollard, and as Giles's hand was hurt
the Red-faced Man climbed up it, though Giles tried to prevent
him.

'Now then, Giles,' he said, 'give me the fox — I mean the
dog, and I will drop it down. Great Heavens! how this tree stinks.
Has there been an earth here?'

'Not as I knows of, Squire,' said Giles sullenly.

Grampus stretched his hand down into the hollow of the
pollard and dragged up a rotting fox by its tail.

'Giles,' he said, 'you have been killing more foxes and
hiding them in this tree. Giles, I dismiss you at once and without
a month's wages.'

'All right, sir,' said Giles, 'I'll go, and I prays you'll find
some one what will keep your hares which you must have, and
your pheasants which you must have, and your partridges which
you must have, without killing these varmints of foxes what eats
the lot.'

The Red-faced Man descended from the tree holding his
nose and looked at Giles. Giles sucked his bleeding hand and
looked at him.

'Foxes are very destructive animals,' said the Red-faced
Man to Giles, 'especially when one shoots and keeps harriers.'

'They are that, sir,' said Giles to the Red-faced Man, 'as
only those know what has to do with them.'

'Put the other in, Giles,' said the Red-faced Man, 'and
when you have time, throw some soil on to the top of the lot. This

place smells horrible. And look you here, Giles,' he added in a voice of thunder, 'if ever I find you killing a fox upon this property, you will be dismissed at once, as I have often told you before. Do you understand?'

'Yes, Squire, I understand,' answered Giles, 'and I'll see to the burying of them this same afternoon, if the pain in my hand will suffer it.'

'Very well,' said the Red-faced Man, 'that's done with – except the cubs. As you have killed the vixen you had better stink the cubs out of the earth. I daresay they are old enough to look after themselves – at any rate I hope so. And now, Giles, we must shoot some of these hares when we begin on the partridges next week. There are too many of them, the tenants are complaining, ungrateful beggars as they are, seeing that I keep them for their sport.'

At this point I thought that I had heard enough, and slipped away when their backs were turned. For, friend Mahatma, I had just seen a fox shot, and now I knew what shooting meant.

About a week later I knew better still. It came about thus. By that time the turnips I have mentioned, those that grew in the big field, had swelled into fine, large bulbs with leafy tops. We used to eat them at nights, and in the daytime to lie up among them in our snug forms. 'You know, Mahatma, don't you, that a form is a little hollow which a hare makes in the ground just to fit itself? No hare likes to sleep in another hare's form. Do you understand?'

'Yes,' I answered, 'I understand. It would be like a man wearing another man's boots.'

'I don't know anything about boots, Mahatma, except that they are hard things with iron on them which kick one out of one's form if one sits too close.' Once that happened to me. Well, my form was under a particularly fine turnip that had some dead leaves beneath the green ones. I chose it because, like the brown earth, they just matched the colour of my back. I was sleeping there quite soundly when my sister came and woke me.

'There are men in the field,' she said, her eyes nearly starting out of her head with fear, for she was always very timid. 'I'm off.'

'Are you?' I answered. 'Well, I think I shall stop here where

I shan't be noticed. If we begin jumping over those turnips they well see us.'

'We might run down the rows, keeping our ears close to our backs,' she remarked.

'No,' I said, 'there are too many bare patches.'

At this moment a gun went 'bang' some way off; and my sister, like a wise hare, scuttled away at full speed for the wood. But I only made myself smaller than usual and lay watching and listening.

There was a good deal to see and hear; for instance, a covey of partridges, troublesome birds that come scratching and fidgeting about when one wants to sleep, were running to and fro in a great state of concern.

'They are after us,' said the old cock. 'I remember the same thing last year. Come on, do.'

'How can I with all these young ones to look after?' answered the hen. 'Why, if once they are scattered I shall never find them again.'

'Just as you like, you know best,' said the cock. 'Goodbye,' and away he flew, while his wife and the rest ran to a little distance, scattered and squatted.

Presently, looking back over my shoulders without turning my head, as a hare can, I saw a line of men walking towards me. There was the Red-faced Man whom Giles called Grampus behind his back and Squire to his face. There was Giles himself, with his hurt hand tied up, holding a kind of stick with a slit in it from which hung a lot of dead partridges whose necks were in the slit. One of them was not dead or had come to life again, for it flapped in the stick trying to fly away. He held these in the hand that was tied up, and in the other, oh, horror! was a dead hare bleeding from its nose. It looked uncommonly like my mother, but whether it were or no I couldn't be quite sure. At least from that day neither my sister nor I ever saw her again.

'I suppose you haven't met her coming up this big white Road, have you, Mahatma?'

'No, no,' I answered impatiently, 'I have already told you that you are the first hare I have ever seen upon the Road. Please get on with your story, or the Lights will change and the Gates be opened before I hear its end.'

Just when I saw her I was thinking of running away, but the sight terrified me so much that I could not stir. You see,

Mahatma, I really loved my mother as much as a hare can love anything, which is a good deal.

Well, beyond Giles was, who do you think? That dreadful boy, Tom, with a gun in his hand too. Did I say that they all had guns, except Giles and some beater men, only that Tom's was single-barrelled? Then there were others whom I need not describe, stretching to left and right, and worst of all, perhaps, there was Giles's great black dog, a silly-looking beast which always seemed to have its mouth open and its tongue hanging out, and to be wagging a big tail like the fox's, only black and more ragged.

As I watched, up got the old hen partridge and one of her young ones and flew towards me. The Red-faced Man lifted his gun and fired, once, twice, and down came first the mother partridge and then the young one. I forgot to say that Tom fired too at the old partridge, which fell dead quite close to me, leaving a lot of feathers floating in the air. As it fell Tom screeched out:

'I killed that, father.'

This made the Red-faced Man very angry.

'You young scoundrel,' he said, 'how often have I told you not to shoot at my birds under my nose? No sportsman shoots at another man's birds, and as for killing it, you were yards under the thing. If you do it again I will send you home.'

'Sorry, father,' said Tom, adding in a low voice with a snigger, 'I did kill it after all. Dad thinks no one can hit a partridge except himself.'

Just then up jumped my father near to Giles, and came leaping in front of the Red-faced Man about twenty yards away from him.

'Mark hare!' shouted Giles, and Grampus, who was still glowering at Tom and had not quite finished pushing the cartridges into his gun, shut it up in a hurry and fired first one barrel and then the other. But my father, who was very cunning, jumped into the air at the first shot and ducked at the second, so that he was missed; at least I suppose that is why he was missed.

Giles grinned and the Red-faced Man said, 'Damn!'

'What does 'damn' mean, Mahatma? It was a very favourite word with the Red-faced Man, but even now I can't quite understand it.'

'Nor can I,' I answered. 'Go on.'

Well, my poor father next ran in front of Tom, who shot too and hit him in the hind legs so that he rolled over and over in the turnips, kicking and screaming.

'Have you ever heard a hare scream, Mahatma?'

'Yes, yes, it makes a horrid noise like a baby.'

'Wiped your eye that time, Dad,' cried Tom in an exultant voice.

'I don't know about wiping my eye,' answered his father, turning quite purple with rage, 'but I wish you would be good enough, Thomas, not to shoot my hares behind, so that they make that beastly row which upsets me' (I think that the Red-faced Man was really kind at the bottom) 'and spoils them for the market. If you can't hit a hare in front, miss it like a gentleman.'

'As you do, Dad,' said Tom, sniggering again. 'All right, I'll try.'

'Giles,' roared Grampus, pretending not to hear, 'send your dog and fetch that hare. I can't bear its screeching.'

So the great black dog rushed forward and caught my poor father in its big mouth, although he tried to drag himself away on his front paws, and after that I shut my eyes.

Then a lot of partridges got up and there was any amount of banging, though most of them were missed. This made the Red-faced Man angrier than ever. He took off his hat and waved it, bellowing:

'Call back that brute of a dog of yours, Giles. Call it back at once or I'll shoot it.'

So Giles called, 'Nigger. Come you 'ere, Nigger! Nigg, Nigg, Nigg!'

But Nigger rushed about putting up partridges all over the place while Grampus stamped and shouted and every one missed everything, till at last Tom sat down on the turnips and roared with laughter.

At length, after Giles had beaten Nigger till he broke a stick over him, making him howl terribly, order was restored, and the line having reformed, began to march down on me. For, Mahatma, I was so frightened by what had happened to my father, and I think my mother, that I didn't remember what he, I mean my dead father, had told me, always to run away when there is a chance, as poor hares can only protect themselves by flight.

So as I had lost the chance I thought that I would just sit tight, hoping that they would not see me. Nor indeed would they if it hadn't been for that horrible Tom.

During the confusion the mother partridge which the Red-faced Man had shot had been forgotten by everybody except Tom. Tom, you see, was certain that he had shot it himself, being a very obstinate boy, and was determined to retrieve it as his own.

Now that partridge had fallen within a yard of me, with its beak and claws pointing to the sky, and when the line had passed where we lay Tom lagged behind to look for it. He did not find it then, whether he ever found it afterwards I am sure I don't know. But he found me.

'By Jove! here's a hare,' he said, and made a grab at me just as he had done in the furze bush.

Well, I went. Tom shot when I wasn't more than four yards from him, and the whole charge passed like a bullet between my hind legs and struck the ground under my stomach, sending up such a shower of earth and stones that I was knocked right over.

'I've hit it!' yelled Tom, as he crammed another cartridge into his single-barrelled gun.

By the time that it was loaded I was quite thirty yards away and going like the wind. Tom lifted the gun.

'Don't shoot!' roared the Red-faced Man.

'Mind that there boy!' bellowed Giles.

'I was running down between two rows of turnips and presently butted into a lad who was bending over, I suppose to pick up a partridge. At any rate his tail . . .

'Do you call it his tail, Mahatma?'

'That will do,' I answered.

Well, his tail was towards me; it looked very round and shiny. The shot from Tom's gun hit it everywhere. I wish they had all gone into it, but as he was so far away the charge scattered and six of the bullets struck me. Oh! they did hurt.

'Put your hand on my back, Mahatma, and you will feel the six lumps they made beneath the grey tufts of hair that grew over them, for they are still there.'

Forgetting that we were on the Road, I stretched out my hand; but, of course, it went quite through the hare, although I could see the six little grey tufts clearly enough.

'You are foolish, Hare; you don't remember that your body is not here but somewhere else.'

'Quite true, Mahatma. If it were here I could not be talking to you, could I? As a matter of fact, I have no body now. It is — oh, never mind where. Still, you can see the grey tufts, can't you? Well, I only hope that those shots hurt that fat boy half as much as they did me. No, I don't mean that I hope it now, I used to hope it.'

My goodness! didn't he screech, much worse than my father when his legs were broken. And didn't everybody else roar and shout, and didn't I dance? Off I went right over the fat boy, who had tumbled down, up to the end of the field, then so bewildered was I with shock and the burning pain, back again quite close to them.

But now nobody shot at me because they all thought the boy was killed and were gathered round him looking very solemn. Only I saw that the Red-faced Man had Tom by the neck and was kicking him hard.

After that I saw no more, for I ran five miles before I stopped, and at last lay down in a little swamp near the seashore to which my mother had once taken me. My back was burning like fire, and I tried to cool it in the soft slush.

V

The Coursing

Quite a moon went by before I recovered from Tom's shot. At first I thought that I was going to die, for, although luckily none of my bones were broken, the pain in my back was dreadful. When I tried to ease the agony by rubbing against roots it only became worse, for the fur fell off, leaving sores upon which flies settled. I could scarcely eat or sleep, and grew so thin that the bones nearly poked through my pelt. Indeed I wanted very much to die, but could not. On the contrary, by degrees I recovered, till at last I was quite strong again and like other hares, except for the six little grey tufts upon my back and one hole through my right ear.

Now all this while I had lived in the swamp near the sea, but when my strength returned I thought of my old home, to which something seemed to draw me. Also there were no turnips near the swamp, and as the winter came on I found very little to eat there. So one day, or rather one night, I travelled back home.

As it happened the first hare that I met near the big wood was my sister. She was very glad to see me, although she had forgotten how we came to part, and when I spoke of our father and mother these did not seem to interest her. Still from that time forward we lived together more or less till her end came.

One day – this was after we had made our home in the big wood, as hares often do in winter – there was a great disturbance. When we tried to go out to feed at daylight we found little fires burning everywhere, and near to them boys who beat themselves and shouted. So we went back into the wood, where the pheasants were running to and fro in a great state of mind.

Some hours later, when the sun was quite high, men began to march about and scores of shots were fired a long way off, also a wounded cock-pheasant fell near to us and fluttered away, making a queer noise in its throat. It looked very funny stumbling along on one leg with its beak gaping and two of the long feathers in its tail broken.

'I know what this is,' I said to my sister. 'Let's be gone before they shoot us. I've had enough of being shot.'

So off we went, rushing past a boy by his fire, who yelled and threw a stick at us. But as it happened, on the borders of the property of the Red-faced Man there were poachers who knew that hares would come out of the wood on this day of the shooting and had made ready for us by setting wire nooses in the gaps of the hedges through which we ran. I got my foot into one of these but managed to shake it off. My sister was not so lucky, for her head went into another of them. She kicked and tore, but the more she struggled the tighter drew the noose.

I watched her for a little while until one of the poachers ran up with a stick.

Then I went away, as I could not bear to see her beaten to death, and that was the end of my sister. So now I was the only one left alive of our family, except perhaps some younger brothers whom I did not know, though I think it was one of these that afterwards I saw shot quite dead by Giles. He went over and over and lay as still as though he had never moved in all his life.

Death seems a very wonderful thing, Mahatma, but I won't ask you what it is because I perceive that you can't answer.

After this nothing happened to me for a long while. Indeed I had the best time of my life and grew very strong and big, yes, the strongest and biggest hare of any that I ever saw, also the swiftest of foot. Twice I was chased by dogs; once by Giles's black beast, Nigger, and once by that of a shepherd. Finding that I could run right away from them without exerting myself at all, I grew to despise dogs. Ah! little did I know then that there are many different breeds of these animals.

One day in mid-winter, as the weather was very mild and open, I was lying on the rough grass field that I have spoken of which borders a flat stretch of moorland. On this moorland in summer grew tall ferns, but now these had died and been broken down by the wind. Suddenly I woke up from my sleep to see a number of men walking and riding towards me.

They were tenants and others who, although the real coursing season had not yet begun in our neighbourhood, had been asked by Grampus to come to try their greyhounds upon his land. Those of them who walked for the most part held two long, lean dogs on a string, while one or two carried dead hares. They were dreadful-looking hares that seemed to have been bitten all over; at least their coats were wet and broken. I shivered at the sight of them, feeling sure that I was going to be put to some new kind of torture.

Besides the men on foot were those on horseback, among whom I recognised the Red-faced Man and my enemy, the dreadful Tom. Most of the others were people called farmers, who seemed very happy and excited and from time to time drank something out of little bottles which they passed to each other. Giles was not there. Now I know that this was because he hated coursing, which killed down hares. Hares, he thought, ought to be shot, not coursed.

Whilst I watched, wondering what to do, there was a shout of 'There she goes!' and all the long dogs began to pull at their strings. Off the necks of two of them the collars seemed to fall, and away they leapt pursuing a hare. The men on the horses galloped after them, but the men on foot remained where they were.

Now I was afraid to get up and run lest they should loose the other dogs on me, so I lay still, till presently I saw the hare coming back towards me, followed by the two dogs whose noses almost touched its tail. It was exhausted and tried to twist and spring away to the right. But as it did so one of the dogs caught it in its mouth and bit it till it died.

'That was a rotten hare,' said Tom, who cantered up just then, 'it gave no course at all.'

'Yes,' puffed Grampus. 'Hope the next one will show better sport.'

'Hope so too,' answered Tom, 'especially as it is Jack and Jill's turn to be slipped, and they are the best greyhounds for twenty miles round.'

Then the Red-faced Man gave some orders and Jack and Jill were brought forward by the man whose business it was to slip the dogs. One of them was black and one yellow; I think Jack was the black one – a dreadful, sneaking-looking beast with a white tip to its tail, which ended in a sort of curl.

'Forward now,' said Grampus, 'and go slow. There's sure to be another puss or two in this rough grass.'

Next second I was up and away, and before you could count twelve Jack and Jill were after me. I saw them standing on their hind legs straining at the cord. Then the collars fell from them and they leapt forward like the light. My thought was to get back to the wood, which was about a minute's run behind me, but I did not dare to turn and head for it because of the long line of people through which I must pass if I tried to do so. So I ran straight for the moorland, hoping to turn there and reach the wood on its other side, although this meant a long journey.

For a while all went well with me, and having a good start I began to hope that I should outrun these beasts, as I had the shepherd's dog and the retriever. But I did not know Jack and Jill. Just as I reached the borders of the moor I heard the patter of their feet behind me, and looking back saw them coming up, about as far away as I was from Tom when he shot me.

They were running quite close together and behind them galloped the judge and other men. There was a fence here and I bolted through a hole in it. The greyhounds jumped over and for a moment lost sight of me, for I had turned and run down near the side of the fence. But Tom, who had come through a gap, saw me and waved his arm shouting, and next instant Jack and Jill saw me too.

Then as the going was rough by the fence I took to the open moor, always trying, however, to work round to the left in the hope that I might win the shelter of the wood.

On we went like the wind, and now Jack and Jill were quite close behind me, though before they got there I had managed to circle so that at last my head pointed to the wood, which was more than half a mile away. Their speed was greater than mine, and I knew that I must soon be caught.

At last they were not more than two yards behind, and for the first time I twisted so that they overshot me, which gave me another start. Three times they came up and three times I wrenched or twisted. The wood was not so far away now, but I was almost spent.

What was I to do! What was I to do! I saw a clump of furze to the left, a big clump and thick, and remembered that there was a hare's run through it. I reached it just as Jill was on the top of me, and once more they lost sight of me for a while as they ran round the clump staring and jumping. When they saw me again on the further side I was thirty yards ahead of them and the wood was perhaps two hundred and fifty yards away. But now I could only run more slowly, for my heart seemed to be bursting, though luckily Jack and Jill were getting tired also. Still they soon came up, and now I must twist every few yards or be caught in their jaws.

I can't tell you what I felt, Mahatma, and until you have been hunted by greyhounds you will never know. It was horrible. Yet I managed to twist and jump so that always Jack and Jill just missed me. The farmers on the horses laughed to see my desperate leaps and wrenches.

But Tom did worse than laugh. Noting that I was getting quite near the wood, he rode between me and it, trying to turn me into the open, for he wished to see me killed.

'Don't do that! It isn't sportsmanlike,' shouted the Red-faced Man. 'Give the poor beast a chance.'

I don't know whether he obeyed or not, as just then I made my last double, and felt Jill's teeth cut through the fur of my scut

and heard them snap. I had dodged Jill, but Jack was right on to
me and the wood still twenty yards away.

I could not twist any more, it was just which of us could get
there first. I gathered all my remaining strength, for I was mad,
mad with terror, and bounded forward.

After me came Jack, I felt his hot breath on my flank. I
jumped the ditch, yes, I found power to jump that ditch where
there was a rabbit run just by the trunk of a young oak. Jack
jumped after me; we must both have been in the air at the same
time. But I got through the rabbit run, whereas Jack hit his
sharp nose against the trunk of the tree and broke his neck. Yes,
he fell dead into the ditch.

I crawled on a few yards to a thick clump and squatted
down, for I could not stir another inch. So it came about that I
heard them all talking on the other side.

One of them said I was the finest hare he had ever coursed.
Others, who had dragged Jack out of the ditch, lamented his
death, especially the owner, who vowed that he was worth £50
and abused Tom. Tom, he said, had caused him to be killed − I
don't know how, but I suppose because he had ridden forward
and tried to turn me. The Red-faced Man also scolded Tom.
Then he added:

'Well, I am glad she got off, for she'll give us a good run
with the harriers one day. I shall always know that hare again by
the white marks on its back; also it is the biggest I have seen for a
long while. Come on, my friends, the dog is dead and there's an
end of it. At least we have had a good morning's sport, so let's go
to the Hall and get some lunch.'

The Hare paused for a little, then looked up at me in its comical
fashion and asked:

'Did you ever course hares, Mahatma?'

'Not I, thank goodness,' I answered.

'Well, what do you think of coursing?'

'I would rather not say,' I replied.

'Then I will,' said the Hare, with conviction. 'I think it
horrible.'

'Yes, but, Hare, you do not remember the pleasure this
sport gives to the men and the dogs; you look at it from an

entirely selfish point of view.'

'And so would you, Mahatma, if you had felt Jack's hot breath on your back and Jill's teeth in your tail.'

VI

The Hunting

The Hare sat silent for a time, while I employed myself in watching certain shadows stream past us on the Great White Road. Among them was that of a politician whom I had much admired upon the earth. In this land of Truth I was grieved to observe certain characteristics about him which I had never before suspected. It seemed to me, alas! that in his mundane career he had not been so entirely influenced by a single-hearted desire for the welfare of our country as he had proclaimed and I had believed. I gathered even that his own interests had sometimes inspired his policy.

He went by, leaving, so far as I was concerned, a somewhat painful impression from which I sought relief in the company of the open-souled Hare.

'Well,' I said, 'I suppose that you died of exhaustion after your coursing experience, and came on here.'

'Died of exhaustion, Mahatma, not a bit of it!'

In three days I was as well as ever, only much more cunning than I had been before. In the night I fed in the fields upon whatever I could get, but in the daytime I always lay up in woods. This I did because I found out the shooting was over, and I knew that greyhounds, which run by sight, would never come into woods.

The weeks went by and the days began to lengthen. Pretty yellow flowers that I had not seen before appeared in the woods, and I ate plenty of them: they have a nice flavour. Then I met another hare and loved her, because she reminded me of my sister. We used to play about together and were very happy.

'I wonder what she will do now that I am gone.'

'Console herself with somebody else,' I suggested sarcastically.

'No, she won't do that, Mahatma, because the hounds

'chopped' her just outside the Round Plantation.'

I mean they caught and ate her. You think that I am contradicting myself, but I am not. I mean I wonder what she will do without me in whatever world she has reached, for I don't see her here. Well, I went to the little Round Plantation because I found that Giles seldom came there and I thought it would be safer, but as it proved I made a great mistake. One day there appeared the Red-faced Man and Tom and the girl, Ella, and a lot of other people mounted on horses, some of them dressed in green coats with ridiculous-looking caps on their heads.

Also with them were I don't know how many spotted dogs whose tails curled over their backs, not like greyhounds whose tails curl between their legs. Outside of the Plantation those dogs caught and ate my future wife, as I have said. It was her own fault, for I had warned her not to go there, but she was a very self-willed character. As it was she never even gave them a run, for they were all round her in a minute. Then they made a kind of cartwheel; their heads were in the centre of this cartwheel and their tails pointed out. In its exact middle was my future wife.

When the wheel broke up there was nothing of her left except her scut, which lay upon the ground.

I had seen so many of such things that I was not so much shocked as you might suppose. After all a fine hare like myself could always get another wife, and as I have told you she was very self-willed.

So I lay still, thinking that those men and dogs would go away.

But what do you think, Mahatma? Just as they were going the boy Tom called out:

'I say, Dad, I think we might as well knock through the Round Planatation. Giles tells me that the old speckle-backed buck lies up here.'

'Does he?' said Grampus. 'Well, if so, that's the hare I want to see, for I know he'd give us a good run. Here, Jerry' (Jerry was the huntsman), 'just put the hounds into that place.'

So Jerry put the hounds in, making dreadful noises to encourage them, and of course I came out, as I did not wish to share the fate of my future wife.

'That's him!' screeched Tom. 'Look at the grey marks on his back.'

'Yes, that's he right enough,' shouted the Red-faced Man. 'Lay them on, Jerry, lay them on; we're in for a rattling run now, I'll warrant.'

So they were laid on and I went away as hard as my legs would carry me. Very soon I found that I had left all those curly-tailed dogs a long way behind.

'Ah!' I said to myself proudly, 'these beasts are not grey-hounds; they are like Giles's retriever and the sheep dog. They'll never see me again. So I looped along saving my breath and heading for a wood which was quite five miles off that I had once visited from the Marsh on the sea-shore where I lay sick, for I was sure they would never follow me there.

You can imagine, then, Mahatma, how surprised I was when I drew near that wood to hear a hideous noise of dogs all barking together behind me, and on looking back, to see those spotted brutes, with their tongues hanging out, coming along quite close to each other and not more than a quarter of a mile away.

Moreover they were coming after me. I was sure of that, for the first of them kept setting its nose to the ground just where I had run, and then lifting up its head to bay. Yes, they were coming on my scent. They could smell me as Giles's curly dog smells the wounded partridges. My heart sank at the thought, but presently I remembered that the wood was quite close, and that there I should certainly give them the slip.

So I went on quite cheerfully, not even running as fast as I could. But fortune was against me, as everything has always been, for I never found a friend. I ran along the side of a hedgerow which went quite up to the wood, not knowing that at the end of it three men were engaged in cutting down an oak tree. You see, Mahatma, they had caught sight of the hunt and stopped from their work, so that I did not hear the sound of their axes upon the tree. Nor, as my head was so near the ground, did I see them until I was right on to them, at which moment also they saw me.

'Here she is!' yelled one of them. 'Keep her out of covert or they'll lose her,' and he threw out his arms and began to jump about, as did the other two.

I pulled up short within three or four yards of them. Behind were the dogs and the people galloping upon horses and in front were the three men. What was I to do? Now I had stopped exactly in a gateway, for a lane ran alongside the wood. After a moment's pause I bolted through the gateway, thinking that I would get into the wood beyond. But one of the men, who of course wanted to see me killed, was too quick for me and there headed me again.

Then I lost my senses. Instead of running on past him and leaping into the wood, I swung right round and rushed back, still clinging to the hedgerow. Indeed as I went down one side of it the hounds and the hunters came up on the other, so that there were only a few sticks between us, though fortunately the wind was blowing from them to me. Fearing lest they should see me I jumped into the ditch and ran for quite two hundred yards through the mud and water that was gathered there. Then I had to come out of it again as it ended, but here was a fall in the ground, so still I was not seen.

Meanwhile the hunt had reached the three men and I heard them all talking together. The end of it was that the men explained which way I had gone, and once more the hounds were laid on to me. In a minute they got to where I had entered the ditch, and there grew confused because my footmarks did not smell in the water. For quite a long time they looked about till at length, taking a wide cast, the hounds found my smell again at the end of the ditch.

During this check I was making the best of my way back towards my own home; indeed had it not been for it I should have been caught and torn to pieces much sooner than I was. Thus it happened that I had covered quite three miles before once more I heard those hounds baying behind me. This was just as I got on to the moorland, at that edge of it which is about another three miles from the great house called the Hall, which stands on the top of a cliff that slopes down to the beach and the sea.

I had thought of making for the other wood, that in which I had saved myself from the greyhounds when the beast Jack broke its neck against the tree, but it was too far off, and the ground was so open that I did not dare to try.

So I went straight on, heading towards the cliff. Another mile and they viewed me, for I heard Tom yell with delight as he stood up in his stirrups on the black cob he was riding and waved his cap. Jerry the huntsman also stood up in his stirrups and waved his cap, and the last awful hunt began.

I ran – oh! how I ran. Once when they were nearly on me I managed to check them for a minute in a hollow by getting among some sheep. But they soon found me again, and came after me at full tear not more than a hundred yards behind. In front of me I saw something that looked like walls and bounded towards them with my last strength. My heart was bursting, my eyes and mouth seemed to be full of blood, but the terror of being torn to pieces still gave me power to rush on almost as quickly as though I had just been put off my form. For as I have told you, Mahatma, I am, or rather was, a very strong and swift hare.

I reached the walls; there was an open doorway in them through which I fled, to find myself in a big garden. Two gardeners saw me and shouted loudly. I flew on through some other doors, through a yard, and into a passage where I met a woman carrying a pail, who shrieked and fell on to her back. I jumped over her and got into a big room, where was a long table covered with white on which were all sorts of things that I suppose men eat. Out of that room I went into yet another, where a fat woman with a hooked nose was seated holding something white in front of her. I bolted under the thing on which she was seated and lay there. She saw me come and began to shriek also, and presently a most terrible noise arose outside.

All the spotted dogs were in the house, baying and barking, and everybody was yelling. Then for a minute the dogs stopped their clamour, and I heard a great clatter of things breaking and of teeth crunching and of the Red-faced Man shouting:

'Those cursed brutes are eating the hunt lunch. Get them out, Jerry, you idiot! Get them out! Great heavens! what's the matter with her Ladyship? Is any one murdering her?'

I suppose that they couldn't get them out, or at least when they did they all came into the other room where I was under the seat on which the fat woman was now standing.

'What is it, mother?' I heard Tom say.

'An animal!' she screamed. 'An animal under the sofa!'

'All right,' he said, 'that's only the hare. Here, hounds, out with her, hounds!'

The dogs rushed about, some of them with great lumps of

food still in their mouths. But they were confused, and all went into the wrong places. Everything began to fall with dreadful crashes, the fat woman shrieked piercingly, and her shriek was:

'China! Oh! my china-a. John, you wretch! Help! Help! Help!'

To which the Red-faced Man roared in answer:

'Don't be an infernal fool, Eliza-a. I say, don't be such an infernal fool.'

Also there were lots of other noises that I cannot remember, except one which a dog made.

This silly dog had thrust its head up the hole over a fire such as the stops make outside the coverts when men are going to shoot, either to hide something or to look for me there. When it came down again because the Red-faced Man kicked it, the dog put its paws into the fire and pulled it all out over the floor. Also it howled very beautifully. Just then another hound, that one which generally led the pack, began to sniff about near me and finally poked its nose under the stuff which hid me.

It jumped back and bayed, whereon I jumped out the other side. Tom made a rush at me and knocked the fat woman off the thing she was standing on, so that she fell among the dogs, which covered her up and began to sniff her all over. Flying from Tom I found myself in front of something filmy, beyond which I saw grass. It looked suspicious, but as nothing in the world could be so bad as Tom, no, not even his dogs, I jumped at it.

There was a crash and a sharp point cut my nose, but I was out upon the grass. Then there were twenty other crashes, and all the hounds were out too, for Tom had cheered them on. I ran to the edge of the lawn and saw a steep slope leading to the sands and the sea. Now I knew what the sea was, for after Tom had shot me in the back I lived by it for a long while, and once swam across a little creek to get to my form, from which it cut me off.

While I ran down that slope fast as my aching legs would carry me, I made up my mind that I would swim out into the sea and drown there, since it is better to drown than to be torn to pieces.

'But why are you laughing, friend Mahatma?'

'I am not laughing,' I said. 'In this state, without a body, I have nothing to laugh with. Still you are right, for you see that I should be laughing if I could. Your story of the stout lady and the dogs and the china is very amusing.'

'Perhaps, friend, but it did not amuse me. Nothing is amusing when one is going to be eaten alive.'

'Of course it isn't,' I answered. 'Please forgive me and go on.'

Well, I tumbled down that cliff, followed by some of the dogs and Tom and the girl Ella and the huntsman Jerry on foot, and dragged myself across the sands till I came to the lip of the sea.

Just here there was a boat and by it stood Giles the keeper. He had come there to get out of the way of the hunting, which he hated as much as he did the coursing. The sight of him settled me – into the sea I went. The dogs wanted to follow me, but Jerry called and whipped them off.

'I won't have them caught in the current and drowned,' he said. 'Let the flea-bitten old devil go, she's brought trouble enough already.'

'Help me shove off the boat, Giles,' shouted Tom. 'She shan't beat us; we must have her for the hounds. Come on, Ella.'

'Best leave her alone, Master Tom,' said Giles. 'I think she's an unlucky one, that I do.'

Still the end of it was that he helped to float the little boat and got into it with Tom and Ella.

Just after they had pushed off I saw a man running down the steps on the cliff waving his arms while he called out something. But of him they took no heed. I do not think they noticed him. As for me, I swam on.

I could not go very fast because I was so dreadfully tired; also I did not like swimming, and the cold waves broke over my head, making the cut in my nose smart and filling my eyes with something that stung them. I could not see far either, nor did I know where I was going. I knew nothing except that I was about to die, and that soon everything would be at an end; men, dogs – everything, yes, even Tom. I wanted things to come to an end. I had suffered so dreadfully, life was so horrible, I was so very tired. I felt that it was better to die and have done.

So I swam on a long way and began to forget things; indeed I thought that I was playing in the big turnip field with my mother and sister. But just as I was sinking exhausted a hand shot down into the water and caught me by the ears, although from below the fingers looked as though they were bending away from me. I saw it coming and tried to sink more quickly, but could not.

'I've got her,' said the voice of Tom gleefully. 'My! isn't she a beauty? Over nine pounds if she is an ounce. Only just in time, though,' he went on, 'for, look! she's drowning; her head wobbles as though she were sea-sick. Buck up, pussie, buck up! You mustn't cheat the hounds at last, you know. It wouldn't be sportsmanlike, and they hate dead hares.'

Then he held me by the hind legs to drain the water out of me, and afterwards began to blow down my nose, I did not know why.

'Don't do that, Tom,' said Ella sharply. 'It's nasty.'

'Must keep the life in her somehow,' answered Tom, and went on blowing.

'Master Tom,' interrupted Giles, who was rowing the boat. 'I ain't particular, but I wish you'd leave that there hare alone. Somehow I thinks there's bad news in its eyes. Who knows? P'raps the little devil feels. Any way, it's a rum one, its swimming out to sea. I never see'd a hunted hare do that afore.'

'Bosh!' said Tom, and continued his blowing.

We reached the shore and Tom jumped out of the boat, holding me by the ears. The hounds were all on the beach, most of them lying down, for they were very tired, but the men were standing in a knot at a distance talking earnestly. Tom ran to the hounds, crying out:

'Here she is, my beauties, here she is!' whereon they got up and began to bay. Then he held me above them.

'Master Tom,' I heard Jerry's voice say, 'for God's sake let that hare go and listen, Master Tom,' and the girl Ella, who of a sudden had begun to sob, tried to pull him back.

But he was mad to see me bitten to death and eaten, and until he had done so would attend to no one. He only shouted,

'One . . . two . . . three! Now, hounds! *Worry, worry, worry!*'

Then he threw me into the air above the red throats and gnashing teeth which leapt up towards me.

The Hare paused, but added, 'Did you tell me, friend Mahatma, that you had never been torn to pieces by hounds, "broken up," I believe they call it?'

'Yes, I did,' I answered, 'and what is more I shall be obliged if you will not dwell upon the subject.'

VII

The Coming Of The Red-Faced Man

'As you like,' said the Hare. 'Certainly it was very dreadful. It seemed to last a long time. But I don't mind it so much now, for I feel that it can never happen to me again. At least I hope it can't, for I don't know what I have done to deserve such a fate, any more than I know why it should have happened to me once.'

'Something you did in a previous existence, perhaps,' I answered. 'You see then you may have hunted other creatures so cruelly that at last your turn came to suffer what you had made them suffer. I often think that because of what we have done before we men are also really being hunted by something we cannot see.'

'Ah!' exclaimed the Hare, 'I never thought of that. I hope it is true, for it makes things seem juster and less wicked. But I say, friend Mahatma, what am I doing here now, where you tell me poor creatures with four feet never, or hardly ever come?'

'I don't know, Hare. I am not wise, to whom it is only granted to visit the Road occasionally to search for someone.'

'I understand, Mahatma, but still you must know a great deal or you would not be allowed in such a place before your time, or at any rate you must be able to guess a great deal. So tell me, why do you think that I am here?'

'I can't say, Hare, I can't indeed. Perhaps after the Gates are open and your Guardian has given you to drink of the Cup, you will go to sleep and wake up again as something else.'

'To drink of the cup, Mahatma? I don't drink; at least I didn't, though I can't tell what may happen here. But what do you mean about waking up as something else? Please be more plain. As what else?'

'Oh! who can know? Possibly as you are on the human Road you might even become a man some day, though I should not advise you to build on such a hope as that.'

'What do you say, Mahatma? A man! One of those two-legged beasts that hunt hares; a thing like Giles and Tom — yes, Tom? Oh! not that — not that! I'd almost rather go through everything again than become a cruel, torturing man.'

As it spoke thus the Hare grew so disturbed that it nearly vanished; literally it seemed to melt away till I could only perceive its outline. With a kind of shock I comprehended all the horror that it must feel at such a prospect as I had suggested to it, and really this grasping of the truth hurt my human pride. It had never come home to me before that the circumstances of their lives — and deaths — must cause some creatures to see us in strange lights.

'Oh! I have no doubt I was mistaken,' I said hurriedly, 'and that your wishes on the point will be respected. I told you that I know nothing.'

At these words the Hare became quite visible again.

It sat up and very reflectively began to rub its still shadowy nose with a shadowy paw. I think that it remembered the sting of the salt water in the cut made by the glass of the window through which it had sprung.

Believing that its remarkable story was done, and that presently it would altogether melt away and vanish out of my knowledge, I looked about me. First I looked above the towering Gates to see whether the Lights had yet begun to change. Then as they had not I looked down the Great White Road, following it for miles and miles, until even to my spirit sight it lost itself in the Nowhere.

Presently coming up this Road towards us I saw a man dressed in a green coat, riding-breeches and boots and a peaked cap, who held in his hand a hunting-whip. He was a fine-looking person of middle age, with a pleasant, open countenance, bright blue eyes, and very red cheeks, on which he wore light-coloured whiskers. In short a jovial-looking individual, with whom things had evidently always gone well, one to whom sorrow and disappointment and mental struggle were utter strangers. He, at least, had never known what it is to 'endure hardness' in all his life.

Studying his nature as one can do on the Road, I perceived also that in him there was no guile. He was a good-minded, God-fearing man according to his simple lights, who had done many kindnesses and contributed liberally towards the wants of the poor, though as he had been very rich, it had cost him little thus to gratify the natural promptings of his heart.

Moreover he was what Jorsen calls a 'young soul', quite young indeed, by which I mean that he had not often walked the Road in previous states of life, as for instance that Eastern woman had done who accosted me before the arrival of the Hare. So to speak his crude nature had scarcely outgrown the primitive human condition in which necessity as well as taste make it customary and pleasant to men to kill; that condition through which almost every boy passes on his way to manhood, I suppose by the working of some secret law of reminiscence.

It was this thought that first led me to connect the new-comer with the Red-faced Man of the Hare's story. It may seem strange that I should have been so dense, but the truth is that it never occurred to me, any more than it had done to the Hare, that such a person would be at all likely to tread the Road for many years to come. I had gathered that he was comparatively young, and although I had argued otherwise with the Hare, had concluded therefore that he would continue to live his happy earth life until old age brought him to a natural end. Hence my obtuseness.

The man was drifting towards me thoughtfully, evidently much bewildered by his new surroundings but not in the least afraid. Indeed there none are afraid; when they glide from their death-beds to the Road they leave fear behind them with the other terrors of our mortal lot.

Presently he became conscious of the presence of the Hare, and thoughts passed through his mind which of course I could read.

'My word!' he said to himself, 'things are better than I hoped. There's a hare, and where there are hares there must be hunting and shooting. Oh! if only I had a gun, or the ghost of a gun!'

Then an idea struck him. He lifted his hunting-crop and hurled it at the Hare.

As it was only the shadow of a crop of course it could hurt nothing. Still it went through the shadow of the Hare and caused it to twist round like lightning.

'That was a good shot anyway,' he reflected, with a satisfied smile.

By now the Hare had seen him.

'*The Red-faced Man!*' it exclaimed, 'Grampus himself!' and it turned to flee away.

'Don't be frightened,' I cried, 'he can't hurt you; nothing can hurt you here.'

The Hare halted and sat up. 'No,' it said, 'I forgot. But you saw, he tried to. Now, Mahatma, you will understand what a bloodthirsty brute he is. Even after I am dead he has tried to kill me again.'

'Well, and why not?' interrupted the Man. 'What are hares for except to be killed?'

'There Mahatma, you hear him. Look at me, Man, who am I?'

So he looked at the Hare and the Hare looked at him. Presently his face grew puzzled.

'By Jingo!' he said slowly, 'you are uncommonly like — you *are* that accursed witch of a hare which cost me my life. There are the white marks on your back, and there is the grey splotch on your ear. Oh! If only I had a gun — a real gun!'

'You would shoot me, wouldn't you, or try to?' said the Hare. 'Well, you haven't and you can't. You say I cost you your life. What do you mean? It was my life that was sacrificed, not yours.'

'Indeed,' answered the Man, 'I thought you got away. Never saw any more of you after you jumped through the French window. Never had time. The last thing I remember is her Lady-ship screaming like a mad cockatoo, yes, and abusing me as though I were a pickpocket, with the drawing-room all on fire. Then something happened, and down I went among the broken china and hit my head against the leg of a table. Next came a kind of whirling blackness and I woke up here.'

'A fit or a stroke,' I suggested.

'Both, I think, sir. The fit first — I have had 'em before, and the stroke afterwards — against the leg of the table. Anyway they finished me between them, thanks to that little beast.'

Then it was that I saw a very strange thing, a hare in a rage. It seemed to go mad, of course I mean spiritually mad. Its eyes flashed fire; it opened its mouth and shut it after the fashion of a suffocating fish. At last it spoke in its own way — I cannot stop to explain in further detail the exact manner of speech or rather of its equivalent upon the Road.

'Man, Man,' it exclaimed, 'you say that I finished you. But what did you do to me? You shot me. Look at the marks upon my back. You coursed me with your running dogs. You hunted me with your hounds. You dragged me out of the sea into which I swam to escape you by death, and threw me living to the pack,' and the Hare stopped, exhausted by its own fury.

'Well,' replied the Man coolly, 'and suppose I, or my people, did, what of it? Why shouldn't I? You were a beast, I was a man with dominion over you. You can read all about that in the Book of Genesis.'

'I never heard of the Book of Genesis,' said the Hare, 'but what does dominion mean? Does this Book of Genesis say that it means the right to torment that which is weaker than the tormentor?'

'All you animals were made for us to eat,' commented the Man, avoiding an answer to the direct question.

'Very good,' answered the Hare, 'let us suppose that we *were* given you to eat. Was it in order to eat me that you came out against me with guns, then with dogs that run by sight, and then with dogs that run by smell?'

'If you were to be killed and eaten, why should you not be killed in one of these ways, Hare?'

'Why should I be killed in those ways, Man, when others more merciful were to your hand? Indeed, why should I be killed at all? Moreover, if you wished to satisfy your hunger with my body, why at the last was I thrown to the dogs to devour?'

'I don't quite know, Hare. Never looked at the matter in that light before. But — ah! I've got you now,' he added triumphantly. 'If it hadn't been for me you never would have lived. You see *I* gave you the gift of life. Therefore, instead of grumbling, you should be very much obliged to me. Don't you understand? I preserved hares, so that without me you would never have been a hare. Isn't that right, Mr — Mr . . . I am sorry I have forgotten your name,' he added, turning towards me.

'Mahatma,' I said.

'Oh! yes, I remember it now — Mr — ah — Mr Hatter.'

'There is something in the argument,' I replied cautiously, 'but let us hear our friend's answer.'

'Answer — my answer! Well, here it is. What are you, Man, who dare to say that you give life or withhold it? You a Lord of

life *you*! I tell you that I know little, yet I am sure that you or
those like you have no more power to create life than the world
we have left has to bid the stars to shine. If the life must come, it
will come, and if it cannot fulfil itself as a hare, then it will
appear as something else. If you say that you create life, I, the
poor beast which you tortured, tell you that you are a presump-
tuous liar.'

'You dare to lecture me,' said the Man, 'me, the heir of all
the ages, as the poet called me. Why, you nasty little animal, do
you know that I have killed hundreds like you, and,' he added,
with a sudden afflatus of pride, 'thousands of other creatures,
such as pheasants, to say nothing of deer and larger game? That
has been my principal occupation since I was a boy. I may say
that I have lived for sport; got very little else to show for my life,
so to speak.'

'Oh!' said the Hare, 'have you? Well, if I were you, I
shouldn't boast about it just now. You see, we are still outside of
those Gates. Who knows but that you will find every one of the
living things you have amused yourself by slaughtering waiting
for you within them, each praying for justice to its Maker and
your own?'

'My word!' said the Man, 'what a horrible notion; it's like a
bad dream.'

He reflected a little, then added, 'Well, if they do, I've got
my answer. I killed them for food; man must live. Millions of
pheasants are sold to be eaten every year at a much smaller price
than they cost to breed. What do you say to that, Mr Hatter?
Finishes him, I think.'

'I'm not arguing,' I replied. 'Ask the Hare.'

'Yes, ask me, Man, and although you are repeating yourself, I'll answer with another question, knowing that here you
must tell the truth. Did you really rear us all for food? Was it for
this that you kept your keepers, your running dogs and your
hunting dogs, that you might kill poor defenceless beasts and
birds to fill men's stomachs? If this was so, I have nothing more
to say. Indeed, if our deaths or sufferings at their hands really
help men in any way, I have nothing more to say. I admit that
you are higher and stronger than we are, and have a right to use
us for your own advantage, or even to destroy us altogether if we
harm you.'

The Man pondered, then replied sullenly:

'You know very well that it was not so. I did not rear up pheasants and hares merely to eat them or that others might eat them. Something forces me to tell you that it was in order that I might enjoy myself by showing my skill in shooting them, or to have the pleasure and exercise of hunting them to death. Still,' he added defiantly, 'I who am a Christian man maintain that my religion perfectly justified me in doing all these things, and that no blame attaches to me on this account.'

'Very good,' said the Hare, 'now we have a clear issue. Friend Mahatma, when those Gates open presently what happens beyond them?'

'I don't know,' I answered, 'I have never been there; at least not that I can remember.'

'Still, friend Mahatma, is it not said that yonder lives some Power which judges righteously and declares what is true and what is false?'

'I have heard so, Hare.'

'Very well, Man, I lay my cause before that Power — do you the same. If I am wrong I will go back to earth to be tortured by you and yours again. If, however, I am right, you shall abide the judgment of the Power, and I ask that It will make of you a hunted hare!'

Now when he heard these awful words — for they were awful — no less, the Red-faced Man grew much disturbed. He hummed and he hawed, and shifted his feet about. At last he said:

'You must admit that while you lived you had a first-class time under my protection. Lots of turnips to eat and so forth.'

'A first-class time!' the Hare answered with withering scorn. 'What sort of a time would you have had if some one had shot you all over the back and you must creep away to die of pain and starvation? How would you have enjoyed it if, from day to day, you had been forced to live in terror of cunning monsters, who at any hour might appear to hurt you in some new fashion? Do you suppose that animals cannot feel fear, and is continual fear the kind of friend that gives them a "first-class time"?'

To this last argument the Man seemed able to find no answer.

'Mr Hare,' he said humbly, 'we are all fallible. Although I

never thought to find myself in the position of having to do so, I will admit that I may possibly have been mistaken in my views and treatment of you and your kind, and indeed of other creatures. If so, I apologise for any, ah – temporary inconvenience I may have caused you. I can do no more.'

'Come, Hare,' I interposed, 'that's handsome; perhaps you might let bygones be bygones.'

'Apologise!' exclaimed the Hare. 'After all I have suffered I do not think it is enough. At the very least, Mahatma, he should say that he is heartily ashamed and sorry.'

'Well, well,' said the Man, 'it's no use making two bites of a cherry. I am sorry, truly sorry for all the pain and terror I have brought on you. If that won't do let's go up and settle the matter, and if I've been wrong I'll try to bear the consequences like a gentleman. Only, Mr Hare, I hope that you will not wish to put your case more strongly against me than you need.'

'Not I, Man. I know now that you only erred because the truth had not been revealed to you – because you did not understand. All that I will ask, if I can, is that you may be allowed to tell this truth to other men.'

'Well, I am glad to say I can't do that, Hare.'

'Don't be so sure,' I broke in; 'it's just the kind of thing which might be decreed – a generation or two hence when the world is fit to listen to you.'

But he took no heed, or did not comprehend me, and went on:

'It is an impossibility, and if I did they would think me a lunatic or a snivelling, sentimental humbug. I believe that lots of my old friends would scarcely speak to me again. Why, putting aside the pleasures of sport, if the views you preach were to be accepted, what would become of keepers and beaters and huntsmen and dog-breeders, and of thousands of others who directly or indirectly get their living out of hunting and shooting? Where would game rents be also?'

'I don't know, I am sure,' replied the Hare wearily. 'I suppose that they would earn their living in some other way, as they must in countries where there is no sport, and that you would have to make up for the shooting rents by growing more upon the land. You know that after all we hares and the other game eat a great deal which might be saved if there were not so many of us. But I am not wise, and I have never looked at the question from that point of view. It may seem selfish, but I have to consider myself and the creatures whose cause I plead, for something inside of me is telling me now – yes, now – that all of them are speaking through my mouth. It says that is why I am allowed to be here and to talk with you both; for their sakes rather than for my own.'

'If you have more to say you had better say it quickly,' I interrupted, addressing the Red-faced Man. 'I see that the Lights are beginning to change, which means that soon the Road will be closed and the Gates opened.'

'I can't remember anything,' he answered. 'Yes, there is one matter,' he added nervously. 'I see, Mr Hare, that you are think-ing of my boy Tom, not very kindly I am afraid. As you have been so good as to forgive me I hope that you won't be hard on Tom. He is not at all a bad sort of a lad if a little thoughtless, like many other young people.'

'I don't like Tom,' said the Hare, with decision. 'Tom shot me when you told him not to shoot. Tom shut me up in a filthy place with a yellow rabbit which he forgot to feed, so that it wanted to eat me. Tom tried to cut me off from the wood so that the running dogs might catch me, although you shouted to him that it was not sportsmanlike. Tom dragged me out of the sea and blew down my nostrils to keep me alive. Tom threw me to the hounds, although Giles remonstrated with him and even the huntsman begged him to let me go. I tell you that I don't like Tom.'

'Still, Mr Hare,' pleaded the Red-faced Man, 'I hope that if it should be in your power when we get through those Gates, that you will be merciful to Tom. I can't think of much to say for him in this hurry, but there, he is my only son and the truth is that I love him. You know he may live – to be different – if you don't bring some misfortune on him.'

'Who am I to bring misfortune or to withhold it?' asked the Hare, softening visibly. 'Well, I know what love means, for my mother loved me and I loved her in my way. I tell you that when I saw her dead, turned from a beautiful living thing into a stained lump of flesh and fur, I felt dreadful. I understand now that you love Tom as my mother loved me, and, Man, for the sake of your love – not for his sake, mind – I promise you that I won't say anything against Tom if I can help it, or do anything either.'

'You're a real good fellow!' exclaimed the Red-faced Man, with evident relief. 'Give me your hand. Oh! I forgot, you can't. Hullo! what's up now? Everything seems to be altering.'

As he spoke, to my eyes the Lights began to change in earnest. All the sky (I call it sky for clearness) above the mighty Gates became as it were alive with burning tongues of every colour that an artist can conceive. By degrees these fiery tongues or swords shaped themselves into a vast circle which drove back the walls of darkness, and through this circle, guided, guarded by the spirits of dead suns, with odours and with chantings, descended that crowned City of the Mansions before whose glory imagination breaks and even Vision veils her eyes.

It descended, its banners wavering in the winds of prayer; it hung above the Gates, the flower of all splendours, Heaven's very rose, hung like an opal on the boundless breast of night, and there it stayed.

The Voice in the North called to the Voice in the South; the Voice in the East called to the Voice in the West, and up the Great White Road sped the Angel of the Road, making report as he came that all his multitude were gathered in and for that while the Road was barred.

He passed and in a flash the Gates were burned away. The ashes of them fell upon the heads of those waiting at the Gates, whitening their faces and drying their tears before the Change. They fell upon the Man and the Hare beside me, veiling them as it were and making them silent, but on me they did not fall. Then, from between the Wardens of the Gates, flowed forth the Helpers and the Guardians (save those who already were without comforting the children) seeking their beloved and bearing the Cups of slumber and new birth; then pealed the question:

'Who hath suffered most? Let that one first taste of peace.'

Now all the dim hosts surged forward since each outworn soul believed that it had suffered most and was in the bitterest need of peace. But the Helpers and the Guardians gently pressed them back, and again there pealed, no question but a command.

This was the command:

'DRAW NEAR, THOU HARE.'

Jorsen asked me what happened after this justification of the Hare, which, if I heard aright, appeared to suggest that by the decree of some judge unknown, the woes of such creatures are not unnoted and despised, or left unsolaced. Of course I had to answer him that I could not tell.

Perhaps nothing happened at all. Perhaps all the wonders I seemed to see, even the Road by which souls travel from There to Here and from Here to There, and the Gates that were burned away, and the City of the Mansions that descended, were but signs and symbols of mysteries which as yet we cannot gasp or understand.

Whatever may be the truth as to this matter of my visions, I need hardly add, however, that no one can be more anxious than I am myself to learn in what way the Red-faced Man, speaking on behalf of our dominant race, and the Hare, speaking as an appointed advocate of the subject animal creation, finished their argument in the light of fuller knowledge. Much also do I wonder which of them was proved to be right, a difficult matter whereon I feel quite incompetent to express any views.

But you see at that moment I woke up. The edge of the Road on which I was standing seemed to give way beneath me, and I fell into space as one does in a nightmare. It is a very unpleasant sensation.

I remember noticing afterwards that I could not have been long asleep. When I began to dream I had only just blown out the candle, and when I awoke again there was still a smouldering spark upon its wick.

But, as I have said, in that spirit-land whither I had journeyed is to be found neither time nor space nor any other familiar thing.

Only a Dream...

Footprints – footprints – the footprints of one dead. How ghastly they look as they fall before me! Up and down the long hall they go, and I follow them. *Pit, pat* they fall, those unearthly steps, and beneath them starts up that awful impress. I can see it grow upon the marble, a damp and dreadful thing.

Tread them down; tread them out; follow after them with muddy shoes, and cover them up. In vain. See how they rise through the mire! Who can tread out the footprints of the dead?

And so on, up and down the dim vista of the past, following the sound of the dead feet that wander so restlessly, stamping upon the impress that will not be stamped out. Rave on, wild wind, eternal voice of human misery; fall, dead footsteps, eternal echo of human memory; stamp, miry feet; stamp into forgetfulness that which will not be forgotten.

And so on, on to the end.

Pretty ideas these for a man about to be married, especially when they float into his brain at night like ominous clouds into a summer sky, and he is going to be married tomorrow. There is no mistake about it – the wedding, I mean. To be plain and matter-of-fact, why there stand the presents, or some of them, and very handsome presents they are, ranged in solemn rows upon the long table. It is a remarkable thing to observe when one is about to make a really satisfactory marriage how scores of unsuspected or forgotten friends crop up and send little tokens of their esteem. It was very different when I married my first wife, I remember, but then that marriage was not satisfactory – just a love-match, no more.

There they stand in solemn rows, as I have said, and inspire me with beautiful thoughts about the innate kindness of human nature, especially the human nature of our distant cousins. It is possible to grow almost poetical over a silver teapot when one is going to be married tomorrow. On how many future mornings

Harry Furniss's Christmas Annual, 1905.

shall I be confronted with that teapot? Probably for all my life; and on the other side of the teapot will be the cream jug, and the electro-plated urn will hiss away behind them both. Also, the chased sugar basin will be in front, full of sugar, and behind everything will be my second wife.

'My dear,' she will say, 'will you have another cup of tea?' and probably I shall have another cup.

Well, it is very curious to notice what ideas will come into a man's head sometimes. Sometimes something waves a magic wand over his being, and from the recesses of his soul dim things arise and walk. At unexpected moments they come, and he grows aware of the issues of his mysterious life, and his heart shakes and shivers like a lightning-shattered tree. In that drear light all earthly things seem far, and all unseen things draw near and take shape and awe him, and he knows not what is true and what is false, neither can he trace the edge that marks off the Spirit from the Life. Then it is that the footsteps echo, and the ghostly footprints will not be stamped out.

Pretty thoughts again! and how persistently they come! It is one o'clock and I will go to bed. The rain is falling in sheets outside. I can hear it lashing against the window panes, and the wind wails through the tall wet elms at the end of the garden. I could tell the voice of those elms anywhere; I know it as well as the voice of a friend. What a night it is; we sometimes get them in this part of England in October. It was just such a night when my first wife died, and that is three years ago. I remember how she sat up in her bed.

'Ah! those horrible elms,' she said; 'I wish you would have them cut down, Frank; they cry like a woman,' and I said I would and just after that she died, poor dear. And so the old elms stand, and I like their music. It is a strange thing; I was half broken-hearted, for I loved her dearly, and she loved me with all her life and strength, and now – I am going to be married again.

'Frank, Frank, don't forget me!' Those were my wife's last words; and, indeed, though I am going to be married again tomorrow, I have not forgotten her. Nor shall I forget how Annie Guthrie (whom I am going to marry now) came to see her the day before she died. I know that Annie always liked me more or less, and I think that my dear wife guessed it. After she had kissed Annie and bid her a last goodbye, and the door had closed, she spoke quite suddenly: 'There goes your future wife, Frank,' she said; 'You should have married her at first instead of me; she is very handsome and very good, and she has two thousand a year; *she* would never have died of a nervous illness.' And she laughed a little, and then added:

'Oh, Frank dear, I wonder if you will think of me before you marry Annie Guthrie. Wherever I am I shall be thinking of you.'

And now that time which she foresaw has come, and Heaven knows that I have thought of her, poor dear. Ah! those footsteps of one dead that will echo through our lives, those woman's footprints on the marble flooring which will not be stamped out. Most of us have heard and seen them at some time or other, and I hear and see them very plainly tonight. Poor dead wife, I wonder if there are any doors in the land where you have gone through which you can creep out to look at me tonight? I hope that there are none. Death must indeed be a hell if the dead can see and feel and take measure of the forgetful faithlessness of their beloved. Well, I will go to bed and try to get a little rest. I am not so young or so strong as I was, and this wedding wears me out. I wish that the whole thing were done or had never been begun.

What was that? It was not the wind, for it never makes that sound here, and it was not the rain, since the rain has ceased its surging for a moment; nor was it the howling of a dog, for I keep none. It was more like the crying of a woman's voice; but what woman can be abroad on such a night or at such an hour – half-past one in the morning?

There it is again – a dreadful sound; it makes the blood turn chill, and yet has something familiar about it. It is a woman's voice calling round the house. There, she is at the window now, and rattling it, and, great heavens! she is calling me.

'Frank! Frank! Frank!' she calls.

I strive to stir and unshutter that window, but before I can get there she is knocking and calling at another.

Gone again, with her dreadful wail of 'Frank! Frank!' Now I hear her at the front door, and, half mad with a horrible fear, I run down the long, dark hall and unbar it. There is nothing there – nothing but the wild rush of the wind and the drip of the rain from the portico. But I can hear the wailing voice going round the house, past the patch of shrubbery. I close the door and listen. There, she has got through the little yard, and is at the back door now. Whoever it is, she must know the way about the house. Along the hall I go again, through a swing door, through the servants' hall, stumbling down some steps into the kitchen, where the embers of the fire are still alive in the grate, diffusing a little warmth and light into the dense gloom.

Whoever it is at the door is knocking now with her clenched hand against the hard wood, and it is wonderful, though she knocks so low, how the sound echoes through the empty kitchen.

There I stood and hesitated, trembling in every limb; I dared not open the door. No words of mine can convey the sense of utter desolation that overpowered me. I felt as though I were the only living man in the whole world.

'*Frank! Frank!*' cried the voice with the dreadful familiar ring in it. 'Open the door; I am so cold. I have so little time.'

My heart stood still, and yet my hands were constrained to obey. Slowly, slowly I lifted the latch and unbarred the door, and, as I did so, a great rush of air snatched it from my hands and swept it wide. The black clouds had broken a little overhead, and there was a patch of blue, rain-washed sky and with just a star or two glimmering in it fitfully. For a moment I could only see this bit of sky, but by degrees I made out the accustomed outline of the great trees swinging furiously against it, and the rigid line of the coping of the garden wall beneath them. Then a whirling leaf hit me smartly on the face, and instinctively I dropped my eyes on to something that as yet I could not distinguish — something small and black and wet.

'What are you?' I gasped. Somehow I seemed to feel that it was not a person — I could not say, *Who* are you?

'Don't you know me?' wailed the voice, with the far-off familiar ring about it. 'And I mayn't come in and show myself. I haven't the time. You were so long opening the door, Frank, and I am so cold — oh, so bitterly cold! Look there, the moon is coming out, and you will be able to see me. I suppose that you long to see me, as I have longed to see you.'

As the figure spoke, or rather wailed, a moonbeam struggled through the watery air and fell on it. It was short and shrunken, the figure of a tiny woman. Also it was dressed in black and wore a black covering over the whole head, shrouding it, after the fashion of a bridal veil. From every part of this veil and dress the water fell in heavy drops.

The figure bore a small basket on her left arm, and her hand — such a poor thin little hand — gleamed white in the moonlight. I noticed that on the third finger was a red line, showing that a wedding-ring had once been there. The other hand was stretched towards me as though in entreaty.

All this I saw in an instant, as it were, and as I saw it, horror seemed to grip me by the throat as though it were a living thing, for as the voice had been familiar, so was the form familiar, though the churchyard had received it long years ago. I could not speak — I could not even move.

'Oh, don't you know me yet?' wailed the voice; 'and I have come from so far to see you, and I cannot stop. Look, look,' and she began to pluck feverishly with her poor thin hand at the black veil that enshrouded her. At last it came off, and, as in a dream, I saw what in a dim frozen way I had expected to see — the white face and pale yellow hair of my dead wife. Unable to speak or to stir, I gazed and gazed. There was no mistake about it, it was she, ay, even as I had last seen her, white with the whiteness of death, with purple circles round her eyes and the grave-cloth yet beneath her chin. Only her eyes were wide open and fixed upon my face; and a lock of the soft yellow hair had broken loose, and the wind tossed it.

'You know me now, Frank — don't you, Frank? It has been so hard to come to see you, and so cold! But you are going to be married tomorrow, Frank; and I promised — oh, a long time ago — to think of you when you were going to be married wherever I was, and I have kept my promise, and I have come from whence I am and brought a present with me. It was bitter to die so young! I was so young to die and leave you, but I had to go. Take it — take it; be quick, I cannot stay any longer. *I could not give you my life, Frank, so I brought you my death — take it!*'

The figure thrust the basket into my hand, and as it did so the rain came up again, and began to obscure the moonlight.

'I must go, I must go,' went on the dreadful, familiar voice, in a cry of despair. 'Oh, why were you so long opening the door? I wanted to talk to you before you married Annie; and now I shall never see you again — never! never! *never!* I have lost you for ever! ever! *ever!*'

As the last wailing notes died away the wind came down with a rush and a whirl and the sweep as of a thousand wings, and threw me back into the house, bringing the door to with a crash after me.

I staggered into the kitchen, the basket in my hand, and set it on the table. Just then some embers of the fire fell in, and a faint little flame rose and glimmered on the bright dishes on the dresser, even revealing a tin candlestick, with a box of matches by it. I was well-nigh mad with the darkness and fear, and, seizing the matches, I struck one, and held it to the candle. Presently it caught, and I glanced round the room. It was just as usual, just as the servants had left it, and above the mantelpiece the eight-day clock ticked away solemnly. While I looked at it it struck two, and in a dim fashion I was thankful for its friendly sound.

Then I looked at the basket. It was of very fine white plaited work with black bands running up it, and a chequered black-and-white handle. I knew it well. I have never seen another like it. I bought it years ago at Madeira, and gave it to my poor wife. Ultimately it was washed overboard in a gale in the Irish Channel. I remember that it was full of newspapers and library books, and I had to pay for them. Many and many is the time that I have seen that identical basket standing there on that very kitchen table, for my dear wife always used it to put flowers in, and the shortest cut from that part of the garden where her roses grew was through the kitchen. She used to gather the flowers, and then come in and place her basket on the table, just where it stood now, and order the dinner.

All this passed through my mind in a few seconds as I stood there with the candle in my hand, feeling indeed half dead, and yet with my mind painfully alive, I began to wonder if I had gone asleep, and was the victim of a nightmare. No such thing. I wish it had only been a nightmare. A mouse ran out along the dresser and jumped on to the floor, making quite a crash in the silence.

What was in the basket? I feared to look, and yet some power within me forced me to it. I drew near to the table and stood for a moment listening to the sound of my own heart. Then

I stretched out my hand and slowly raised the lid of the basket.

'I could not give you my life, so I have brought you my death!' Those were her words. What could she mean — what could it all mean? I must know or I should go mad. There it lay, whatever it was, wrapped up in linen.

Ah, heaven help me! It was a small bleached human skull!

A dream! After all, only a dream by the fire, but what a dream. And I am to be married tomorrow.

Can I be married tomorrow?

RIDER HAGGARD

Henry Rider Haggard was born in Bradenham, Norfolk, England in 1856. He had an inconsistent education, moving between various schools and failing to gain entrance to both the army and Foreign Office. Haggard was in South Africa between 1875 and 1882, before returning to England, where he studied law and was called to the bar in 1884. However, by this stage his attention had already turned to the writing of novels, and in September of 1885 he published the novel for which he is most famous, *King Solomon's Mines*. Two years later, Haggard published *She* (1887), which was extraordinarily popular, and remains one of the best-selling books of all time, having never been out of print. Haggard followed this with eight more novels, all of which were highly popular. He was made a Knight Bachelor in 1912, and a Knight Commander of the Order of the British Empire in 1919. Haggard died in London, England in 1925, aged 68.